PRAISE FOR *A LEGEND OF THE FUTURE* BY AGUSTÍN DE ROJAS

"Finally, we have the chance to read a landmark work from one of Cuba's greatest science fiction writers.... If you like intensely psychological sci-fi that deftly piles on the suspense, this novel's for you.... Agustín de Rojas authored a trilogy that pushes the boundaries of our imaginations.... You'll want to prepare yourself for *Legend*. It's been compared to Clarke's *2001*, and like that remarkable text, de Rojas's will blow your mind in a good way.... The boundaries between dream and reality, and then between human and machine, almost melt away as the story progresses. And it is de Rojas's skillful manipulation of those boundaries that makes *Legend* so addictive."

—*SF Signal*, 4.5-stars

"Philosophically dense and hallucinatory in the manner of later Philip K. Dick.... *Legend* works as both suspenseful survival sci-fi (much like the current Matt Damon film *The Martian*) and a philosophical reflection of what it means to be human.... A strong blend of hard science and psychological fiction, *A Legend of the Future* should prove engrossing for admirers of Philip Dick or Stanislaw Lem."

—Blogcritics

"Tightly written prose manages to firmly grasp the reader, the pace is steady and the quality of the writing superb. It's unforgiving and demanding but also worth the effort. I loved this brief glimpse of science fiction from a mindset free of western constraints. *A Legend of the Future* is a remarkable glimpse not only into a vision of the future but more importantly into a culture very different from western capitalism. It's also a stark reminder about some of the more serious problems that a country in the stranglehold of a communistic country face. A worthy addition to anyone's science fiction collection."

—SFBook.com

"At last, they are finally publishing science fiction from Cuba.... Let me assure you, it is a pity that it took so long!... What really sells this story is not the situation (which is terribly reminiscent of *2001* and *Tau Zero*), but the psychological focus on the characters.... I came to admire de Rojas's lesson conducted with the crew of the Sviagator: namely, how the limits of individual humanity can only be surpassed through cooperation and dependency upon our fellow man—sometimes at great personal sacrifice. If *A Legend of the Future* is idealistic science fiction, colored by the politics of its age, then it is idealistic science fiction at its best—concerned with the fate of mankind among the stars."

—*Portland Book Review*

"Agustín de Rojas is widely considered the Asimov of Cuban science fiction thanks to his award-winning trilogy in the 1980s.... *A Legend of the Future* is a brisk, fascinating piece of social science fiction and a sharp indictment of capitalist greed.... A wild, unpredictable ride.... Fascinating."

—*Necessary Fiction*

"The characters are put in situations, through changes, only possible in SF, but the psychological exploration of death, desires, thoughts, and values among deeply emotional-connected people struggling to find a way to survive catastrophe is relatable and human. It's a fantastic book, well-plotted and paced, that plays with some traditional SF rules and gambits, while ever-exciting in the new avenues it creates."

—Three Percent Blog

"A subdued psychological drama enhanced by speculative elements about human psychology (fans of Joss Whedon's TV show *Dollhouse* will find a couple of points of resonance) topped off with an overwhelming awareness of mortality.... It's a novel that shows the dizzying range of fantastical situations that can emerge from a ground-level view of ideological conflict's aftereffects."

—Electric Literature

"Reading through [*A Legend of the Future*], I was reminded of books like *Solaris*, and interestingly, of Jeff Vandermeer's *Annihilation*."

—io9

"This is the first English translation of a novel by de Rojas (1949-2011), considered the father of Cuban science fiction. Influenced by Ray Bradbury and Isaac Asimov, *A Legend of the Future* tells the tale of a space mission to Titan, a moon of Saturn, during a potentially apocalyptic war between superpowers back on Earth. Along the way, the spaceship's crew is drawn into an experiment of reconditioning that may remind some readers of the ideological indoctrination reinforced to this day in Castro's Cuba."

—Chicago Tribune

AGUSTÍN DE ROJAS

THE YEAR 200

*Translated from the Spanish
by Nick Caistor and Hebe Powell*

RESTLESS BOOKS
BROOKLYN, NEW YORK

First Restless Books paperback edition July 2016

ISBN: 978-1-63206-051-8
Library of Congress Control Number: 2016939491

Cover design by Edel Rodriguez
Typset by Tetragon, London

Printed in the United States of America

1 3 5 7 9 8 6 4 2

Ellison, Stavans, and Hochstein LP
232 3rd Street, Suite A111
Brooklyn, NY 11215

www.restlessbooks.com
publisher@restlessbooks.com

This book is dedicated to those who choose fear.

"That was the way with Man; it had always been that way. He had carried terror with him. And the thing he was afraid of had always been himself."

—C.D. SIMAK

"From the materialist point of view, everything is very simple: man, and only man, is the constructor and creator of other men. In every sense."

—S. DOLETSKI,
THOUGHTS ON THE ROAD

"The road is split before us, and we must choose."

—T. MAULNIER,
VIOLENCE AND CONSCIENCE

CONTENTS

THE YEAR 200

When Hydra Awakes

1

A LEAD-210 ATOM (or more precisely, its nucleus) is unstable. Sooner or later it will emit a beta particle, and it will become an atom of bismuth-210. Bismuth-210 isn't stable either, and it has to eject another two particles from its nucleus (one alpha, the other beta) before it turns into a stable atom, lead-206. This process can take fractions of a second, or thousands of years. In the case of a single atom of lead-210, no one can predict at what moment it will decay. However, if there is a large enough number of atoms (let's say several hundred thousand...which is not as many as it may seem, since one gram of lead-210 contains close to three thousand trillion atoms) things are different. After twenty-two years, half of them will have decayed, and in another twenty-two years only a quarter of the original number of lead-210 atoms will remain; it's a natural clock. An alpha-particle detector positioned close enough to the atoms at the start will go crazy, but as the years go by the amount of alpha particles registered will steadily diminish. There will be fewer and fewer lead-210 atoms that have not already turned into stable lead-206, which does not emit alpha particles. The day will come when the particles emitted are so few that the detector, not sensitive enough to record them anymore, stops responding and shows zero radioactivity.

The limits of the detector's sensitivity can be determined when it is manufactured. It can be established—and in fact was established—so that when less than two thousandths of the original mass of lead-210 remained, it would be unable to detect the residual radioactivity. It was not hard to install an auxiliary mechanism designed to awaken Hydra when the detector showed zero radioactivity...

2

Hydra IV was the first to awake.

The bionic brain tested its internal circuits.

They were functioning.

The self-sufficient energy system was working normally. The long period of inactivity had not damaged the complex cybernetic systems that would allow it to gather data and make decisions; it could undertake the first phase of the program.

In the upper part of Hydra IV a small flap opened and almost immediately closed again.

The exploratory microrobot cyber had emerged.

The cyber explorer measured about seven centimeters long and two in diameter. Its cylindrical shape made it look like an old pencil—thick and rather short. It began pushing its way upward through the earth as directly as it could. Hydra IV was not aware it had been buried ten meters deep two centuries earlier, but the robot explorer had been programed to push in the direction opposite the pull of gravity.

Eight meters up, the microbot discovered that the earth it was climbing through was growing increasingly damp. It communicated this information to the electronic brain and continued on its way. At first, the soft soil helped its climb. Soon, though, it became a hindrance; the mud offered no secure points of contact to help its ascent.

After pushing through eleven meters of earth, the microbot's pointed tip no longer met any resistance. It advanced a little further, until four centimeters of its front end stuck out of the mud. Its external analyzers' protective covers slid back, and it was able to register and transmit the characteristics of its surroundings to Hydra IV.

The bionic brain processed the information. It was plain that there were more than twenty meters of water above the exploratory microrobot. The conditions were unfavorable for carrying out the second part of the program. However, Hydra decided to make another attempt (it had a certain autonomy of action in carrying out its tasks and was ready to employ it). It ordered the exploratory microbot to move across the solid (or rather, half-solid) surface in search of higher ground.

Shuddering slightly, the microbot finally freed itself fully from the sticky mud and fell onto one side. It advanced, half sunk in the mud, tracing wider and wider circles around the bottom of the lake...

An hour later, Hydra IV ordered the explorer to return. Nowhere within a fifty meters' radius did the land stand higher than the water. There was no sense exploring at any greater distance; the explorer did not have sufficient resources to carry out the required task, and it was impossible to move on to the second phase of the program. Everything has its limits...

The exploratory microbot returned to Hydra IV through the same flap from which it had emerged. The bionic brain reactivated the automatic system that protected against intruders and waited. It would wait until someone arrived and uttered the password in what was already a dead language (although no Hydra could be aware of this detail). It did not know when this person would arrive—or if they would ever even appear. That was of no interest to the Hydra. The order stored in its memory should the second phase of the program not be carried out was to wait, and the Hydra would wait.

3

Five months later, some hundred kilometers away, another exploratory microbot reached the surface.

Hydra II had awoken.

The bionic brain studied the data received.

These were promising. The microbot had emerged a short distance from the highest point of a small mound; according to the microbot, which emerged on its southwestern flank, it was approximately three meters and sixteen centimeters above the surrounding plain and some forty meters in circumference. The mound was covered in grass and dotted here and there with medium-sized rocks, most of them with diameters of between thirty and sixty centimeters. The plain around it had other irregular outcrops, none of them as high as this one, at least in the immediate surroundings that the microbot could survey. Bushes, or something that through the infrared rays seemed very much like them, filled the landscape. According to the amount of light recorded, it was nighttime—a cloudy, moonless night, which, Hydra II decided, was perfect for carrying out a closer inspection of the terrain without risk of being discovered.

Guided by its microradar, the microbot slid down the gentle incline to the base of the mound and began its circumnavigation, avoiding the thickest bushes (which is what they were, definitely).

When it reached the eastern side of the mound, it discovered an oddly shaped area devoid of vegetation. As far as the microbot could determine it ran from southeast to northwest in irregular curves. It was on average a meter wide. Beyond it there was more grass and bushes.

The explorer moved toward the area to study it more closely.

The surface was earth. It was not damp and lumpy, like the soil under the grass, but dry and compacted. The sample the microbot collected for analysis disintegrated into fine dust when handled. The bionic brain gave orders for the microbot to explore this ribbon of bare earth, and it did so. As it advanced, it became aware of small depressions in the ground's surface, occurring apparently at random—at least based on the data collected. Unfortunately, these depressions were superimposed on each other, making a detailed examination impossible. The explorer had to travel to the edge of the ribbon before it found a single isolated print. It was the shape of an irregularly lengthened ellipsis, narrowing slightly in the upper third. Or possibly in the lower third. There was insufficient information to assess the meaning, if it indeed had one.

The microbot carefully measured the consistency of the earth and the size of the depression.

It must have been caused by a weight (not a very heavy one, about twenty-five kilograms at most) that had been pressed down for a moment and then lifted.

The order came for the probe to move on. It continued its progress along the path. Now it turned once more, moving into the mound, where the path cut out a large chunk, forming a miniature ravine. The wall on the side of the mound reached about two meters high; the separated fragment was a little more than a meter and a half tall. Further on, the path left the mound and wound its way between other small hillocks.

The probe received the order to return. The bionic brain had decided it now had sufficient information to initiate the second phase of the program. Hydra II had to work quickly, making the best use of the time available before the darkness of the night lifted.

Ferhad's Adventure

1

ALMOST UNNOTICED, the level of the fog had sunk so that by now it barely reached Ferhad's waist. When he saw the rags the hero was wearing to protect himself from the cold, Bennie clenched his fists angrily. How Ferhad had suffered in the dungeons of Castle Danger! Just thinking of what awaited him if he was recaptured made the hairs stand on the back of Bennie's neck. Oh no, it could not happen. He had to escape, he *must* escape... He looked further on, his heart in his mouth. Yes, there they were, wonderfully close now: the Black Mountains. Ferhad only had to cross them, and he would be safe. Beyond the Enchanted Valley, the Wizard Bohz had much less power, and Ferhad could face him as an equal...

Bennie held his breath. What was that green whirlwind heading straight for Ferhad? What could he do? How could he avoid being turned to stone, like so many others who had dared defy the all-powerful Bohz? There's no way I can warn you... What? Oh, good, very good. Ferhad had come to a halt, freezing so that he looked like just another one of the countless statues dotted all over the Enchanted Valley. The whirlwind swept past only a few centimeters from his chest, unaware that its master's bitterest enemy was right there.

Bennie laughed to himself, relieved. What great luck that these whirlwinds could only sense moving objects... Ferhad was on the move again. Perfect, the fog barely covered his thighs now. Bennie could see the entrance to the ravine not far off. He would soon be through it, and... But could it be there were even more whirlwinds than before?

Fearful, he bit his lips. Bohz surely must have discovered that his prisoner had escaped, and was mobilizing his shadowy army to recapture him. He knew only too well the danger that a free Ferhad represented for him, with all that he knew of his secrets... But the hero was almost out of his reach; now that the fog was only as high as his knees, the whirlwinds would not be able to touch him. Or would they? Hurry up, Ferhad, hurry up... Bennie urged him on silently.

A flash of red light blinded him for an instant. What was that? He peered through half-closed eyes. Everything appeared normal... Then another blinding light, yellow this time! Bennie realized what it was: the Spell of the Seven Colors! His lips curled scornfully. Ferhad wouldn't fall into that trap. Yes, he knew how to counter the spell, but if he did so, Bohz would immediately know where he was. Ferhad wasn't that stupid... Smiling to himself, Bennie watched him go on his way, pausing with eyes closed just before the explosion of another cascade of color: dark blue, orange, purple, pale blue, green... Bennie laughed under his breath. Give up, old man Bohz? Are you convinced yet that Ferhad is cleverer than you?

The hero had already begun his climb toward the mountain pass, free at last from the treacherous fog. Only a short distance now and he would make good his escape... But it was not certain yet. With a shudder, Bennie remembered the lookouts. It went without saying that Bohz had already alerted them to the prisoner's escape, adding a few threats about the horrible fate of any who let him get away... Quivering with emotion, Bennie saw the hero glance back one last time at the Enchanted Valley. Nearby, Bennie could see the dark mass of Castle Danger, the countless green whirlwinds swirling in between the stony heads of their victims poking out from the everlasting gray fog. A yellow sky hung above this gloomy landscape, unchanged by day or night... Bennie could feel a shiver run down his back; the evil saturating the valley was palpable, real.

Turning around again, Ferhad stepped into the ravine. Now he had to search for Heen, The Elf with Far-Seeing Eyes, and the fearsome Brattnir, the Dwarf with the Hammer. Together, the three of them could... Be careful, Ferhad! The lookout!

Bennie's eyes could hardly follow the hero's sudden leap backward. Where he had been standing only a second before, the giant spider was writhing in the midst of clouds of dust, laboriously rising to its feet. Still dripping from its half-open jaws was the black venom that would have paralyzed Ferhad instantly, leaving him defenseless in its power... Attack it as quickly as you can, before it has time to recover!

Bennie struggled to control himself. No, not that way; his hero would never attack someone unable to defend themselves. He would wait until it was able to face him, and then... Bennie licked his lips, parched from the anticipation of the forthcoming duel. Ferhad was drawing—oh so slowly!—his sword. How it glittered!

Freshly restored, the giant spider withdrew to its corner, its evil little eyes glinting with anger and fear. It was clear that the speed of Ferhad's reaction had confused it. If this were added to the warnings Bohz must have given them about the fugitive's skill in combat... Quickly, Ferhad! Attack it before it flees!

Anticipating Bennie's thoughts by a fraction of a second, Ferhad had leapt forward, brandishing his gleaming sword threateningly.

The giant spider's possible escape route was cut off, so it would have to fight...

All at once, Ferhad and the giant spider disappeared.

In their place Bennie saw the image of a well-known female face.

"Oh no, Mom!" he groaned. "Couldn't you have chosen another moment?"

Ignoring his protest, the holographic projection asked with apparent seriousness, "Aren't you Ben Slidell?"

"No!"

The hologram clicked her tongue.

"That's a shame. I'll have to tell Winnie not to..."

Bennie immediately recovered his own personality.

"Winnie? Why didn't you say so?" Without waiting for her reply, he removed the inductive visor from his eyes. Why had Winnie come so early? he wondered as he struggled with the sensoheadset. What time was it anyway?

"What time is it, Duende?" he asked out loud.

The reply flashed quickly through the air.

"It is fourteen hours and twenty-two minutes on the eighth of No—"

"That's enough," Bennie said, interrupting the prodigious cybernetic intelligence. He got up from the armchair and walked to the closest wall. He hadn't realized it was so late...

"Duende! Clothes!" he ordered.

The wall slid open. Two slender arms emerged from inside, holding in their pincers a white tunic with a red belt. Bennie shook his head.

"Not that. I want a brown one."

Ferhad always wore brown tunics.

2

"Winnie..."

The young girl's eyes rose quickly toward the spot where the tree trunk split into two heavy branches. The three-dimensional image of Donna Slidell's head reappeared in the divide.

"I've told him. Do you want to come in and have something to drink while you're waiting?"

The girl refused politely.

"No thanks, Aunt Donna, we're late. Perhaps on our way back..."

Aunt Donna nodded.

"As you wish, sweetheart."

The head disappeared.

Winnie settled back onto the stone she had been sitting on, her eyes fixed once again on the tree trunk.

She waited.

A minute later, her foot began to tap rhythmically on the carpet of fallen leaves. If Bennie didn't appear soon, they would arrive late to the park...and just the day that the individual *avispas* competitions were about to start. Their Uncle Trainer had warned them...

The bark of the tree slid back silently, revealing a broad oval cavity inside and Bennie's rising head. The force fields pushed him upward, revealing little by little his elegant chestnut-colored tunic, secured at the waist with a broad black belt. His boots were also black and almost reached his knees.

Without waiting for his feet to reach the ground. Bennie jumped out of the elevator.

"Last one to reach the meadow is a cybo!"

Ten seconds later their figures vanished between the trees. Donna Slidell disconnected the sim-dow with a maternal smile. Her beloved, marvelous Bennie... There was no denying he could be exasperating at times, but at others—like now—he could be a real tonic for her spirit...

She sighed, and the smile faded. These unproductive periods disturbed her—especially the present one. She couldn't recall another this lengthy and depressing. It had already been two months—or was it three?—of constant efforts, focusing her knowledge and imagination as hard as she could, but to no avail... Could it be that her inspiration had dried up forever?

She gritted her teeth. That remained to be seen.

She concentrated again on the central panel of her desk. Deriaguin's articles were always stimulating; the audacity of his thoughts had often sparked ideas for her. And his prose was so clear...

"A call for you, Donna."

Damn it.

"Who is it?"

Something like a throat being cleared came through the invisible loudspeaker. The tone of her question had not exactly been friendly.

"I... I don't know the person," stuttered the household brain.

It seemed she was destined not to work today.

"It doesn't matter, Duende." He wasn't to blame for the call... And one had to take into account how sensitive the latest models of domestic guardians were.

She made the connection.

The face of a middle-aged man was observing her with a frown from the sim-dow screen.

"Is this the emotional engineer Donna Slidell?"

Donna raised her eyebrows slightly.

"No, I'm Donna Slidell, the environmental engineer," she said, stressing the syllables of *en-vi-ron-men-tal*, but the stranger did not back down.

"My name is Mifflin. Giles Mifflin, philosopher. I am currently looking for a new place to live, Slidell. Somewhere pleasant and peaceful; that is what I need for my meditation..."

Donna smiled to herself. In general she did not like refusing requests from people wishing to live in Tranquil Grove, but in this case... She brusquely interrupted his explanation of all the demands his new place of residence would have to fulfill.

"I'm sorry, Tifflin..."

"Mifflin," the man corrected her in a hurt tone.

"All the dwellings here are occupied at the moment, and none of them are likely to fall vacant in the immediate future."

Mifflin lowered his puzzled eyes to something she could not see through the sim-dow. He raised them again almost at once.

"There must be some mistake, Slidell. In the housing lists there are only twenty units marked here."

"Which is correct. That's the number of dwellings in Tranquil Grove."

"Twenty units in five hectares?"

"Exactly, that's why it's called tranquil."

The man blinked. He had obviously lost much of his original confidence.

"Oh, yes..." he stammered. "But I don't think the difference between twenty and twenty-one is significant, Slidell. We could..."

By now, Donna had classified the man (every environmental engineer was necessarily something of a psychosociologist). He must be one of those mystics who think they are the navel of the world.

She thought about what she should do now. It would not be ethical to suggest he wait for a unit to fall vacant; it was obvious Mifflin would not get through the compatibility tests with his future neighbors. There was only one solution... She took a deep breath.

"I'm sorry to disappoint you, Mifflin, but twenty is the optimal number. Only an environmental specialist could grasp the basis of the calculations that led to this conclusion, and you are not one. It seems to me it would be useless for you to waste your time..." And mine, she thought to herself. "...listening to arguments you wouldn't understand. The only thing I can suggest is that you go and see Rickenbacker. Arnold Rickenbacker," she pronounced his name slowly and clearly, "the environmental engineer. He is a specialist in the construction of hermitages. If you don't like his designs, you could ask him to recommend other people who specialize in that area. He knows it better than me."

Giles Mifflin had enough time to recover his lofty disdain. "Thank you," he muttered coldly, and cut the communication.

Donna leaned back in her chair. She felt terribly tired, and it was no wonder; being an environmental engineer was no easy task. Environmental, not emotional, as that idiot had said. How could anyone not distinguish between "emos" and "enviros"? At least emotional engineers did not have to put up with arbitrary requests like this one... Yet there were some undeniable similarities; both kinds of engineering (the only ones left on Earth) demanded from their practitioners that very special sensitivity to beauty, which linked to a deep understanding of keys unlocking the instinctive fibers of humanity and arousing emotions that, when skillfully manipulated by those who created them, culminated in an enrichment of both the individual and the collective universe, new sensory-intellectual experiences (or possibly intellectual-sensual ones, as the correct term was still being debated)... But that was where the similarity ended.

The creations of emotional engineers could be—and needed to be—aggressive, incisive, like real magnets that it was practically impossible to escape from, but they were only bearable for a few minutes at a time...or, in the best of cases, a few hours. Any longer exposure would render the recipient emotionally unresponsive or even drive them mad. No, the "enviros" had to be much more subtle...

Besides, it was not simply a question of the emotional needs of those who inhabited the dwellings, laboratories, or parks; other limiting factors had to be taken into account. Looked at in this way, the work of environmental engineers was almost as complex as that of the analysts; they needed to know about ecology (it was preferable that the biological surroundings suffer the least possible impact), cybernetics (it was no easy matter to decide on the best configuration of domestic service systems; a home that required too little attention from its resident was as inconvenient as one that demanded too much), and psychosociology (the layman could have no idea about the differences in taste that normally existed between two clients with apparently similar characteristics)... The complete list of qualities an environmental engineer had to possess would be almost limitless. And this wonderful work—that required as much subtlety as energy, as much inspiration as cool calculation—was her profession. Or would it be more accurate to say "had been"?

Donna chewed her lip. She needed a break; in her current state of mind she would not get anywhere.

She used the controls on her desk to switch off the images of a calm sea... She could no longer hear the rhythmic slap of the waves on the nonexistent beach (a rhythm she herself had carefully chosen to create the maximum soothing effect while at the same time minimizing disruption to her creative faculties). For a brief moment her studio appeared as it really was: a room with bare walls constructed fifteen meters underground.

She connected the sim-dow system, and the wood murmured around her.

She stood up. Bennie would of course have left his room in a mess; that was what always happened when Winnie surprised him watching a feelie movie.

Risky Decisions

1

ALL AT ONCE, Bennie came to a halt—so suddenly that Winnie almost collided with his back.

"What's wrong?" she asked. She wasn't happy; they were still in the middle of the plain, barely halfway to the park, and she was worried they would not arrive in time for the competitions. On the other hand, although they had been running at a regular pace that allowed them to cover long distances almost without tiring, she was beginning to find it hard to catch her breath, so on second thought a rest wasn't such a bad idea.

Without looking back at her, Bennie raised a hand calling for silence. He was closely scrutinizing the small hillock in front of them.

Intrigued, Winnie asked again, unconsciously lowering her voice, "What's wrong, Bennie?"

"An ambush," the boy muttered over his shoulder in what he hoped sounded like a growl.

Winnie's eyes gleamed. "What shall we do?" she asked, putting on a worried look.

The young warrior did not even bother to reply. With his arms folded across his chest, he was examining the scene of the imminent combat... He frowned with displeasure; there was no way to avoid it.

The path went through the center of the mound, turning a corner that made it impossible to see the exit on the other side... Concealed at some point on the way, the lookout would be waiting...

"Bennie, is the ambush on the path?"

He nodded, his thoughts elsewhere.

"In the part that crosses the little hill?"

Bennie nodded a second time, pleased at how quickly his charge had understood the situation.

"What if we went around instead?"

Bennie briefly considered her alternative... No, he decided: that would ruin everything. "No," he whispered fiercely, turning his head. "It's surrounded by quicksands."

Tremendously excited, Winnie went closer until she was almost breathing down his neck.

"So what can we do?" she asked.

"Just our luck we didn't bring a single wasp with us," the young warrior grunted. He peered at Winnie with great concern. How could he make sure the princess reached the castle? He couldn't delay any longer or his pursuers would catch up with them. There was only one solution.

He gave a whispered order. "Follow me, Winnie. But keep your distance. Let me go three paces ahead at least. And try not to make any noise. We may take him by surprise. Got that?"

All this time, Hydra was trying to evaluate the situation. There were two of them. According to its program, the ideal sample size was one, but until now seven groups had gone by, each with between two and five. It had let them all pass. Should it do the same with these two? All the data suggested there was only a small possibility of coming across an isolated individual.

One boot edged slowly forward, then the other, just as silently. Bennie paused, trying to hear something, any sound that might tell him where the lookout was lying in wait. All he could hear was his own racing heartbeat. He looked ahead to where the bend began, and with it, danger... He tried to think calmly. What would Ferhad have done in this situation? He recalled the feelie movie and bit his bottom lip, annoyed at himself. He was behaving in the worst possible manner. Ferhad knew that the ravine was guarded by his enemies, and yet he had not slunk along it like a cornered rat. No, he had strode boldly into it, with apparent nonchalance but without letting his guard down for a single instant... Now Bennie thought about it, it was obviously the best way. Only in that way would the giant spider become overconfident and attack Ferhad directly, without taking any precautions. Bennie smiled a hard smile. This lookout would soon see who he was dealing with. He strode on, glancing quickly to each side. There was no way they would catch him unawares...

Horrified, Winnie felt a lump rise in her throat. Had Bennie gone crazy? How could he walk into the lion's den so unconcernedly? Yet she also quickened her step; better to follow him than to remain on her own. The sudden sound of falling earth paralyzed her for a moment. What could have happened? Abandoning all caution, she ran to the bend where her friend had vanished a second earlier.

Standing on top of the steep right-hand edge of the curve, Bennie was staring at the far side. He had turned pale.

Slightly reassured, Winnie found enough voice to speak.

"What happened, Bennie?"

The boy swallowed hard before replying.

"Nothing serious, Winnie... Just a small landslide over there." He pointed with a trembling hand to the far side of the path.

Winnie looked in the direction he was pointing.

33

She could see signs of the recent slip in the wall of the mound opposite them. Part of the path was covered with damp earth and rocks.

"It fell just as I was passing through," Bennie said.

Winnie looked up at him admiringly.

"How did you manage to get up there?"

It was a hard question to answer. In all truth, Bennie himself had no idea.

"Well...by jumping, obviously," he replied with a shrug. That must be somewhere near the truth, he thought, looking down. His problem now was a different one: how was he to get down? The almost vertical face of bare earth offered no footholds, and in order to live up to his recently acquired reputation, he would have to jump down again, but his legs were trembling so much he wasn't sure he could do it. It was at least a meter and a half high, he told himself after a swift calculation. No, better not to run any risks...

He walked a few steps along the top to regain confidence in his lower limbs, while at the same time trying to find somewhere lower. Finally, he jumped, landing on hands and feet next to his friend.

"Let's take a look at that cave, Winnie," he suggested, brushing off his knees.

"What cave are you talking about?"

"That..."

Bennie broke off in surprise. He was staring at the irregular patch of damp earth that showed where the landslip had occurred. How odd! From where they stood, there was no sign of the cave.

He walked up to the fresh mound of earth.

It was not that high, and the rocks weren't that big. If he had stayed on the path, all he would have regretted was getting his boots dirty. But yes, there was the entrance to the cave; his eyes had not deceived him.

"Come and look, Winnie. It's here."

They had to kneel down to see inside it. It was not very deep. At the far end, something shone feebly.

"Do you think it's a cave prairie dogs use?"

Bennie automatically sniffed the air. The smell of a den inhabited by wild animals (or tame ones, for that matter) was unmistakable, but there was no trace of one.

"If it ever was, they haven't used it for a long time," he assured Winnie, examining the diameter of the entrance. "Besides, dogs' caves are much narrower. I could easily climb inside this one myself. Yes, I'll try. I want to know what's gleaming at the back there."

Winnie grabbed him by the tunic belt to stop him. When he turned angrily toward her, she simply asked, "What if the roof falls in?"

Her question made Bennie think. He looked up at the earth wall above his head. It was almost, if not quite, two meters high. Winnie had made a good point; if it came down, he would be trapped. But would it collapse? He felt the top of the cave with his hand. It seemed solid. He punched at it; a few loose clods fell off, but nothing more.

"I think it's firm enough, Winnie," he said. "Besides, if it weren't, it would have come down with the landslide." He smiled at her reassuringly, before concluding, "Keep an eye on me when I go in. If you spot any danger, shout to me, alright?"

He dropped to his hands and knees and started into the cave.

Winnie instinctively raised a hand to her wrist strap. All she had to do was take it off for an alarm to sound back at her home.

She didn't remove it. It would take them too long to reach here. By then Bennie would already be back out, and if he learned she had made such a fuss... He already made fun of her for wearing the security strap; she didn't want to make it even worse.

She looked at her friend's feet in front of her, still in the cave entrance. Luckily, it wasn't very deep...

Twenty-eight kilos.

Enough light shone in over Bennie's shoulder for him to be able to make out what had attracted his attention; it was a gleaming rock crystal.

He stretched his hand out toward it. Perhaps he could pull it out. It was really pretty, Winnie would like it.

Hydra activated the sample-collecting system.

Raising a hand to his lips, Bennie sucked instinctively on his finger. He had to be careful; these rocks had sharp points and edges.

MASCULINE GENDER. APPROXIMATE AGE: NINE YEARS. USE VARIANT A.

Bennie took the piece of rock in both hands, trying to pull it out of the cave's back wall. It didn't budge. Perhaps if he tugged harder...

Inside what appeared like a piece of rock crystal, a microcapsule slid along a slender channel up toward where the temperature of the crystalloid metal wall had risen slightly, and came to rest by an injector outlet.

VARIANT A PREPARED.

ACTIVATE.

Bennie grimaced. He'd been pricked. Muttering to himself, he changed the position of his injured right hand. He'd sacrifice both of them rather than leave that stubborn rock there. Perhaps if he used the other one as a lever?

Hydra activated its camouflage plan.

"Bennie, earth is coming loose!"

A clod hit him on the back of the neck. Then another. A trickle of sand ran down his back. Bennie crawled backward as fast as he could. Would he get out in time?

A hand grasped him by the edge of his tunic and pulled hard at him. Half-blinded by the cloud of dust, he stood up outside the cave.

"Get back!"

Winnie made him get away from the collapsing cave wall and the cloud of soil and sand still growing in its interior.

"Only you would think of going in there, knowing there could be another collapse... Why were you in there for so long?"

"There was a rock crystal. I tried to pry it out, but I couldn't..."

Winnie's eyes flashed.

"Idiot! You were the one who caused the landslide!"

There was no answer to that. He would do better to examine his right hand; the scratches hardly hurt anymore, but...

"Did you hurt yourself?" she asked anxiously. "Let me see..."

The two of them looked at the palm of his hand.

"This is where I was cut...and here, too."

Winnie inspected the tiny punctures. She pressed the fleshy part of his index finger between her fingers, but no blood appeared. She did the same with the second cut, at the base of his thumb, but nothing came out there either.

By now the microcapsule had reached the capillary network, and the bloodstream was taking it away from its entry point and into the body. Now it was merely a matter of time. There would be times when it collided with the walls of veins, and it would take time to become unstuck and continue its erratic journey. Sometimes it would take the wrong route out of the heart or the aorta and be forced to make a lengthy detour. Sooner or later, though, it would find itself in an artery. From there it would climb to the brain and once there activate the location system for its final destination: the frontal lobe... It would reach its goal and remain there until it died. It was all a question of time.

Relieved, Winnie let go of her friend's hand.

"It's nothing, two scratches that are almost invisible." She ran a stern eye over Bennie's disheveled appearance and said, "Let me get the dust off you; you can't turn up at the park looking like that."

A couple of minutes later, Winnie looked him up and down for the hundredth time. Good, he didn't look perfect, but he would do.

"I think you're okay now," she said. She remembered the competitions and added, "We have to hurry, Bennie. Shall we have another race?"

The boy stopped gazing sadly at the spot where the cave entrance had been. The new pile of earth had completely covered it. A shame about the rock crystal.

"If you like, Winnie," he said, preparing himself for the start.

2

Her hands trembling with excitement, Donna removed her sensoheadset. Don't be silly, she told herself, Fawcett was bound to have registered the idea already. And if not him, then some other emotional engineer. It was absurd to think they hadn't already discovered this treasure.

And yet she asked out loud, "Duende, connect me to the Central Archive, would you? Environmental Projects please, as quickly as possible."

During the short wait, she forced herself to think calmly. Even if nobody had registered the idea already, there remained another question: are Ferhad's adventures popular enough to justify such a project? Of course, Bennie liked them, but what about the child public in general?

"Environmental Projects here. I'm listening…"

Normally, Donna would have immediately asked the Archive to adopt Duende's voice; she couldn't bear the new basic female voice they used. It was so sweet, so exquisitely modulated, so perfect... It was as inhuman as you could wish. She thought her household brain's voice was much better; sometimes it sounded gruff, at other times it was uneven, because it followed a random program. That gave Duende something imperfect and human; it was as if it made it closer, more familiar. But on this occasion she was so excited that she asked straight out, "Projects, has any idea been registered to create a recreational park using the environmental framework of the feelie film," she looked at the label in her hands, "number 23-SD-VII-C? To be more precise, using the Enchanted Valley?"

The answer came instantaneously: "No, that has not been registered." Then, in a tone of friendly inquiry, Projects went on: "If you would like to do so..."

"Yes, I would like to." Donna could hardly keep from crying out with joy; they had all been blind, blind.

"Consider it done. Will there be anything more?"

"No..." Then, recalling the question about popularity, she quickly corrected herself. "I mean, yes, there is. Transfer the connection to Socio-emotional Statistics, would you?"

"At once..."

A second later, the sur-human voice replied: "Socio-emotional Statistics here. What would you like to know?"

Donna was surprised at how different Statistics was from Projects. Although they both used the same basic female voice, Projects sounded much more emotional, richer in suggestive tones; it evoked an imaginative person, someone with a lively, curious mind. Statistics, on the other hand, seemed more sober, thoughtful even; it gave the impression of seriousness, of self-absorption... Donna smiled at her train of thought. An imaginative cyber brain. A self-absorbed cyber brain. She had to admit that the enviro who had invented these differences in the basic female voice was a maestro.

"What is the level of acceptance of feelie film 23-SD-VII-C among its target public?" she asked.

She waited anxiously for the answer. For feelie films, the C public comprised children between the ages of nine and twelve. This was the group that, apart from adults, showed the widest range of tastes. It would be asking a lot to find more than ten percent of positive reactions.

"Positive reaction, thirty-nine percent; very positive, twelve percent."

Donna couldn't believe her luck.

"And how widely has it been distributed in Zone IV?"

This was the other danger. Some films were accepted almost universally by the public for which they were intended, but the total of those interested could be too small to justify such a large-scale environmental project. Of course, this tended to happen only among adults, but it could be that Ferhad was still at the stage of initial distribution, seen by only a select group chosen from among fans of this kind of adventure. If that were the case, the favorable percentages would not justify any wider distribution.

"The distribution of the film is not complete..."

"Oh, no!"

"Until now, it has reached only eighty-seven point four percent of the category C public in this Zone. The data supplied show only the reaction of sixty-nine point six percent of the total target population."

Donna gave a satisfied smile. The sample size was big; it was reasonable to assume that the levels of approval would be similar when its distribution was completed. If that were so, the project could reach such a high priority she felt giddy just thinking about it. She had to go on asking.

"Statistics, I should like to know what level of priority an environmental project based on this feelie film would have."

"Please supply the ecological requirements."

Her luck was definitely up. Two months earlier she had been in Reserve 18-IV to try to get some rest and possibly an idea or two. None had occurred to her (fortunately, she could now say), but she had seen, at the very edge of the reserve, a small valley that would fit perfectly. She tried to recall its characteristics.

"I would need a valley about three or four kilometers long, and about two kilometers wide, perhaps a little more." Donna did not entirely trust her memory, and so she added, "A small valley like the one in Reserve 18-IV, very close to its western or possibly southwestern limit. In fact, that one itself could be used...if there's no objection, that is."

She waited. Her request would require numerous internal consultations in the Central Archive. They would need to identify the valley on the basis of her imprecise description, consider the ecological impact of separating it from the rest of the reserve, estimate the probable demand for the environmental theme park, and examine her past record as an environmental engineer. Unconsciously, Donna held her breath for the seven or eight seconds it took for the reply to arrive.

"Your project will be given a provisional level two priority. As you know, the definitive classification will only be provided once the fully completed project has been presented," announced Statistics, with an unmistakably respectful tone to the voice.

Good gracious! Level two!

"Yes, yes, thank you so much for everything, Archive."

"It has been a real pleasure attending to you, Engineer Slidell."

The green light flashing above the control panel to show the Central Archive was connected faded out.

Level two priority!

Donna had never before reached higher than level four, and that had only happened twice (although she had never gone lower than level six either).

She relaxed in her chair, enveloped in a happy glow. Priority two... Well, now she had to keep it at that level. That meant she could finish the park in a matter of months. What was she thinking? In weeks, Donna.

When she had calmed down slightly, she considered the next steps to be taken. This wasn't a project she could undertake on her own; she would need to gather a good team of assessors. First of all, she would need a good cyberneticist. If the people in the valley were going to do everything she intended, it would have to be a leading light, such as Carvalho... Why not him himself, in fact? This was not an offer to be rejected out-of-hand: a level two project! Of course, there was no way of knowing how busy he was. If he didn't have the time, there was always Daskevich. He might not be as brilliant as Carvalho, but he was good, and Donna was sure he would drop whatever he was working on to be involved in a level two priority project. Besides, they had already worked together when they designed those laboratories. They knew each other and got along well; they could understand one another without having to explain everything, and that was important. She decided not to contact Carvalho; old Dask would know what to do...

"Duende!"

"I'm listening, Donna."

"Open a new folder. Call it 'The Enchanted Valley.' First heading, 'possible assessors: cybernetics, Yuri Daskevich; emotistics...'"

She paused. No, Ogabe wouldn't do. Child emotistics had its own characteristics, and she didn't know anyone who worked in that field. She would need to find more information... She sat up straight in her seat. Why hadn't she thought of it before?

"Duende, leave the new project aside for a moment. I want you to find out who the author of..." She glanced down again at the label. "...the feelie film 23-SD is. And quickly, please; I need it now."

It was obvious. Who better than the creator of Ferhad to assess her? It was just a shame that her knowledge of the inside world of feelie films was so negligible. Perhaps the code name hid one of those stars constantly besieged by offers of the most interesting work... But in the worst case, he would surely be able to recommend a good emotional engineer to assist her. After all, it meant bringing one of his creations into reality.

"I have the information you asked for, Donna."

"Proceed."

A rectangular cube appeared out of the wall nearest her. Donna took hold of it and began to scrutinize the smiling stereoscopic image of a young man's face.

"23-SD is the code name the emotional engineer Sidney Barrow uses to register his creations. He is thirty-four years old and has specialized in category C feelie films. So far, he has made seven. He has not taken part in any environmental projects. Do you require any further information?"

"Wait a moment, Duende."

She had never heard the name before. That didn't mean much though; he could still be terribly famous among those who knew about this kind of thing... No, he couldn't be that famous. Up until now no one had used any of the environments he had created; that was an important fact. Now she understood why Ferhad had escaped the attention of the children's enviros... He wasn't so pale, after all; it was simply an effect of him having such dark hair and eyes.

She turned the hologram in her fingers and looked at it from the front. He had a pleasant smile, but there was something melancholy about his look that... well, that had nothing to do with work. What else had Duende told her?

Hmm. Seven feelie films in fourteen years. He had not been that prolific. Or had he? Perhaps it took a long time to create a feelie film.

Donna decided she needed to know more. With her eyes still on the hologram, she asked, "What is his popularity rating?"

"Among the category C public for feelie films, he's considered second level."

Second level. Not excellent or mediocre, simply good. Well, she could talk to him.

"Do you know anything else that might interest me, Duende?"

"Well... Yes, possibly. He likes to play with children. And at the moment, he doesn't have a partner."

Donna's cheeks flushed. She looked up from the hologram.

"That information does not interest me," she pointed out sharply.

She put the hologram away in the front pocket of her tunic. She would continue working in her study. She needed to create a model of the park in her simulator before she spoke to Dask, and...

She paused outside the elevator door, with the sensoheadset under her arm.

"Duende?"

"I'm listening."

"Include Darrow among possible emotistic assessors."

"I will do so, engineer."

Duende's tone was respectful. Possibly too respectful?

Donna pursed her lips and entered the elevator; she was not going to let Duende's suspicions deprive her of the right assessor.

In the Realm of Emotions

1

SIDNEY DARROW approached the simulator, intrigued. Perfect: that was the only way to describe it, he decided. He had to admit she knew how to do things.

He remained silent for a while, lost in his contemplation of the replica of Castle Danger. He was pleased to see there was not a single battlement missing, even though the model was so small. But the most important success in his view was that the tiny maquette had kept the gloomy, threatening aspect of the original. Only the mist was absent...

"Weren't you able to reproduce the mist?" he asked, raising his eyebrows inquiringly at the young blonde woman standing beside him.

"Oh, yes... If you want to see it..." Donna replied hurriedly, stretching a hand out toward the top part of the simulator control panel.

A thin gray mist immediately began to cover the Enchanted Valley, while wisps of whitish cloud began to pour from the walls of the tiny castle, as if driven by gusts of wind.

"I didn't connect it before so that you could appreciate all the details better."

The effect took Sidney's breath away. He gestured to show his satisfaction. The model was almost as good as his own, which was much larger, and she had constructed it in only three hours—if she had not been exaggerating slightly, that is. He smiled broadly at her. Even if it had taken her longer, it would be worth working with her, and perhaps...

Blushing, Donna looked away and busied herself smoothing a nonexistent crease in her green tunic.

Sidney smiled again. Some people thought being shy was a defect, but he disagreed. He looked down at the model once more. No need to embarrass her any further. Yes, she had been right not to start the mist; now he couldn't make out the terrain, apart from the mountains. But, what was this?

He leaned forward to get a better view. No, he wasn't mistaken; that gorge should not be there. Nor that other one. They had obviously been working too quickly. He would have to tell her so.

"I think there are more gorges than there should be, Slidell." Pointing with his finger until he almost touched the model, he explained, "Here you can see one, two...five gorges, but the Enchanted Valley has only three."

Bending over (perhaps too close; she realized her hair was brushing against his shoulder, and moved away slightly), she pointed to another part of the maquette.

"I think you've missed this other entry point, Darrow," she said, turning her candid gray eyes on him. "In fact, the model has six entry gorges. Each of the original ones has been duplicated on the other side of the valley. Ah, and you can call me Donna, everybody does."

"So why has the original been altered?"

Silly me, thought Donna; she shouldn't have forgotten Sidney's lack of experience in this kind of environmental scheme.

"If there were only three entry points, the park could only receive some five hundred visitors a day; but if we want to meet the projected demand, we need to double that."

Sidney blinked in astonishment.

"But..."

Donna held up her hand to interrupt him; all too often people thought that enviros were magicians.

"Let me explain. There's no other way to do it, believe me." She operated the control panel nimbly, and a screen appeared covered in numbers and diagrams. She brought it closer to him and explained.

"The park will only be open from eight in the morning to ten at night. Any longer is impossible." She cut short her companion's second attempt to speak, raising her hand again in a manner that was delicate but imperious. "Yes, I know. The dome we will use to simulate the golden sky makes the park independent of sunlight and meteorological phenomena, so in theory it could stay open twenty-four hours a day, but in practice we have to keep to this timetable. We have to abide by the time the public—that is, the children—need to sleep. Is that clear?"

Fearing he might never get a word in, Sidney simply nodded weakly. After all, he had to try to see things from her viewpoint. That was the only way they could understand each other and work well together.

Donna went on in a calmer tone.

"Alright, so we've established that the park will work for fourteen hours a day. It's obvious that the actual opening hours will be less, let's say approximately twelve hours. It seems to be impossible to guarantee a satisfactory adventure in less than two hours. So, in order to resolve the problem of admitting a thousand visitors in those twelve hours..."

Sidney could not contain himself any longer.

"But...that's absurd!" he burst out. Donna's astonished look made him soften his tone somewhat, but he continued forcibly.

"The mere idea of seeing Ferhad shepherding a hundred children through the Enchanted Valley like a tourist guide..." His renewed anger made him lose the thread. "It's pitiful! Such a disappointment! What kind of adventure can it be under those circumstances?"

Donna struggled to hold back a smile. Remember, he has no experience, she told herself. But he was obviously sensitive; they could understand one another. She continued more gently, almost as if apologizing.

"I never ever thought of allowing children to enter in big groups, Darrow... They'll come in one by one, or at most in pairs of friends. I also realize that any larger numbers would prevent it being a real adventure."

Still not convinced, Sidney shook his head.

"How do you expect to reconcile this individual adventure with a thousand child visitors a day?"

Donna gave a broad smile.

"That's the job of an enviro, Darrow. But before I go into detail, think what would happen if only one or two children entered the Enchanted Valley at the same time and no new visitors were allowed in until they had left. The park could only cater to a dozen children a day. Then what would we do with the hundreds of thousands who want to come, if only once, and wouldn't be able to? We'd have to build thousands of Enchanted Valleys, wouldn't we?" She paused for him to take this in, before going on. "Even discounting the amount of energy and materials needed, where would we find the space on Earth to make so many Enchanted Valleys?"

Sidney said nothing.

"Alright, so let's move on to how to solve the problem. How can we make each and every one of the children who enter the Enchanted Valley feel that they are alone there, with their hero Ferhad? Where had we gotten to?" She glanced at the screen. "Ah, yes; we have twelve hours for them to explore the Valley. The idea is to leave an interval of ten minutes between each visit. We calculate that any less time would make it impossible to avoid the children seeing one another and destroying the illusion of a real adventure. However, with our park, I think it will be possible to reduce this to six minutes without any problem; the gorges are full of bends, and once the children have emerged from them there is the constant mist covering everything. In my view, that means there is no risk of the visitors seeing each other. In this way, we can guarantee there will be seven hundred and twenty independent visitors through the six entry points each day."

Frowning, Sidney interrupted her.

"But how many Ferhads will we need?"

Donna rolled her eyes up to the ceiling.

"I hadn't considered that detail yet, but I think a hundred and fifty should be enough. Perhaps a few more in reserve."

Sidney collapsed into the nearest armchair. A hundred and fifty Ferhads was too much for him.

Donna understood. She rested a sympathetic arm on his shoulder.

"I can imagine how you feel, Darrow. But we're obliged to observe these things from the wings. I don't know if that means anything to you."

Sidney nodded, his face expressionless.

"We studied ancient theater, too, Slidell."

"Perfect. From our point of view, it's a real nightmare to have to find a hundred and fifty Ferhads. But for every child who enters the Valley there'll be just one of the hero they worship. Do you follow me?"

Sidney nodded again, somewhat reassured. Donna suddenly realized she still had her hand on his shoulder and quickly withdrew it; her gesture could be misinterpreted. This was a work relationship, nothing more.

"Well then, where were we? Oh, I remember: seven hundred and twenty visitors. Alright, let's say that forty percent are pairs of children, and the rest..."

Sidney raised his hand in protest.

"Please, no more figures. Do you guarantee that six entry points are necessary?"

It was Donna's turn to nod her head.

"Fine, then so be it. I have only one problem with that. Isn't there a danger that the children will see there are more gorges than there should be?"

"Impossible," replied Donna firmly. "Don't forget that because of the mist they won't be able to see further than a hundred meters. And when they come out of a gorge, which is the only point when their ability to see won't be restricted, the opposing gorge will be at least two kilometers away. Even if at that very moment another Ferhad appeared with another visitor, they wouldn't be able to spot them. The mist clouds rise to the upper strata of the air, and prevent anybody seeing into the distance."

"So... How many children will be in the Valley simultaneously?"

"By the time there's a steady flow, there will be a hundred and twenty visitors at the same moment. If we factor in those who come in pairs, that makes a total of around one hundred and sixty children."

"Couldn't there be a chance encounter between any of them?"

Donna dismissed the idea with a wave of her hand.

"All the adventures are programed, Darrow. The control cyber brain will make sure we avoid any such clash. Incidentally, we've now come to the part where your collaboration will be vital." Remember he knows nothing about environmental projects. "Did you ever visit this kind of park when you were a child?"

"Yes, but..."

"Were the adventures you had there identical to the ones you knew about from feelie films?"

A smile reappeared on Sidney's face.

"There's no need to beat about the bush, Donna, at least not over this. I read up on it before I came. I'm aware only a few children are satisfied with a simple rehash of the adventures they already know, and so I came prepared to discuss how many alternatives I have to create. However, I'm worried about how many daily visits there will be. Do I have to come up with a hundred different adventures?"

Donna smiled back at him.

"No, it won't be that many. I think five or six will be sufficient. Of course, you'll need to make sure no incidents are repeated, but from those main outlines the cyber brain will be able to combine the different elements to create more than three hundred alternative adventures. I'm afraid that will be the toughest job for us. We'll have to revise them all, and get rid of the least interesting parts. In reality, we will only need half that number, or a few more."

Donna neglected to mention all the work it would take to fit more than a hundred adventures that could be going on simultaneously in the Valley, nor that they would have to select the most appropriate adventure to fit the possible psychological profile of every child visitor... There was no point scaring Sidney off.

"I don't think it will be that difficult..." he began, but a voice coming from the nearest wall interrupted him.

"Mom, where is my sensoheadset?"

Donna quickly switched off the simulator; she didn't want Bennie to see the model. Perhaps, if they worked hard and well, the park would be ready in time for his birthday.

Turning to the wall-screen, Donna smiled at her son.

2

It's difficult to advance blindly, guided only by the weak, irregular electrical impulses that pass through the brain at brief intervals, at every moment having to avoid yet another new dendrite, another thick axon...

They paused beside the tree. Winnie looked up from the ground and across at the melancholy Bennie. She sighed. What could she do? She tried to encourage him.

"You shouldn't worry. We can all have an off-day." When she saw that Bennie's face only darkened still further at her words, she bit her lip. That obviously wasn't the way to do it. "I'm sorry, Bennie," she whispered. "Really sorry."

"Thanks, Winnie."

An embarrassed silence.

"See you tomorrow then," she said with a forced cheerfulness.

"See you tomorrow," he muttered, then stepped inside the tree without so much as a backward glance. As he slid gently down the black hole, he remembered yet again what had happened that unfortunate afternoon. Twice—*twice*—his wasp had bumped into the sides of the dome before it completed the compulsory exercises. And as a result, he came in last. He stared down at his hands. It had all been his fault; by struggling with that stupid rock crystal he had lost the sensitivity of his skin, the muscular control needed to steer a wasp.

He controlled himself. Alright, that was in the past. He raised his eyes and looked defiantly at the door to his room. There was nothing he could do about what had happened, but tomorrow...tomorrow would be another day, he promised himself as he stripped off his tunic. What he needed now was a good bath.

Leaving his clothes strewn on the floor—he would pick them up later—he went over to the shower corner, his back to the wall.

"Shower, Duende," he said.

A wall of light separated him from the room. A thousand pores opened in the wall, and out of them poured jets of water. He turned around, enjoying the cold darts on his chest.

"Soap," he commanded, and the liquid beating against him turned soapy. He began to carefully scrub his skin.

This was it.

Settling among the neurons, the microcapsule stuck firmly to the axon's myelin coating. Analyzing the composition of the extra-cellular liquid, it compared the results with the rhythm and frequency of the brain waves. It decided they were satisfactory; there were clear signs of tiredness, even though the subject was still awake. Even taking into account the individual variability of human beings, there could be no doubt that the normal hour for sleep was close. The program had been completed; it could perish.

And it did.

The thin protective layer split in all the planned zones, and from inside the dead capsule tiny drops of the narcotic began to ooze out.

"I've finished, Duende."

The wall of light disappeared. Feeling fresh and revitalized, Bennie walked over to his bed with a spring in his step. He had time to finish watching Ferhad's adventures before supper.

He crouched down and thrust his hand into the wall, feeling for the sensoheadset. It wasn't there. He blinked. In the end, taking a shower hadn't been such a good idea. All the day's accumulated tiredness was surfacing.

"Duende, where is my sensoheadset?"

"Donna took it."

"And she didn't put it back?"

"No, she took it with her."

Bennie's head wobbled. His eyelids insisted on closing. It would be best to... No, before he went to sleep, he must at least find out...

"Put me through to my mom, Duende."

The wall in front of him transformed into a three-dimensional image of his mother's study.

"Mom, where's my sensoheadset?"

Donna switched off the simulator quickly; she didn't want Bennie to see the model...

Turning to the wall-screen, she smiled at her son.

"Oh, I forgot to give it back. It's here, come and get it if you like. That way you can meet..." she said, smiling affectionately at Sidney, "...a new colleague of mine. Are you coming?"

Struggling to free himself from the cobwebs of sleep, Bennie drew a hand across his face.

"Oh, no, I'm very tired. I need to go to bed. I just wanted to know..." This really wasn't a good day. The smile his mother gave the unknown visitor suggested that in all likelihood he would soon have a new father. Too sleepy to protest, he could only wish to himself that this one was better than the previous one. Or at least than the one before last.

He yawned a huge, long yawn and said goodnight.

"See you tomorrow, Mom." He switched off the wall and struggled to find his way to bed.

3

No doubt about it, Sidney was good news. How quickly he had entered into the spirit of the project, despite his lack of experience!

Donna carefully finished folding her green tunic and handed it to the wall.

"Take this, Duende."

She walked through the darkness toward her bed, which was visible thanks to the phosphorescent gleam floating above the force field. It occurred to her that it was too small. But could a single bed be any bigger?

As she lay down, the phosphorescence faded. Donna was thankful for the underlying dark; it would help her sort out what was going on inside her. First of all, she asked herself whether she was in love. In love? In love with Sidney? Or was this simply a result of her loneliness?

Seven months had gone by since she and Shelby had ended their relationship. Seven months.

Perhaps there was a relation between her loneliness and her lack of ideas... No. The idea for the Enchanted Valley had occurred to her before she met Sidney. Besides, that wasn't the problem; she had to work out what she felt for him.

He was physically attractive to her, but that wasn't a sufficient reason; she was not an animal. She needed to think about him as a person.

He wasn't the kind who overwhelmed you, someone who openly displayed his qualities, but he *did* have them. He was a real human being. Sensitive. And he loved children. So? Was all this a reason for loving him, or was it because she was alone? Solitude is a bad counselor, she told herself, recalling how only a month before she had been at the point of getting back together with Ogabe.

There was no arguing that her relationship with Ogabe had been marvelous, full of love and understanding; it had perhaps been the best she had known (so far). It wasn't for nothing that it had lasted more than a year. Perhaps that was why Shelby had lasted for such a short time; he couldn't compare. That was also why she had considered trying again with Ogabe and would have done so if she hadn't remembered that these things never worked a second time around. She knew that only too well; when she had decided to get back with Bennie's father Tahar, there had been...

Just a moment. What had all this got to do with her present predicament? That concerned Sidney and her, and no one else. Well, there was Bennie as well, of course. He was already big, and very intelligent. That would make everything more difficult, from a certain point of view...

She turned over in the invisible bed. Perhaps she ought to wait and define her feelings more precisely. But what if Sidney posed the question before she did? What could she say to him?

Well, that he should wait. She set her mouth. He should wait until she could see clearly what...

The last drop of the narcotic had dissolved in the extra-cellular liquid and was now swiftly destroying the interior lining of the perished capsule. A crack soon appeared. Then another, and another... The NEMOs escaped through the growing holes and made their way to the places they had to occupy in order for them to once again be what they had been two hundred years before...

"Donna, are you asleep?"

Caught unawares in the midst of her reflections, she sat up startled in the bed.

"Is something wrong, Duende?"

The domestic brain took some time to answer.

"Well... I'm not sure it's anything important, but it is unusual."

"Just tell me what's happening, Duende."

"Bennie cried out."

"Did he fall? Hit himself? Is he hurt?"

"Not as far as I can tell. He's asleep."

"Ah... It must only be a nightmare."

"Possibly, but I didn't like the sound he made."

Donna could not help but smile. Duende occasionally overdid it with his concern for Bennie, but it was better that way than the opposite... At any rate, there was no harm in finding out exactly what had happened.

"Did you record his cry?"

"Of course. Would you like to hear it?"

"Yes, proceed."

Duende cried out loud.

Donna leapt out of bed and ran toward the wall separating her from her son's room.

V

An Intruder in Tranquil Grove

1

ANTICIPATION OF THE PLEASURE to come sent tiny shivers down Thomas Babson's spine as he approached the human figure stretched out on his workbench. The semidarkness in the interrogation room meant he could not tell whether it was a man or woman. But that didn't matter, he thought with a smile. He began to rummage in his toolbox. He laid the neurovibrator to one side; this time he didn't have to worry about any possible marks. What lay on the bench was waste material. Officially, it was already dead—in a traffic accident, if he wasn't mistaken. And the thing trembling with fear and cold on the table did not know this...yet.

He straightened up, clutching the tools he had chosen, the smile still playing around his lips. It was moments like this that gave life meaning, he told himself. To be able to work at leisure, without bothering about having to ask questions and get answers.

Where should he begin? His brow wrinkled in thought. He had to make sure the experiment lasted; he didn't often get a chance like this. He remembered the previous week's case with distaste. They had been in too much of a hurry then, and that should not be allowed to happen this time.

He chose a foot. The right foot.

He leaned over slowly and deliberately. It was good to increase the patient's nervousness; that led to the best results—especially if he stayed silent. Not a word, whatever the future corpse might shout, say, or sob. As he had observed on previous occasions, the psychological effect of such an attitude was quite surprising. Sometimes, even the toughest could not bear it; the lack of questions during torture disconcerted them, made them lose their internal balance, and then...then, he carried on working. The recorders functioned automatically. All he had to worry about was keeping the patient alive for as long as possible. And conscious, of course. But that completely coincided with his own interests.

Okay, here was the foot. God, how it trembled; he couldn't ask for anything more promising.

He checked the strap around the ankle and was happy with it. It was solid but not too tight. It was always counterproductive to cut off circulation; a limb would then lose most of its feeling.

He licked his lips. Should he start with the big toe? Or the smallest one? It was incredible, all the nerve endings in a foot that people didn't even know about. Chuckling to himself, he laid the instruments out in a neat row on the bench. It was supposed to be best to progress from smaller to larger... So he'd start with the little toe.

He placed the instrument on the required spot, taking more time than was strictly necessary. Unlike a novice, thank God he was well aware of the psychological value of the first impact on the patient's nervous system. Ready. Now, apply a slight pressure... Good.

His smile broadened. It was all going smoothly; he couldn't have asked for a better reaction from his patient. A cry like that would make a rock shudder.

He lit a cigarette. Still holding the match, he hesitated. He could press it against some delicate part of the body. No, it wasn't the right moment yet. He limited himself to threatening with it, here, there, and there, with rapid movements, always making sure that the terrified eyes could see him as he savored the way the flesh of the defenseless body cringed at each move he made. That was enough; if he carried on threatening without doing anything, the effect would be lost. He would play that game again the next time he lit up. Except that then, the thing on the bench would not be expecting to be burnt, and when the match touched its skin... He coughed, leaning forward so that it would not see the gleam in his eyes, and dropped the match on the floor.

He watched it sputter and die out in the puddle of water. Or possibly of blood... He would have to complain; the cleaning team had not been doing its job properly recently. For heaven's sake, he wasn't demanding the sterility of an operating room, but at the very least there should be no water near the table. He might slip at a crucial moment, and then who would be responsible for a premature death?

Annoyed, he turned back to the bench. For the moment, the person who would answer for the lack of cleaning was right there in front of him. Let's look at that foot... It was no longer trembling. Good, good; it had reached the phase of panic rigidity. The next cry would be even better.

He bent over again. A little more pressure...

He pulled back. What was going on? Could it have fainted?

He grimaced with disgust. Such a soft case would hardly offer him any pleasure.

He looked at the face lying there.

The eyes were open.

Had it died already? A heart attack? He went closer to get a better look. No, it was breathing normally. Too normally, he said to himself; by this stage the breathing ought to be rapid, panting even. Perhaps it was in a trance.

He passed his hand in front of the patient's face. It did not blink but was not in a hypnotic trance either. Its eyes had moved and were now focused on him. Was that a smile he saw?

He turned his attention back to the right foot. Perhaps the instrument wasn't properly connected. He checked the installation meticulously. Everything in order.

He wiped the blood from his hands. He was worried; he really did not like what was happening. Alright, he'd try again. Seriously this time. Then we'd see if it was still smiling.

He pressed down on the instrument.

No reaction.

He gradually increased the pressure until it reached the maximum. Blood spurted into his face. He looked over again... Nothing! The leg muscles had not even contracted. Perhaps this time it really had fainted... Christ! It was still smiling!

Clenching his teeth, he removed the instrument. Perhaps it had lost all feeling in that leg.

He realized his hands were shaking. He couldn't work properly like this. For a long minute he concentrated on breathing deeply and rhythmically. He looked down at his hands; that was better.

He picked up his instruments. He would try an arm. The left one, to be more certain.

Three minutes later, he raised his head. His forehead was covered in sweat. A quick glance confirmed his fears; that damned thing tied to the bench was still smiling.

Unable to control himself, he punched the insolent mouth. The flesh split open, and blood poured out, but the smile was still there.

Was that thing laughing at him? At Thomas Babson?

A blind rage swept over him. Seizing a surgical knife, he began to stab at random; the thing must feel pain somewhere.

He cut, stabbed, cut, made a deeper incision... Then he moved to another intact spot.

Another. And another, and another...

He stopped, overcome with a sudden fear; could he have cut the...?

He stepped back, his eyes fixed on the mound of bloody flesh. It was sitting up on the table, free from its bonds. He moved back more and more rapidly... His back touched the wall. Without taking his eyes from the thing walking toward him, he frantically clutched at the damp wall. He was searching for the door lock but couldn't find it.

Of course, it wasn't there. The door was on the far wall. How could he have made such a mistake?

Now that thing was between him and the door, walking toward him.

Perhaps he could edge past it. He slid silently along the wall. The thing changed direction, following him. God almighty, how could it do that with no eyes?

His shoulder bumped into a new obstacle. He turned his head to see what it was.

The side wall.

He was trapped in the corner.

You're stupid, he thought. So stupid. All he had to do was shout for help, and someone...

Then he remembered that the interrogation room was sound-proofed. He turned desperately to face his pursuer.

The handless stumps were waving in front of his face...

He cried out in terror—and woke up, shouting.

2

When she reached Bennie's room, Donna slowed down; she didn't want to alarm him. She walked silently over to his bed and leaned over to look at her son.

It was too dark to see his face.

"More light, Duende," she whispered.

The room became a little brighter. Donna peered at the young boy's face. It was tense and covered in sweat. Bennie was panting. It must have been a nightmare. A terrible nightmare, she told herself, recalling his cry. Should she wake him up?

Before she could do so, Bennie writhed in the bed and cried out again.

Donna was paralyzed with fear; this cry was completely different from the other one. She had never thought it possible to hear such an explosion of animal terror out of a human mouth. Out of a child's mouth. Out of her son's mouth...

As he continued to scream, Bennie's eyes opened. For an instant Thomas Babson gazed fearfully into Donna Slidell's moist eyes.

Then he fainted.

The process was not complete. Many of the NEMOs had still not reached their target.

Bennie opened his eyes again and peered up at his mother.

"What...what happened?" he stammered.

Donna impulsively flung her arms around him.

"Calm down now, don't be frightened... It was nothing; it was only a dream, a bad dream, my little one."

Bennie ran his tongue over his parched palate. A dream? A nightmare? Yes, he seemed to recall there had been something like that... But no, he couldn't remember what it was; it had slipped

from his mind when he woke up. But it had been something...
something bad.

He clung to his mother.

"Mom!"

"What is it?"

Bennie raised his eyes.

"Can I sleep with you?" he begged.

"Of course you can, my love. Come on... Up you get!"

Donna lifted him as she always used to. How heavy he was,
quite the little man already...

"Let us through please, Duende," she whispered.

Crossing the wall, they found themselves in Donna's room. She
walked as softly as she could; from what she could tell from the
steady rhythm of his breathing, Bennie had fallen asleep again.
Poor little thing.

She lay carefully in the bed and placed the boy beside her.

The light in the room dimmed again, without disappearing
altogether. Donna smiled gratefully. Duende knew what he was
doing. If Bennie happened to wake again, he wouldn't find himself
in darkness and would be able to see his mother beside him.

She kissed his hot child's cheek and prepared for sleep.

3

Around midnight, the wind rose, a damp, wet wind. The clouds
came chasing after it and hid the stars.

The wind died down. Then it began to rain, a light, persistent
rain.

At first, the giant trees stoutly defended Tranquil Grove, but
little by little the raindrops penetrated the dense foliage, dripping

from leaf to leaf, joining up, racing to form a complex aerial network of tiny cascades that fell noisily onto the mossy ground.

The layer of humus and dry leaves soaked them up anxiously. The dry beaten earth of the paths became muddy, rapidly dissolving...

The first puddles appeared and began to grow.

The wind blew again; the clouds were needed elsewhere. The stars gradually came out once more, paler than before, as if freshly washed; the day was dawning.

The branches were still dripping when, out of a hundred hiding places, the guardians of the grove began to appear.

They snaked along the muddy paths and began to drink avidly. They drank and drank, swelling up monstrously. One after the other they crawled to the hidden drains, vomited their loads, then, agile and slim once more, they went back to work.

Soon all the paths were dry.

The guardians returned to their dens.

The first rays of the sun filtered through the leaves, speckling Tranquil Grove with light.

It was the start of another day.

———————

VI

A Play of Images

1

BE CAREFUL, the doctor had warned. She was cold, impersonal...
and attractive. Not pretty, but attractive. Devilishly attractive. He
would have to submerge himself in the flood of someone else's
memories, dive deep down, and take care he did not get carried
away, because then Thomas Babson would vanish. Forever. She
spoke without ceasing to smile, but her gaze was chilly. A typical
professional smile, he thought. Very professional. Very attractive.
Of course, he could also reject those memories, she said, her small
hand chopping through the air energetically. Destroy them. But
that would be risky. Very risky. Almost certainly mortally dangerous. She did not recommend it. Thomas Babson was going to wake
up in a very different world. Completely different. My God, she
couldn't imagine how different, he sighed.

He half-opened his eyes. Blue. Everything was blue: pale blue,
dark blue, and every imaginable shade of blue in between, plus a
few more. And they didn't stay still; the myriad subtle tones circled,
gyrated, merged into one another, and seeped into the walls, the
ceiling, the floor, in rhythmic, hypnotic waves.

Shuddering, he closed his eyes again and sobbed; this blue
inferno was nothing compared to the memories that insisted on
floating to the surface. God Almighty, the world could not be like
that!

Yet it was precisely in those memories (the doctor had insisted) that the key to his survival lay. It was very possible he was the first to wake up. He would be alone and vulnerable. Back then he had struggled not to laugh in the doctor's face. Him, Thomas Babson, vulnerable? But that was then. Now he was not laughing anymore. Now he was clenching his tiny infant fists. He mustn't forget that his chances for survival depended on making it seem as though he was still the same individual whose body he had possessed (that Bennie, that cursed Bennie, so naive, so credulous, so stupid) so that then he could...

"Are you feeling ill, my love?"

2

To some extent, Donna felt guilty with regard to Bennie. Hadn't he been the center of all her maternal love, for the past six months at least? And now the Enchanted Valley was coming between them—and possibly Sidney as well. Above all, Sidney. Bennie was very intelligent, and knew her well. She couldn't be sure that when he saw them together he hadn't noticed something. And just now, that same morning, instead of waiting for him to wake up so that they could play the early morning games he enjoyed so much, hadn't she got up stealthily and gone down to her study to finish the chemical formula for that damned fog? (Oh, yes, now it's as impermeable sonically as it is visually. It has no toxic elements. Satisfied, Donna? Have you got something new you can show Sidney and impress him with when you see him this afternoon?) And after that, hadn't she become absorbed in designing possible alternative routes to get into Castle Danger, forgetting to instruct Duende to tell her when Bennie got up so that they could have breakfast together as always?

All of this meant that Duende's anxious call had prompted her remorse. It was her own behavior, her shameful neglect of her son, that explained Bennie's strange behavior.

Bennie, who was curled up in a corner of his room, at times sobbing and groaning, at others trembling in silence, refusing to look at the Blue Symphony she had created especially for him.

She stepped into the elevator. She would not use the intercom. Enough substitutes; there is nothing like a mother's embrace, her kiss, lots of kisses.

When she entered her son's room, her heart skipped a beat. To see Bennie crouching in the corner, shaking all over, as if he were a stranger in his own home! It was too much for her.

"Are you feeling ill, my love?"

Donna! She would discover him immediately, unless... He tried to control his mounting panic; stay calm, he told himself, stay calm or you're a dead man.

"Very ill, Mom..." he managed to say. Good, very good, he told himself. You got the tone just right; it was Bennie's unmistakable voice.

Donna came to a halt in the middle of the room. She could be to blame... But then again, she might not be. She had to find out as quickly as possible.

"Could it be... Could it be you're angry with me?"

Babson hesitated. Was her question a trap? Did she suspect him? There was only one way to find the right answer. Fearfully, he ventures into the quicksands of someone else's memories... No, he decided. Possibly his search had been too quick and superficial, but something as important as a quarrel between Bennie and his mother would have been immediately obvious.

Even so, his voice reflected his uncertainty when he replied.

"No, Mom, it's not that."

Donna frowned. Why had it taken him so long to respond?

"Look into my eyes, Bennie," she asked in a voice that was both gentle and firm.

Babson forced himself to open his eyes.

Good God! Where had the blue walls gone? He blinked as he gazed at the trees all around him. He instinctively felt for the ground beneath him. No, there were not stones or soil there, just the soft, flexible floor made of some kind of plastic he could not identify. He understood: three-dimensional screens. That was what the supposed walls were. Relieved, he raised his eyes and saw Donna's worried face.

"Are you sure you're not angry with me, Bennie?"

"Of course not, Mom!"

The answer came out automatically. Thomas was beginning to get used to the situation.

"So why are you like this?"

"I've already told you, Mom!" (Be careful, not that tone of voice!) "I feel very sick."

Donna came and squatted beside him. She put her warm arm around his childish shoulders.

"Sick in what way exactly?"

Babson improvised.

"I feel dizzy—as if I had vertigo, Mom. Everything is spinning around."

Donna bit her bottom lip. This was unusual; Bennie had always had an iron constitution. She would have to find out what was wrong.

"Duende, bring the health module," she said.

Babson could not help being startled; a silvery rectangle had suddenly materialized in between two trees. It sped toward them, changing into a shiny oblong box almost two meters long that miraculously came to a halt alongside Donna. She had not even blinked. Babson understood; those wall-screens were not in fact solid. Possibly the floor wasn't either; they were all force fields (he had to find this description in Bennie's memory) that, depending on the instructions given to the cyber brain in charge of the house, which was in fact the house itself, could be permeable or solid. He knew that this explanation was dreadfully incomplete; these fields went beyond his knowledge of physics and were obviously also beyond the boy's comprehension—even though he was a boy of this era. If Bennie had been able to get used to them and to use them, so could he...

Donna's voice roused him from his thoughts.

"Let me help you, my love."

The woman lifted him easily from the floor. Why? Was she going to put him on that box? On the health module? What on earth was that anyway?

The information flowed docilely from Bennie's memory; the health module was a miniaturized amalgam of all the clinical diagnosis cybernetic systems had been aware of in his own time, plus a lot more... A lot more? How much was this "a lot more"? Was it capable of discovering that Bennie no longer existed?

Terror ran like wildfire through all the fibers of his taut body. No, he couldn't allow himself to be examined by this machine; he had to refuse, to get away...

Too late; it was already too late. He was enveloped in something invisible, which made it impossible for him to move, and now he was gradually sinking inside the box. His throat contracted spasmodically, but no sound came from his mouth. His lips were paralyzed, too.

Donna waited for Bennie's body to disappear completely inside the health module. Then she waved her hand across the front edge of the box, and a keyboard emerged; she didn't want Bennie to hear the health module's replies. She typed on the polished keys, and her instructions appeared in black and white on the top.

CHECK HIS PHYSICAL CONDITION, HEALTH MODULE. WRITE RESPONSES.

Before her fingers could leave the keyboard, the reply had already flashed up:

INSTRUCTIONS RECEIVED.

Donna prepared to wait. Not for the analysis as such; that would already be complete, of course. The wait was because the health module would need to translate these results into a language that she (no expert in physiology) could understand.

Almost five seconds went by before new writing appeared.

PROFUSE PERSPIRATION.

Pause.

PANTING BREATH.

Pause.

ABNORMALLY RAPID PULSE.

Pause.

EXTREMELY IRREGULAR VARIATIONS IN BODY TEMPERATURE.

A longer pause.

QUESTION: ANY ADDITIONAL INFORMATION?

Donna typed quickly.

BENNIE SAYS HE FEELS DIZZY, VERTIGO.

And waited.

INFORMATION FROM PATIENT COINCIDES WITH OBSERVATIONS MADE.

Exasperated, Donna typed again.

BUT WHAT IS WRONG WITH HIM?

The health module replied evenly.

NO ORGANIC CAUSE.

Donna blinked uneasily. If there was no organic cause, the problem must be mental. Should she consult the sociopsychologist?

The expert would cure Bennie of course (and would also yet again recommend she had another child, and go on about her alleged over-protection of her son). But did that many women have two children? She did not think siblings were really that necessary. She herself did not have any... And on a playground Bennie could meet as many companions of his own age as he wished. What good would a child he had nothing in common with do him? It couldn't compare with Winnie, for example. And anyway, was it so easy to have a child? She would need to meet a suitable father first... Perhaps the health module could offer a different solution.

WHAT DO YOU RECOMMEND?

The health module had obviously been expecting that question; even before she finished making it, Donna saw the black letters appearing on the surface of the box.

FOR THE MOMENT, PHYSICAL AND MENTAL REST. ALSO SUGGEST CONSULT SOCIOPSYCHOLOGIST.

Donna let out a sigh. It was inevitable.

THANK YOU, HEALTH MODULE.

The printed letters vanished, and Bennie's limp body surfaced from inside the box.

Thomas Babson had fainted.

VII

The New Frontier

1

HYDRA II WAS IN A STATE halfway between sleep and waking; it was waiting. Waiting and deliberating.

There were few possible choices. It could go back to the experimental subject, either when he was on his own (in which case everything would be fine) or accompanied by undesirable onlookers (in which case it would activate the self-destruction mechanism, a small white flash, barely visible from the moon, that would destroy both Hydra and the intruders), or not go back.

In that case (which was the most interesting), it would need to start over again. Anticipating this, Hydra II had already chosen the next subject (if it proved necessary). This was the person who had accompanied the first one earlier. This subject had appeared twice on the path again today; the first time heading northwest, the second (obviously returning) heading southeast. On the first occasion, the subject had paused for seven seconds to look at the spot where the trap had been laid. The second time, the person had not stopped at all. It was reasonable to suppose that the subject made this journey on a regular basis; it had done so on two consecutive days. Accessibility to this second experimental subject was the first point in favor.

In addition, to judge by the subject's appearance compared to that of the first one, it belonged to the opposite sex, which would be very convenient for Hydra, as Variant B was applicable only to females. This would of course need verifying and was not a decisive factor, as Variant C was applicable to both sexes, but probabilities indicated the individual was likely to be female. In the age when Hydra was buried, the sex of a nonadult individual could be recognized by external characteristics. The key was the mass of fine threads of organic matter that grew from the individual's top part: if it was relatively long, it belonged to a representative of the male sex, and if short, of the female sex. But these terms could have become inverted, as the case of the first experimental subject seemed to suggest, or it was no longer a determining feature. Those long (dark-colored, almost black) strands proved nothing; they merely pointed in that direction.

In fact, what had made Hydra II decide to choose her (or possibly him) was the fact that this subject had witnessed the first experimental individual's capture. Nothing indicated that s/he had understood what had really happened, but Hydra's program established as a basic principle that it should reduce any risk of being discovered to the minimum so that it could immediately avoid one potential danger by using her/him as the second experimental vessel.

And yet there was a problem—a serious one, and the reason behind Hydra's deliberations. S/he had seen how the basic trap functioned. Hydra would have to create another one.

It appeared that her/his weight was similar to that of the first experimental subject, although that would have to be verified. If Hydra placed a weighbridge beneath the path, it could accurately determine this, and at the same time would obtain a representative sample of the users of this particular path. This could then be compared with the table of weights stored in its memory. (If Hydra were capable of feeling emotions, it would have had to express its profound distaste at having to use the weight of an individual as a criterion of relative maturity, based on tables that had not been drawn up on the basis of the real population it would have to deal with, but it could not argue with its own program—at least, not too directly.)

So Hydra would have to determine the sex of the subject. It had noticed in the zone under consideration that there was a lack of tiny creatures feeding on the internal liquids of the beings that interested them. On first thought, this was a serious obstacle to the application of the mosquito sampling method. However, if the question was considered in more depth, this was in fact another advantage; the subject pricked by the sample collector would not have prepared defense mechanisms, and the risk of the destruction of the collector would be practically nil. That would make it possible to keep the "mosquito" in reserve to use as Variant B (or Variant C if necessary) on the chosen subject.

Hydra's speculations were interrupted by information transmitted from the cyber sentinel posed on top of the hillock; someone was coming along the path, and, to judge by the infrared spectrum (fortunately the night was also very dark), it could very well be the desired experimental subject.

Hydra II gave the order to verify (as cautiously as possible) whether or not there were other beings present within the field of observation.

The answer was negative.

Despite this, Hydra prepared for the worst; it knew very well that there were many ways of seeing, feeling, and acting at a distance.

2

Another stumble, another fall. Babson cursed fluently under his breath. The darkness prevented him from seeing not only the path but also whether there was somebody on it who might be shocked at the incomprehensible sounds issuing from his mouth (either his new tongue was lacking in sufficient expletives or Bennie was extraordinarily unaware of this aspect of linguistics). He stood up, dusting off his tunic. He had to check how far away he was from his goal.

He raised his hand to the transparent band fixed around his head and pressed the correct spot.

A beam of light shot from the front and disappeared almost at once, but in Babson's trained memory a photographic image of momentarily glimpsed landscape remained. He studied it. Yes, that was the hillock. The path now led straight to it, and there did not seem to be much rough ground in between, although Babson had learned by painful experience that this was not very reliable information.

He thrust one foot forward carefully and made sure it was firmly planted on the ground. Now the other one...

He had been lucky despite everything. He had managed to convince that silly Donna that she should postpone the visit to the sociopsychologist to the next day, arguing that all he needed was rest. In fact, she had not really insisted they should go that same evening.

His lips twisted in a sardonic grin. It had only been later that he realized the real reason, when she came up and smothered him with her affection, asking if he felt well enough to be left on his own for a couple of hours. "Duende will be looking after you, my love, and he'll inform me at once if there is any problem. I'll come straightaway... You see, yesterday I made a work commitment with Darrow..." Ha! A work commitment! He had agreed, of course. Perhaps too quickly, but that damned old woman was capable of staying if he insisted the way Bennie would have done, and he needed as long as possible to gain more control over his new identity. She hadn't fooled him with her "work commitment." No, he wasn't that idiot Bennie, who had imagined that the "thing" was only just beginning. Such naivety made him cringe; although he, Thomas Babson, had only half as much experience, it was enough for him to know almost beyond a doubt that something had happened between the two of them the night before. He knew that twinkle in the eyes only too well.

He licked his suddenly dry lips. That Darrow must have had a good time. Donna might never see thirty again, but no one would think that from the way she looked.

Irritated, he cut short this train of thought. Christ, this was some joke! Being a little kid again, a boy scarcely nine years old and incapable of satisfying a woman... Although, thinking it over, he still had some possibilities; there was that little Winnie. She wasn't bad looking. And if she were half as naive as Bennie, it wouldn't be difficult to... Of course, he would have to go about it carefully; that innocence was double-edged. But she was still a real possibility. Even though someone more mature and experienced would be better, someone like Donna. Why not her, after all?

He smiled. Not a bad idea. She was quite hot... Of course, he would have to proceed with caution; Donna might be silly, but...

He stumbled and fell once more. He got back to his feet, cursing. Proceed with caution... Damn it, that was what he needed to do at this very moment.

He pressed the band on his head.

The hillock was right in front of him.

He looked around carefully. Perfect, there was no light to be seen. He needed to keep his own beam on if he was to find the right spot. He adjusted the controls until the band was only emitting a faint glow, and entered the gap—or, as Bennie had called it, "the ravine." Ha!

The light shone on the mound of fallen earth. Yes, that was the entrance. He kneeled down and whispered, "Hydra! I'm here."

No reply.

He raised his childish brows. Why? Ah, of course. Hydra needed the password in order to respond.

"Time is the new frontier," he said. Heavens, what did that mean? No doubt about it, all the passwords were absurd.

A stone fell from the front of the mound. Babson went over to it.

The stone had left a cavity exposed. His light did not illuminate the interior; all he could see was a dark circle. He stuck his hand in. Hmm... There was something solid and smooth in there...

"Report," Hydra ordered in a metallic voice.

3

Donna pushed the diagrams away. She was worried and found it impossible to concentrate. Why was Bennie taking so long?

She pursed her lips, annoyed with herself. She should never have allowed him to go out at night. But he had looked much better—almost normal, she would have said. But what if he felt dizzy again, out there on his own?

She glanced at the control panel. The green light was still on; he was alright. Stubborn child, she thought with a smile. He had insisted Duende not look after him; he was "big now." He had even made her promise nothing would follow him, even at a distance. Fine, she had kept her promise; nothing was following him close or at a distance... Only the monitor was going with him. Concealed in his headband, it kept a constant check on his body functions and transmitted them to the health module. As long as the green light was on, she had nothing to worry about. If it went off, or even before it had time to go off, Duende would send a cybo after him that was much faster and more efficient than she was. Despite this, he was staying out too long; she ought to go and find him. Duende could tell her where to look... Gracious... Had the light gone off?

"Bennie has just arrived," Duende calmly informed her.

Donna relaxed.

"Is he coming here?" she asked.

"Yes."

The household brain barely had time to reply before the door to her room opened.

Bennie looked a little pale... Heavens, even taking the elevator made him feel dizzy! She really shouldn't wait any longer; she would take him to the sociopsychologist the very next day.

"Good evening, my little man. How was your walk?"

"Wonderful, Mom..." Damned hair, it was almost impossible to see Donna's neck. "In fact, I feel a whole lot better."

He gently slid his hand over the woman's hair, drawing it back. Yes, now he could see...

Donna shook her head, and the blonde mane fell back over her shoulders.

"I'm so glad, sweetheart. I was very worried about you today."

"Oh, Mom! It was nothing serious, and now I really do feel fine," he said, carefully pushing back her hair once more.

Donna absent-mindedly stroked her son's back. If he only knew...

That evening she had been very cold toward Sidney. She had not been impolite, of course; she was simply marking the limits. Work colleagues, fine, but nothing more... Oh, and Sidney had taken it so well! It was a shame, a real shame. But, she sighed, what sacrifice would a mother not make for her child?

Yes, there was the carotid. Now, flexing his little finger, he could...

Bursting with maternal pride, Donna peered down at the blonde head nestling against her shoulder. He was so affectionate... And his hand was so soft as he caressed her hair, the back of her neck... What was that? Something had pricked her.

"Bennie, have you got something in your fingernails?"

Bennie looked surprised and examined his hand.

"No, Mom... Or rather, yes, this one is a bit split, can you see?" He held out his little finger to her. "It must have been when I tried to move that rock."

"Yes, I see. Duende will sort it out in a second. What, you're going already?"

Bennie had straightened up and moved away from her. He was smiling.

"Yes, I have to get to bed early." Now he could clearly see the small red dot on her skin, exactly above the carotid. "I want to feel completely well in the morning. I've lost the whole day today."

"Yes, but don't forget that tomorrow we have to go to the socio-psychologist, sweetheart."

"Oh no, so that means I'll miss another session with the Master?"

Babson hated the very idea of going into the cybernetic instructor's cabin, but that stupid Bennie loved it. He would have to play the part whether he liked it or not. And anyway, by tomorrow... He smiled to himself. By tomorrow, Donna (or to be more precise, Donna's body) would have different ideas. Very different ones.

"I don't think that's a problem, sweetie. You could spend the afternoon session with the Master. I don't think you're well enough to go back to the park yet."

"Yes, perhaps," he conceded, as if reluctantly. Then he said goodnight with a sigh. "See you in the morning, Mom."

Donna smiled at him affectionately.

"See you tomorrow, son."

4

For Candy (her real name was Candice Stow, but very few in the Imperial Secret Service knew or remembered this) the Hydra Project was the ideal solution to her problems.

Now that she had turned forty, after an adventurous and surprisingly lengthy career in the Service, she found herself facing a choice between an unhappy retirement and certain death.

She had not always succeeded in emerging from operations unscathed (while it was true that modern bioprosthetics were almost indistinguishable from real limbs, her efficiency was still no greater than that of a normal limb belonging to a normal person, and an agent had to be much more than a normal person), and her reflexes were nothing like those that the young girl had possessed when she entered the Service at barely eighteen. Besides, her body—or to be more precise, what was left of it—was no longer suitable for any new impersonations; the renovation techniques had not been designed for such unusually long periods. Normally, an agent did not get beyond their fifth change of appearance; Candy was on to her twelfth.

The only thing that had permitted her to compensate, up to a certain point (already in the past, unfortunately), for the increasing deficiencies of her body and to continue to operate was her mind, which had been enriched by all her varied experience.

If she retired, she could become an instructor... But to tell the truth, she didn't like the idea. To pass on the knowledge acquired at such a high cost to swarms of still-green kids who for the most part were incredibly dim but still possessed what she had lost (a young, intact body with rapid reflexes and that could put up with half-a-dozen remodelings), for a salary that was barely a third of her present one and would make it impossible to continue with those "operations" of her own that provided her with such a high proportion of her current income (instructors did not have the same leeway as first-class agents)... No. Becoming an instructor did not attract her.

And yet she was aware she shouldn't continue to work as an agent. If she succeeded in coming out of the next operation alive (and she never got any of the easy ones), it would be a miracle, and she knew there weren't that many miracles in her profession. She had no interest in dying. Despite the fact that she was maimed and prematurely aged, she was barely forty years old; she could live as many years more. And living was very pleasant, if you had enough money...

Money.

A lot had come her way, legally or illegally, and had slipped through her fingers again with astonishing speed. She did not regret anything; she had lived very well. Besides, no agent was that worried about the distant future; very few of them even lived to see it.

However, she had reached the point where she could see it; it was ugly and undesirable.

What was she to do? Set up on her own? No. That would have only been possible in her younger days, if she hadn't been so good at her job. The Service had not been as keen to do without her talents at that time as they were now. No one would employ her nowadays for their confidential business; she was old and weary. She should not have any illusions, and she didn't, which was perhaps the key to her longevity. She knew how to assess her own worth coldly; she knew what she could and couldn't do.

In spite of all her doubts, she could not come up with a suitable alternative. Sooner or later she would have to become an instructor. Better sooner, if she wanted to stay alive.

Yet she put off the decision as long as she could. She avoided one summons after another while she made more and more adjustments to her battered body. At least she would be at the height of her physical capacities (so painfully diminished now) when the moment came. Eventually there would be a summons she could not ignore, and then she would see. If she were offered a simple operation (which was almost impossible, as the legendary Candy was not given unimportant tasks), she would accept. If it were a hard one, the moment would have arrived to become an instructor.

That was why the news that she had been incorporated into a new project did not please her at all. Incorporated, without the usual prior discussions to assess her suitability for the job—a bad sign, she told herself. A very bad sign.

The security measures surrounding the Institute of Special Investigations only served to reinforce her initial negative impression. It was impossible to leave there without proper authorization, and it was unlikely they would give it to her if she refused to take the job. The project was so secret that not even its code name was accessible to anyone not taking part in it—the worst possible sign.

She obediently submitted to the control tests. These were not like the ordinary ones; nobody seemed concerned or upset by her obvious physical drawbacks. Instead they seemed silently pleased at her mental agility at taking in the simulated situations and finding the best solutions (solutions her tired body would never be able to put into practice) to every unexpected problem. Well, she had no reason to disappoint them; perhaps they had already decided to move her to the category of instructor.

This idea left her feeling slightly depressed.

When it was time for the final interview, she was prepared for the worst. It was then that she finally learned the name of the project, Hydra, and realized it would be impossible for her to refuse to take part and stay alive. But would anybody in their right mind reject such an opportunity?

For as long as she was part of Hydra she could live almost eternally (and also be eternally young).

Could she ask for anything more?

After all, the task awaiting her was not that different from much of her normal work; it could be seen as a new technique of impersonation. And it had many advantages; it wouldn't be necessary to suffer the tortuous series of operations to lengthen or shorten her limbs (those she still had), reshape her thorax or pelvis, add or remove fatty tissue, change the color of her skin, her hair, or eyes (this last one was especially painful; she had undergone seven changes to the color of her irises, and it had affected her eyesight considerably), restructure her facial bones, change the skin on her fingertips (something that was undoubtedly necessary, but also harmful; despite the care those carrying out the operation took not to damage the nerve-endings, her fingers had lost all sensitivity), or modify the cartilage in her nose and ears. She would receive a new body, together with a cast-iron story (a completely authentic one) that she would not have to memorize in interminable sessions, because it had already been implanted in her mind, ready to be used whenever she needed it.

She let herself be led docilely into the next room and get strapped down without protest; she obeyed all the instructions instantly (Sit down. Relax. Take deep breaths...), and when the anesthetic spread through her brain, she fell asleep without offering the slightest resistance, with a smile on her lips.

When you are asleep, two hundred years pass quickly.

In fact, when she woke up, she thought she had only just fallen asleep. Then suddenly she remembered that she was—or ought to be—in a body that was not hers and that in her mind there ought to be unknown memories, belonging to a strange world. She sighed. She had to start work. First she had to explore this new brain...

She felt rather disappointed when she found she wasn't as young as she had hoped. There was not much difference between thirty-five and forty, at least at first glance. But when she turned over in bed, simulating waking up as normal, she realized the difference was immense; this new body was complete and very well looked-after. She could sense how flexible it was and liked the rapid way it obeyed instructions.

"Is something wrong, Donna?"

What was that voice? Wasn't she alone?

She controlled herself. Above all, show no surprise. She shook off the rigidity that had gripped her and flexed gently, yawning, while she searched desperately through her new memory... It's Duende, she sighed with relief.

"No, nothing," she answered. "I was just stretching." She spoke automatically; her mind was busy reviewing Duende's history. "I've got a lot of work ahead of me today." She shuddered. How could Donna be so blind? Duende was an intelligent being! If she wasn't very careful, he might find her out. She couldn't do her work if he could see and sense her; she would have to behave exactly like Donna, and that was dangerous, very dangerous, because if she didn't assert herself as the dominant personality soon, she would run the risk of disintegrating and dying. She needed time to think.

"You can begin the session with the biostimulator, Duende."

That was usually Donna's first act when she woke up. When she had not asked for it, and turned over so clumsily in bed, Duende's curiosity had been aroused. She mustn't make the same mistake again; she had to follow Donna's routine until she could find a way to neutralize this domestic spy.

A warm wave caressed her whole body. She opened her eyes. The bed had disappeared, and it was as if she were floating in mid-air. Obviously scientific progress had continued!

The feeling of warmth spread through all her body, reaching every nerve and muscle fiber. It really was very pleasant... She concentrated again. There must be some way to get rid of Duende. That's it! She smiled. After all, Donna did have a sense of privacy.

She waited calmly until the session with the biostimulator finished. Then she bounded out of bed. She felt extraordinarily fresh and revitalized; it was a shame equipment like this had not existed in her own time. The long, boring sessions of fitness training could have been avoided. Those ten minutes in the biostimulator were equivalent to at least two hours of intense exercise and had not made her feel tired in the least. No, she felt as if she were capable of the heaviest physical task there and then. It was no wonder Donna's body was in such good shape. Right, now to get rid of the cyber brain.

"What time is it, Duende?" she asked casually.

"It's eight twenty-one in the..."

Candy did not let him finish.

"Heavens! Is it that late already? Sidney must be about to arrive."

She walked quickly to the door. She mustn't give Duende time to reflect; artificial brains think so rapidly...

"To the control room, please," she said, stepping into the elevator.

Despite the psychological preparation she had undergone, the unpleasant sensation that she was falling, however slowly, through space almost made her feel sick. She clenched her teeth. Luckily, the door to the study had already gone by, and the entrance to the control room was gliding toward her.

She jumped into the tiny cabin and went over to the central control panel. Not too quickly, she told herself. Calm yourself; you may be in a hurry, but it should not seem like a question of life and death, even if it is.

"Are you going to disconnect me, Donna?"

A note of surprise (and possibly something else) in Duende's voice.

Candy's hand, or more precisely her new hand, paused a few inches from the switch. Slowly, she repeated to herself. Besides, she could never react as quickly as a cyber brain; she had to fool him, not fight him.

She put on an expression of surprise.

"Of course, Duende." She smiled shyly. "Oh, I get it. I forgot to tell you that Sidney is coming here to live."

Tense, she moved her hand toward the switch once more. Damn it, Duende would find it hard to swallow a story like that. That puritan Donna did not usually act so quickly, if ever; it took her weeks, if not months, to decide to have sex with a new partner, and Duende must know that better than anyone. Of course, there was always the possibility of her falling head-over-heels for somebody, but could a cyber brain understand that?

Her fingers touched the smooth surface of the knob. A small turn to the left... That was it.

She breathed out with relief. Fine, there was no longer any danger. Now, to work... Let's see. How had she come to take over this particular body?

She searched deep in her memories of the previous day.

Bennie. It must have been him. There was no other explanation for his behavior. So, the fact that she had been sown by a child almost certainly meant that she was the second person to wake up.

She had the job with the heaviest responsibility: to sow the latent minds from her Hydra (Hydra II, if she remembered correctly) among the most suitable targets in this society. She needed to think that over carefully; she shouldn't hurry.

First and foremost, she needed to see Bennie, to determine whether she really was the second to wake up. And then to find out where Hydra was hidden. She turned around, ready to leave the control room.

Next to the door was a small plate covered in buttons. She sighed. It was a shame to have to do without Duende. To judge by Donna's memories, he knew the secret of how to turn this house into a paradise. Now she would have to constantly go to one or another of these control points to achieve what she wanted, instead of just asking for it out loud. Oh well, sacrifices had to be made.

She pushed the button controlling Bennie's room and stepped into the elevator.

As the elevator climbed slowly, Candy continued examining Donna's memory; she was bound to find lots of useful things in there.

Hmm... Yes, that park. The Enchanted Valley: that was a good idea. She was sure she could make use of it. She was still deep in thought when she entered Bennie's room.

A

This is the first part of a test. It is strictly your own work; you must complete it on your own, without discussing your answers with anyone. If you do not wish to complete it, continue to the next page.

I. Put an X beside what you consider to be the correct answer:

  1. Regarding the character of Thomas Babson:

      a) he is completely monstrous and unreal
      b) I know people just like him
      c) I have no opinion

  2. Concerning the relationship between Donna Slidell and Sidney Darrow, do you think that:

      a) she felt an incipient love for him
      b) it was all due to her loneliness
      c) she ought to give it a try to see what happens

  3. On the basis of what you have read so far, do you think this book is:

      a) cruel: Bennie and Donna should not die like this
      b) fantastic: the kind of adventures you love
      c) too realistic for your taste

TURN TO THE NEXT PAGE

II. Read the following verse carefully:

> *We're dying every hour*
> *Every minute of deaths is the rhythm of our life*
> *We're losing the golden dream of youth*
> *So what is still ours?*

—BOB DYLAN, "HANDS OFF"

1. Do you see any relation between the feelings expressed in this poem and Donna Slidell's problems?
2. Do you see any relation to your own problems?

This test will continue later. You may change your answers at any moment.

GO TO THE NEXT PAGE

VIII

In the Hermitage

1

AGAINST A RAPIDLY DARKENING SKY, the clouds were tinged with red one after another, streaks of scarlet against a violet background. In ecstasy, Shari held her breath: so much beauty! To think there were blind people who could not see the miracle hidden in the simple, daily repetition of a sunset. Optical laws, it was said. Diffracted light—and they were satisfied. My God, such vanity! That stupid desire to explain everything, know everything—that was the only real mortal sin. Establishing and re-establishing laws and theories that collapsed time and again, as though mocking their vain enterprise, merely meant they grew further and further from the Divine Presence. The Creator of all existence only accepted those who looked with pure eyes, eyes constantly ready to worship His works, as they had been offered them...

She sighed, and bit her bottom lip.

She was sinning. She always lapsed back into sin. At this very moment, instead of being thankful for and enjoying His infinite goodness, had she not allowed herself to be overwhelmed by feelings of bitterness and grief? She was wasting the brief, precious minutes when she could contemplate His works, that essential preparation so that she could progress, amazed and full of reverence for the grandeur of Creation, to internal contemplation...to the contemplation of the sacred spark that the all-powerful Hand had planted within her body, her immortal soul, so that she could come to know and worship it.

She drove the impure thoughts from her mind. She must not think, only feel—perceive the beautiful, be enthralled by all that surpassed her understanding...

She started to breathe heavily. Your works are so beautiful, my God! I give thanks to you, thanks, thanks... Falling to her knees, she forced her eyes closed. I am waiting for you! Here I am, desirous of You, my Divine Beloved! She began to froth at the mouth. I can see you! I can see you! I can feel you!

Her body convulsed. She fell to the stony floor of the observatory and writhed spasmodically, banging against the low wall separating her from the abyss. From the world below. From the two tiny dots—one bigger than the other—that were climbing the narrow mountain trail up to the hermitage perched on the edge of the cliff.

The convulsions gradually subsided.

Exhausted, Shari Gwinnett lay stretched out on the cold floor. The divine ecstasy had passed... Oh, how brief it had been! And yet how lengthy!

She struggled to turn her sweat- and saliva-covered face upward. She sobbed quietly. Her soul was as black and empty as the night sky after the infinite joy it had experienced. All she had left was the recollection of the Divine Union to console and encourage her. She could feel a welcoming stupor gradually take hold of her body... Yes, she needed rest. Reaching the mystic heights was too much for her wretched material shell. She had to take care of it; that, too, was one of the Lord of the Universe's creations.

She slipped imperceptibly into a deep sleep.

The two dots had turned into human figures that were still climbing.

2

The loud metallic vibrations echoed through the reception room and resounded between the rough-hewn walls until they reached the cells.

Brother Kevin raised an irritated eyebrow. Who could it be? He went reluctantly to the visiting room. It was obviously somebody unaware of the hermitage rules; otherwise they would not have come at nightfall and interrupted the meditation hour.

Another loud clanging made him quicken his step. The stranger might also distract the other brothers. He walked across the visiting room and connected the outside viewer.

The image of the newcomers appeared on the screen.

There were two of them. The woman, young, small, and fragile looking, was holding the hand of a young boy of around ten. They both looked tired from the climb.

"What do you want, woman?" Brother Kevin asked coldly.

Blinking, she raised her clear gray eyes to look at the hooded figure floating in the air in front of the hermitage door.

"I should like... I should like if possible to see Shari. Shari Gwinnett."

The monk's face became even more frozen.

"I'm sorry, woman. Those of us who live here have renounced our earthly ties and have no intention of renewing them," he replied, raising his hand to cut the communication.

Grasping his intention, Candy quickly said in a pleading voice, "Brother, if I could just leave her a message."

Her psychological calculation had been correct; that word 'brother' had made Kevin pause, and the rest was a matter of curiosity. Apparently, this was still a very human weakness.

The stereo-image made up its mind.

"Alright, you can give me the message." Woman, sister? Kevin cleared his throat to hide his confusion. "I'll make sure she gets it."

Timidly lowering her gaze, Candy hid her smile.

"Tell her..." she hesitated, as if she found it hard to find the words, "tell her I came in search of the Truth." She emphasized the last word so that the capital letter was plain.

The monk's face lit up.

"Yes... Yes, I'll tell her at once." He impulsively manipulated the invisible controls. "Please come in and wait."

The metal door creaked open.

"It's too cold to be out there." The three-dimensional image moved through the air across the threshold, showing the two newcomers the way with his hand. "And the climb up the mountain is tiring. Really tiring." The incorporeal hand traced a caress on Bennie's head. "Especially for a little boy, isn't that right?"

Babson nodded his agreement and walked inside. Brother Kevin showed them a stone bench.

"You may sit here while I fetch the reply from sister Shari... I'm sorry, what's your name? I'm afraid I've forgotten it."

"Donna, Donna Slidell... I'm sure Shari will remember me."

"Very well, Donna... Sit here and wait."

The three-dimensional image disappeared.

Candy sat next to Babson. She gazed with pretend admiration at the bas-reliefs covering the stony walls (that monk did not appear to suspect her, but in her line of work precautions never came amiss), and her mouth set in a firm line. This was bad, bad... Apart from the door they had come in through, there was only one other in the room, and that did not look easy to force. If Shari also decided to use the viewer to talk to her... No, that wouldn't be logical. The thought of a possible disciple, especially as it concerned a former acquaintance who had not approved of her mystic vocation, would

undoubtedly lead her to come in person. She only had to wait...
and rest; that climb had been really exhausting.

She stroked the back of Babson's neck and could feel the tension there.

"Relax, sweetheart..." she whispered softly.

Babson glanced up at her, then rested his head on her shoulder.
Candy could tell the effort he was making to breathe normally, and
frowned. He was a dreadful agent, no doubt about it. Fortunately,
he could pass in his new identity; it was normal for a young boy to
be impressed by this fantastically ancient hermitage.

She closed her eyes and pretended to be dozing. Only an expert
eye would have noticed the slight tensing of different areas of her
skin as the muscles rhythmically tightened and relaxed. The task
ahead of her seemed an easy one, but it was always good to be
prepared for any eventuality, and she would be.

3

Shari came running down the steps. Here you have the Lord's
answer, you of little faith. You were complaining about how many
spiritually blind people there were, while He was lifting the veil
from the eyes of someone she had believed would never see...

As she reached the bottom of the stairs, she almost bumped
into Brother Kevin.

"Where is she?"

"I brought her into the ante-room, sister. Would you like...?"

"Of course I would. Who can refuse to greet the lost sheep who
has returned to the fold? Not me, brother..."

They exchanged joyful smiles.

"Good, then I'll go and see her," said Shari, heading for the door.

"Wait, sister..." said Kevin, and Shari turned to him with a perplexed look.

"She's not alone," the monk explained.

"She isn't?"

"She has a young boy with her."

Shari wrinkled her brow. Who could it be? She searched in her memory... Bennie, of course.

"In that case..."

"Wouldn't it be advisable for me to accompany you, sister?"

She had to admit Kevin was right.

"Yes. Come with me, brother."

As she entered the ante-room, Shari spread her arms wide in joy.

"Blessed is the day we meet again, my dear Donna."

Donna got up, looking surprised.

"Shari! What a pleasure to see you! But..." Confused, she looked across at Kevin. "I thought that..."

"What? Oh yes, we have cut our earthly ties, my dear. But we will not reject anyone who is searching for the way of Truth... My, how big and handsome little Bennie is!"

Visibly embarrassed, Babson rose from his seat. Shari pinched his cheek affectionately.

"I can still see him taking his first steps... I'm glad to see you, too, little man," said Shari, smiling at him. Turning to Donna, she added, "Although perhaps it would be better if..."

Yes, everything was working out perfectly... Donna laid her hand on Babson's shoulder.

"Sweetheart, didn't you want to..." She looked apologetically toward Shari. "I'm sorry, but he needs to..."

"Of course, of course, we understand," said Shari hastily. She gestured toward Kevin.

"Brother, could you take him?"

Trying to appear more kindly, Kevin approached Babson.

"Are you coming, young man?" he asked, holding out his hand.

Babson took it roughly and entered the hermitage with the two women looking anxiously after him (although each for very different reasons).

"Perhaps afterward you'd like to see what the hermitage is like," Kevin suggested as they crossed the threshold.

"Oh, yes!"

Donna chewed her lips; Babson should not seem so anxious.

The door to the hermitage closed behind them, leaving the two women facing each other in silence.

All of a sudden, Candy threw herself into Shari's arms and burst into tears.

"Yes, go on, cry, it will do you good, my dear," crooned Shari. "Tears of repentance are the most precious offering we can make to the Lord." While she was speaking, she led Donna over to the nearest bench. How small and fragile the new sister in the Lord was! "You can't imagine how happy I am that you've discovered the lies of the world."

Still sobbing, Candy agreed, and they sat down together.

"You did well to come and see us, Donna. There are so many who, thinking they are following the right path, instead only increase the weight of their sins and make it hard to discover the tiny flame we are struggling to keep alight here."

As she pretended to listen, Candy was wondering how long it would take Bennie to carry out his part of the plan.

4

Babson came out of the toilet adjusting his tunic. Keven greeted him with a broad smile.

"Should we start the tour?"

"I'd love to, uncle."

They set off side by side along the corridor dug into the rock face. Kevin pointed to a side corridor and explained, "That's the way to the prayer room, little one."

"And where do you sleep?"

Kevin raised his head to the ceiling.

"Up there. We have twelve cells."

Babson shuddered. Twelve? Could the information Candy had received be wrong? Even if only half the cells were occupied, he couldn't complete his task.

"Twelve?" he asked nervously. "I didn't think there were that many people living here, uncle."

Kevin's face darkened for a brief moment. He didn't like to remember the latest schisms with those rebels who thought they could hear the Voice of God better than Shari, and who one by one had abandoned the true path. Yet the cells were still there, thanks to sister Shari's unshakeable belief that new, more faithful disciples would come to take the place of the lost sheep. Anyway, there was no point mentioning all that to Bennie, for the moment at least. So he answered, quite sharply, "No. They're not all occupied."

"And...how many people live here, then?"

"Three. Sister Shari, Brother Simon, and me."

Relieved, Babson licked his lips. Candy's information was correct.

"I'd like to meet Brother Simon, uncle," he murmured.

This idea pleased Kevin. He was well aware he was not very good when it came to dealing with children. It was possible that Brother Simon (who must have finished his meditation by now) would get on better with Bennie.

No doubt about it; all too often the Lord's inspiration came from the mouths of the innocent. He stroked Bennie's tousled hair with gratitude.

"That's not a bad idea, little one. Come on, we'll go and see him."

They walked back along the main corridor until they came to another side one. Kevin headed down it. Babson looked around him: he had to fix the route in his memory. If everything went according to plan, he would have to come back alone, and he had no wish to get lost in this tortuous labyrinth cut into the mountain.

"What are you staring at? It's this way."

"Yes, uncle." Babson ran to catch up to him and explained, "I stopped to get a good look at the engravings on the walls; I like them a lot."

Kevin nodded approvingly.

"It was sister Shari who designed them. Can you see, they represent..." He pointed to the figure of a man surrounded by fantastic beasts. "...the struggle of believers against earthly temptations."

Slowing down, Kevin launched into a detailed description of all the vices and sins represented in the bas-reliefs.

Babson listened patiently; after all, he had brought it upon himself. Damnation! To have to listen to all that nonsense. He peered ahead and his eyes opened wide with astonishment... Stairs? These madmen took their asceticism much too far! It could well even be that they lit fires in their cells to keep themselves warm.

They climbed the steps.

Fortunately, there were no murals here, so that put a stop to the endless flow of explanations from the crazy monk leading him.

Babson could feel the growing itch in his fingers. My God, how keen he was to go into action. They quickened their step. It would be soon, very soon...

5

"And what happens? They stumble and fall. Each new barrier is higher and stronger, because He does not want His mysteries to be revealed along the way that the serpent has traced. But they insist, heedless of the divine wrath they are provoking, and reach abominable extremes that revolt all those who still have human feelings. I have not lost hope that those cybos will be the camel that breaks..."

Candy cast a furtive glance in the direction of the inner door. Why was Bennie taking so long? He had already had more than enough time... Her eyes returned to Shari. If her experience was anything go by, this crazy woman was about to have a fit of hysterics. It wouldn't be easy to subdue her, in spite all her knowledge; Donna's body might be strong and agile, but it was too small and thin. The mystic was a head taller than her and weighed almost double. If you also took into account the incredible strength of a maniac, the outcome was by no means clear... What was that? Shari had stopped talking and was staring at Donna, waiting for her reply. What could she say? She should have been paying closer attention.

"God is our only salvation," she murmured.

"That's very true, but what is to be done with the blasphemers, those who insist on living in sin, despite His warnings? The most terrible of punishments will fall upon them; they will lose their immortal souls."

The inner door opened slowly.

Candy's muscles tensed unconsciously. What if that idiot had failed?

At that moment, Babson's smiling face appeared in the crack of the door. He winked at her.

Candy sighed with relief. Now the only one left was this crazy mystic sitting next to her. She put on a worried look and exclaimed, "Bennie! What are you doing?"

Without appearing to have heard her, Shari went on undaunted with her monologue, apparently hypnotized by her own words.

Bennie settled in the doorway, obviously enjoying himself.

Candy weighed the alternatives.

A direct attack? No. Shari's reaction was unpredictable; she might offer no resistance, or fight back equally well, her reflexes and strength galvanized by her hysteria. Ask Babson for help? No again; that would be to lose face with him. In the long run, that would be more dangerous than risking a fight with this lunatic. Better continue with the prepared variant.

With a look of terror on her face, she shouted, "No, Bennie!"

This time the note of alarm in her voice pierced Shari's consciousness. The nun began to raise her head...

Like a startled dove taking flight, Candy's hand rose silently, rapidly, until it struck like lightning just below the mastoid, then fell back gently into her own lap. All this took no longer than a single heartbeat. Candy sat motionless, watching Shari's body slowly topple over, a growing look of surprise spreading across her face.

Babson resisted an urge to applaud. No doubt about it, Candy was a true master.

IX

The Triumvirate

1

A SLIGHT CONTRACTION of his leg muscles, and Stephen Houdry could no longer see the spectators' faces. An imperceptible hand movement, and his eyes left the stars and the clear night sky, briefly surveyed the clipped lawn ten meters below him, then sought and found the other flying figure. Nellie was approaching him at top speed, converted into a human arrow by the energy-saturated air. Energy, he thought. That was the key.

Buoyed up by the changing lines of the force field, he swooped in a wide circle. Nellie and he flew shoulder-to-shoulder, mingling in such an incredible cascade of figures that they could almost feel on the backs of their necks the bated breath of the hundred men and women watching their aerial dance.

So much energy, at almost no cost... And the thermal pollution was next-to-nothing. If only they had known about techniques like these. Stephen shrugged, mentally rather than physically, otherwise he would have risked crashing to the ground. No point thinking about what might have been. Better to concentrate on the present moment, to enjoy to the fullest the physical pleasure of flying and being able to look, as they turned and turned, at Nellie's pink, happy face...

All of a sudden, darkness, and the gravitational field became a soft, swaying cradle... An urgent message. *The* urgent message, he corrected himself, hearing the distant sigh of disappointment from the crowd at this interruption to the show.

Donna's delicate features appeared on his retina, and from some unknown location gentle electronic pulses reached his auditive nerves.

"I'm sorry, Harry, but again, Bennie..."

Candy left her sentence unfinished; there was no need to complete it.

Candy's boss smiled at her (with lips that shortly before had belonged to Harry Mergenthaler, a promising young psychosociologist in charge of Control Point IV-18-085-03) and replied, "Don't worry, Donna. I'll be right there."

As far as they had been able to determine, there was no system that could register what they said through their holo-visors, and yet Stephen thought—and Candy completely agreed—that you could never be too cautious.

"Merlin, I have to leave at once," Stephen signaled to the gravitator's brain. Donna's image disappeared, replaced by Nellie's inquisitive face, gradually getting further and further from him as Merlin brought him back down to the ground.

"I'm sorry, my love. It's an emergency," he explained.

Nellie agreed with a sigh.

"Let me down, too, Merlin," she asked.

Stephen's feet sank into the grass. Raising his head sharply, he protested, "No, Nellie. I know how much you like to fly, so don't..."

Nellie interrupted him. "I don't like flying alone, my love."

Stephen pursed his lips as a sign of concern.

"It's going to be hard for me to finish quickly, sweetheart."

Nellie landed next to him. She rested her hand on his shoulder.

"That doesn't matter, Harry. I'll wait for you at home."

They exchanged a rapid, warm kiss, and he strode off among the men and women stretched out on the grass, who were already watching enthralled as a fresh couple performed acrobatic maneuvers high in the sky.

Once he had escaped the circle of spectators, Stephen raised his left hand to his mouth and told the ring on his finger, "Come here, Hermes."

The final phase of his work was beginning. If there had been some way of avoiding it... But no, everything had been meticulously planned. He didn't know where the other Hydras were. Or even how many of them there were. If he did not awaken the Three, someone else would. Besides, he had already collected them, and the mere thought of destroying...

An icy flash seared his brain once more. He stumbled, and his face contorted as he felt the cold sweat pouring out of him. But this time he managed not to fall, to keep his balance. No one could see him like this...

Little by little, his brain began to function again. Except about that. That was completely unthinkable.

He smiled a bitter smile. If he had known he would be the victim of his own creation, he would have... But then someone else would have done it. They would have taken his place in the ranks of the immortals. He had to accept the price, to submit to being conditioned in order to do his job. His job. To wake up the Three... And if he so much as toyed with the idea...

He paused his train of thought right there. Not again. He hadn't the slightest desire for his brain to disintegrate. Besides, it was time for the Hermes to arrive.

He raised his eyes in the darkness.

In the distance it looked like a shooting star. As it drew closer it was more like a white drop—or teardrop—of light.

The Hermes craft had been designed for their beauty as well as speed.

It descended in front of him and hovered about twenty centimeters above the ground. Stephen went over to it, touched the wall panel, and disappeared inside the oval door that opened and then closed silently behind him.

He sat at the controls. Reaching underneath, he pulled out a small gray box. It was intact.

He opened it and contemplated the three slender diadems inside. The Three Brains... Who could they be? One of them was surely Dahlgren. The other two...

Whoever they might be, to him they were three all-powerful brains. Who were irremediably two hundred years behind. None of them would have the chance he had had to merge with the brain and memory of one of the human beings who lived on this disconcerting Earth. To realize that nothing was as simple as they had thought it was two hundred years earlier. As he himself had thought. But how could he tell *them* that? How could he make them understand that their hypotheses about the long-term instability of the Federation had been completely misplaced?

He shook his head sadly. His task was no easy one; to see and comprehend the terrible change in the conditions they were expecting to find required great mental flexibility. Greater than the Three might possess, whoever they might be. And yet if he didn't manage to persuade them, everything would be lost. Without a doubt. And he would be, too, of course. If only he could get them to see that the only possibility, the last chance...

He sighed and closed the box, then put it away. It would all depend on who the Three were.

He bent over the controls and tapped in the coordinates for Shari's hermitage.

2

The three diadems had gradually lost their silver shine and were now almost black.

Three bodies began to stir on the stone floor, about to awaken.

"You can go now. Wait for me in the control room," said Houdry.

Candy headed silently for the door, leading Bennie-Babson by the hand. His dark childish eyes glanced constantly behind him, full of curiosity.

Stephen was relieved to see them go. The tiny, cold professional killer and that mindless degenerate disguised as a boy got on his nerves. He felt something similar toward all the rest of the crew of his Hydra. Of course, that was how the small shock force had to be: cold, practical, cunning, and ruthless. Yet he was not sure he could ever get used to the mortal aura they gave off whenever they quit their protective disguises. No doubt about it, it had been wise to create the deep conditioning technique; he would never have been able to lead such a disparate group had he not known that in the deepest recesses of their minds a blind obedience to his commands had been implanted.

He walked among the three prone bodies and took the diadems from their heads one by one. Soon the Three... A strange sensation made him look behind him.

The woman had opened her eyes and was staring at him.

3

"Who can they be, Candy?" insisted Babson, almost running to keep up with her as they went down the dark passageway.

"I don't know; the leader didn't tell me anything."

Candy stifled a sigh. It was true Stephen had not told her anything, but that had not stopped her reaching her own conclusions. She had eyes, and a trained brain, and she knew that two plus two made four; it was the Leaders who were waking up in the hermitage chapel. But that fool Babson was unable to realize something so obvious. My God, what a partner she'd been given. Luckily (for him) he was no more than a child. If Babson had been implanted in an adult, she would have had to kill him by now. He was too irrational for her to be able to trust him. At least that helped him adapt more or less adequately to the role of Bennie. Ah, the control room at last. All those dratted corridors...

The boy and the woman entered the room. It was not very different from the rest of the hermitage: the same walls covered in rough bas-reliefs; the same lofty ceiling, almost lost from view in the constant semidarkness; the cold gray flagstones; a few uncomfortable stone benches. But here, too, were the controls for the hermitage maintenance and surveillance systems, as well as what had made Candy in such a hurry to arrive: a biostimulator (a primitive design, like everything else here).

"Check the stereo-visors, Thomas," she ordered. She started removing her tunic.

"But we've already activated the automatic surveillance system," Babson complained.

"Check it," Candy said sternly, taking off her boots.

As she bent and stretched her naked body, she could feel Babson's avid eyes on her. That was another problem.

"What are you waiting for?" she grunted, stretching out in the pod.

With difficulty, Babson took his eyes off the body on the metal bed and turned to the controls.

Problems: she had plenty of those. She connected the biostimulator. As the warm waves flowed through her muscles, easing her tension and tiredness, she thought back on everything that had happened since she had woken.

It has been a fruitful month. It had not been easy to implant eight minds in carefully chosen bodies without losing a single one of them. Also, developing the Enchanted Valley, at a speed not even Donna would have dreamed of (with the necessary modifications, of course) had been a real feat. And all of that without raising the slightest suspicion. Although they need not have taken so many precautions: the people of this age were so trusting. Careful. Overconfidence could ruin everything. These people might be careless to the point of naivety, but their scientific knowledge was so advanced that they could become dangerous. Very dangerous...

She turned her head. From the control panel, Bennie was peering over his shoulder at her, eyes smoldering.

She shut her own eyes. Let him look if he wanted to.

She relaxed her mind; she needed to rest that, too. It was almost certain that Stephen would leave them there to attend to the Leaders as they became accustomed to the new world. In that case, there would be questions. And she would be asked for advice. She had her reputation to look after, and if possible to increase...

The pod stopped vibrating. Refreshed, Candy climbed out, picked up her clothes, and began to dress.

"The biostimulator is free, Thomas," she told him, smoothing down her tunic.

"Aha..."

Her mind automatically classified his grunted reply: *animal*. She turned quickly toward the control panel.

Crouching behind the chair, Bennie's body was moving jerkily. His eyes were greedy, shiny, fearful.

She turned her back on him, unconcerned, and put on her boots. If he had found a way to get some release without bothering her, so much the better: that was one problem less.

4

Stephen Houdry came to a halt in front of the woman. She had opened her eyes and was staring at him.

"That was some nightmare," she murmured as if to herself in a quaking voice. She looked around the chapel and frowned, then pushed herself into a sitting position. Her eyes examined her new body curiously, and she shook her head. "And by the looks of it, not everything was a dream," she commented, her voice normal now.

"To whom do I have the honor of speaking?" she asked coldly, looking up at the man standing in front of her.

In an automatic gesture, Stephen stood to attention.

"I am Stephen Houdry, the captain of Hydra II. My congratulations, madam."

The woman visibly relaxed. Crossing her legs, she went on.

"Your appearance has improved noticeably in the last two hundred years, my dear. I hope the same can be said of me. Are there any mirrors in here?" She glanced around the walls, then raised her eyebrows. "I doubt it," she said, answering her own question. She went on in a light-hearted tone. "But I don't think your politeness has improved much, Stephen."

Stephen stared at her open-mouthed. My God! Could it possibly be? No, there was no logic to it. *Her*, one of the Three? And yet her way of talking, her gestures...

"Don't you recognize me yet?" she asked, and burst out laughing.

Her laugh was unmistakable.

"Doctor Golden?" said the still incredulous Stephen.

She nodded, with a broad smile.

"That's right, sweetheart. I'm Sybil Golden—in spirit, if not in body," she joked, running her hands over Shari's prominent breasts. "And the body doesn't seem too bad. But until I can find a mirror, I'll have to rely on your good taste."

Standing up, Sybil Golden stretched like a cat, and went on:

"You don't understand? I don't blame you. Your poor mind could never understand the reason why a simple section head in the old research institute could rise so far." She laughed and shook her head, her long hair waving across her face. "Nice hair..." she said approvingly, pushing it back with one hand. "Well, did you manage to carry out your instructions? What are the initials of the former owner of this body?"

Thoughts whirled through Stephen's brain.

"S.G." he answered automatically. "Her name was Shari Gwinnett." Good God! Had he faced all those difficulties finding the right place just because this madwoman had conditioned him to look for a woman with the same initials as her? He gradually grew less indignant. Perhaps that was a clue.

"Sabrina!" snapped a gruff voice.

Sybil and Stephen turned as one to look at the man half sitting up on the floor. This time Stephen had no doubt. That icy gaze, one so sure of its own power... He clicked his heels together smartly.

"At your orders, my President. I'm happy to see you again, Mister..."

The president, His Highness Patrick Maynard Dahlgren, did not deign to reply. He frowned as he stared at Shari-Sybil-Sabrina? (Stephen could sense a dim light flashing at the back of his mind: Sabrina? A Sabrina S.? Perhaps...)

"What were you talking about?" Dahlgren asked the woman.

"Oh, nothing important, my dear." Sybil replied, tilting her head coquettishly to one side. "Just your Sybil's typical feminine gossip, that's all."

(Had she pronounced her name Sybil with a little more emphasis than the rest of the sentence? And had the president blinked slightly when he heard it? Be that as it may, whatever it was must be a secret. And knowing or imagining secrets was dangerous, truly dangerous, so Stephen made sure his face revealed nothing.)

The president continued staring at the woman for a few seconds longer. (Why did he allow her to speak to him with such familiarity?) Then he shrugged his shoulders.

"Anyway, that's not important now," he muttered (but Stephen noticed the way he looked at her out of the corner of his eye). Turning to the third, still motionless body, he shook one of the shoulders. "Ryland! How long do you intend to go on sleeping?"

(Ryland? Of course. Ryland Kern, the head of the Imperial Security Service. Who else could the third diadem be? But it was incomprehensible that Sybil... Sabrina?)

Ryland Kern opened his eyes. They were not cold and authoritarian like Dahlgren's. Nor smiling and slightly crazed, like Sybil's. (In appearance only; Stephen knew Sybil well—or had thought he did.) They were two dark pools, completely inexpressive.

"I hope this isn't some dungeon, Dahlgren," said Ryland, scarcely moving his lips.

The president looked quizzically over at Stephen, who quickly answered, "No, sir. We're in the chapel of a hermitage."

"How many inhabit it?" Kern asked rapidly.

"Only you three."

Ryland Kern nodded his head approvingly.

"And you are?"

Stephen stiffened still further.

"Stephen Houdry, captain of the Hydra II, sir."

The president's eyes drifted up to the ceiling, trying to remember.

"Hydra II... Hydra II..." He looked again at the man standing to attention in front of him. "Planted in the region of the former BosWash, if I'm not mistaken."

"That's right, sir."

"Good... Very good," Dahlgren took a few steps, with a satisfied air. "So the city must still exist. I'm glad, I always liked the old metropolis. It's a real symbol."

"I'm sorry, sir, but it's not there."

Dahlgren came to a halt.

"What's not there?"

"BosWash, sir. There are only woods and meadows where it once stood."

The president's face hardened. Kern intervened to calm him down.

"Well, I suppose Houdry isn't to blame. I think we'd do better to ask him for a report on the current situation, don't you think?"

The president hesitated a moment, then agreed.

"Your report, Houdry."

"The ten members of Hydra II have been successfully implanted in new bodies, sir. None of them has been discovered, and no one suspects our existence. We have no news about the other Hydras; we don't know if any of them have woken up. But I'm afraid that the situation we've found is very different from what we expected, sir. Perhaps it will be easier to understand if I give you an overall view of what has happened in the past two hundred years..."

X

An Unexpected World

1

DAHLGREN'S EYES were open wide, demonstrating his real astonishment.

"So, Houdry," he asked. "You say there's no central government? And no armed forces? Not even police?"

"That's right, sir."

Sybil looked thoughtful.

"But there has to be some system of coordination," she commented after a short silence.

"That's true, Doctor. Naturally enough, there is a need to distribute resources among the different projects and to decide which of them will take priority, and the ones that are not feasible..."

"Keep it short, Houdry," Dahlgren interrupted him.

"Yes, sir. Central coordination is carried out by the Integrated Cybernetic System (ICS). All the cyber brains of today, big and small, are connected to one another, creating a huge network that covers the entire planet."

"And where is this coordination center located?" asked Kern.

"I don't know, sir. Strangely, based on the information I have, the Central Archive does not seem to be in any specific location."

Kern scratched his new beard.

"We will need to investigate that," he said.

"Houdry, there's something that doesn't convince me in all this," Sybil interjected. "I'm not sure, but there must be some people who don't agree with the ISC's decisions. It's impossible to satisfy everyone, and the people whose projects are rejected can't be happy. They must protest in some way or another. By saying, for example, that as machines, computers are incapable of appreciating this or that highly important factor that is intrinsic to their project, or something of that sort..."

"You're not wrong, Doctor. That used to happen often at first, but it had been anticipated. Even before the ISC was set up, there was an overseeing body: the Supreme Council."

Dahlgren smiled.

"Ah, so there's still a government."

Stephen shook his head.

"I'm sorry, but I think the name has confused you. This isn't the old Supreme Council of the Communist Federation, although it does descend directly from it. But it has so few real powers I would not go so far as to call it a 'government.'"

Anticipating Dahlgren's reply, Kern stepped in first.

"Houdry, why don't you explain to us what its functions are, who its members are, and how they are chosen? I think that would help us see more clearly."

"Of course, sir. Well, the current function of the Supreme Council is to consider the appeals against the ISC's decisions. Those who wish to protest can turn to it, giving the reasons for their complaints. The council asks the ISC for a report detailing the reasons why the project in question has been rejected or postponed. Then in a hologram session that is open to anyone interested in the matter, it is debated and a decision taken. Apart from in a very few cases, the ISC has always been right; I cannot recall any successful appeal over the past twenty years. Naturally therefore, the number of people challenging its decisions is fewer and fewer. The last appeal was a year and a half ago. As a result, the council has become little more than ornamental, and its members have dwindled to seven."

"How are they chosen?"

"It's quite complicated. Each of the members of the council represents one of the seven world zones. But not just that; they also represent the sexes, essential professions, different age groups. The ISC proposes a candidate from the zone to be elected that year. If anyone objects and says that the candidate does not possess the necessary requirements, then the ISC proposes another one."

"What if that one is also rejected?"

Stephen shrugged.

"In fact, I can't recall any candidate ever being rejected. What I outlined was simply a hypothetical case."

Kern waved a hand to silence him.

"I think that's enough, Houdry. We're not interested in this council. I'm afraid we're going to have to concentrate on the ISC. Our cybernetic experts will have to study the ways of penetrating and controlling it. That will allow us to act."

Houdry took the chance of intervening, even though nobody had directly asked his opinion.

"I understand, sir. But I don't think that can be the way—at least, not the main way."

Kern leaned forward, a smile of curiosity on his face.

"Explain what you mean, Houdry."

"One of my men was planted in the brain of one of today's cybernetic experts. When I asked him about such a possibility, his reply was a categorical no. Sir, almost all the more complex models are designed by cybos. Any human cybernetics engineer is like a gyro-mechanic faced with a spaceship. He might be able to carry out a few minor repairs, but when it comes to altering its internal structure... No chance. At least, that was his opinion."

Kern stroked his beard.

"So then the true rulers of everything are the cybos, Houdry."

"On the contrary, sir. Allow me to remind you that they are forbidden even to reproduce biologically."

"But, isolated on their island, I think they can probably avoid those regulations, can't they?"

"They cannot leave the island, but humans can go there, and do. The Institute of Psychosociological Studies has set up a network of observation posts there; all the cybos are checked regularly. They don't have any real power, Doctor."

"I think that's the key..." Sybil muttered to herself.

"What is? The cybos?" Dahlgren cut in, obviously irritated. "I'm afraid that Houdry's explanation doesn't leave any room for doubt, my dear."

"No, not the cybos," Sybil agreed. "I mean that Institute of Psycho-Sociological Studies, my dear Patrick."

Stephen could feel his pulse start to race; he was about to get what he wanted.

The wrinkles on Dahlgren's brow gradually eased. He smiled.

"You're right, Sybil. That's where we can strike, and strike hard." He got up from the stone bench. "If we can't control the decision-making mechanisms, we still have the possibility to change these people's way of thinking—and thus undermine the foundations of their power. What do you think of the idea, Ryland?"

"I like it, Dahlgren. But we shouldn't neglect the ISC," the head of security replied drily.

"Of course, of course," Dahlgren admitted. "But in my view, this approach is very promising. More than that, I think it is the key to this absurd society of sheep without ambition. It takes a huge psychological operation to mutilate the minds of an entire planet, to make them feel satisfied with their lives without knowing the pleasure of struggle and triumph. It's clear; we have to give virility back to this world of eunuchs. And what has been done thanks to psychosociology can be undone thanks to psychosociology," he concluded triumphantly. He turned toward Stephen. "Do you think it's feasible, Houdry?"

Stephen pretended to think before he replied.

"Yes, sir. I think that's the best way forward." Just in time, he remembered Kern's position. "Of course, we mustn't neglect the ISC. I think that the more alternatives we have..." he said, leaving his last sentence unfinished.

Dahlgren smiled.

"Don't worry, Houdry," he said encouragingly. "I still remember the old refrain: don't put all your eggs in one basket. But I've no doubt that the psychosociological basket is the most promising."

"I think the main lines we need to follow have been established," Sybil commented, rising from the bench. She looked at Houdry. "All we have to sort out are the practical aspects. We need to take in more information, assimilate it, and then prepare the tactical details. I suppose you have already prepared a way for us to learn their 'tongue.' If we don't know it, it will mean we're blind, deaf, and dumb."

"Yes, I anticipated that. I've created a learning program that will guarantee you speak their language within five days. I've already copied it to the hermitage's cyber brain."

Kern interrupted him.

"Into the cyber brain, Houdry? Won't the ISC be surprised to find the program there?"

Stephen smiled reassuringly.

"There's no danger, sir. The model of cyber brain they had here is as antiquated as the building itself. It's not connected to the ISC; I've already checked."

Dahlgren nodded, obviously pleased, and complimented Stephen.

"Good work, Houdry. And I don't mean for simply setting up the program. Does anyone want to ask him any more questions?"

Sybil shrugged.

"I think that's enough for now, Dahlgren," Kern said.

Stephen was still standing at attention. The president turned to him.

"Then we won't keep you any longer... Wait!"

Stephen came to a halt as he made to leave.

"I think we are going to need some of your subordinates here, until we've gotten used to the local conditions."

Houdry agreed.

"I brought two with me, sir. They can stay with you."

"Who are they?" Kern wanted to know.

"Candace Stow and Thomas Babson."

"Candy, isn't it? You have a good agent under your command, Houdry."

"Yes, sir. May I go now? I can't stay much longer; that might arouse suspicion."

Dahlgren waved his approval.

"Yes, you may go, Houdry."

Stephen turned on his heel and left the chapel.

He felt both satisfied and concerned.

Satisfied, for having succeeded in making it seem that the right proposal came from the president himself. He was well aware that if he had suggested it himself, it would not have been accepted; a foot soldier should never know more than a general.

His concern came from the mystery of Sybil-Sabrina.

He knew this wasn't an urgent problem, despite that reference to his "poor mind"... It would be better to accept the miraculous rise of Sybil Golden... Sabrina S., like...

The answer—or rather, the glimmerings of an answer—came to him so forcefully he came to a halt halfway down the passageway. Sabrina G.... Sabrina Glaspel! The neurophysiologist. The sister of Nevin Glaspel, Ryland's predecessor as head of security. And brother and sister had died shortly before Patrick Maynard Dahlgren became Imperial president... Patrick Maynard Dahlgren, who bewildered and annoyed his closest allies, systematically distancing himself from them.

Sabrina Glaspel, the brilliant neurophysiologist from the Institute of Special Investigations.

Sybil Golden had entered the institute following Sabrina Glaspel's death. Sybil Golden was also a brilliant neurophysiologist—although she was completely unknown until she arrived there.

There was another piece of information that fitted into this jigsaw puzzle. There had been several unexplained deaths in the neurophysiology section: Browne, for example. All of them had known Sabrina Glaspel at least somewhat.

Okay. So let's imagine that Sabrina Glaspel had discovered the principle of psychotransducers (which had come as a surprise to him; he had been aware of the project on dominant NEMOs, but the diadems—that is, the psychotransducers—appeared to operate in a different manner...even though possibly based on the same principle, that of modifying the structure of the NEMO, and yet it appeared as if the diadems left nothing of the original personality).

Where was he? Oh, yes, Sabrina Glaspel discovering the principle of the diadems. And immediately telling her brother about it, who would have spotted all its possibilities. Such as becoming Patrick Maynard Dahlgren, the president...

He stepped into the control room.

Candy and Babson rose to their feet simultaneously; it wasn't hard to see they were bored by the long wait. Stephen conveyed his instructions to them quickly and concisely. They were to stay in the hermitage, to attend to the newcomers' needs. Neither of them objected.

Stephen left the control room, once again absorbed in his own thoughts.

It all made sense now. Using his position as head of Imperial Security, Nevin Glaspel had taken over Dahlgren's body. In order to avoid any suspicion, Sabrina Glaspel had also changed bodies—or possibly had simply wanted to recover her youth.

And so they would have gone on, transferring to a new body whenever the old one was wearing out, ruling the Empire eternally... But the Empire was not eternal.

Foreseeing its imminent and inevitable collapse, the pair of them prepared their escape, developing the principle of psychotransducers. Of course, the diadems were useless for such a lengthy leap through time; they destroyed the original NEMOs. And if they had no memories in the new world, if they could not speak the language, they would be revealed straightaway. The logical solution was the injectable NEMO project; these would take over from the original ones but would not suppress them completely. The information would be saved, and the transported being would adapt quickly to any environment. Yes, it all made perfect sense.

Houdry closed the hermitage door behind him. He was surprised to see it was still night. Glancing down at his ring, he saw it was two hours before dawn. He would need them to sleep; Harry Mergenthaler had a lot of work in the morning.

As he walked toward the Hermes, he tested the validity of his hypotheses, weighing up different alternatives. He confirmed they did not fit—at least not from the information he had.

He entered the Hermes and settled at the controls.

"Take me home," he ordered.

So what use was what he had discovered?

None at all. Now, anyway. In the time of the Empire, it would have been a precious, invaluable piece of information, but here it was unimportant who led the triumvirate, Maynard Dahlgren or Ryland Kern. And yet he couldn't help feeling satisfied. So he had a "poor mind," did he? Well, with a minimum of information he had succeeded in solving the Sybil-Sabrina mystery—a problem that had no practical significance, whereas there were others that were urgent.

Nellie, for example.

She had been a perfectly satisfactory partner for Harry Mergenthaler, there was no doubt about that. But for Stephen Houdry...

It was true that as far as the techniques of love were concerned, she was impeccable (possibly *too* impeccable). She was affectionate, understanding. But she didn't have what he needed.

Habits developed over more than thirty years cannot be changed. He had always been very selective and had never liked "mass-produced" females. He always preferred to implant his own programs in them, ones he had created and gradually perfected from one to the next, up to the enchanting Gayla. It was a real shame she wasn't here; she would have made a good partner. And there was no way he could program Nellie; she would know straightaway. That would lead to a scandal, and everything would be given away. And as for programming one of his subordinates, good God, that was unthinkable! They had such repulsive minds... Sybil then?

He stared at the dark night through the front window. If he wanted to save his own skin, he shouldn't even dream of that possibility. At least not until the exact role of each of the triumvirate had been defined.

The corners of his mouth lifted in a smile. If the experience he had gained during the sixty-eight years he had lived under the Empire served for anything, it was to be able to foresee where conflicts might arise. And he knew he could wager that among those three there would soon be more than enough of them. Could he tell who would emerge the winner? To position himself alongside him before his victory became too obvious would be incredibly useful. But the outcome was still uncertain. And there was always the possibility of making a mistake. No. Better to wait for them to settle everything amongst themselves; that was not his problem.

His problem was Nellie.

The Hermes began to descend slowly outside his house.

2

The chapel door swung shut behind Stephen Houdry.

Kern shook his head thoughtfully.

"I never thought Ryder would have dared go so far as to destroy a whole continent..."

"Are you praising him or criticizing him?" asked Sybil, raising her eyebrows.

"I'm criticizing myself, dearest. I should have brought him with us, or eliminated him. If the other consuls had followed his example, we would have woken up on a dead Earth."

"Or more precisely, we would never have woken up," she corrected him. "What are you thinking, my love?" she asked, turning to Dahlgren.

The president stirred.

"I'm wondering how trustworthy Houdry is," he replied.

Sybil folded her arms.

"I think you've forgotten that I vouched for him."

Dahlgren waved away her answer with a brusque movement of his hand.

"You vouched for him two hundred years ago. Now there's another element inside him. Perhaps I didn't phrase the question properly. Tell me, who can vouch for the part that isn't Houdry in Houdry?"

Reassured, Sybil smiled.

"The security conditioning, which he himself invented."

"You didn't understand. I'm not worried about his security, but his way of thinking. How is he influenced by the sheep that inhabited his body before him?"

Screwing up his eyes, Kern interjected.

"What are you suggesting, Dahlgren?"

The president shrugged.

"I'm not suggesting anything. I simply did not like the way he talked about what had happened while we were asleep. Houdry showed a complete lack of analytical distance over the version *they* gave. In my opinion, he accepts deep inside that the normal state of a man is to be a sheep. Do you follow me?"

Kern settled on the bench.

"Yes, I do," he said. "But I think it's inevitable, Dahlgren. Nothing is for free. Through Houdry we've been given firsthand information that is indispensable but distorted by the spirit of the time we find ourselves in. It's inevitable when we use injectable

NEMOs. That's precisely why we chose to use psychotransducers to get here; it means our ability to come to correct judgments is unaffected, and we can correct any errors. Don't you agree, Sybil?"

For a brief instant, Dr. Golden considered the possibility of telling them that the situation as Houdry had described it indicated that the soundness of their judgment was more than questionable, since they had been unable to imagine what was going on around them. Then she sighed.

"I agree, Ryland," she answered.

It made no sense to start a fruitless argument; she knew the two men only too well. Besides, there were the other problems she had glimpsed during their meeting, which needed careful analysis... Later on. When they were alone.

The president spoke again.

"Well, there are several matters that need sorting out. For example, our general lines of action. It seems to me that in the current conditions, we should not wake up any more Hydras. Far from it. I propose we inhibit them until we are properly prepared to go into action."

"I'm not too sure why you're suggesting that, Dahlgren."

It was predictable that Ryland should react in this way, Sybil thought. Most of his direct subordinates were in the Hydras, the people he could trust...

"I think the reasons are obvious, Kern," she said. "The more of us there are, the greater the likelihood we'll be discovered. At the moment, we're in a delicate situation: without any concrete plans, not yet adjusted to the environment, lacking all the necessary information. I think that the ten members of Hydra II can guarantee we get the information we need and provide sufficient help to carry out the first tasks. Of course, if you're planning some big initiative straightaway..."

It took Kern several seconds to reply.

"No. I agree with you."

You're in the minority, Sybil corrected him mentally. Then she went on.

"What we need first and foremost is psychosociologists and cyberneticists, so that they can help us analyze the situation. Don't you think so, Patrick?"

Before Dahlgren could reply, Kern butted in.

"I've no doubt we will need your specialists, Sybil. But they're not properly conditioned."

"You know very well I didn't have the time or the opportunity, Kern."

"I know. That's why I need to make some adjustments before waking them up."

"You've already done that, sweetheart. You yourself personally approved each of the candidates before you put the diadems on."

A cold smile played around Ryland Kern's lips.

"Yes, I did approve them. But, to quote Dahlgren, that was two hundred years ago."

Sybil frowned.

"I don't understand what Patrick had to say has got to do with our specialists."

"A lot. I approved them on the basis of the information I had two centuries ago. I can now bring that information up to date and correct any errors in time."

"Bring the information up to date? How?"

"I suppose the past is still conserved. The data on the agents and informers the Federation had amongst us must be kept somewhere," the head of security explained.

"It won't be that easy to find, Kern," replied Sybil. "Don't forget that all the information is controlled by the ICS. You'll need to have a very good reason for searching for them, if you don't want to arouse suspicion."

"I don't think that will be too much of a problem. Just suppose that a historian is interested in writing about espionage and counter-espionage in the last days of the Empire... And, naturally enough, he suffers a tragic accident. Things like that are perfectly normal, aren't they?"

Sybil searched for some flaw in Ryland's argument but couldn't find one.

"That sounds alright," she said reluctantly.

"I think so, too," said Dahlgren, a glint of amusement reflected in his eyes. "I think we're all in agreement," he continued. "For the moment, we'll use only Hydra II. We'll gather the information we need, bring ourselves up to date. Then, as our plans develop, we can awaken the other Hydras and the specialists."

The sound of knocking on the door interrupted him.

"Come in."

"Allow us to introduce ourselves: Candace Stow and Thomas Babson," said Candy in a steady voice.

3

Sybil inspected the room from the threshold.

It was narrow and gloomy, a real cave, she told herself. Well, she'd have to learn to adapt.

"Thank you, Babson. You may leave."

The boy stood to attention.

"At your service, Doctor Golden," he said, then wheeled around and marched off down the corridor.

It was only with great effort that she succeeded in shutting the heavy door. She ran a critical eye over it: heavy, but not very secure. The hinges were already buckling under the weight. Well, she hoped she would never be besieged in there.

She walked over to the bed—or rather, over toward what laid claim to being called that—and stretched out on it, to the sound of suspicious creaks.

No doubt about it: the former occupants of the hermitage had a tendency to exaggerate. Too ascetic for her tastes, she thought as she looked up at the small barred window high in the wall. She folded her hands behind her head and tried to get comfortable. She needed to think; there were too many flaws in the original plan.

First of all, the predictions of the psychosociologists (Stephen among them) had been wrong. They had been convinced that once the Empire had disappeared, the Federation, having lost the external reason for its existence, would disintegrate into a hundred small states. But the nationalists had not behaved as expected. More seriously still, the assumption as to the basic constancy of the human personality had also been a mistake. From what Stephen had said—and above all, from what had come from the mind that his body had previously possessed, as Nevin had correctly observed—came a depressing conclusion: that the communist theorists had been right. It had proved possible to alter—and alter significantly—the composition of personal values, the very focus of the meaning of life. She still did not understand how it had been done, but it was a fact. And that made their goal, the goal of the entire Hydra Project, really difficult to achieve. It would require a long-term (very long-term) effort until they could achieve relative security, and that meant the danger of being discovered was increased.

Infiltrating the key positions in the Institute of Psychosociological Studies, planning and carrying out a slow process of massive reversion, was something that could only appear simple to Nevin and Ryland, because they weren't scientists.

Nevin and Ryland. That was the other problem, one that was much more urgent and immediate.

All those years as president of the Empire had definitely not done Nevin much good. He had changed a lot for the worse. It was a shame she hadn't realized this sooner, to be forewarned about it. But a mere section head from the Institute of Special Investigations did not have many opportunities to meet the highest authority in the empire. And when she did so, it was just the two of them. Until now she had not been aware of all the negative aspects he had developed in his dealings with his subordinates: irritability, contempt. His sense of what was possible and what wasn't had also been affected. It was true he still had his intuition. He could still tell when an idea was worthwhile, but he was no longer able to grasp them instantaneously. Poor Stephen had had a hard time trying to suggest the idea that they should infiltrate the IPS, but if she hadn't said so directly, Nevin would not have seen it. That was it: Nevin Glaspel was willing to listen to her or Kern, but he did not consider anyone lower down in the hierarchy worthy of his attention. That was bad. And she doubted whether she could correct it. That being so, Ryland Kern was a danger. He would never have been able to rival the old Nevin Glaspel, but he was clearly stronger than the present Patrick Maynard Dahlgren. She would bet anything that Ryland would try to topple him. But as far as she could tell, Nevin thought he was as untouchable as when the Empire existed. He was amused by the arguments between her and Ryland, thinking he was still the decisive factor.

Unfortunately, there were more than just the three of them involved: Kern's former subordinates had to be taken into account. They were the only disciplined, combative force, and his specialists would never resist him, if the worst came to the worst. Besides, it was very likely that many of them had been secretly in Ryland's pay from before. So, in conclusion, in the long term Ryland held all the trump cards. He could afford the luxury of waiting until everything was properly organized, and then strike; she and Nevin would vanish.

Her specialists were useful, even essential, but she wasn't. Quite the opposite.

She looked up at the window. There were few stars left in the sky; day would soon be dawning. It had been a long night...

She turned restlessly on the narrow bed. She had to prepare herself for the struggle and decide what methods to employ against Kern.

Should she talk to Nevin? Warn him?

That would be useless. He was too sure of himself. He would see her warning as an attempt by her to take over, to play the principal role. He would not think he was in any danger until it was too late.

Perhaps if she abandoned him, she could save herself. But how to go over to Ryland's side? By becoming his lover?

She examined her body.

An acceptable physique. A pretty face...but nothing out of the ordinary, nothing that could guarantee her a place alongside Ryland. Possibly if she changed bodies...

No. She shouldn't have any illusions. Ryland would always see her as an adversary in the struggle for power. He would accept an alliance, but only until he got rid of Nevin—that is, of President Dahlgren. Then it would immediately be her turn. There was no other solution: she would have to stay with Nevin.

She considered the possibility of pretending to side with Kern, only to betray him at the last moment. That was too fanciful; Ryland would never trust her enough to reveal his plans to her. At least not the most important ones.

She sat up on the bed, legs crossed under her, elbows on her knees, and head in her hands. She was making the same mistake as Nevin: she was only taking the three of them into account. She had to look further, to consider all the elements in play. There was an old principle she could possibly apply: sometimes the strongest point became the weakest.

If she could only make Ryland's former subordinates go over to the rival camp. Not all of them, obviously; some he trusted, who at the right moment…

She shook her head in annoyance. She was forgetting the security conditioning. None of the members of the Hydra II could even dream of attacking any of the Three. Although this also counted against Ryland: whatever he was planning to do, he would have to do it on his own.

Unless he was counting on some of her specialists already having gone over to his side. Perhaps his current opposition to them being woken up was no more than a trick designed to deflect attention from that possibility. She couldn't discount that possibility; she would have to be suspicious of her own subordinates. Not good.

In any case, she would have to act as quickly as possible, before the other Hydras and the specialists sleeping in them could come into play. Hydra II, Stephen Houdry: those were the elements she could use. Especially Houdry; she didn't know the others in the Hydra. She knew only that they were former members of the Security Services, and people Ryland Kern felt he could trust. It was lucky that her proposal to put psychosociologists in the Hydras had been approved by Kern. They would obviously be better able to understand the new situation. But that was all water under the bridge; the important thing was that she knew Stephen, the head of Hydra II, quite well.

She stretched out on the bed again.

Stephen Houdry... He might have the physique of a young, athletic man of little more than thirty, but his mind was still that of Stephen Houdry, deputy head of the psychosociology department in the ISI. Stephen Houdry, fat, wrinkled, bald, and, above all, cautious. He had needed to be throughout his sixty years in order to survive. It would be difficult for him to be daring now. She could undo his conditioning so that he was capable of acting against Kern. He could do the same with his subordinates for them to eliminate the president. But the cautious, cowardly Stephen Houdry would never be brave enough to take her side. He would prefer to remain out of the struggle, waiting for the victor to emerge. She couldn't count on him. So whom could she turn to?

Let's see. Stephen must have his weaknesses. That would be a good starting point to get a hold over him, until he was committed to her to such an extent that he could not back out, and then use him as a tool to destroy Ryland Kern. Wait a second: first of all, what weaknesses did he have?

He didn't do drugs. He didn't have any perversions... Just a moment: there were women. Or more precisely, prostitutes. The word was that he had particularly refined tastes in that area. He did not use ordinary prostitutes. He preferred to have one to himself, a concubine, and to program her behavior in bed personally. At least, that was what people said. And it was true that he always had a strikingly beautiful girl in his bungalow. Over the years, he had not seemed to want variety. That must be partly a question of cost; not even the elite members of the ISI could allow themselves the luxury of keeping multiple concubines or changing them with any frequency. Yes, that was his weak point. According to what he had told them, in this age there were no prostitutes, much less the possibility of programming sexual behavior. Anyway, he would never dare program one of today's women; the risks of being discovered were too great. He would be, he must be, unhappy. If she could only find a way to satisfy him, by offering him, for example, one of the specialists waiting among the diadems. She could program her without any risk. No, there would be a risk. She would be offended at being programed like a common prostitute and would turn against the project. It was too dangerous. And, even if that could be avoided, Stephen would not feel he was in her debt. As soon as Kern had checked the past of all the specialists, they would be available to all the leaders of the Hydras, and Houdry would get the idea for himself. She would not be compromising him. He could choose one who would like being programed. He knew the psychological profiles of almost all the ISI specialists; that had been part of his job. Yes, he would find one of them who was willing.

With a sigh, Sybil turned over again in the bed and looked up at the window. The sky was brightening already.

Alright, she ought to get some sleep. She was too exhausted to think properly. Perhaps there was some way...

She yawned. First, to sleep.

She stretched out on the mattress, trying to find the softer spots. She closed her eyes. She still had time; Kern wouldn't act immediately, he didn't have...

Her thoughts unraveled. Without realizing it, Sybil Golden slipped gently but quickly into sleep.

Outside, the new day was dawning. Warm. Beautiful.

XI

Dealing in Souls

1

THEY PLUNGED SILENTLY through the darkness. Down, further down.

The bands of light threw silvery beams over the rough, undulating walls, so that for a fraction of a second they picked out a thousand hidden shades of ocher and gray before they returned to eternal night.

All of a sudden, a black disk-like shape appeared.

The men touched the sensors on their belts, and the hum of the degravitators became audible—like three buzzing, irritating insects. Suspended in mid-air, they rotated slowly.

Stephen raised a hand to his mouth.

"Can this be it?" he asked, and the echo repeated: "...be it?"

The electronic capsule vibrated in his ear.

"Diameter?"

Stephen measured it with a look.

"No more than a meter," he replied, uncertain. "It's an almost round opening."

"How far down are you?"

He glanced at his wrist.

"A hundred and eighty meters."

A sigh came from far away.

"No. It must be further down."

Stephen's hand pointed downward.

Further down.

The three men renewed their descent. Above them, the mouth of the small lateral tunnel disappeared from view.

"This one?"

Stephen's voice sounded hopeful.

"Possibly... Depth?"

"Two hundred and eight."

Above them, a whispering...

"It might be. Is it round?"

"Almost."

"Diameter?"

"More than a meter...but not as much as a meter and a half."

"There's no other one nearby?"

The beam of light from Houdry's forehead moved up and down, all around.

"No, no others."

Another pause.

"You'll have to explore, Stephen. Go in on your own. Don't forget the password."

"Of course. I don't want to be crushed to death."

Stephen Houdry motioned to the other two men to wait. He put his hands on the stone edge and pushed his way in.

"The new frontier is time," he said, repeating the phrase over and over almost at a shout until the words echoed around the stony walls. Childish nonsense, he told himself. The frontiers disappeared centuries ago. But we still love those old expressions. We are children. Children playing at bringing back the past. Stupid children...

The walls did not collapse.

Good, very good: the acoustic sensors are still working. Or it might be that this wasn't the cave. No. It had to be this one.

The walls sloped inward, blocking his path.

It was the end of a blind tunnel.

He felt tentatively with his hands at the rocks; they moved, and a space opened in front of him.

The black box glinted in his luminous beam.

Remember: don't try to open it.

He moved his hand carefully over the smooth surface, brushing off a nonexistent layer of dust.

"Well?"

The voice from above sounded impatient.

"It's here."

"Perfect. Hurry up, it's getting late."

"I'll hurry, don't be so impatient."

The capsule didn't bother to respond.

Grasping one of handles, Stephen began to pull it toward him. It was heavy; Lambert and MacGray would have their work cut out.

2

There was no moon, and the stars were shining intensely, as if this were the first time, but Sybil was not looking. She was staring at the opening among the rocks. Down below, tiny gleams of light kept appearing and disappearing, growing as they neared the surface. Coming closer. Sybil knelt down to get a better view.

She began to make out the figures. There were two of them, joined together by something long, flat, and rectangular. They were climbing out slowly, with difficulty. A third man was ahead of them, rising quickly toward the bright night sky.

Stephen rose above the opening, then gently landed next to Sybil, still breathing heavily. Busy watching the box rise, Sybil didn't move.

Now Lambert and MacGray emerged, barely rising above ground level and then leaving their load almost at the edge of the hole with a sigh of relief.

Sybil went toward them without a word. She stroked the edge of the box, and it opened.

They all peered inside.

In the narrow space between the thick sides they saw the pale gleam of fifty or so folded bands and a small pile of little metal sticks.

MacGray shook his head in disbelief. Lambert muttered a scarcely disguised protest.

"It would have been better to empty it down below."

A smile played briefly around Sybil's mouth.

"This box can only be opened when it is close to certain mental frequencies," she said, without looking at any of them. "Otherwise..."

She left the rest to their imagination, as she stroked the folded bands and counted them. She knew that the three men were staring at the small metal sticks, the thin strips that fit easily into a closed hand, because they knew what was lurking inside them, ready to burst out at the slightest pressure: death.

Lambert and MacGray's hands moved nervously as they remembered.

Sybil closed the box and straightened up agilely.

"It's too heavy," she said to Stephen. "Your Hermes won't be able to carry them all."

Stephen Houdry turned to his men.

"I'll stay here. You take the box to the hermitage, leave it there with Doctor Golden, then come back for me."

The two men bent down, carefully lifted the box, and moved off toward the spot where the Hermes, a darker shape in the night, stood.

They clambered inside and stood in the entrance, waiting for Sybil.

She shook her head.

"I'll stay. I need to talk to Houdry."

Stephen could sense his men's invisible smiles through the gloom. He didn't like it. He turned toward Sybil, but something in her eyes brought him up short. This was not a flirt; it was far worse, but he could not refuse without taking sides in some way or other. Alright, there was nothing stopping him from listening to her, and then. Then he would see.

Despite this, he felt an uncomfortable wrench in his solar plexus.

"Didn't you hear her?" he shouted roughly to his men. "You can go."

The Hermes lit up, and an instant later it rose gracefully from the ground. Then it turned in a gentle curve and sped off toward the hermitage.

Sybil had sat down on a rock. She signaled for him to come over.

"Don't be frightened. I'm not going to attack you," she said. There was a smile around her mouth, but her eyes were cold. "Put your light out; it's not necessary."

Stephen switched it off and sat beside her. Now Sybil did look up at the stars.

"See? The night is more beautiful like this. Tell me, Stephen, what happened with Nellie?"

Stephen stirred uneasily on the rock. This was not how he was expecting the conversation to start.

"Nothing special…just the usual. Even in these days. We didn't get along," he said, and decided to add a small lie: "It was already coming to an end before I arrived."

"Are you sure?" asked Sybil, looking him straight in the eye. Stephen looked away. "Remember, Houdry, I know you."

He shrugged.

"I don't see what that has got to do with work, Sybil. As I said, it's normal these days. A couple doesn't last longer than six months, a year at most."

Sybil let out a sigh.

"Stephen, Stephen… You're a psychosociologist. A good one, I think. So tell me, can habits acquired over half a century change?"

He didn't reply.

"You see? You haven't told me everything about your separation from Nellie. And it seems to me you have a serious problem. What chance do you have of finding a woman to your taste here?"

"None," Stephen replied drily.

She agreed, thoughtfully.

"It's so obvious that even a novice in psychosociology like me can see it. And doesn't that lack affect you?"

"Yes, it does."

"See? And you didn't want this conversation."

"I still don't see why it's necessary."

Sybil smiled.

"Perhaps I can help you."

Stephen raised his head sharply.

"You? I don't see how. Unless, that is…"

"No way, Stephen. There's no way I'm going to let you program me. I still have my prejudices."

Stephen leaned back on his hands and took a deep breath.

"What then?"

"Not so fast, darling. Tell me, would it be possible to program a woman from this time?"

"No, she would realize what was going on."

"Then everything would be lost. I agree. What about one of your subordinates? Candy, for example?"

Stephen could not help smiling.

"Candy? That's absurd. I need a woman, not a killing machine."

"That's what I thought. So the present-day women are no use to you, nor are the ones in the Hydras. Is that right?"

"I didn't need to talk to you to reach that conclusion myself," replied Stephen, obviously annoyed. He made to stand up, but Sybil quickly put out a hand to stop him.

"Don't be in such a hurry to dismiss my help, darling," she said icily.

Stephen sat down once more. A smile returned to Sybil's face.

"What if I told you there's a third possibility?"

He turned to look at her. She was staring up at the stars.

"Tell me, did you see what was in the box?"

Stephen Houdry shivered.

"Yes, the lasers."

"You didn't look hard enough. There was something else."

"Yes, bands. Similar to..."

His eyes widened inquisitively; she nodded.

"Yes, you're right. They're diadems, too. Psychotransducers, and they are loaded. There are women there, Stephen."

Houdry stood up again; this time, Sybil did not stop him.

"Who are they?"

"There are all kinds. Neurophysiologists, nonspecialists, psychosociologists, cyberneticists, futurologists. Unfortunately, none of them has been programed. We didn't see the need."

Stephen sat down again. Slowly.

"Then we haven't gotten anywhere, Sybil," he muttered. "None of those women would want to be programed. If I tried... Well, you can imagine the risk. Everything could be discovered." He turned to Sybil in exasperation. "Why are you doing this to me? I don't understand."

She put an arm around his hunched shoulders.

"Don't be so downhearted. I wouldn't have mentioned any of this if I didn't have a proper solution for you, darling." Saying this, she felt with her free hand inside her tunic and pulled out one of the bands. "See? Here it is."

Stephen looked down at the psychotransducer. It was glinting softly in the darkness.

"How do you know she'll allow herself to be programed?" he asked, an edge of anxiety in his voice.

Sybil turned the band between her fingers, admiring it.

"She'll accept because she is Bright Eyes."

"That's what you're off..." he said, then came to a halt.

"I see you've understood, darling. The only woman who could be programed without realizing what was going on, would be one whom no man has never, ever approached with amorous intent."

Stephen nodded and swallowed hard as he remembered. That face! *Face?* Well, he had to call it something. Those purple scars extending back into her thin, spiky hair the color of bleached corn and descending to the carefully covered neck, suggesting an even more complex geography of horror beneath. That shapeless mouth and eaten-away nose. And to top it all, what served as eyes: two glittering black disks, shining out of those surroundings. That was "Bright Eyes." Yes, only her... her mind, that is. Placed in another body.

"Part of my job was to select these specialists, Stephen. I had to study their files closely... Alice Welland. 'Bright Eyes' (if ever there was a misnomer...) suffered the accident that left her like that when she was seven. What do you think of my solution?"

Stephen's hand reached out toward the band. Sybil quickly snatched it out of his reach. Then she went on, smiling placidly.

"Not so fast, darling. You must have realized that my concern for you isn't exactly charity."

Stephen took another deep breath.

"I'm very grateful to you, Sybil, but I can wait for her. I imagine Ryland will be very interested in your concern for me."

The smile spread across her mouth.

"I wouldn't recommend you wait too long. The diadem could be broken, or get lost, while you were doing so."

He tried to throw himself at her, but stopped at once, a grimace of pain on his face...

Sybil shook her head.

"I think you're making a mistake trying to use force, darling. You more than anyone should know what conditioning is."

Stephen nodded, as if to himself, huddled on the rock.

"I'd like to be able to give you time to think it over, Stephen. I know you don't like hasty decisions. But in fact, we don't have much time. Even if you agree now, that would give you less than twenty-four hours to find a body for our sweet Alice."

Silence.

"I need to explain it properly to you. I don't want you to miss the opportunity. There's no one else like her. No one you can condition without her finding out. That means you need to be extremely cautious with her. The box with the psychotransducers in it has very special properties. Inside it, the diadems can last, and do last, for centuries. Outside it, they only last twenty-four hours. As soon as they're taken out, a process of decomposition begins... In the case that interests us, it has already started. For twenty-four hours, it's not serious, but after that..."

Stephen had hidden his face behind his hands.

"Okay, you win," he said dully. "What do you want me to do?"

"Nothing impossible, darling. Do you know something? The conditioning technique you developed always appealed to me. I've studied it, but unfortunately only in theory... I'd like to see it applied."

"On whom?"

"On you," said Sybil, then added hastily. "Yes, I know you've already been conditioned, but I don't know enough to do it with someone who is intact. I want to begin with you."

"What would you do?"

"Suppress part of your conditioning. To be precise, the part protecting Ryland."

Stephen shook as though struck by a thunderbolt.

"Do you imagine I don't know what you're after?" he stammered. "I can't even think of something like that."

Sybil looked at him with feigned sincerity.

"That's because you have evil thoughts. Before I start, I have to warn you of what would happen if Ryland were to find out that your conditioning regarding him has been deactivated. What would he do to you, Stephen?"

"I don't know... Please, hurry up, start soon, or I'll explode."

Sybil Golden wiped the smile from her face. Now she was cold, professional.

"Fine, let's get started. Look into my eyes."

Stephen took his hands from his face.

"Good, that's good... Remember, you have to help me, or I won't be able to do it. I'm not an expert like you, darling."

3

The Hermes descended silently over the hermitage. It remained floating in the air, ten centimeters from the top ledge. The hatch opened, and Sybil jumped nimbly out.

Turning a smiling face to the interior of the Hermes, Dr. Golden waved.

"See you soon, darling. And thanks for everything."

Reluctantly, Stephen Houdry briefly waved his hand in reply. He could feel his men staring at his back. Too bad; he was committed now. Better for them to think it had been nothing more than a romantic tryst.

Sybil Golden disappeared beneath the arches.

Stephen shut the hatch and returned to the captain's seat. First he would take MacGray home, and then Lambert. He needed to do this before dawn, so he had to hurry.

The Hermes rose swiftly, pressing the men back in their seats.

Stephen punched in the directions to MacGray's house, then sat back. Feeling inside his tunic, his hand found the diadem. It was warm... "Bright Eyes," he thought with a smile.

He would have to hurry. Only one day to find the body. Who would be the most suitable?

Perhaps that girl...the one from the week before. What was her name? He struggled to remember, but couldn't. No matter. He could look for her name in the files. Then he would need to think of whom to prepare to get rid of Ryland Kern. It could be MacGray himself. Or better still, Candy. He needed someone efficient—and quick.

XII

Alice's Eyes

1

"...BECAUSE WE ARE FOLLOWING a path strewn with corpses. But don't weep for them; to offer a tear, a single tear to each of the dead, you would need ten lifetimes. Remember, you have only one. Use it to reach your final goal. That will be your best tribute to those who died." Aisha's voice trembled as she finished her reading.

A hand groped toward her in the semidarkness of the room.

"Why are you crying?" asked Vern. He turned toward her and held her tightly. "Don't cry. It hurts me."

The girl struggled to control her feelings.

"Don't say that, my love," she replied, her voice still thick with tears. "I would never, ever want to harm you."

Instinctively, their bodies sought each other.

The vague light in the room lessened, until it was gone. Then gradually, it returned.

"I don't know why I feel so good next to you," Vern murmured.

Aisha didn't hear him. Her hand was stroking his chest over and over again.

"Do you know why I was crying?" she asked all at once.

His eyes still shut, Vern shrugged.

"I suppose it was because of those dead. That's silly, though. Even that old author says as much. Not even ten lives..."

Aisha sighed.

"I wasn't crying for them."

"Who for, then?"

"For myself."

The man's eyes opened.

"I don't understand you," he said with a smile. "You're not dead."

"I'm afraid," she whispered, and a sob struggled to rise in her throat. She choked it back and said, "I'm afraid of dying without reaching it."

Vern gave a short laugh.

"I'd like to know what you can't reach," he said.

She looked at him and smiled for a moment.

"I wish I had your confidence, my love."

Vern sighed and sat up in the bed, facing her.

"Aisha, I don't know why you chose that profession." He shook his head, with a concerned look. "I never thought that emotional engineering could be so destructive."

"It isn't."

"Yes it is. It's enough just to look at you. At night, of course. By day, you're a different person; you personify happiness, beauty, and the will to live. This job is killing you. Why don't you change it?"

Aisha's face fell.

"I can't change it, Vern. I can't leave it. I am what I am because of it. It doesn't bring death, it brings life. My life. Do you understand?"

"No, I don't." Vern replied sharply. His look softened. "Perhaps it's better that I don't. To accept you as you are, with that aura of strangeness, of mystery that you have. So that you can go on being my little goddess. I love you so much, Aisha," he said, plunging his face into her breasts.

Aisha stroked his hair tenderly, staring into nothing.

"What time is it?" she asked, frowning.

A young girl's voice answered.

"Eight o'clock and thirty-seven minutes, Aisha."

For a second, her body stiffened, then she became a whirlwind of activity. Raising Vern's surprised head, she slid out of the bed and called out urgently.

"Clothes, Elf, and ones that are easy to put on."

A semitransparent tunic appeared out of the wall.

Vern sat on the edge of the bed.

"Why such a hurry?"

"I forgot I have a meeting with Harry at nine," Aisha replied, the words tumbling out as she quickly pulled on the tunic.

"Harry?"

Aisha paused. She glanced at him and smiled.

"Sometimes I forget what you're like. Silly, Harry Mergenthaler is my psychosociologist."

Vern gazed up at the ceiling. He knew that if he went on looking at Aisha's young, firm body he wouldn't be able to think, and he needed to remember something... That was it.

"But didn't you see him last week?"

"Yes, but he called me early this morning, while you were asleep. It seems my analysis turned up something odd." She looked up at Vern radiantly. "Perhaps it was my love for you." Impulsively, she nestled close to him and kissed him on the cheek. "I must be a unique case," she concluded with a smile.

Vern stretched out his hands to grasp her.

She moved away, shaking her head with a playful look.

"No, my love. I'll be late..." she warned him.

2

Stephen Houdry examined the diadem for the hundredth time.

Could he have made a mistake? No. It was as shiny as ever. He had followed Sybil's instructions to the letter, and now, inside the psychotransducer, the mind of Bright Eyes had fused with his conditioning. A special conditioning; not even Gayla's could compare. And in that body, for God's sake!

His breathing had accelerated.

He swallowed the saliva that had filled his mouth. Stay calm, he told himself, and glanced at the time on the wall. She must be almost there. She must find you the same as ever: calm, friendly. She mustn't be suspicious in any way.

He looked at the walls. The green-blue waves were moving rhythmically, expanding, contracting. The blue tone needed lowering a little; it was too cold for Aisha Dewar. The green had to predominate. He pushed the controls and briefly surveyed the result. Yes, that was the exact tone. He closed his eyes; he had to avoid the hypnotic effect of the colored walls and keep his mind alert, even though he had not slept. He had to wait calmly.

He waited.

He opened his eyes to glance quickly at the time, then shut them again: 9:12 a.m. She was taking too long. Could something have happened to her?

No. At six that morning she was perfectly normal, to judge by her voice. It was impossible for something to have happened to someone like her in only three hours. What if something had really gone wrong?

He gripped the chair arms. That possibility could not be excluded, however remote.

In that case, he would have to look for another woman. But none of the others were like Aisha. There was no other body like hers. But if something had happened to her, who could it be?

In his mind, he quickly ran through the memories of the person Harry Mergenthaler used to be. No, not that one. This one, possibly... He clenched his teeth. He shouldn't give up so quickly. Aisha Dewar was a typical emotional engineer. Temperamental, impulsive. It wouldn't be unusual for her to get caught up in a new task and arrive late. But what if she didn't turn up?

He got up from the seat and walked from one end of the cubicle to the other, staring at the floor the whole time to avoid the hypnotic walls.

Aisha...

It was 9:21.

His hands picked up and dropped the stereograms one after another. Faces, bodies. Faces, more bodies. This one, perhaps... No. *No.*

He straightened up, teeth still clenched.

Calm. Stay calm. He mustn't let his nerves get the better of him. She could still...

"You have a visitor, Harry," said the door.

Stephen took a step toward it, then came to a halt.

No, not like that. He had to relax, to be the cheerful, calm Harry she knew. He took another deep breath.

That was it.

He ordered the door:

"Open." For one anxious moment, he was struck with doubt. His smile froze. What if it wasn't her?

The door opened.

On the threshold, cheeks aflame, panting for breath, stood Aisha Dewar.

"I'm sorry, Harry," she said in a rush. "I couldn't help being late."

He stepped to one side, inviting her in.

"It's not important," he said. "I know how absorbing your work is."

Her cheeks became even pinker.

This detail didn't escape Stephen's trained eyes as they walked to their seats. He sighed. If it wasn't work, there could only be one other reason with Aisha Dewar. Which meant a further complication. Fine, he would resolve that when the moment came.

Aisha took a seat, glanced at the walls, and smiled.

"You've got the room looking really nice today, Harry."

Stephen said nothing.

She settled back in her chair, still gazing at the whirling greenish colors.

"Do you know something, Harry?"

"What's that?"

"I finally found it."

Stephen nodded silently. He had been right.

Turning her head away from the pulsing sea of colors, Aisha looked at him.

"I know what you're thinking, you don't need to tell me. 'There goes Aisha again, fooling herself.' But not this time, Harry, not this time."

"I believe you."

Aisha shook her head. The shiny silver strands swirled around her shoulders.

"No, you don't believe me," she said with a sigh, and turned her head back to the walls. "You can't believe me, because I've said the same thing to you so often. But this time it's true." She wrung her hands, trying to find the right words. "It's so different..."

You mean, always the same, thought Stephen. What remained of Harry Mergenthaler inside him writhed with compassion. Why had Aisha Dewar set herself that impossible goal? *An eternal love.* Could there ever be two more incompatible terms?

Stephen casually pushed Harry Mergenthaler back into the void. His sentimentality would only get in the way—although, after all, what he was about to do was a charitable act. For Aisha Dewar to die now, just when she thought she had found true love, before disappointment set in yet again, would be an act of mercy. How often can a human being set off on the search for the impossible?

And Aisha Dewar was human. Impossible to imagine what she would be like when she lost hope once and for all. The ancients knew that, for sure: "Those whom the gods love die young."

"Harry?"

"Yes?"

"What was the problem? The problem with my analysis?"

Stephen focused his attention on her.

She had unclasped her hands, which were now lying on her lap. She was gazing at the wall, and her eyes were blinking increasingly rapidly. Everything is going well, he said to himself, but there's still a way to go.

"I don't want to alarm you for no reason, Aisha," he said soothingly. "There must be some mistake with the instruments. We'll do another test today, different from the previous ones."

"What...is it like?"

Aisha had stopped blinking. She was staring at the waves of color flowing in and out...

"In one way, it's already started."

"Already...started..."

Stephen leaned forward in his chair.

"You need to relax. Completely."

"I...feel...sleepy. Very..."

"Yes, just relax. Go to sleep," whispered Stephen, and waited.
A minute went by.

Two.

"Aisha?"

No reply.

He reached out and prodded her shoulder. No reaction.

Stephen sighed and got up from his seat.

3

The flower.

The hand, the tiny childish hand firmly clasping the flower stem.

People.

People walking quickly, always quickly. Tall, very tall. People close by. People in the distance.

Tiredness.

Tiredness in her legs, her short legs, having to hurry, always hurry. The other hand, in hers. Her mother's hand.

Tiredness in her stiff arm.

Why such a hurry?

"Mama..."

"What is it?"

"Is there far to go?"

From on high, a clear gaze, a weary smile.

"Not far, my love. We're almost there."

Almost where?

Shouts.

Fear invading her breast again.

The silhouette running, separating from other silhouettes, coming closer.

Fear, cold and sticky, rooting them to the spot.

The silhouette grew. Turned into a man. The man: unruly beard, disheveled, long hair. Crazy, inhuman eyes.

The bottle, being shaken.

The other silhouettes moving back, away.

Terror flowing toward her from the restless heart of the crowd.

The bottle coming closer to her face.

The drops glittering yellow in the sun.

The drops, slowly aiming for her skin.

The acid, reaching her face, reaching her eyes...

Her eyes!

Alice Welland woke up, gripped by the old horror. Instinctively, she raised her hands toward her eyes, the eyes which should not be there.

They were there.

Incredulous, she felt the soft eyebrows. The closed eyelids—eyelids! With the tips of her fingers she could feel the drops of moisture flowing from them. Tears? Could she cry again? No, it couldn't be. This must be another dream. Another nightmare, far crueler than the previous one.

She cried harder, and the tears ran down a strange face. Why didn't she wake up? She couldn't take any more...

"Have you woken up?"

What was that voice?

She searched through her memory. She didn't recognize it. Yet it was somehow familiar. It brought back distant memories: children running, the sky, the green landscape.

Removing her hands from her eyes, she opened them, curious to see who was talking to her.

What?

She could see!

She was really seeing! There were colors, the colors she had forgotten so long ago, ever since she had been condemned to live in that horrific gray universe.

She found it hard to focus; everything seemed too close. The colors, the marvelous colors were blurred, ran into each other.

"Bit by bit, Alice. You have to get used to it gradually. Close your eyes."

Alice obeyed reluctantly. But what was she seeing now?

She smiled.

She had forgotten. It had been so long that she had forgotten the streaks of light, the flashes of brightness in the dark that appeared when you closed your eyes.

A hand clasped her bare shoulder, and she felt a gentle warmth spread through her. She had no idea why, but it felt very pleasant.

The lovely voice spoke again.

"Carry on crying. Don't stop, it will do you good."

She understood that she was still crying. That she had not stopped since she had woken up.

His hand on her warm, shaking skin, Stephen waited for the tears to be exhausted.

Her last, dry sobs.

The woman's body slowly relaxed.

Stephen waited. Just a while longer...

"Alright," he said finally. "You can open them again."

The eyelids trembled hesitantly, then opened wide, showing two green, astonished pools.

Alice Welland looked out.

Everything was still slightly blurred. She blinked, to clear her vision of the remaining tears. The world took on a dazzling clarity.

"No problems?"

"No," replied Alice, and with surprise realized this wasn't her voice. What had happened to her?

"Who are you?" she asked uneasily. "What am I doing here? What have they done...?" She fell silent, because her eyes had for the first time fallen on the man talking to her. She felt a strange sensation grow inside her, spreading through her body in pleasant waves.

Before he replied, Stephen took his hand from her shoulder. There was no longer any need for it; the conditioning was entering its final phase.

"I'll try to answer your questions one by one," he said, smiling. "My name is Stephen..."

Stephen! What a lovely name.

"The reason why you, why we are here, is more difficult to explain. It's a special project. The project is..."

Alice no longer heard him, or rather was no longer listening. She could still hear his voice vibrating inside her, and this unknown sensation became increasingly intense, unbearably strong, inexplicably pleasant. Her eyes drank in every feature of Stephen's face as he talked. She stared avidly at his arms, his white tunic, his legs...

"Alice!"

Startled, she came out of her dream.

"What?"

Stephen moved his head from side to side, smiling.

"Nothing. I can see you're not listening to me."

"No, no, carry on talking. I like to hear your voice," said Alice hastily, then blushed. "What were you saying?"

"No, I'll continue with the explanations later. It would be better if you got dressed now."

Got dressed?

Alice lowered her eyes to her body and discovered she was naked.

And it wasn't her body either; it was...beautiful.

Instinctively, she tried to cover herself with her hands, but something inside her made her stop almost at once. Her heart beat faster.

"Stephen..." she whispered faintly.

"What's wrong?" asked Stephen Houdry, bending over her. At once her breathing became irregular, as if something were pressing down on her chest.

"Ah, I understand. You got scared when you saw you were floating in mid-air, didn't you? There's no need to be; it's only a gravitational generator."

What was it she was feeling? Where had these unknown desires come from?

Alice made one last, desperate effort to control herself, to control her restless body, but she failed.

Her hands reached out impulsively toward the man bending over her.

"Stephen, Stephen..."

"What is it?"

"You don't understand. You don't understand anything..." she groaned, as she enveloped the man in her arms and pulled him down to her with all her strength.

XIII

Work for Monsters

1

"THAT, IN ESSENCE, is the origin and scope of the Hydra Project," Stephen concluded.

Alice said nothing. She was supported by the invisible force field, her eyes fixed on the ceiling. Her legs were drawn up and folded over each other. The left one moved rhythmically on the right one.

"Don't you have any questions?"

The left leg stopped moving.

"Were the psychosociologists' predictions confirmed?"

Something close to admiration shone in Stephen's eyes.

"I don't know how you did it, but you hit the nail on the head. That is the precise problem."

Alice shrugged.

Stephen gave a sigh of satisfaction and lay down beside her.

"Now I'm sure you'll be able to help me."

She turned her head to look at him.

"How?"

Stephen automatically made note of the anxious tenderness in her eyes. The conditioning was providing unexpected advantages.

"We have to adapt the plan to the new situation, Alice," he explained. "The internal struggles and the splitting of the Federation into small states has not taken place. To tell the truth, we were wrong. The communist theoreticians were right: it is possible to suppress mankind's competitive spirit. Or, to be more exact, they succeeded in sublimating it into expressions that are compatible with their system." He spread his arms to indicate his frustration. "In fact, I don't know how to describe it. It's hard even to imagine the existence of a world like the one outside here…" He pointed to the walls. "It's the complete, absolute negation of…" He paused to see if she was looking at him, but Alice's eyes had strayed elsewhere. "Fine. I'll supply you with all the details you need to understand. So that you can judge and advise me. I have to confess that I'm unsure; perhaps what is left of Harry Mergenthaler inside me makes it impossible for me to analyze it with proper objectivity. But you don't have that drawback; you're an impartial observer, without prejudices…"

"You're wrong there."

Stephen gave a faint smile.

"That's true," he admitted. "But I need you anyway. You're the best generalist who ever crossed the threshold of the Institute of Special Investigations."

Alice's gaze returned to Stephen's face.

"Really?"

"Really. And normally, that isn't something we tell the person involved; it could make them conceited."

Alice touched his shoulder.

"Thank you, darling."

Stephen shook his head.

"Let's get back to work…"

Then a pleasant-sounding voice came out of the wall.

"You have a visitor, Harry."

2

Vern stopped outside the door.

"What brings you here?" asked the cyber control.

"I want to see Harry Mergenthaler."

"Your name, please..."

"Vern Miller."

Silence.

Vern paced nervously up and down the path outside the house.

It was very old-fashioned; it could have been built a century earlier. It was well-maintained, and in the dawning light it looked almost new. But the right angles of the multicolored polyhedron could not disguise the rancid, unmistakable odor of time.

The door opened.

A tall, thin man with dark hair and light-colored eyes appeared.

"You wanted to see me?"

Vern went up to him.

"Yes."

The man glanced at him, then told him to come in.

They went into the hallway.

Stephen Houdry led him into a small room.

"This is where I attend to my patients," he explained. He sat down and invited his visitor to do the same.

From his seat, which was as antiquated in style as the house, Vern studied the room. It was small, with iridescent walls, and was empty apart from the two chairs placed facing each other.

"Well then?" asked the psychosociologist.

Vern moistened his lips.

"I'm looking for someone... Aisha Dewar," he said, trying to find answers to his questions in the other man's face.

Stephen looked attentive. Polite.

Vern took a deep breath. He went on.

"I last saw her yesterday morning. At her home. She told me she had an appointment with you."

"That's true. She came here."

Stephen could see the young man gripping the arms of his chair.

"And...do you have any idea where she went afterward?"

Stephen Houdry did not reply.

It was plain that Vern was growing increasingly tense. In the end, he could contain himself no longer.

"I know she's here, Mergenthaler. I asked the Central Archive, and it informed me she was."

"Yes, she's here."

Vern leaned forward in his seat.

"I want to see her."

"She doesn't want to see you."

The young man blinked.

"I'd prefer her to be the one who told me that," he replied after a while.

How boring it is sometimes to know human beings so well, Stephen told himself. He removed his hand from the tunic pocket and held it out to Vern.

The young man hesitated for a second. He looked Houdry in the eye and made up his mind. He took the disk from him and pressed its sides.

The disk vibrated musically, and the hologram appeared on its top surface, gradually forming Aisha's beautiful face.

"Vern..." the image murmured, then stopped, as if she didn't know what to say.

When he saw her moving her head in a gesture he knew so well, Vern unconsciously bit his bottom lip. The image went on.

"We have to separate, Vern. Believe me, it's best for both of us."

Looking at the hologram, Stephen felt proud of a job well done. Yes, he had been able to use all the stereo-videos of Aisha Dewar, but that had only been the raw material. It was an art, selecting the right fragments and editing them so that it looked as though it were really her who was saying this.

"I'm sorry, I feel so guilty."

The image could not go on. She broke down in sobs.

Stephen settled in his chair, waiting for the final touch.

Aisha recovered her composure and took a deep breath.

"We shouldn't see each other again. Never again," she said passionately. "We would only hurt each other, a lot..." She paused, staring intently into nothingness before concluding, "Goodbye, Vern."

The hologram faded.

Vern carefully placed the blank disk on the arm of his chair. He stood up and walked over to the door. He halted on the threshold and said over his shoulder:

"Tell her... Tell her she can go home. I won't bother her again."

Before replying, Stephen looked away.

"She's thinking of staying here."

Even though he couldn't see him, Stephen could sense how the young man's body was trembling.

The door closed silently behind him.

3

Alice's gaze turned away from the hypnotizer.

"Who was it, my love?" she asked with curiosity.

"Nothing important," Stephen answered, removing his tunic. "Work matters."

"Difficult?"

Stephen gestured noncommittedly.

"Not really. And they're already resolved," he said, lying back on the force field.

"I'm glad," said Alice.

Slowly, she began to stroke his body.

He moved away from her.

"Not now, my love. We have to work."

Aisha sighed and lay back on the bed.

"This is one of our main problems," said Stephen. "I have to carry on with Harry Mergenthaler's work. I don't have a moment to study the situation, to think... And we've hardly had time to draw up even an outline of the strategy we want to follow." He could tell his companion was paying closer attention now. She was a good generalist, he thought. She knew when something was important. "In other words, to refashion the mental attitude of the inhabitants of this era. What has been done can be undone." He looked across at her puzzled face. "I know you realize it's not an easy task, my love."

"I realize that," said Alice in a flat voice.

"You'll have to assimilate a huge amount of information and analyze it carefully. Then come to the correct conclusions, and from them, work out what tactics we need to follow, and how to make the necessary adaptations subtly. To return these people's instincts to their original channels without them realizing that an alien hand is leading them there. Almost impossible, don't you think?"

"So it seems."

"But it's the only solution, Alice."

Aisha took a deep breath, like someone about to dive into the sea.

"Are you sure...really sure, there is no alternative?"

Stephen thought before replying.

"No, there definitely isn't."

Silence.

"But I don't think I'll have the time to do the work either."

"Why?"

"Because of this," said Alice, touching her face. "I also have to represent somebody in this world, don't I? And in fact, I'm not sure I can do that. I don't even know the name that this body had...I mean, the one it has."

Stephen shrugged.

"That's not a problem."

"It isn't?"

"No," Stephen said with a smile. "The body you have used to belong to an emotional engineer. She was called Aisha Dewar... Nobody will be surprised if you cease having anything to do with the people you know or don't produce anything for years. Crises like that are not unusual for 'emos,' as they like to call themselves. Even if you change your profession and become a psychosociologist or a mystic or whatever, that wouldn't be unusual either."

Alice's eyebrows rose doubtfully.

"If you say so..."

Stephen smiled.

"I've plenty of reasons for saying so. I was your psychosociologist for years, Aisha."

"Aisha... It's a pretty name."

"Yes, like the person who was here before," Stephen said without thinking. He touched her arm and felt her suddenly stiffen. "But you don't need to worry about that, my love. It was you or her. Two people don't fit into one body. You, we, have to be practical."

All of a sudden, Aisha pressed herself against him, forcing him to fall quiet...

Several minutes later, Stephen spoke again.

"That's good, but don't forget, today we have to work. Once we've got a bit further with the task of ours, then we can spend more time like this."

"Whatever you say, my love," Alice whispered, her lips still swollen. "I'll do whatever you wish."

"I know," Stephen replied with a smile, and then continued in a more serious vein: "The first thing you need to do is to learn their language."

Alice nodded forcefully.

"I will."

"After that, you can gather information: psychosociology, history, anything you need. You can ask the Central Archive without arousing any suspicions. We need to know everything."

"The Central Archive?"

"Ah, I forget sometimes that you're like a newborn in this age. The Central Archive is where all the information from the ICS, the Integrated Cybernetic System, is stored. I'll give you more details about it later on. For now, your interest in these things will be further justified by the fact that you're with me. It's logical for you to want to know about my work, isn't it?"

"Yes, that sounds okay... But what if I run into someone I used to know? I can't always stay within these four walls, Stephen."

"That's true," he agreed. "But it's not difficult, my love. I have all the data regarding Aisha Dewar. You can study it, get to know what she was like..."

Once again he could feel her flesh growing taut against him...

Surprised, he glanced at her.

"Do you feel sorry for her?" He shook his head. "I thought you were tougher."

Alice sighed.

"Well, I'm not."

"Now you're worrying me," he said with concern. "You know as well as I do that you generalists are, and have to be, both cold and practical. If they allowed their emotions to interfere with their work..." A timid smile of apology played around her lips. "...it would be chaos. I know that, but..." She hesitated. "Perhaps it's because I have this body now. Because I'm a person again." The smile died. "Do you know how I became a generalist? The best in the institute, according to you?"

"No, tell me," replied Stephen, focusing all his attention on her. Something wasn't working properly.

Alice covered her face in her hands. Then she began talking, in a flat voice.

"Until the age of six I was a normal, ordinary child. At least, I think I was. But then, after that drug addict had..." She shuddered. "Everything changed then, Stephen. I had become a monster. A blind monster, that no one could look at without being horrified. No one, not even my mother, do you understand?"

"I understand," he said.

"I lost everything. Everything, not just light and colors. My parents couldn't afford to get me natural eyes, or a new skin. Even for those ghastly black disks they had to get into debt for years. I sometimes used to think it would have been better if they hadn't bought them. When I saw myself in a mirror for the first time with them inserted, it almost drove me mad. I didn't need to see colors to realize what the faces of everyone looking at me were saying."

Stephen took her by the hands.

"Don't hold back," he said. "Weep. I understand."

Her mouth began to tremble.

"Do you really understand me?"

"Yes."

"I'd like... I'd like to ask you, Stephen... What do you feel for me?"

Fear and hope mingled in her panting breath.

"Love," the man's voice said sincerely, surprising Stephen. Alice raised his hand to her mouth and covered it with kisses.

"Oh, my love... I was so afraid that..." She looked straight at him. "Do you forgive me?"

"For what?"

"For having distrusted you, my love. For having thought that... that it was only desire, only instinct that..."

"No, Alice, it isn't only instinct."

She laughed, pressing his hand against her beating chest.

Stephen's smiled. What was happening to her? He should have been more careful with Harry Mergenthaler.

Alice dried her tears and went on, her voice restored.

"Let me carry on telling you, so that I can let it all out, my love. I want to give you everything I have inside me, what I've never been able to tell anyone. No one is interested in a monster's problems, are they?" she asked pensively. "After what happened, I was living in a cage. I was shut in behind my metal eyes. I could see all the others living, playing, and working happily in a world I had no access to." Her voice quivered. "That I would never have access to. I could even become rich, but I would never, ever, be able to get rid of those dreadful black disks. Did you know that to install them they had to make a direct connection with the visual center of my brain? They changed it, deformed it until it was unable to function with normal eyes ever again."

The old horror shone through her gaze once more... Stephen couldn't look.

"I don't think my parents knew that. They did what they thought was best for me. They had no idea, so I can't blame them. But there I was, in my cage, desperate but unable to reach the world outside; all I could do was look at it, engrave every one of its details inside me... So that's what I did. I studied; I studied a lot, trying to get to understand it better. And I could go further than others, because there was nothing to distract me. Nothing. I had no friends. I had no love. I didn't even have dreams. And I learned. I learned so much I didn't have to choose a profession, it chose me. You know there have never been enough generalists, and that they're needed... There was a test at my school. I won a grant. Next to nothing, but I didn't need money to have a good time, because I never did. Do you understand why I'm telling you all this?"

"No," admitted Stephen.

Alice tenderly patted his hand, still resting on her breast.

"Don't worry about that, my love. I find it hard to understand myself as well. We can try together, perhaps that way we will succeed. This body," she said, touching herself, "means that I've at last escaped from my cage. But will I be able to analyze and understand as I used to, now that I am a flesh and blood creature?"

Stephen did not reply.

"Flesh and blood," Alice repeated, as though to herself. "Do I scare you, my love?"

"Why?"

Alice's eyes peered shyly at him.

"For being the way I am...when we make love, I mean."

"No, I like it. I like you a lot."

She let out a long breath.

"I was so worried... I do such odd, strange things when I..." She smiled with embarrassment. "I even thought that they were, I don't know...perversions of some sort. That everything I had repressed during all those years of forced virginity had become twisted up in some horrible way. But if you like it..."

"I already told you, my love: I like everything you do, I really do."

She tried to embrace him, but Stephen held her back with his hand.

"Not now, my love, remember..."

"No, it's not that. I only wanted to hug you, out of love. I owe you so much, darling."

"Not that much."

"Yes, that much and a lot more."

Pushing against his hand, she brought her face up to his chest and rubbed her nose on it. Then she drew back, smiling.

"You see? I can control myself, my love."

"So I see," replied Stephen, smiling back at her.

Alice sat back on the force field.

"So tell me, what should I do now?"

Lying back on the invisible force field, Stephen folded his hands behind his head.

"You need to study, to learn their language, so that you can start work in earnest."

Alice picked up the hypnoinductor and deftly placed it over her eyes. Then she lay back again, adjusted the straps around her head and fell willingly into the hypnotic trance. Her lips began silently to form the words of the unknown language.

Stephen surveyed the motionless girl with furrowed brow.

Take the cold, logical mind of a generalist. Add to it a series of sexual compulsions...then get away as quickly as possible, he thought. He should have foreseen it, but the consequences of Alice's conditioning were unpredictable. That could be very useful, or very dangerous. He would have to be very careful with her—and with himself.

Harry Mergenthaler's idealistic head was rearing itself at the most unfortunate moments. Or was it because he had a young man's body again? With intact glands that released torrents of hormones into his bloodstream, clouding his brain, leading him to forget his experience... Yes, he would need to be careful about himself as well.

Love for a conditioned woman. He couldn't be so stupidly childish. But he knew what he had to do.

Being a psychosociologist had its advantages, he told himself as he stood up. Nothing simpler for him than to put in place the proper therapy and completely erase that troubling emotion.

XIV

The Need for Doubt

1

THE HERMITAGE WALLS had vanished behind panels and consoles.

Multicolored dots zigzagged across some of the screens; others were covered with constantly changing figures; still more were dark. Flashing lights, leaping from bulb to bulb, column to column, in an unpredictable pattern.

The eyes of Patrick Maynard Dahlgren (or Nevin Glaspel, or, since a little earlier, Brother Simon) looked around with annoyance.

"This shouldn't be in the hermitage, Sabrina."

Sybil (or Sabrina, or Sister Shari) was still leaning over the main controls, studying the data.

"I know, my love. And please, call me Sybil."

"We're on our own, aren't we?"

"Yes, but we have to keep the habit. Always, as you know."

"Anyway, who cares about that now?"

Straightening up in her seat, Sybil gave her brother a worried look.

"You need something to take your mind off things, Patrick."

He was walking up and down the cell that had now become a laboratory, touching the gleaming equipment.

"Why don't you look at the chronoregisters Stephen brought?" Sybil suggested. "They will give you more information about..."

"You are the ones who are supposed to look for information; I think and decide..." He halted. His face relaxed, and the old smile Sybil liked so much appeared. "I'll be frank. I can't bear those registers. I can't stand seeing what mankind has become, those effeminate eunuchs," he concluded angrily.

Sybil got up from her seat and went over to her brother.

"I can understand how you feel. That's why I think you need to take your mind off it. Do something, anything, until the moment to act arrives."

Dahlgren glanced over his shoulder at his sister. He smiled sourly.

"What should I do?" he asked.

"I've no idea," Sybil admitted. "You have to discover that for yourself. Look, you could do the same as Ryland..."

"Ryland is doing his job. He took over the body of that Brackenbury to find out whether there are any spies among your specialists."

"Why did he do that himself, instead of using one of his men?"

Patrick smiled.

"That information is too important, Sybil. Ryland was right not to trust anyone."

Sybil shook her head.

"No, Patrick. Don't forget that the people in the Hydras are conditioned to protect us. None of them would hide any names, not even their own mother's. If Ryland took over that historian's body, it was to escape from this." She gestured around the room. "To escape from this dreaded hermitage, if only for a few days. Living here knocks everyone off balance, unless they have something definite to do. That's why I set up this laboratory. Don't worry, as soon as we can wake up the specialists, I'll transfer it somewhere else. But in the meantime, working here saves me from going crazy out of boredom."

Patrick nodded in agreement.

"I see... And what exactly are you doing?"

"For now I'm just checking the equipment. And learning how to operate it. These machines are sophisticated; science has moved on, my love. But we can do almost anything we need to with them," Sybil explained enthusiastically.

"And after you've installed everything?"

"I don't know," she replied doubtfully. "Possibly I'll try to become an expert in the conditioning technique. And to try to perfect it. According to our agreed strategy, we'll have to progressively change the mentality of these 'effeminate eunuchs,' as you call them. That's not going to be easy."

"Others have already done it, my love...and in the opposite direction, which seems to me much more difficult."

"Which means that there are people who might realize that something strange is going on."

Patrick looked pensively at the equipment.

Sybil lifted her hand from his back. She walked back over to the seat in front of the main controls.

"That's why I'm doing this. Also to try to protect my sanity," she explained, coming to a halt. She turned to look back at her brother. "I've had an idea."

"Tell me."

"Would you like to learn the conditioning technique?"

Patrick raised his hands in doubt.

"I have to confess that I know its general principles quite well, but as for its..."

A metallic whistle came from the main control panel.

Sybil hurried across to it and read the figures it was showing.

"A ship is coming... A Hermes," she said, as her hands moved over the controls.

"What are you doing?" asked Dahlgren, standing behind her.

"I'm sending the acknowledgment," replied Sybil, still staring at the screen. "If it's Stephen..."

The screen lit up. Stephen Houdry's face stared out at them.

"Permission to land?" he asked.

"Yes."

The screen went dark.

"Sybil, isn't it dangerous to use this communication channel?"

"Why?" she asked, leaning back in her seat.

"It could be detected."

"No," she said, smoothing down her hair. "We use directional antennae. The waves are focused in such a way that only the recipients can receive them. Besides, in this world they no longer use anything as primitive as Hertzian waves to communicate with one another. They're not economical."

"I hope you're right," said Patrick, heading for the door.

"Darling!"

"What is it?"

"When you've finished with Stephen, could you send him to me? I want to take advantage of his experience in conditioning."

Patrick agreed from the doorway.

"I'll bring him to you," he added. "I'd like to hear his explanations as well..."

Sybil swiveled around in her chair and gave her brother a forced smile.

"I'm afraid we'd bore you, Patrick. I want to talk about very technical details with him; you wouldn't understand a thing."

A knowing smile appeared on Patrick's face.

"As you wish, my beloved sister."

2

Stephen strode into the laboratory.

"Sit down," said Sybil, pointing to the seat next to her. He obeyed.

"Your report?"

"What would you like me to report on?"

"What news about the plan to get rid of Kern?"

Stephen shook his head.

"I haven't had time to..."

"Five days weren't enough to condition one of your subordinates? Stephen, Stephen, don't forget I know a bit about conditioning. You can do it in an hour."

Stephen spread his arms apologetically.

"Living here, you can't understand my situation, Sybil. I have to do all Harry Mergenthaler's work. And take care of Alice." Seeing the look on Sybil's face, he hastened to explain. "Not in the way you think—at least, not only that way. I've given Alice the task of processing all the information we need to work out the best tactics to reach our goal."

"Alright, alright... And you also have to direct your men and bring all this here," said Sybil, sweeping her arm around the laboratory, "and do everything else we ask of you."

Stephen nodded at each example she gave.

"But even so, you could find an hour!"

Stephen moistened his lips. Sybil leaned her cheek on her elbow and gave him a bored look.

"Well, what have you got to say?"

"Well..." Stephen thought rapidly. "The president ordered me to send someone to fetch Ryland Kern tomorrow. You know that he's..."

"I know, go on."

"I could prepare that man to do...that job. And afterward, everything would seem like an accident. Even the person doing it would be convinced of that; it's not hard to program. What do you think?"

Sybil's mouth tightened.

It seemed like the ideal solution. To get rid of Kern far away from there. With no witnesses. A typical accident. But the information he might have found was important. He could be right—that there was a spy inside the Hydra Project. What then?

"No," she decided. "We'll have to wait until he returns."

Stephen grimaced.

"As you wish."

"And yet, there's something we can use from your idea. It would be very convenient for Ryland's death to look like an accident, even to the person who kills him."

"That can be arranged."

"Could you implant a latent conditioning?"

"What do you mean?"

"I want you to condition someone. It doesn't have to be the person who goes to fetch him tomorrow. It could be any of your subordinates, and the conditioning shouldn't become effective until after tomorrow—say, the day after tomorrow."

"That's possible."

"Of course, the conditioning would only start working when Ryland and the...instrument are alone."

"Obviously. If another conditioned person were there, it could fail, because he would be bound to defend Ryland."

"Exactly. Will you do it?"

"I will."

Smiling, Sybil pointed a threatening finger at him.

"Try not to fail, darling."

"No, I won't fail," Stephen said hastily. He was well aware what Sybil's smile meant.

She settled back in her seat.

"Tell me about the work Alice is doing."

"She's tremendous, Sybil," Stephen replied in a proud voice. "She's learned their language in only two days. And since then, she is spending twelve hours a day in a hypnotic trance, absorbing information about all that's happened in the past two hundred years. She's doing the work of at least ten specialists."

"For what reason?"

He gave her a puzzled look.

"You know very well: to work out how, using what psychosociological manipulations, we will be able to restore a normal mentality to the inhabitants of this time, without being discovered...at least, not until the process is sufficiently advanced."

"But she isn't a psychosociologist."

"No, of course not. I'm the psychosociologist. But on my own, with all the work I have, I wouldn't be able to weigh out all the factors properly. Or even get a superficial idea. In fact, it would take a team of specialists. But since I don't have one, I'm using a generalist as a consultant."

"So I see. And how has the conditioning you gave her influenced her ability to work?"

Stephen's broad smile revealed his teeth.

"In a positive way, Sybil. Highly positive. It adds an extra, very powerful, motive for her to make every effort to complete the job I've assigned her."

Sybil looked at him thoughtfully.

"I thought that as a rule sexual conditioning got in the way of other kinds of work."

"That's true. Especially for intellectual work. When the subject knows she has been conditioned in that way, it produces a high level of internal tension between the programed emotions and their conscious ego. But Alice Welland doesn't know she has been conditioned. I think that all the feelings and desires she is experiencing come from her."

Sybil was still staring at him.

"Are you completely sure that what you have said is true?" she asked, stressing her words.

A look of surprise crossed his face.

"Of course. Why do you ask?"

"Because if that's so, I don't think you're an objective observer. The fact that she satisfies your personal needs prejudices you in her favor."

"You could be right," Stephen admitted.

Sybil leaned forward in her chair.

"Think about it, then answer this question: Can you trust the work Alice is doing, even though she is conditioned?"

Stephen understood how much depended on his reply and was suddenly anxious. Did Sybil know something he didn't? Something to prove he was wrong? If that was the case and he insisted on supporting Alice... Calm down, he told himself. She simply wanted to be sure. It was a great responsibility to work out the campaign of action, and she wants all those involved to offer an objective point of view. She knows me well; she doesn't know Alice. And the conditioned Alice, still less. Besides, she's right to a certain extent. It's quite possible I am prejudiced in her favor. I have to evaluate, calmly and objectively, the work she is doing. Let's see, yesterday...

3

"Don't confuse desire with reality," Alice had said, with obvious sadness.

Stephen's arms were raised to the ceiling.

"How else am I to interpret the data you yourself have given me?" Standing up, he went over to her screen and pointed to the glinting numbers. "It's clear: fifty years ago, the population of Earth was approximately five billion. Now there are five hundred thousand fewer—a ten percent reduction in only five decades..."

"The optimal size of Earth's population is only three billion, Stephen."

He waved his hand to dismiss her objection.

"There must have been some justification, Alice. I don't think we're that crowded on Earth."

"But the energy requirements..."

"They have enough energy for thousands of years!" Stephen exploded, drawing a hand across his face. "And it's not only that raw data. There's also the level of reproduction. Less than two children per woman..." He searched on the screen for the exact figure. "One point eighty-eight, and it's going down slightly more each year. Do you want more figures?" His hands moved over the keyboard. "Fifty years ago, there was a paradise, the Ancient Land, Eden, or whatever it's called by a little more than a million of what they call 'primitives.' Now there are five million... Discounting the mortality rate, four million men and women have turned their backs on civilization, and voluntarily returned to the past—to plow the earth, tend flocks, weave their own clothes, and use torches for light. Why?"

He looked over at Alice, but she was staring at the floor. He went on.

"And what about the cybos? Fifty years ago, they didn't exist. Now there are twelve thousand of them. Twelve thousand people who have renounced being human. Twelve thousand people who have had cybernetic systems implanted in their brains, arguing that they needed to know more, to discover more. No, Alice," Stephen said more calmly, "if all these aren't symptoms of decadence, of this absurd society falling apart, then I know nothing about psychosociology."

"Symptoms of decadence, or a crisis of growth?" asked Alice, without raising her eyes from the ground.

Stephen's eyes narrowed.

"What do you mean by 'a crisis of growth?'"

Alice shrugged.

"I mean I don't know yet what the real cause of all these phenomena is. They indicate a change, it's true, but what sort of change?"

Stephen sighed.

"You're getting lost in subtleties, Alice."

Her face crumpled.

"Don't you understand, my love? I want so much to help you, not to fail you..." she said, her voice faltering.

"I know, I know..." he said, trying to soothe her.

Alice took his hand and kissed it. She went on uncertainly.

"You want everything to be turned backward... That's fine. But if we can't be sure what factors have produced this crisis, if we don't know where this society is heading, anything we do could have consequences diametrically opposed to the ones you want. Now do you follow what I'm trying to say?"

Stephen nodded pensively.

"I understand... You want to discover what the essential problem of this society is. Or, as they call it, the fundamental contradiction."

Alice straightened in her seat.

"Exactly. And you shouldn't allow your wishes to lead you astray. You believe that this society is unsustainable, that it contradicts the basic instincts of human beings, because that is what you want to believe."

Stephen slumped in his chair.

"You're right. I want to believe it," he muttered.

Alice's eyes gleamed.

"My love…"

"What?"

"No, nothing. Nothing that's related to all this," she said, shaking her head.

He twisted his mouth in a mixture of annoyance and understanding.

"That comes later. We have to finish our work first. So, what are you proposing?"

"I'm not proposing anything yet," she said. "I need more data."

"What data?" asked Stephen in surprise. "I thought you had enough already."

"Only about the terrestrials who are…let's call them normal. The 'normals.' And they're only a part of humanity now."

"The others are insignificant minorities. All together they only represent a hundredth of the 'norms' as you call them."

"But their influence on the norms can't be discounted. At least not if we want to do a thorough job."

"You're right. What do you need?"

Alice raised her hand and bent the first finger.

"First of all, data about the solar-system groups: their history, composition, tendencies." She bent her middle finger. "Secondly, information about the Auroran Mentagroups," she said, and folded down the remaining two fingers. "And third and fourthly, more data on the cybos and privos."

Stephen nodded his head.

"You can ask for all that," he said, pointing to the screen.

Alice got up slowly from her chair.

5

"Can you trust the work Alice is doing, even though she is conditioned?" asked Sybil. She kept a close eye on the changing expression on Stephen's face as he contemplated his reply.

Sybil waited patiently. This wasn't the moment to rush him. He had to consider his answer carefully; the plan of action had to be drawn up by people who were completely trustworthy. People who didn't make mistakes, or...

Stephen took a deep breath. He looked up at Sybil.

"Yes, we can trust Alice Welland," he said firmly.

XV

An Exhaustive Revision

1

...**NOT TO BRING BACK** the Saturn-I expedition. It was decided to abandon the excessively ambitious plans of the Institute of Cosmic Studies. Its directors were replaced...

...the next year (three before the Era of Humanity) the Sol-III probe was launched, destined for the recently discovered planetary system of Altair. That same year the ICS's budget was cut, particularly the funds for the Cosmic Academy. With the readjustment of the plans for expansion through the solar system to more realistic proportions and goals, the medium- and short-term needs for groups were much less...

...groups were sent to Earth for the first time in the year 1 before the Era of Humanity—1,758 graduates out of 9,690. (The readjusted expansion plans adopted the previous year, which caused a disproportion between the number of graduate groups and those really needed...)

...reconstruction needs following the fall of the Empire. As a result, in the year 1 of the Era of Humanity 5,128 groups out of a total of 9,973 were assigned to Earth, especially to the most devastated areas of the fallen Empire...

...considering how valuable these groups were in such unusual work conditions, given that their internal stability and efficiency was in no way affected by them, it was decided to raise the number of entrants to the Cosmic Academy in order to use them intensively in reconstruction work. Out of those graduating this year (the year 2 of the Era of Humanity) 8,324 groups were assigned to Earth and 1,682 to the different bases in the solar system...

...in the year 3 of the Era of Humanity, no group from among the new graduates was assigned to the solar system. The number of entrants to the Cosmic Academy began to rise again...

...in the middle of the year 9 of the Era of Humanity, the first antigroup literature appeared:

> We have all watched, with undisguised admiration, the videograms of those groups working in truly infernal conditions, living amongst the degenerate products of the Imperial Era and attending to that human detritus, without being able to spot the slightest sign of the repugnance which—let us confess it—you and I as normal men and women would be unable to repress. And they can work for year after year without losing an ounce of their incredible efficiency, in an environment we would not be able to bear for more than a day. "We have to increase the number of these groups as soon as possible!" you will say. That's what I used to tell myself, before I had the misfortune—or the good fortune—to come into close contact with one of those famous groups (and later with several more). Those who have had a similar experience will understand me. Those who haven't, try to get close to a group. To talk to them. To share their leisure moments (if they have any; I haven't been able to prove that yet). Just try it.
>
> Sooner or later, you will feel the same shudder run up and down your spine as I did. And you will ask yourself, "Are they human?"

Don't hesitate. Confront the question. Find the answer.

You and I are, I think, human beings. Fallible. We can make mistakes (and we do so only too frequently). But we recognize our errors; that's how we grow. We have feelings (which can also be mistaken). We search for, and occasionally find, the twin soul we need so much... And this search, this process of making mistakes and trying again, enriches us. We learn what hope means, and doubt, and despair. Happiness, too. That is how we shape ourselves. As human beings. As normal men and women... But what about the groups?

The groups are not like that.

We have to admit that they are the most perfect result of social engineering (if such a science exists). They are created when they are adolescents, almost children, carefully selected from among millions of possible candidates. Computers and specialists measure, weigh, calculate, then say, "These." They get them together, and wait. They have no way out. They are made for each other. And they don't need anyone else. *They can get along fine without you or me. To be more precise:* without humanity. *They only need each other. They are self-sufficient.*

*You and I can change friends, even people we love. They can't. We are not enclosed in a magic circle; we can roam with complete freedom over all Earth. Every day we can meet, or have the possibility of meeting, somebody who is interesting, attractive, as human as we are. Every day a new love can spring up... Not even the despair caused by a disappointment can deprive us of hope, the hope of finding happiness, tomor-*row—because we are human beings.

The groups experience none of that. You don't believe me? Try to infiltrate one, to be one among them... You won't succeed.

Yes, they will be polite, but between you and them there will be an invisible...and impenetrable wall. Remember, the computers said they don't need you, and the computers are not wrong: they don't need you.

This brings us to the secret concealed behind one of the groups' most praised virtues: their ability not to make mistakes in situations that would make you or I freeze with horror or pity. Do you know why they don't make mistakes? Because they don't have any emotions. *They are as cold and efficient as machines. You and I make mistakes because we are human, but the computers have never let them be that. They have never allowed them to search for themselves. They have not permitted them to suffer or to be happy during that search. They have not grown. They have not been allowed to grow. They are just like computers: cold and efficient.*

I feel sorry for them. I can't help it. They are as perfect as machines. We have to be honest and admit it: they are our mistake (yes, ours, it's not only the psychosociologists who are to blame; we should have foreseen the consequences of the ill-fated idea of creating groups in the first place). But now we must correct that mistake.

The creation of groups has to stop!

Possibly you think that I am exaggerating. That, alright, the invasion of groups this ancient Earth is suffering from can and should be put a stop to. We can agree that we don't need them here. But, in order to conquer the cosmos...

It is true. The cosmos demands we pay that price (for now; perhaps in a century or two we will discover a cheap and rapid way to travel through it without the need for groups). The cosmos now *demands that we sacrifice those children. That we prevent them from becoming human beings.*

*That we convert them into groups so that they can drag
themselves around the solar planets (the stars are still far
off) because normal human beings like you or me cannot do
so. We would go mad if we were far from Earth, far from
humanity, because we are* human. *But to reach the distant
stars, we are now being asked that our own children cease
to be human.*

*I don't know whether you are willing to pay that price.
I am not.*

2

When Stephen opened the door, the explosion of noise almost
knocked him over.

The notes rushed one after another, and the colors gallop-
ing across the walls did their best to keep up with them. In their
midst, Alice's body was moving, stretching, contracting, following
the deafening rhythm, seeming to disappear in one spot, only to
reappear in another...

He forced his way in, overcoming the dense wall of music and
light. He went over to the controls of the living room and switched
them off.

Silence.

Alice stopped in mid-step and looked at him in surprise.

"Oh, it's you! I'm sorry, I didn't realize you had come in," she
said, and came bounding over to him.

Stephen glanced disapprovingly at her naked body. She was
glistening with sweat. Thick drops of it fell from her chin, her
breasts, from the tufted pubic triangle, onto the floor.

"What were you doing?" he asked.

Pushing her wet locks back from her eyes, Alice tried without much success to dry her face with her hands.

"Exercises. I try to stay fit."

"I think the biostimulator would be more economical."

"In what sense?" asked Alice, tilting her head to dry her hair better.

"It would take you less time. And you don't sweat," said Stephen, wrinkling his nose.

Alice went over to the corner of the room.

"Shower," she commanded. A wall of light hid her from Stephen.

There was the sound of falling water.

Her muffled voice reached him

"I'm sorry, my love, but I'm afraid I'm old fashioned about some things." She poked her head through the curtain of light. "What did you want to see me about?"

"About this," he said, holding out two thin, semitransparent bands.

"What are they?" she asked.

"Finish your shower and I'll explain."

The sound of water ceased and was replaced by a hum of hot dry air.

Stephen sat down.

A minute later, Alice appeared, fresh and smiling. She walked over to him. When she had a good look at his face, her smile vanished. She kneeled in front of him and put her hands on his thighs.

"I'm sorry, my love. I didn't know you disliked it so much."

Stephen shrugged without looking at her.

"I really do need it," she said, pleading with him. "I'm overloaded with work. That creates nervous tension, and the biostimulator doesn't help."

"Alright, don't mention it anymore. Let's get on with what's important," he said, waving the two bands in the air.

"What are they?"

"Safety devices."

"Against what?"

Stephen dropped the bands into her hands. She examined them curiously.

"Just suppose that due to some unfortunate coincidence we are found out," he explained. "We cannot continue with these bodies; we'll have to change them."

Alice stared blankly at him.

"Look here," he said, tracing with his finger a yellowish line that was almost invisible down the center of the band. "This is the one you have to place around your head." He gave it back to her and pointed at the other one. "And this is the one you have to put around the head of the body you want to transfer to. Don't mix them up, whatever you do."

"I won't," Alice whispered.

"The new body must be unconscious. Have you been trained in self-defense?"

"Yes."

"You have to make sure you're alone with the person in a secure place. The transfer process lasts about five minutes. During that time you'll be unconscious too."

"What if the other body wakes first?"

Stephen waved his hand.

"It won't. The transfer can only go one way. The body that had been yours will be empty. Ah, and you can return to it. If you have put it to sleep, up to a week later. Otherwise, you mustn't take more than five or six hours. Do you understand?"

Alice nodded.

"Good. How is your work going?"

A faint smile appeared on her face.

"Quite well," she told him. "I'm going through the history of the groups."

Stephen looked at the time on the wall.

"I have to go," he said, and patted her on the shoulder. "Let me get up, sweetheart."

They both stood up.

"Carry on with your work," he said, heading for the door.

"Yes," replied Alice.

She watched him leave. She stood there for a long while, staring at the closed door. Her arms hung limply by her sides.

3

...achieving economic autonomy, the solar-system groups take over the running of the Cosmic Academy from the year 11 of the Era of Humanity.

...the increase in number of those entering the Cosmic Academy comes to an end: whereas in the year 13 900,648 candidates entered, in the year 14 there were only 874,798. Unlike the previous drop in numbers, this one is not caused by budget restrictions, but by the refusal to enter by family members and the candidates themselves...

No. Don't think about that; concentrate.

...make known among the groups the forecast by the Shorojov Group in the year 15 of the Era of Humanity...which said that the minimum permissible number of candidates for admission to the Cosmic Academy was six hundred thousand if the population of groups in the solar system was to be kept stable. Taking account of the growing antigroup attitude on Earth, admissions from that source are likely to dry up within ten years. At that point, in the best possible scenario, the annual total would not be more than four hundred thousand. Therefore the groups would not meet the required number to be stable. There will be a gradual reduction in the number of groups formed each year, and the continuation of the groups will lessen, so that they will completely disappear in a time span of no more than...

Don't think! Do what he's asking you. Do it out of the love you feel for him.

...attempt to avoid the extinction of the groups, in the year 16 the Solar Directorate approves the project to be carried out by the Dubinin Group, specialized in genetic engineering... based on the discovery made by the De Vries Group concerning the genetic conditionality of telepathy, the Dubinin Group conceives the idea of a virus that will carry the telepathy genome that can be transmitted to human beings...on the assumption that the existence of telepathic members in the pre-groups would allow them to be better adjusted, so that a success rate of almost a hundred percent could be expected in the transformation of pre-groups into groups, whereas this figure is currently somewhere between thirty and thirty-five percent. This would cut the critical figure put forward by the Shorojov Group by approximately half...

...unexpected rise, given the working conditions, of the birth rate among the groups: in the year 17 this was 0.12 children per female...

...in the year 19, the second phase of the colonization of Venus. The emigration of those groups resident on Earth to the new planet begins... The birth rate of the groups rises to 0.13...

Why does it have to be like this, my love?

...concerning the future plans for the development of Earth, the Supreme Council enters into negotiations with the leadership of the groups (known as the Solar Directorate) in order to slow the rhythm at which the groups are leaving Earth for Venus...agreement reached in the year 21 of the Era of Humanity regulating the migration to Venus: there will be groups on Earth until the year 33...

Ask me to do something else, anything else!

...regard as pessimistic the conclusions of the Shorojov Group; in the year 22 the birth rate of the groups had reached 0.16 and the proportion of pre-groups entering versus groups graduating from the Cosmic Academy had risen above fifty percent thanks to the improvements made in the techniques of group formation. At that time there was a conservative estimate that the critical minimum number of entrants to the Academy was five hundred thousand, and few doubted it would be reduced further still...

...definitive accord between Earth and the groups in the year 23 of the Era of Humanity... In summary, its main points established the complete autonomy of the groups, the closure of the Terrestrial Cosmic Academy in the year 53 (from the year 48 on, there would be no more terrestrial entrants), the maintenance of the flow of scientific and cultural information between Earth's Supreme Council and the groups' Solar Directorate...It also covered other less important matters such as not increasing the number of groups in the lunar bases and the transfer, before the year 53, of the Stellar City from its orbit around Earth to another around Venus...

...the conclusion of the Dubinin Group's work, arrived at in the same year as the definitive agreement between Earth and the groups had been reached, created a difficult situation for the Solar Directorate... evaluating the consequences for the better relations with Earth that the appearance of telepathic groups in the solar system would produce, and the fact that they would no longer be necessary for the survival of the groups, as had been believed at the moment when the project was authorized, the Directorate decided to order the Dubinin Group to cease work immediately on this project, to hand over all the information gathered for archiving, to destroy the viruses already produced, and to leave Europa Base...

I can't go on anymore!

4

Alice slowly undid the straps of the hypnoinductor around her head. She removed it and rubbed her eyes.

Sitting on the bed, she manipulated the room controls, and the side wall turned into a mirror.

She peered at herself in it.

Purple lines under her eyes. Her face was gaunt, the skin stretched over her cheekbones...

It's true, I can't go on, she thought.

She got up from the bed and went over to the door.

Timidly, she approached Stephen's work cubicle. It was empty.

She explored the entire house... Deserted.

He had left again.

"Tell me when Harry returns," she told the door cyber control.

She walked back into the disconnected living room. She sat at the controls...

Sound.

Light.

She took a deep breath, then blew it slowly out.

A little more.

The music grew louder, harsher.

The colors on the walls began to move.

More...

The sound waves vibrated through the air, and the walls were bursts of color.

More...

More.

XVI

Alice's Choice

1

THE GRASS AND SOFT GROUND came to an end, and there were rocks under his feet. With a snort of satisfaction, Ryland came to a halt. He contemplated the nearby cliff edge, the sky growing dark, the loneliness, and sat down carefully on one of the rocks. His hands rubbed his bony, aged legs.

He wanted to return to the hermitage—soon, so that he would no longer be this lonely old man. Lonely in the hermitage? That was a joke. Only Brackenbury had been lonely there. How had that man been able to bear it for so many years? Ryland Kern shook his head; there was no possible explanation, but it didn't matter. What mattered was that no one would think his death odd. His resignation, as they called it now.

Something glinted far off in the sky. Ryland peered more closely. The setting sun was shining off something coming closer. He got up slowly from the rock.

The Hermes approached the rocky ground and hovered few centimeters above it. A blonde head appeared at the entry hatch.

"Lower," Ryland ordered. Those old, stiff legs of his...

The Hermes was almost brushing the rocks.

Ryland raised himself up to the oval hatch opening and entered the ship.

From the pilot's seat, Savell nodded briefly at him.

"Where is he?" asked the head of Imperial Security.

Savell jerked his thumb over his shoulder at the long oblong box. Ryland lifted the lid and looked down at the body that had belonged to Brother Kevin (a young body again, thank heavens!). He touched it, then quickly withdrew his hand.

"He's still cold," he grumbled.

The Hermes pilot left his seat and came over to the open pod.

"That is to guarantee maximum preservation, sir," he explained, turning the green disk on the side of the pod.

Ryland sat on a seat by the wall. The decrepit body he was using did not allow him to wait standing up.

Brother Kevin's face took on color, and they could hear him breathing.

"Ready, sir."

Ryland Kern took the pair of diadems out of his breast pocket. He examined them closely, then handed one to Savell.

"Put it on him," he ordered.

The pilot carefully raised the empty body and slipped the psychoconductor over his hair.

Ryland took a deep breath. It was safe, he told himself. He had already done it once...twice, if he counted the first awakening. But it wasn't easy to overcome the fear of getting lost forever in darkness. He looked down at the diadem he was holding to reassure himself: yes, the yellow line was there.

He tried to make sure he was sitting firmly in his seat. He had to avoid any risk of slipping or falling, of dropping the diadem while...

He closed his eyes and slipped it on his head.

Savell looked at the two unconscious bodies and began to whistle an old song.

Five minutes later, Brother Kevin's eyes opened, and Ryland Kern smiled at him.

"Everything alright, sir?"

Ryland nodded vigorously.

"Now to get rid of that," he said, pointing to the floppy empty body.

Savell went back to the pilot's seat. Ryland leapt nimbly from the pod and sat next to Brackenbury's body.

"Shall I take off?"

"Yes."

The Hermes rose smoothly, and flew to the nearby precipice.

"Help me," said Ryland.

Savell got up and took Brackenbury's other arm. Between the two of them they dragged him to the hatch.

"Now!"

The body fell, twisting around and around, down into the darkening valley. Ryland watched it fall.

It landed, bouncing off the rocks. All that was left far below was a tiny, feeble dummy, scarcely visible.

"Head for home, Savell."

Ryland sat next to the pilot. A job well done... When Sybil found out... He smiled. No one would have thought it, he told himself, feeling through the tunic material the badge where the names were engraved.

2

...to find out whether the telepathic contamination in Europa Base was accidental or deliberate.

The mere idea that someone deliberately disobeyed an order from the Solar Directorate is inconceivable to any of today's groups, and it was the same back then. In order to understand how this happened—or did not happen—it is necessary to transfer one's mind to that era and look at the specific situation of Europa Base and its inhabitants.

Europa Base was chosen for several reasons. Firstly, it was big enough to provide the Dubinin Group with necessary material conditions to do their work. At the same time, it was small enough so that, if any dangerous genetic material escaped, it would only affect a small number of people.

While it is true that other bases, such as the Ceres, Astra, or Tsiokolski, were similar in this respect, after studying the psychological profiles of the groups living at those bases, the Solar Directorate decided that the members of Europa Base were the ones most likely to accept running a risk of affecting not only themselves but also their descendants. (Remember that at this time the Solar Directorate was convinced that the groups ran a real risk of becoming extinct and that creating telepathic groups was almost the only hope of avoiding this.)

When the Dubinin Group reached this moon of Jupiter, in the year 16 of the Era of Humanity, Europa Base comprised nineteen groups (a total of 127 adults).

The Dubinin Group called everyone together and informed them of their project, of the hope it signified for the survival of the groups, and of the danger they would face if they agreed to the experiments being carried out there.

After that, the Dubinin Group returned to the ship in which they had come. They waited inside until all the preparations for their return were complete. By the third day, everything was ready, and so they met again with the inhabitants of the base to learn their decision.

There were 127 votes in favor.

From that moment on, Europa Base was isolated from the solar system. During seven earth years, no new groups arrived.

The adolescents approaching the age of fifteen were put into strict quarantine before they left for the Cosmic Academy on Mars...

The members of the local groups—astronomers, radio-physicists, planetologists—went on with their usual work, observing and studying the gigantic red planet in Europa's sky. However, it is not hard to imagine (it can only be imagined, as none of them is still alive, and they never spoke to anyone about those seven years) that Jupiter was no longer the center of their attention, that they were dependent on the success or failure of the Dubinin Group's experiments, that they dreamed of the future society of telepathic groups and the salvation of groups as a whole (remember when this was)...until one day they received the order to suspend all work and to destroy the telepathic viruses already obtained.

We can understand that the Solar Council's decision was the only correct one, since we know what happened afterward. But the members of Europa Base did not have the proper perspective: they could not foresee the consequences. We shall never know if the leak of telepathic viruses that affected them all was accidental or deliberate; all those who were there when it happened are already dead.

Fortunately, the Dubinin Group had strictly followed the pre-established rules concerning the viruses; these were unable to live outside human bodies any longer than a month. In addition, those that penetrated the inhabitants of Europa Base could not be transmitted to anyone else apart from their own descendants. The spacecraft that arrived to pick up the Dubinin Group and the youngsters who were to enter the Cosmic Academy that year did not further disperse the telepathic contamination. It arrived three months after the destruction (and partial leak) of the viruses.

The contamination could not be discovered in time. The 106 adolescents under the age of fifteen, as well as the fourteen adults still in the latter stages of their reproductive period (which in those days was between the ages of twenty and twenty-nine) were all carriers of the telepathic genome, but its effect could not yet be detected. The new genes were still at their embryonic stage. It was only in their children, when they had finished growing, that the action of the viruses was detectable. This is why it took so long to identify it and what made the decision that followed an inevitable one...

The first two telepaths were born in the year 24 of the Era of Humanity. The following year, a third one... After that, there was a long gap; the adults in Europa Base had come to the end of their normal reproductive period, and there was a wait until the next generation completed the Cosmic Academy.

The fourth telepath was not born until the year 30. After that, their number grew rapidly; by the time that the two first telepaths entered the Cosmic Academy in the year 38, eighty-six of them had been born.

We need now to introduce a parenthesis.

In the year 43 (by which time there were 267 telepaths), a report was received from the stellar probe Sol-III. This spoke of Aurora, an uninhabited planet suitable for colonization in orbit around Altair. The debates began.

Since the first stellar probes had been launched, great strides had been made in our knowledge of the laws governing society. It was known that in order to guarantee that their descendants would be able to find an adequate group, each society had to contain at least three million individuals of reproductive age. How could those three million be transported ten light years away, with all the support they needed?

The solar system's resources would be exhausted just by sending a tenth part of that number. What would become of the millions left behind?

The Solar Directorate studied the possibility of suggesting to Earth that Aurora be colonized, but it very soon became evident that this was impossible as well. It was true that the Earth dwellers did not have to guarantee adequately sized groups to their descendants; only a little more than a thousand colonizers would offer the necessary genetic viability. However, it was social limitations that came to the fore with them. To create a stable, autonomous society capable of advancing as one in the knowledge of the universe, the low efficiency of those not integrated into groups demands a large population: no fewer than five million Earth dwellers would be necessary. It made no sense to send a few thousand of them to regress socially or to become intellectual parasites of Earth and the solar system, with an inevitable time lag of twenty years.

There was no alternative.

The Solar Directorate archived the construction of interstellar spacecraft capable of colonizing Aurora.

In the following year (the year 44 of the Era of Humanity) one of the two first telepaths, who was in the last year of the academy, showed signs of telepathic rapports with the other members of his group.

This did not attract much attention; although rare, phenomena of this kind were no great surprise then or now. They are usually transitory.

In the year 45, the groups with the first two telepaths graduated. The power of the developing telepathy was already creating interest, especially as the telepaths were occasionally establishing mental contact with individuals belonging to other groups.

The group of the third telepath (in that case, a female telepath) graduated in the year 46. She and the older one who had not yet entered into action established mental contact with other members of their groups and soon reached the level of the first one.

Studying these unusual telepaths, the psychosociologists discovered to their surprise that all three of them came from Europa Base and were the only ones born there in the years 24 and 25. The Solar Directorate came to know of this strange coincidence and had no doubt as to the cause: viruses had leaked during the Dubinin Group's experiments.

Investigations were immediately carried out to determine the extent of this telepathic contamination.

By the year 47 it was established that the contamination was limited to the inhabitants of the base in the year 23, and 184 non-telepathic carriers who were still alive had been identified (32 still in the reproductive phase) as well as the 390 telepaths already born. This news spread rapidly through the solar system and produced two kinds of reaction: there were those who approved of telepathic groups' existence (a minority, based fundamentally in the asteroid belt and the satellites of the most distant planets) and those who rejected them (the majority: almost all of Venus and most of the inhabitants of Mars).

The psychosociologists characterized this negative attitude toward these "mentagroups" as a reaction against the mental contacts the first three telepaths occasionally established with members of other groups. This violation—however involuntary—of the internal privacy of each group was bound to produce an unfavorable reaction.

The defenders of the mentagroups argued that the rapports outside the groups had been produced because of a lack of adequate training for the three original telepaths but that if these latter helped, then the new telepaths would be able to control their mental contacts and limit them to the members of their own groups. Their adversaries questioned whether a greater training of the telepathic faculty would lead to a lessening of mental contacts outside these groups or, on the contrary, to them intensifying beyond all control.

The tensions created by the mentagroups were too serious for the Solar Directorate to accept them without a qualm, but they had few options, and the first three mentagroups were assigned to the Cosmic Academy on Mars to train pre-groups with embryonic telepaths.

The definitive solution was proposed by the Arakata Group, which specialized in psychosociology and included the third telepath. They put forward the hypothesis that the formation of groups including one or two telepaths would permit the creation of psychological profiles that would very probably be incompatible otherwise. This would lessen the compatibility demands for forming a stable group. According to their calculations, with the telepathic element introduced, the minimum size of a society group needed to provide their descendants with an adequate group would fall from three million adults in the reproductive phase to only three thousand.

The Arakata Group proposed that on this basis the mentagroups should be sent to inhabit Aurora.

Several groups specializing in psychosociology disagreed with the Arakata Group's hypothesis. Some doubted whether the effect produced by the participation of a telepath in the formation of a group would allow the creation of psychological profiles with a compatibility level of 0.71 instead of the usual 0.99. Others did not believe that this compatibility effect would reduce, by no less than a factor of a thousand, the size of the population needed for every individual to find adequate groups.

However, the solution proposed by the Arakata Group solved too many problems at once and so could not be rejected out of hand. Following prolonged analysis, the Solar Directorate met with the preexisting mentagroups and those in the process of being formed, and posed to them a fundamental question: Were they ready to accept the Arakata proposal on their own behalf, and on behalf of the other still-embryonic telepaths?

The response was affirmative.

In order for them to enjoy their entire reproductive phase on the new planet, each of the new mentagroups was placed in suspended animation as soon as their training was complete. They would only be brought out of this state on Aurora.

The first spaceship left in the year 53 of the Era of Humanity. It was carrying five groups, made up of thirty-eight individuals (six telepaths among them) together with the resources needed for a detailed exploration of the planet and the construction of the basic installations needed to receive the subsequent expeditions. Four hundred and thirty seven telepaths were left behind on Mars in a latent state.

In the year 58 the second craft left, with 446 members in a state of suspended animation, distributed in sixty-one groups (seventy telepaths among them). The third took off in the year 63, with 179 telepaths in 157 groups, and a total of 1,138 crew members.

The fourth spaceship left with the remaining 189 telepaths (168 groups), and 1,196 hibernating crew, in the year 68.

The first ship reached Aurora in the year 69 of the Era...

Alice snatched the hypnoinductor from her face. She lay without moving on the force field, staring up at the blue ceiling.

3

Why did this have to happen to me, of all people?

Hiding her face in her hands, she turned over. She floated face down in the middle of the room.

How can I understand this world if it isn't mine? If I don't recognize what I dreamed?

Behind her hands, her teeth bit into her lips.

What is my world then?

She turned back again on the invisible lines of the force field.

The world Stephen is in. The world he wants, because I love him.

Her mouth quivered.

But can that world be mine now? I rejected it once, because I hate a world in which everybody thinks of themselves, and only themselves, because then I had hopes... Or was I simply deceiving myself? I hated that world because that crazy drug addict blinded me and destroyed me, and not because of the internal wretchedness, the emptiness inside those around me that they did not realize but still sensed, that forced them to brutalize themselves with drugs, alcohol, sex, to pursue unattainable mirages so as not to remain alone with themselves, so that they wouldn't have to look within and find nothing, nothing at all?

She opened her eyes.

And Stephen?

She clenched her fists.

Was he empty too? But what does that matter if I love him? Yes, love means you can do everything, everything, even renounce your most cherished dreams... What else can I do? she asked herself, and struggled with the answer.

Don't be naive, Alice. You left childhood behind long ago. You won't do anything with words. You'll only make him reject you, with horror and scorn, make him stop loving you. You wouldn't be able to bear that.

Her muscles grew taut.

Does he love you? Does he? Does he really?

She breathed in deeply, then breathed slowly out until her lungs were empty.

Of course he loves me; he told me so. He told me so that time, and I could feel he was telling the truth. I can't have fooled myself to that extent.

She chewed her knuckles.

But he hasn't said it again!

A reddish trickle appeared on her lips and slid slowly, lazily down her face.

That's just how he is, Alice. Dry. Inexpressive. And although you try to control yourself, you stifle him with your love. Perhaps if he felt less secure...

She pulled her bitten hands away from her face.

That's not the question to be asking. Even if he doesn't love me, I love him, and I have to do everything I can for him. That's the question I need to ask: Am I doing the right thing for him by doing what he is asking me to do? Am I doing the right thing in preparing the resurrection of his world? The destruction of this world, which, although it isn't mine (and no, it isn't), is a thousand times better than the previous one?

As calmly as she could, she weighed up her answer.

No, I'm not doing the right thing, she told herself, and got to her feet.

XVII

The Spy Is Discovered

1

THE BELL BUZZED, and Sybil automatically switched on the intercom.

"Yes?" she asked absentmindedly, not taking her eyes off the central control panel.

"Ryland has arrived. We'll wait for you in the chapel," said her brother's voice.

Sybil pressed a button, and the figures disappeared from the screen.

"I'll be right there," she said, and stood up.

She would be in the meeting when Stephen arrived. A shame, she thought to herself. She would have liked to explain her doubts to him while they were still fresh in her mind. Sometimes she thought that the techniques of deep conditioning were too complex and subtle for her... But she would master them. She had to master them, as well or better than Stephen Houdry, if she were to perfect them, make them even more sensitive and indirect so that they could be used without risk in the mental recalibration of four billion human beings.

She quickened her step. Patrick could become impatient. No doubt Ryland had discovered some communist spy among the specialists they had brought with them. Otherwise, he would have just told Patrick. He must have insisted on her being there, the...

She came to a halt for a moment outside the chapel door to gather her thoughts. Who could the spy be?

She went in.

"Hello there, Ryland," she said shortly.

He responded with a nod of the head.

Sybil sat next to her brother.

"Well then?" she asked.

It was Patrick who replied.

"Ryland has discovered four Federation spies, my love."

Sybil raised her eyebrows. Four of them?

Her brother turned to the head of Imperial Security.

"We're all here now. Tell us their names."

Ryland took the list out of his pocket with deliberate slowness.

Pure theater. I bet he knows the names off by heart, Sybil told herself irritably.

"A whole nest of them, Mister President," said Ryland Kern. "But after all, I'm not surprised. I never did trust generalists."

Sybil turned pale.

"Are you feeling alright?"

Although his attention was apparently focused on Dahlgren, Kern's sharp eye had spotted the change in her expression.

Sybil shook her head. She couldn't be sure of her voice.

Ryland put the list down on the table in front of him.

"Here are the names," he said, then read, "Vincent Abbey, Cecil Lang, Edward Norris, and Alice Welland." He looked up at Sybil, smiling.

The smile vanished.

"What's wrong?" he asked.

Sybil managed to control herself. She turned to her brother.

"Patrick, I need to talk to you. Alone."

2

Alice smiled a bitter smile. For the first time, she was glad that Stephen wasn't in the house.

She examined her hands. The healing cream had dried. The purple teeth marks were still visible around her knuckles.

What would her first step be? Who could she talk to?

To a certain extent, it was a problem that this society was so advanced. If only there had still been intelligence services! She would have to manage. Who dealt with all the problems? Who kept this world functioning?

The ICS: the Integrated Cybernetic System.

That was no use. She could tell it all she knew, and it would thank her and archive everything. And the information would be available to anyone requesting it. And the only people who might request it were those who realized there was a problem. No, it was no use turning to the ICS. Who then?

At the back of her mind was the information she had received during the days of her intensive training... At least it could now be useful.

The Institute of Psychosociological Studies?

That seemed like a good idea. It was structured to cover the entire earth and was responsible for training children and adolescents. It also dealt with anticipating and correcting abnormal attitudes and behavior. Yes, that might be the best solution. At least, she couldn't think of any other.

Who could she turn to inside the institute?

She smiled. She could not start at the lower level, as she was meant to; the person responsible for Control Point IV-18-085-03 was Harry Mergenthaler...or, more precisely, Stephen Houdry.

Stephen... I'm sure they'll be able to cure you, my love.

What about the level immediately above him?

No. Stephen had been too discreet. She knew he was the leader of the Hydra, that he had several subordinates. But she didn't know them. She didn't even know how many of them there were. It was not impossible that there was one at the base for whom he worked directly, whose job it was to make sure nobody discovered his true work. If she accidentally went to him, she was done for. She had to forget about Control Point IV-18-085-03.

Another level higher?

Regional Bureau IV-18?

She would be running the risk that they would not attend to her. That they referred her back to the base, or still worse, to the control point. But this risk would only be greater the higher up she went. She couldn't even contemplate going to the Zone IV Bureau.

So the regional bureau was her only alternative. Any higher, and they were almost certain not to listen to her. Lower down, she ran the risk of being discovered by one of the resurrected.

Yes, the regional bureau. Who could she see there?

She went through its organigram in her mind. At the top, the director, and the corresponding council. They dealt with general problems in the region, not individual cases. Not them. Beneath them were three departments. The Information Department. Its functions: to systematize, organize, and control all the psycho-sociological information in the region. To ensure that there was a flow of information from below to above, and above to below. They would not consider an individual case either. The Fieldwork Department. That had an essentially executive function: it followed the directions suggested by the higher levels and simply was unable to attend to an individual case. That left the Department of Special Cases.

No doubt about it, *she* was a special case.

Of course, it would be slightly irregular to appear there without having passed through the previous stages. But she was hoping they would attend to her. If they didn't, she would kick and scream and break everything, and faced with such a special case...

That was it then: the Department of Special Cases.

She looked at the time on the wall. She sighed. She had taken almost a minute to reach this point. It was obvious that her tiredness was catching up with her. She must concentrate.

How could she get to the department?

She had no idea where the regional bureau was located. As usual, Stephen had taken the Hermes with him, and anyway, she did not know how to pilot it. Besides, she had never left the house. All her information about the outside world had come via Stephen, and...

A smile flashed across her face, then vanished. She was annoyed at herself; she wasn't tired, she was silly. The solution was right in front of her: the consultor.

3

Patrick Maynard Dahlgren tried hard to control himself. Despite this, when he spoke his voice throbbed with anger.

"How stupid can you be! Ryland is conditioned as well!"

The woman sitting opposite him bowed her head even further.

He paced up and down the room before speaking to Sybil again, this time in a more even tone.

"Do you think if that wasn't so, he would put so much trust in...?" He paused, biting his tongue. He must at all costs avoid

Sybil suspecting that she, too... "Enough of that. We need to think how to sort the problem out."

Sybil raised her head at once.

"We have to eliminate Alice Welland," she said.

"Agreed. Call... No, wait!"

She halted, halfway to the door.

"We shouldn't be in such a hurry. First we have to bring her here and check whether... No, better not bring her. Let Houdry himself take care of going through every millimeter of her brain, until he is sure she hasn't yet betrayed us."

Sybil's eyebrows arched.

"I think we can rely on the conditioning that Stephen gave her. I've heard she worships the ground he walks on."

"That may be so, but call Houdry, and quickly."

She sat at the intercom. Several seconds went by.

The screen lit up, and it was Alice Welland who was staring out at her.

"What can I do for you?"

Sybil managed to smile.

"Is Harry there?" she asked.

"No. Would you like to leave a message?"

"No. Just tell him Shirley called."

Alice nodded.

"I will. Nothing else?"

"No, nothing else. Bye," said Sybil, and flicked off the intercom.

Patrick Maynard Dahlgren breathed out heavily.

"Where the devil has Houdry got to?" he asked, unable to contain his anger.

Sybil looked at her screen, then straightened in her seat.

"How silly of me! I'd forgotten he was on his way here."

Dahlgren came over to her.

"What time is he supposed to arrive?"

"At nine. That's in fifteen minutes; he must be halfway here by now."

"Sybil..."

"What is it?"

"I didn't like that girl's face."

"She looked normal to me," said Sybil, puffing up her lips. "After all, none of us had seen her before with the body she has now."

Dahlgren shook his head.

"No, sister. Call it what you like—instinct, a hunch—but that woman is hiding something. She's up to no good... How long does it take Houdry to get here from his house?"

"About thirty minutes. Twenty-five, if he hurries."

Dahlgren's face darkened.

"Fifteen minutes until he gets here. Another five to explain, then twenty-five to get back. We have to reach him before he gets here."

"Patrick, the situation's been like this for days. A few more minutes..."

"Can you communicate with him? Right now?"

She shrugged resignedly.

"Not from here. This intercom must be controlled by the ICS, and I doubt whether..."

"Where from, then?"

"From my lab. Using the directional radio."

He took her by the arm and pulled her up from her seat.

Sybil looked at him in surprise. In their new bodies she was taller and heavier than he was.

"What are you waiting for? Run!" said Dahlgren.

Sybil ran. Dahlgren strode along behind her.

He met Ryland in the corridor.

"What's wrong? Sybil..."

"I know, I know. I'll explain later," said Dahlgren. He didn't stop, but instead increased his pace.

He should have foreseen it. He should have foreseen it. He should have foreseen it, he said to himself with each stride. A logical consequence. Too much brotherly love. Nobody was safe enough. Nothing was good enough. For his sister. His little sister... Silly, she was so silly. And him? Silly, too...

He entered the cell transformed into a laboratory.

Sybil was leaning over the central control panel, her hands busy with the buttons. The screen was void.

"Nothing yet?"

Sybil glanced apologetically over her shoulder.

"It needs readjusting. It's set up for closer."

Dahlgren cursed.

Stephen's blurred face appeared on the screen. Sybil straightened up with a look of triumph.

"Ready, Patrick."

Dahlgren pushed her aside and bent toward the screen.

"Can you hear me, Houdry?"

"Yes, sir."

His voice was distorted, almost unrecognizable.

Dahlgren looked angrily at his sister.

"Tune it in better."

She bent over the controls once more. The image became slightly clearer.

"That's the best I can do. It's at the limit of its reach."

"Okay, it's alright like that," said Dahlgren impatiently. He spoke again to Houdry.

"Can you hear me better now?"

"Yes, sir."

His voice came through more clearly.

"Good. Turn around. Go back home as quickly as you can. Arrest Alice Welland. If she resists, don't hesitate to eliminate her. Understood?"

The face on the screen stared back in astonishment.

"She's a communist spy, Stephen!" Sybil explained over her brother's shoulder.

Stephen Houdry's image bent closer to the invisible controls in the Hermes.

"Houdry!"

He looked up.

"Yes, sir?"

"If you have to eliminate her, don't use the laser. The neurotor would be better; it would look like a heart attack. Do you follow?"

"Yes, sir."

"Switch it off, Sybil."

She did as he asked. Ryland came into the lab.

"Sorry if I'm interrupting, but..."

"Who brought you?"

Ryland blinked.

"Where?"

"Here! To the hermitage!"

"Savell, but..."

"Has he already left?"

"No, he's..."

"Go with him. To Houdry's home. He is going to arrest a woman, or, if necessary, eliminate her. Try to get there in time to help him; he hasn't got much experience. Understood?"

"Understood," replied Ryland, and ran to the door, the skirts of his monk's habit billowing behind him.

Patrick Maynard Dahlgren flopped into the nearest seat.

"Sabrina, Sabrina..." he said in a weary tone.

When she heard her old name, Sybil felt a stab to her heart. She fell to the floor beside him and clasped him around his thin waist.

"Will you forgive me, my love? I did it with the best intentions, I could never have imagined that..."

"I know, I know."

Sybil raised her moist eyes to his face. She tried to sound encouraging.

"But you needn't worry, brother. You've done all that you had to; everything will be sorted out, you'll see..."

Dahlgren's hand ran absentmindedly through her golden locks.

"I hope so, Sybil. But please, don't ever do anything like that again without telling me first," he said. Freeing himself from her embrace, he stood up. "I'm going to my cell. I feel tired; I want to rest a while."

Sybil followed with her eyes as her brother's hunched figure made for the door.

Damned traitor... She would take care of her personally. Patrick wouldn't be able to deny her that pleasure.

She adjusted the hood around her head with trembling hands and stood up.

She would teach her. That Alice Welland would moan, repent a thousand times, howl, beg for forgiveness, Sybil told herself, and spat.

XVIII

A Double Pursuit

1

BEFORE THE HERMES had even completed its descent, Stephen leapt out of the hatch and began to run to the house.

A second before he collided with it, the door swung open, and Stephen entered.

Calm. He had to stay calm. He had to take her alive. She mustn't suspect that...

Slowly and painfully he forced his lips into his habitual smile. His eyes. He blinked several times until they had recovered his usual look. Now for his breathing... He tried to control it, to master it. A desperate panting came from his lungs.

No. He mustn't be afraid. *He mustn't be afraid.*

He looked all around him. Where could she be?

In her room?

He took measured paces to the door and opened it gently.

She wasn't there.

Where could she be?

The living room.

He made for it. His footsteps and his heartbeat quickened without him realizing it.

He pushed open the door.

The room was silent. Empty.

Where?

He searched the whole house, opening and closing doors, holding his breath each time and becoming more annoyed, more rushed, more worried as he did so.

He was soon back at the entrance. Alice Welland was not in the house.

He opened his mouth, trying to take in more air, while his mind was trying to deny the inevitable conclusion: Alice had betrayed them. Already.

A flood of fragmentary, disconnected thoughts mixed with a sense of guilt, fear, and anger threatened to destabilize his mind.

He ought to	No,	But who could have known?
have	it was	Who?
guessed.	all	Only Ryland.
Who would pay?	Sybil's responsibility.	
Who would pay?	Not him...	

A sob escaped his lips.

He calmed down. How could it have happened? Alice did not know, had no idea where to go, she had never been out, she would never dare, she couldn't...

The consultor.

She could have asked it. It would have told her all she needed. Yes, that was how...

What could he do now?

Nothing.

No, he shouldn't be defeatist; Alice had not had much time. Half an hour, at most. He had left her quiet in her room when he left. Checking where to go...

Where could she have gone?

Must have taken her some time. Perhaps she had just fled when he was about to arr...

The hopper. A clear image flashed into his mind.

As he was approaching the house in the Hermes, he had seen a hopper heading toward the horizon.

At that moment he had not thought it important. If he had known it was his hopper with Alice fleeing in it, he would have pursued it. The Hermes was faster, and...

What point was there in dreaming about what he might have done?

The hopper must be far away by now, and he had no idea where Alice was heading.

He was momentarily discouraged.

But then, almost at once, hope stirred inside him.

He could find the direction she had taken from the same consultor, and the Hermes's greater speed could still be decisive.

What was he doing, standing there in the entrance?

He ran to the consultor.

"Where did Aisha go?"

The apparatus took almost two seconds to reply.

"Insufficient data."

Stephen took a deep breath. Of course, she was not going to say exactly where it was she was going. But from her questions...

"Reproduce your last conversation with Aisha," he ordered.

Thank heavens he had been so cautious. For a long while, it had seemed to him a waste of time to have instructed the consultor at the start to register all its conversations with Alice, but something (most likely instinct) had stopped him from canceling it.

Alice's voice rang through the room.

"Consultor, how can I get to Regional Bureau IV-18?"

Damn, she was very astute. If she had gone to the base, Maureen would have...

"You can call a transporter and order it to take you there."

"How do I call a transporter?"

"Ask for one at Section Two of the Central Archive."

"I cannot."

"Why?"

"I am not connected."

"My precautions weren't completely wasted," Stephen muttered to himself. "If she had gotten hold of another Hermes..."

"Could I go on foot?"

"That is not recommended. If you want to reach the regional bureau, it is one hundred and eight kilometers away."

A pause.

"Consultor, is there nothing in the house that can be used as a more rapid means of transport than walking? One that will allow me to reach the regional bureau quickly?"

"Yes, there is a hopper."

Curse Harry Mergenthaler and his love of that antiquated sport.

"How can I get one?"

"Ask at the door."

"Consultor, do I need training to pilot the hopper?"

"No. You will only need to tell it to take you to the regional bureau."

"Thank you, consultor. Ah, by the way, I've decided not to go to the bureau. I'll simply go out in the hopper for a while. End of consultation."

Stephen bit his lips. She really was astute. She had foreseen that he would ask the consultor and made that last comment to put him off the scent. Well, we'll see who's cleverer, he said to himself, walking toward the exit to the house. He hesitated for a moment. Should he tell the hermitage what had happened?

A shudder ran down his spine. No, no, that would be wasting time, and every second was precious. He had to stop Alice before she reached the bureau.

He walked on. Besides, he couldn't speak clearly through the intercom; there were the security measures... And anyway, they couldn't do anything. None of his subordinates were closer to the regional bureau than him. If he hurried...

He ran outside.

The Hermes was waiting by the door, shining and serene. He clambered into the cabin and started to push the controls rapidly.

The craft took off at full speed.

Pushed back in his seat, his eyes on the horizon, he traced the invisible line that would lead him to the regional bureau. This meant he did not see the other Hermes approaching the house and landing outside.

2

Savell and Ryland left the craft and walked over to the house.

"We wish to see Harry Mergenthaler," Ryland told the door.

"I'm sorry, he has gone out," the cyber control informed him, and added, "Would you like to leave him a message?"

Ryland stared at the door through narrowed eyes.

"How long ago did he leave?"

"Three minutes ago."

"Was he alone?"

"Yes."

Ryland Kern's fingers disappeared under his beard. What could that mean?

Possibly Houdry had already eliminated her and left for the hermitage to seek help, not knowing it was on its way. Anything could happen with these newcomers. But they would have to verify that...

"We would like to come in and wait for him, door," he said.

"I am sorry, but that is not possible," came the response, in a sorrowful tone. "Harry does not want anyone to come in when he is not here."

Should he leave things as they were?

Ryland recalled Dahlgren's expression when he gave him this task. No, first he had to exhaust every possibility. He turned to Savell and whispered in his ear.

"Do you know the name of the woman who lives with Stephen?"

Savell shook his head.

Ryland spoke to the door again.

"Can we see Mergenthaler's wife?"

"If you mean Aisha Dewar, she has also gone out."

Ryland's eyes widened in surprise.

"When?"

"Seventeen minutes ago."

"Follow me," Kern ordered Savell, striding back toward the Hermes.

They entered the cabin, and Ryland connected the intercom.

"I need to talk to Harry Mergenthaler. He's not at home. He must be flying a Hermes. It's urgent," he said, and waited, shifting uneasily in his seat. If the woman they had to catch—or eliminate—was Aisha Dewar, then things weren't good at all.

The screen lit up, and Stephen Houdry's face appeared.

"Where are you going?" asked Ryland shortly.

Stephen's eyes settled on his for a moment, then quickly looked away.

"To the institute's regional bureau," he muttered, and paused to swallow hard. "I need help, but you're too far away."

Ryland did not like the look on Houdry's face. It had been a mistake to appoint inexpert civilians to take charge of the Hydras, he said to himself angrily.

"We're not far away. We're outside your house." He spoke slowly, emphasizing each word; in the state Houdry was in, it would be hard for him to understand even the simplest thing. "We'll see you at that bureau. Wait for us."

He switched off the intercom.

"Savell, head for the institute's regional bureau," he ordered him grumpily, then settled back in his seat.

3

The blurred patches slowed down, rising up from the ground for a brief moment, and once more became recognizable trees, rocks, and bushes. Then everything started to slide rapidly down and backward once more. Alice sank into her plush seat, feeling her stomach churn yet again. At least it was empty now. Completely empty, she told herself, gazing with disgust at the cabin floor. The hopper had been right, they were traveling too fast. But she couldn't lose a single minute; Stephen might return to the house at any moment, discover she wasn't there, guess what had happened, and who knew what else…

Her head began to spin, leaving her nauseated and incapable of thinking.

A hop… A flight through the air… A landing… Another hop…

She closed her eyes, but it was a vain gesture. Her stomach didn't need to see to feel the sudden leaps and bounds the craft made.

Perhaps she ought to diminish speed a little. Yes, that wouldn't be a bad idea. If she arrived feeling like this, she wouldn't be able to do a thing.

She stretched her hand out to the lever almost hidden in the floor. But then withdrew it, sighing. She would do her best to put up with the nausea; they must be almost there. It was impossible for a hundred kilometers to last forever, she told herself. Then she passed out.

Dim, insistent words penetrated the thick mists of her mind, repeated over and over and gradually acquiring more meaning.

"...arrived. Are you feeling ill? Do you need help? We have arrived. Do you feel ill? Do you need help? We..."

Alice shook her head, trying to clear it. The intense pain forced her to raise her hands to her temples and press hard, to prevent her head splitting open. She said, in a hoarse, scarcely intelligible voice.

"Thank you... I feel fine."

The hopper fell silent.

She fumbled with the safety belt, then rubbed her aching stomach. She felt as if she had almost been wrenched in two. She stretched out her legs gingerly... Yes, they still obeyed her.

Grasping the armrests, she tried to stand up, but a sudden sense of weakness forced her back into the seat.

The hopper spoke to her once more.

"I calculate I should inform the Emergency Service."

"No! Wait!" shouted the girl.

She couldn't lose any more time.

Clenching her teeth, she tried to stand up once more. Successfully this time.

"Let me out," she ordered.

The hatch opened.

Would she be able to climb out?

She had to.

She approached the steps uncertainly and clung to the metal handrails.

One step... That's right. Now the next. Good. Now another one... Had there been this many when she climbed in?

The last one.

Letting go of the handrails, she collapsed onto the soft, thick lawn.

Sleep... She needed to sleep...

"I have contacted the Emergency Service. You shouldn't move from where you are. Wait for..."

Alice Welland cursed loudly. She didn't care that it was in an already-dead language; it made her feel better. She struggled to her knees.

The hopper stood beside her like an irresolute guard, motionless on its single leg.

Alice finally stood up straight. She rubbed her face and eyes, trying to get a proper view of the building in front of her: air, light, and transparent walls rising in gentle curves up to the sky; inside, irregular patches of calm colors creating an enigmatic design.

Don't stand there gawping; there's no time to lose.

She stumbled across to the entrance.

The door did not open.

"What do you require?" it asked courteously.

Alice's voice was slurred.

"To see someone..." she replied. "Someone from the Special Cases Department."

"Do you have an appointment?"

She did not reply at once. She had turned around to lean her back against the transparent door and was gazing at the hopper.

It still stood on its metal leg, with the upper dome still open.

Beyond the hopper, another machine was approaching rapidly, balancing on its three flexible feet and somehow keeping the long, thin cylinder slung between them stable. The Emergency Vehicle, she guessed.

She turned and pushed her face closer to the door.

"No, I don't have an appointment," she whispered. To her own amazement, her voice rose to a passionate cry. "I don't have any damned appointment, but I have to see someone from the Special Cases Department. Isn't that clear?"

The door didn't answer.

Alice brushed the tears from her face.

Behind her, the hopper and the Emergency Service vehicle seemed to be locked in a kind of silent electronic conversation.

A little further off, a Hermes landed. A man's head appeared at the window.

"It's urgent, can't you see? Or are you incapable of telling when something is urgent?" shouted Alice.

The man climbed out of the Hermes and began to hurry over to the bureau entrance.

The two machines appeared to take a decision. The hopper moved away in great leaps. On the way it stepped in front of the hurrying man, forcing him to halt for a moment. The Emergency Service vehicle came toward Alice.

The door ended its silence.

"Enter," it said, and opened slowly, so she wouldn't fall.

Alice staggered, then recovered her balance. She was inside the regional bureau.

The door closed behind her.

"Follow the blue arrow," it added in a neutral voice.

She looked about her and saw it flickering on the wall opposite her.

As if it had been waiting for her to find it, the arrow started moving off slowly.

"Follow it," insisted the door.

Alice did so, setting off down light-filled corridors.

B

This is the second part of the test. It is strictly your own work; you must complete it on your own, without discussing your answers with anyone. If you do not wish to complete it, continue to the next page.

I. Read the following passage:

> *...you should not ask, because there is no answer. Don't look for the meaning of things. You will never find the truth that you betrayed...*
>
> —AUGUSTO ROA BASTOS,
> *I, THE SUPREME*

1. Could the meaning of these words be applied to Alice Welland? Stephen Houdry? Sybil Golden? To you? (If you find it difficult to answer this point, go on to the next one.)
2. In your classroom, a classmate copies the answers to an exam. You tell the teacher. Who is the traitor? You, the person doing the copying, or the teacher who gave him good marks the previous year?

GO TO THE NEXT PAGE

II. True or false:

1. Solitude does not exist.
2. Fear does not exist.
3. Honesty does not exist.
4. Love does not exist.
5. You do not exist.

This test will continue later. You may change your answers whenever you wish.

TURN TO THE NEXT PAGE

XIX

Inside the Regional Bureau

1

CLYDE GREENAWAY'S long, slender fingers uncertainly touched the gilt disks on the table.

There were four of them.

Four.

Four psychological profiles, belonging to four human beings he would need to see that day in order to convince them life was worth living. That there was something that they and only they could do, that they could find pride and satisfaction in what they had already done.

Four.

He pushed the four disks away from him. One fell off and landed on the floor with a crash.

So what does that gesture mean?

You're worn out, Clyde Greenaway. Weary from seeing dull faces on the far side of the desk, staring at you in the faint hope that you can discover the possibility they couldn't or didn't know how to see...

He forced himself to his feet. To walk around the desk. Pick up the fallen disk. Place it back with the others.

Study them, Clyde Greenaway. Find hope in them, show them there's still something they can do on earth...

And passion, what about that? The strength you need to convey to them so that they recover their confidence, their self-assurance. Where's that passion, Clyde?

Without it, you won't be able to do anything. Those who will sit on the far side of the table need that as much as, or more than, the hope of becoming human again, of satisfying the basic need to work, to create... And they, the men and women who will sit on the far side of the table cannot work, cannot create, because they have been left behind, because knowledge has continued its advance, and the unknown, what has not yet been created, has withdrawn far away, too far away for them to be able to reach it... And those people, those human beings who twenty years earlier (or only ten, or possibly five) could have discovered or created in order to feel useful, fulfilled, are now exhausted. Their abilities are feeble, diminished, useless, and living, living for its own sake, without giving, does not make sense...

And it makes no sense, Clyde Greenaway, for you to study those gilded psychological profiles scattered on the table, because even if you do discover in them the latent possibility for them to do something, to be someone, when you tell them, your words will lack conviction, force, passion, because you have poured yourself out day after day to those who have come to ask you for a reason to live, and that reason, offered with empty, insincere words is valueless, and you have given willingly, happily, the only way you can give, without thinking that you are not inexhaustible, that you too are human, and that you gave and gave and gave until you, too, are empty...

Enough self-pity, Clyde. Remember the four who will be coming today, trusting you (no, not you, trusting someone they don't know, someone who is still faceless, who will give them back a future, human dignity, the certainty of being, not simply vegetating). They have not yet given up on this world, because deep in their hearts the last, weak, almost-extinguished hope is still beating. They are coming here in the belief that you will fan that tiny flame and turn it into an inextinguishable fire that will give them color and light for as long as they live... Yes, that's enough self-pity, Clyde Greenaway.

Better to look for the sources of strength and of life within yourself and renew your fire, your passion, your faith, in order to transmit them to those who need it. Go back, to your roots. Remember all you've done, remember what is still left to be done, and let your spirit be reborn out of that memory. Go on, you still have time.

He stood at the big window, looking out without seeing the meadow, the groves of trees surrounding the regional-bureau building.

Go on, begin. Go over your life—your working life, your life of giving, the only real life.

Two years as a psychosociologist at a control point.

Three, attending to special cases at the base.

Two, in charge of special cases in the region...

(Whoa! Not those last two years; those were the ones that emptied you.)

Further back. Go back to the days when you were working at the base. (Those were happy times... Perhaps it would do you good to work there again, even if only for a short while.)

(No, reject that cowardly thought, Clyde. Yes, you can go back, but only in your memory, to regain strength, but you need that strength to go forward, not backward. Don't shrink from your present difficulties, however tough and exhausting they may be.)

The special cases at the base, he thought, and a smile came to his lips. Could they be compared to these? Ah, no; those cases were always, always full of life.

Remember them, Clyde. Concentrate, remember one tough, beautiful one in particular.

Which one?

Jenny.

Yes, little Jenny; that was a difficult case. Truly unusual...

Jenny, the only girl in the whole area of the base whose parents still lived together, when she was already eight years old!

No, she had plenty of reasons to feel abandoned, living surrounded by normal children who knew they were the center of their mothers' only stable emotion and who could regard their relationships with indifference, knowing that they would only be short term, that soon, in a year or two at the most, the man would disappear from their home, and their mother would return to them with even more intense feelings... And Jenny lacked that basic certainty in a mother's love, because for eight years (ten, counting the time before she was born) her mother and father had lived together.

And little Jenny had tried bravely to hide her pain, her insecurity from her parents.

It had been difficult to convince them of the pathological nature of their relationship, to show them that their stability was abnormal, and denied the individual the possibility to develop their own personality.

(A dark dot grew in irregular fashion on the horizon; Clyde's eyes automatically focused and recognized a hopper approaching, and his subconscious mind registered that peace in the meadow had disappeared. Turning back into the room, he went to his seat behind the desk and went on remembering Jenny's case.)

Jenny's parents had refused to acknowledge something as obvious as that the constant growth and enrichment of human personality inevitably brought with it a gradual detachment from the points of contact that formed the basis of love. They claimed that the growth of personality could occur harmoniously between two distinct people, even if they had their own rich and varied interior worlds, and refused to accept that they were the ones who were the exception to the rule. They even used the argument that, if the solar-system groups could stay united throughout their members' long life, why couldn't they do the same?

Their passionate defense of their love might have convinced him, were it not for Jenny. When he revealed their daughter's mental condition, the trauma that the unhealthy prolongation of their union was creating, they gave way. It was only then that they agreed to be emotionally readjusted in order to have their abnormal love terminated.

It was hard work. Truly difficult... But then, when he saw Jenny's joy and happiness once she had become a girl like all the rest...

His fist struck the desk.

It was useless; not even memories like that can restore life to you, Clyde Greenaway. You're facing a real crisis. It was true what everyone said: the first one was the worst. (What's this? Trying to protect yourself in advance from the next ones, Clyde?) And you thought you were invulnerable, didn't you? How naïve you were.

He looked for the time on the wall.

There's still time, Clyde, to find Lardner and tell him you're completely exhausted. Tell him to find a substitute, say you'll go and work somewhere else for a while (possibly as a trainer of youths...or better, of children; you could imbibe their fresh joy).

A female voice interrupted his thoughts.

"Are you the one who attends to special cases?" the voice asked anxiously.

Clyde raised his eyes in surprise; there was still a long time to go before he was due to see his cases.

He examined the girl standing in the doorway before he responded.

Her long white hair was disheveled, and her sleeveless tunic— far too short, it had to be said—was covered with unsightly stains.

Yet her face was beautiful; it was full of excitement, strength, liveliness. This girl was alive, he realized in astonishment. What was she doing there?

"Do you have an appointment for today?" he asked in a mechanical way.

The girl's face was covered with reddish patches, and from her lips came a word he didn't understand. After a visible effort to control herself, she went on, her voice strained.

"No, I don't. To hell with all appointments! *I'm a special case.* Even the guards have understood that. Can't you?"

For the fraction of a second, Clyde considered the possibility of administering her a sedative. However, without knowing exactly why, he rejected the idea.

He smiled.

"Very well. If you're really such a special case, I'll have to see you. Come in and sit down, please."

2

Stephen came to a halt outside the door, fists clenched.

Too late; he had arrived too late.

"What is it you require?" the door asked.

He thought quickly. Should he wait for Ryland? But Alice would start talking at any moment.

"I'm Harry Mergenthaler, a psychosociologist in charge of Control Point IV-18-085-03," he said, and waited impatiently for the door to confirm his identity.

"What do you want, Mergenthaler?"

"I saw a patient of mine enter here. I'd like to know where she has gone."

"She is in the Department of Special Cases. At this moment, Clyde Greenaway is attending to her. Would you like to take part in the interview?"

His hand felt for the neurotor in his pocket. What should he do? If Alice saw him coming into the department, she would be on her guard. There would be a struggle, with unforeseeable results. It would be better to…

"No," he answered. "I'd better talk to the bureau director."

"Come in," said the door, opening in front of him.

Stephen took a step forward, before doubt brought him to a standstill on the threshold:

What if she had already been talking? If this is nothing more than a trap to ensnare me?

"Does my patient have an appointment for today?"

"No."

"So why did you let her in?"

"She was considered an emergency case."

Stephen accepted that. It was logical enough. Looking the way she did, anyone would have considered Alice a special case.

He entered the building.

"Show me the way to the director's office," he said.

"Follow the green arrow."

As he followed the slowly moving arrow, Stephen had time to consider the situation. It would be impossible to arrest her alive here; he would have to eliminate her. And that psychosociologist Greenaway. And the bureau director as well? He shook his head doubtfully. Too many deaths would complicate things. But he could always find an explanation: for example, that Alice (or Aisha

Dewar, more exactly) was a hysteric who suffered from hallucinations, and during one of them, she...

The door to the regional bureau director's office opened in front of him.

Behind an oval table sat an elderly, slightly stocky man with completely white hair.

"Please, come in and take a seat. I understand you want to see me."

In his side pocket, Stephen felt the neurotor's control: level one. That would only knock someone unconscious for a short while, ten minutes at most. More than enough time to...

He entered the room.

3

Savell's hand pointed toward a gleaming dot on the horizon.

"The regional bureau," he announced.

"Get closer, but not too close," ordered Ryland.

The Hermes swooped in a wide circle around the building. Ryland closely inspected the ground around it. There was a Hermes stationed close to the entrance. He noted with irritation that it was the only one he could see; Houdry should not have landed somewhere so visible. That would make his wait too conspicuous. If in fact he had waited.

Ryland's brow furrowed. It was almost certain he hadn't.

He touched Savell's shoulder, and the pilot turned to him. He pointed to a small clump of trees near the front of the building.

"Land behind those trees; they'll protect us from any curious onlookers."

The Hermes descended rapidly at a distance from the building, then glided at ground level toward the trees, making sure they were always between them and the regional bureau. Ryland felt silently satisfied. Thank God, Savell was a professional...

The craft landed softly and came to a standstill.

"Go out," Kern ordered his subordinate. "Stroll over to Houdry's Hermes like somebody who has all the time in the world, and tell him to come here, if he is in the craft."

Savell left the cabin without a word.

Ryland Kern poked his head out of the hatch and breathed in the fresh air. Birds he didn't know were singing in the nearby trees. A good place for a rest, he told himself, then withdrew inside the Hermes.

This was not the moment for his mind to stray. He needed to think what he would do if Stephen Houdry, disobeying his orders, had entered the bureau without waiting for them... something that was unfortunately quite probable.

He stroked the smooth surface of the cabin wall with the palm of his hand. Neither he nor Savell could get into the regional bureau; there was no reason for them to be there. They would have to wait until Houdry came out...after he had caused all the trouble he was capable of.

Ryland rubbed his nose. If only there were someone they could trust inside the regional bureau. Then at least they would have an idea of what was going on, in case the worst happened. If only one of his men had an excuse, thanks to the personality they had adopted in this world, to enable them to get in. Just a moment! There was Houdry's security system. If he remembered correctly, one of his subordinates had been planted in the body of a key specialist at the base, and it would be easy for that person to... Damn it, he couldn't remember the name. He had probably never known it; he had allowed that Houdry too much autonomy, he sighed. But that had been inevitable, at least at the start. While he was familiarizing himself with the situation and dealing with the most pressing problems, he couldn't hope to keep on top of every detail. Well, there was still the hope that Savell knew...

As if summoned by this thought, Savell's head appeared at the cabin door.

"The other Hermes is empty," he said.

Ryland gave a dismissive wave.

"It doesn't matter, Savell. Do you know who the man is that Houdry planted in the base he worked for?"

Savell nodded.

"She's a woman. Maureen Rockne," he said.

"Call her. Tell her to come here and use an excuse to get you inside the bureau."

Savell slipped into the seat in front of the intercom.

The image of a tall, thin woman with thick black hair appeared on the screen.

"Max! How good to see you again!" she exclaimed, eyes shining. "Where have you been?"

"That's not important, Carol," Savell replied with a smile. "You'd do better to ask where I am now."

"Where are you?" asked Maureen Rockne, returning his smile.

"Outside the regional bureau of your institute, sweetheart—the perfect place to have a rest and a conversation. And of course, I thought of you. I said to myself, 'If only Carol were here. If she had something to do at her regional bureau and came over, we could spend some time together.' Is there any chance of that?"

Maureen Rockne thought it over for a moment.

"Well, that might be possible," she said. "I need to go there to check on some inconsistent data. I was thinking of doing it tomorrow, but if you're there..."

"I am, sweetheart, and I'm waiting for you."

"Fine. I'll be there in fifteen minutes. See you then, Max."

"See you soon, Carol...and hurry up."

The woman's smiling face vanished. Savell glanced across at his superior.

"Anything else?"

"No... Will she really take fifteen minutes to get here?"

Savell nodded.

"At least," he added. "But don't worry, she understood how urgent it is."

"I hope so," said Ryland, leaving the cabin. He had done all he could.

He stretched out on his back on the lawn, arms folded behind his head. He stared up at the clear sky, without a single cloud in it.

Pulling his hand from behind his neck, he plucked a blade of grass and put it in his mouth. He began to chew it slowly and rhythmically.

4

Stephen got up cautiously from the floor. His new body was really old. He leaned over the empty shell that Harry Mergenthaler was now and removed the diadem from his head. He stowed it with the other one in the pocket of his new tunic. Then he unclasped Mergenthaler's rigid fingers from the neurotor. His hands were trembling as he adjusted the controls... Level three: complete disruption of the synaptic nerves. It would seem like a heart attack. If he only had to eliminate Alice... What could she have told them already?

He straightened up, feeling his joints creak. He hid the hand with the neurotor in his side pocket. He walked with an old man's gait to the door, which opened in front of him.

He began the trip down the corridors.

He was soon covered in sweat. It would have been better to keep Harry Mergenthaler's body; in this new one, his reflexes and coordination were poor. But there was one compensation: Alice would never be suspicious of an old man who could barely drag himself around.

Although he would have preferred it if Steve Lardner had been a little younger. At least not more than a hundred.

He raised his weepy eyes; there was the Department of Special Cases. He went slightly faster (not too fast; he was already close to the maximum that Lardner's ancient frame could manage).

He stretched out a hand. Without waiting for contact, the door to the department opened respectfully for him to pass.

He paused on the threshold, adopting a look of surprise.

"I didn't know you were busy, Clyde," he said, then glanced over at Alice. "Am I interrupting?"

"On the contrary. I'm glad you're here, Lardner," said Clyde Greenaway. "I think we have a really special case here. I'd like you to listen to...to this girl." He looked toward Alice. "If you don't mind, of course," he added politely.

Alice examined the newcomer suspiciously.

A face covered in friendly-looking wrinkles. His left arm hanging limply by his side. The right one hidden inside the invisible pocket of his long black tunic. His prominent belly shaking with every breath...

"No, I have no problem with him listening."

"Thank you so much, young lady," replied Stephen, stepping into the room.

XX

A Shot Raises the Alarm

1

"IF YOU REALLY ARE a special case, I ought to see you. Please, come in and sit down."

At last, Alice said to herself, and her knees gave way beneath her. Her hand instinctively clutched the doorframe, saving her from falling at the last moment.

Clyde leapt from his seat and strode across the room toward her.

"Do you feel ill?" he asked, grasping her shoulders.

The girl shook her head, eyes tight shut.

"Come over here," said the psychosociologist, unclasping her hands from the frame. He could feel the weight of her body against him.

He led her carefully across to the chair opposite his desk. He pressed a button, and a glass appeared, half full of an amber liquid.

"Drink this," he ordered, handing her the glass.

She did as she was told.

Clyde Greenaway went to the far side of the desk and sat down.

Her hands still shaking, Alice fiddled with the empty glass. Little by little, her voice regained warmth.

"I don't know where to start," she said at length.

"You could tell me your name," Clyde suggested. His hands pressed the lower edge of the desk. Underneath, visible only to him, a blue-tinged tablet slid out. The cyber brain of the Information

Department would have to supply him with all the necessary data as he went along.

The girl raised her head. Her green eyes stared straight into those of the psychosociologist. Clyde could scarcely breathe.

"You won't believe me. You won't be able to believe me."

There was no indication of hysteria in her voice. Clyde noted that she had spoken with complete conviction. With the bitterness of someone who knows that everything she does is useless. Clyde shook his head, annoyed at himself. He had to control his depressed state of mind. He had a job to do, and if his instinct wasn't wrong, it was a job unlike anything he had come across before. He forced himself to smile reassuringly.

"I could at least believe your name."

She shook her head.

"No, you won't believe even that. My name is Alice Welland."

Clyde Greenaway glanced quickly at the tablet under the desktop.

NAME NOT REGISTERED

"I don't see why you have to give me a false name," he said, trying not to sound annoyed. "I won't be able to obtain the information I need to help you."

A sad smile appeared on the girl's lips.

"You see? I told you the truth, and you don't believe me. Now I'm going to lie, and you'll believe me," she said, with a shrug of her shoulders, then went on. "My name is Aisha Dewar."

Clyde's eyes returned momentarily to the tablet.

AISHA DEWAR, EMOTIONAL ENGINEER, TWENTY-THREE

Hmm, an emo, he thought, looking back up at the girl sitting opposite him. The emos and their constant emotional tangle. He ought to study her file in detail, but that was impossible now. He would have to feel his way, at least in this first conversation.

"Good, now we're beginning to understand one another," he said approvingly. "Now, explain to me why you say you're lying when you're telling the truth, and vice versa."

It wasn't right to start like that, he reproached himself as soon as the words left his mouth. Control yourself, Clyde Greenaway; don't let your own problems affect your work. Stay calm and think before you speak.

The girl had raised her hands and was studying them.

"It's true that up to a certain point I am Aisha Dewar," she said, holding her hands out to him. "These were her hands." She delicately touched her face. "This was her face...and this, her body." She sighed. "But the person inside is Alice Welland."

A split personality?

"And who is Alice Welland?"

A mixture of amusement and sadness appeared on her face.

"Alice Welland lived two hundred years ago. A generalist by profession. What you call an 'analyst.' She worked in the Special Investigations Institute of the former Empire. She was an informer for the Communist Federation." Her forefinger pointed at the desk in front of her, more or less where the tablet was hidden. "Ask your computer whether that Alice Welland existed or not. Ah, and I don't know how she died. Possibly in an accident. And don't be surprised that I noticed your tablet; if I hadn't been a good observer, I wouldn't have made a good informer."

Clyde Greenaway took the tablet from its hiding place and laid it on the desk.

"Verify the existence of Alice Welland," he said.

In fact, that wasn't necessary. He was beginning to see it clearly: Aisha Dewar had been doing research to create a work on the last years of the Empire and had discovered the story of someone called Alice Welland. She has chosen her as a protagonist and—seeing what the emos were like—she had come to identify completely with her and lost all sense of reality. Clyde felt cheated. Yes, this wasn't a normal case, but in essence it was a simple one.

ALICE WELLAND EXISTED DURING THE STATED ERA. SHE DIED IN THE EXPLOSION THAT DESTROYED THE SPECIAL INVESTIGATIONS INSTITUTE IN YEAR 1 OF THE ERA OF HUMANITY.

"It's interesting to find out how one died," said Alice.

The psychosociologist leaned back in his seat.

"Very good; Alice Welland existed. Could you tell me how her... let's call it her soul...managed to survive and then took over Aisha Dewar's body? Oh, I'm sorry, I should like to record our conversation. Do you have any objection?"

"No, no objection. On the contrary; please do record it."

"Record our conversation, Information," Clyde ordered.

He would need to study the recording later on, together with her file, to decide how to cure Aisha Dewar of her hallucination.

"The fall of the Empire did not take place due to an unexpected popular uprising, as people believe." The girl was speaking rapidly, as if afraid she didn't have time, but quite clearly. "It was the Empire that prepared the uprising."

"Why?" Clyde could not stop himself asking. What she was saying was too absurd, even for him.

"The Empire had foreseen that it was bound to fall," Alice explained. "But it thought that the factors that made its survival impossible would disappear later on. They believed that the World Communist Federation was unstable, that it would collapse once the Empire had ceased to exist. They saw the Empire as an unintended catalyst for the Federation itself. They thought that after a couple of centuries, the centrifugal forces generated by nationalisms and local interests would bring about not only the complete destruction of the Federation, but also extremely favorable conditions for the reconstruction of the Empire. That would be the ideal moment to reappear, and..."

"Reappear? How?"

The girl slipped a hand inside her tunic. She took something out and laid it on the desk. Clyde picked it up and examined it.

There were two thin bands of some translucent, flexible material. They looked identical, but when he brought them closer, the psychosociologist saw that one had a thin yellow line running down its center.

While Clyde was studying the diadems, Alice went on.

"As I understand it, this is only one of the methods developed by the Special Investigations Institute to transmit the totality of mental characteristics that form the personality—the psychological structure—from one person to another." She pointed at the band with the yellow line on it. "The person wanting to be transferred to another body puts this on. The other one goes on the head of the person whose body one is going to occupy." She showed him how to place one band around her forehead. "See?" she asked. "That's how it's done. The other person has to be unconscious."

"And what happens to the mind of that other person? Does it transfer into the body that you've abandoned?"

Clyde could see how the young girl's entire body shuddered.

"No, it isn't transferred. It disappears, it's destroyed, see?"

Clyde Greenaway swallowed hard.

"Yes, I see," he said.

He was starting to understand. It wasn't surprising that Aisha Dewar suffered such a violent shock. Her imagination was obviously far too fertile. Her description was morbid in the extreme: to deliberately destroy a person's mind, a human being's mind, in order to take over their body. A shiver ran down his spine.

Alice nodded, sympathetically.

"Yes, it's horrible, isn't it? I know that for a man of this era it must seem inhuman, impossible to conceive... I know it's hard to believe me."

"Yes, it is hard," Clyde agreed, and said nothing more. Stay calm. Stay objective. Remember the power of suggestion that emos have.

"There's one thing I don't understand," he said finally. "With this method, you must have been changing from body to body for two centuries now, so why haven't you denounced this...imperial plan before now?"

The girl twisted the glass in her fingers. The light brought unexpected gleams from its faceted surface.

"In fact, I have only inhabited this body for a week. Before that, I can only remember my life during the Empire. I imagine my psyche was 'stored' somehow during the intervening years."

Good. The case wasn't that difficult after all. She had not yet completed the construction of her fantasy...or rather, of her nightmare.

"To tell you the truth, I don't know the details of how the project was managed. To judge by Stephen, I suppose they woke up recently and found themselves...in this world. As is only to be expected, they were confused, as all their predictions had been proved false."

"Yes, they must be pretty confused... And who is Stephen?"

The girl blushed.

"He woke me up. Stephen Houdry, who back then was a psychosociologist at the Special Investigations Institute. You can verify that if you wish."

"No, I don't think that's necessary. What I can't understand is how this Stephen person could have come out of hibernation and lived in this world without being discovered. He must know nothing about it."

Alice shook her head.

"No, he is well informed."

"How?"

"I don't know. I suppose he was transplanted using a different method than mine. Maybe he has retained part or all of the memories of the former occupant of his present body."

"Do you know his name?"

"The former occupant of his body?"

"Yes."

"He's called, or was called, Harry Mergenthaler."

"Profession?"

"Psychosociologist. He works at Control Point IV-18-085-03. From what he's told me, Aisha Dewar was a patient of his. He used that relationship to transfer my mind to her."

Clyde straightened in his seat and rested his elbows on the desk. The case was much more difficult than he thought. Obviously, Mergenthaler had attended to her and tried to get rid of her hallucination. But all he had done was become another part of her fantasy. He would have to move cautiously if he didn't want to become another figure in this imperial conspiracy.

"But how could Stephen Houdry succeed in occupying the body he is in now?" he asked tentatively. "I don't think that Mergenthaler would have put this on his head out of mere curiosity," he said, rolling the band between his fingers.

Alice drew a hand across her face.

"I don't know. That's why I think there must be other methods of transfer, apart from the diadems."

"Diadems?"

"Yes. They call that a diadem," she said, pointing to the band Stephen was holding. "But to get back to the main point: I can understand that you have your doubts about the truth of what I'm telling you. But Stephen hasn't talked to me about the details of the project. He's very cautious."

"Does he suspect you?"

Alice sighed.

"No, I don't think so. You must find it hard to understand the mentality of those who lived during the time of the Empire. Especially those of us who used to work in the institute. It was essential to be discreet, even if you weren't a spy for the Federation. We never told anyone anything unless it was really essential, see?"

"Yes, I think I see. But if that were the case, how did you find out about this project the Empire had? For example, that they thought the Federation would collapse?"

"Stephen had to give me that information. I'm a generalist, remember? He took my mind from wherever it had been and put it into this body for it to analyze the current situation. To find the way that they could achieve their objective and rebuild the Empire in these unforeseen circumstances. I also know that he has several subordinates. He's the captain of a Hydra..."

"A Hydra? What's that?"

Alice shrugged.

"All I can tell you is that the project was called the Hydra Project. And that Stephen Houdry is the captain of a Hydra."

"Of one? So there are more?"

"I'm not sure... I suppose so."

"And couldn't Stephen Houdry be the overall head of that operation?"

"No. He talks about his superiors. I know they exist, but I don't know who they are, or where they are."

Clyde thought this over.

"How did you learn our language?" he asked. "If I'm not mistaken, the Solar language did not exist in the days of the Empire."

"I used a hypnoinductor. It took me two days to learn it."

"I see... And how did you communicate with the people around you while you were doing so?"

"Stephen was the only one I had any contact with. I've been shut up in his house all this time."

Clyde's observant eyes noticed that her cheeks had turned pink again.

"Yes, it's all logical," he said, and leaned back in his seat once more. Too logical, he thought. He had been wrong; her fantasy wasn't at the construction stage, it was already completely elaborated. It had become so much part of her personality that she had even succeeded in forgetting the overall thrust of her initial proposal, and her mind had deliberately limited itself to remembering what this imaginary Alice could know...

"You don't believe me."

There was neither disappointment not anger in her voice; she was simply stating a fact.

He looked across at her and saw her weary green eyes. He said what he had not been thinking of saying.

"You have to understand me, Aisha...or Alice. What you've told me is...pretty fantastic, isn't it? I would need more solid proof that..."

He fell silent; the door to the room had opened. Lardner was staring at them in surprise from the threshold.

Clyde felt relieved; the old fellow could help him with this case.

"I didn't know you were busy, Clyde," he said, then glanced over at Alice. "Am I interrupting?"

"On the contrary. I'm glad you're here, Lardner," said Clyde Greenaway. "I think we have a really special case here. I'd like you to listen to...to this girl." He looked nervously toward Alice. "If you don't mind, of course," he added politely. Aisha Dewar was capable of believing that Lardner was yet another imperial conspirator...

"No, I have no problem with him listening," he heard her say, and let out a sigh of relief.

2

Stretched out face down on the carpet, Maureen Rockne was enjoying the sound of the wind whistling in her ears. Nothing could compare to this sensation of plunging through a wall of air, her fingers poised on the controls, ready to instantly alter course if they met any unexpected obstacle. It was a risk, of course, a marvelous risk, but a tiny one, which she tried to ignore: if a really dangerous obstacle appeared—a bird, another carpet— and she didn't have time to react, the automatic pilot would steer her around it. Even so, the sense of danger was almost real.

In the distance, she spied the ethereal outline of the regional bureau. She sighed and initiated the braking process. Savell must be around somewhere, but probably not that close.

She changed course slightly.

The air resistance had dropped enough for her to be able to sit up on her fragile craft, her legs crossed underneath her. She studied the area around the building.

There was a Hermes on the ground almost directly in front of the entrance.

She shook her head; that couldn't be Savell's. She peered more intently; there was something shining brightly in that little clump of trees.

Yes, it was a Hermes. And a head she knew well was poking out of its hatch.

She braked sharply and came to a halt alongside the silver craft. Before the slender currents of air keeping the carpet a few inches off the ground had fully switched off, she jumped down and ran to the Hermes, removing her protective goggles.

"Here I am. What's wrong?"

Her colleague pointed to a man standing up in the grassy meadow, shaking off the dry blades that had stuck to his back.

"He'll tell you why we need you," said Savell. When she looked inquisitively at him, he explained: "He is one of the Three: Ryland Kern."

She turned toward the approaching figure, automatically smoothing down her short hair.

Ryland got straight to the point.

"Do you have any pretext that could get you inside there?" he asked, pointing his chin toward the regional bureau.

"Yes, I have to check some data in the Information Department. I was going to do so tomorrow, but there's nothing stopping me doing it now."

"Are you able to get around inside the bureau?"

"I've got several friends there."

"Go in. Try to localize Houdry. If you can see him on his own, tell him to come out at once. Have you got that?"

"Yes."

"If you can't find him, try to observe as much as you can. Just observe, don't do anything that might compromise you, even if Houdry is in danger."

Savell and Maureen turned pale simultaneously.

Inwardly, Ryland cursed the protective conditioning. Well, he could use it in his favor.

"You must understand. We, the Three, could be destroyed if we don't find out what is happening in there. If Houdry really does have a problem, there's nothing you'll be able to do. But if you can get as much information as possible about his situation, then we can help him. Do you follow?"

Maureen Rockne licked her lips with the tip of her tongue. She nodded.

"Any doubts?"

"No."

"Repeat your mission."

"Look for Houdry as discreetly as possible. If I can see him alone, tell him to get out immediately. If I can't find him, observe everything that might be related to him."

"Good. Off you go."

Maureen ran toward the carpet, clumsily replacing her goggles.

Stephen is in danger; the Three are in danger...

The carpet rose slowly into the air.

What's wrong with me? Maureen Rockne asked herself, and answered her own question. If they discover Houdry and make him talk, it's goodbye immortality, power, pleasures...

She forced herself to calm down.

It all depends on doing my job. I have to do it well. Fulfill my mission. It's easy, I can do it without a problem...

Her hands gradually recovered their usual agility.

The carpet zigzagged its way between the bumpy surface of the land, heading for the luminous building.

She descended outside the main door.

"Good afternoon, guard," she said with a warm smile.

"Good afternoon, Carol. I wasn't expecting you today," the door greeted her, and slid open.

"I've brought forward my visit," Maureen explained as she went inside. "Anything new in this old hell?" she asked casually.

"Not a lot," replied the door, closing behind her. "Just a few unexpected visitors."

"Anyone I know?" she asked, without appearing particularly interested.

"You must know one of them: Harry Mergenthaler. He works at one of the control points in your base."

Maureen came to a halt in the middle of the hallway, feigning surprise.

"Harry? I ought to see him. Has he left yet?"

"No."

"Do you know which department he went to?"

"He went in to see Lardner."

"Hmmm... I'll try to find him before he leaves."

Maureen strode briskly off toward the director's office. She wouldn't have any problem getting in there; the old man wouldn't be surprised at her going to see him. He saw her as a daughter... She could tell Houdry.

"Can I see Lardner?" she asked.

"Lardner isn't here," replied the door to his office.

Her brow wrinkled. Where could Houdry be?

"When he returns, tell him Carol came to see him. I'll be in the bureau for some time; when I've finished, I'll drop in on him again," she informed the door, then headed for the Information Department.

Why had Houdry gone directly to see the director, whom he hardly knew, rather than turn to her? He knew about her contacts here...

She heard the sound of someone running, and her back muscles tensed. What was going on? Was it Stephen?

A figure appeared in the bend of the corridor in front of her and came running in her direction. Maureen relaxed; it wasn't Houdry. But why was the head of the Information Department in such a hurry?

"What's going on, Alena?" she asked.

"People killed...in Clyde's department," the other woman shouted, without stopping. "Come with me, Carol!"

The two of them sprinted toward the Department of Special Cases.

3

Clyde broke the momentary silence.

"I ought to start by saying, Lardner, that what she has been telling me is...really hard to believe."

The director tilted his head toward the young woman, intrigued. "Oh?" he said, in a friendly fashion. "Fine, I'm willing to listen." Alice bit her lip.

"I know it's not easy," she began. "It would be logical and reassuring to believe that I'm mad, because if what I said were true, you'd lose all your peace of mind..."

Stephen settled back in his chair, trying to find the best position. He was to Alice's left; it wouldn't be easy for him to slip out the neurotor, aim, and fire without making any sudden movement.

"...the Hydra Project, which consists of..."

Lardner's thin lips drew into a line. How this idiot can talk, Stephen thought. Luckily Clyde doesn't believe her...yet.

He took his hand from his pocket. The neurotor was almost completely hidden in his closed fist. The tip protruded no more than a couple of centimeters. Careful... Alice was staring at him too insistently.

He tried to adopt a look of absorbed interest.

Perfect, she was concentrating her attention on Greenaway again. Now he just had to wait for a moment when she got carried away and Greenaway wasn't looking at him. Then, with an imperceptible move of his hand...a heart attack. Sad, but understandable, with all those fantasies on her mind. And then old man Lardner would withdraw, profoundly shocked, to look after Mergenthaler, and his own heart.

He rested the arm with his weapon on the arm of the chair.

A slight turn of the wrist, and the neurotor would be pointing directly at the spy's heart. A slight squeeze, and...

Careful! She was staring at him again. He paused, waiting with bated breath for Alice to look away once more.

Good! He took a deep breath. He was irritated to note that he was still sweating. Too much tension for this decrepit body. He couldn't wait for Alice to get carried away. The damned girl looked astonishingly calm while she talked and talked about things she shouldn't mention.

Now!

His fist turned as quickly as he could manage...

The glass crashed into his knuckles, and the invisible death rays missed their target. A female hand grasped his wrist and twisted so hard that he opened it, crying out in pain.

The neurotor fell to the floor with a metallic crash.

Stephen bent to pick it up, but Alice got there before him. She leapt back and pointed the weapon straight at Houdry's chest.

"No! No! Don't shoot!" came the plea from the old man's throat.

"This is the proof you were looking for, Greenaway," said Alice with an icy smile, not taking her eyes off Stephen.

Behind his desk, the psychosociologist surveyed the scene, wide-eyed.

Alice glanced down at the cylinder in her hand and nodded.

"As I thought...a neurotor. At level three. Was it going to be a heart attack?"

"I've no idea what you're talking about," Stephen replied in a tone of hurt dignity.

"Well, what d'you say now, Greenaway?"

Clyde said nothing.

Alice gave him a concerned glance.

"Do you still think this is a fantasy? Can't you see how scared he is? Do you think what I took from him is a toy? This can kill, Greenaway..."

A pause.

All that could be heard in the room was the old director's rasping breath.

Alice's smile gradually faded.

"You still don't believe me, you idiot? Do you need further proof?"

She began to raise her arm to aim at Houdry.

She can't harm me; her conditioning will stop her. Stay calm, and don't give yourself away.

Her arm was outstretched, pointing straight at Stephen's chest.

But she doesn't know it's me inside this body!

"Don't shoot! I'm..."

The weapon vibrated silently.

Alice went slowly back to her seat. Her eyes met Clyde's.

"That was a mistake, Alice," the psychosociologist said, controlling his annoyance. He pointed to the body slumped on the floor. "We could have gotten more information about the project from him."

Alice stared at him in astonishment for a moment, then she threw her head back and laughed.

"How can you laugh?" asked Clyde, increasingly angry. "You killed a man!"

"Don't worry, I didn't kill him, although he deserves to die. See?" She held out the neurotor. "I set it to level one without him noticing. He's just lost consciousness. We've got five minutes to decide what to do before he comes around."

Clyde smiled.

"Good, but I hope you understand that I have to think things over first. I don't know how to face..."

Lost deep in thought, Greenaway did not finish his sentence. Alice Welland waited patiently.

"There are bound to be others like him nearby, maybe even inside the building, to check whether he succeeded...in silencing you," he said pensively.

"I agree."

"And they don't have a precise idea of what you know?"

"I doubt it."

"The logical thing for them to do if they find out what has happened would be to transfer to other bodies using these...diadems, wouldn't it?"

Alice nodded.

Greenaway sighed.

"So they have to find his dead body here...and mine too, naturally."

"Eh?"

Clyde glanced at her and smiled.

"Don't worry, I'm not suggesting we end our lives," he said, and picked up the tablet from the desk. "Information, put me through to the Central Archive."

The reply flashed up almost at once.

COMMUNICATION ESTABLISHED.

"Archive, this is Clyde Greenaway, a psychosociologist in Bureau IV-18. A crisis situation has arisen, one that I think is unprecedented. I think it requires top priority. To back this up, I suggest you analyze the conversation that has just taken place in the department where I work and the information it contains."

I WILL DO SO.

The pair of them waited. Ten seconds later, and the tablet was covered with writing.

ABSOLUTE PRIORITY PROVISIONALLY GRANTED. SUPREME EARTH COUNCIL TO GRANT DEFINITIVE PRIORITY IN MEETING WITHIN TWENTY-FOUR HOURS.

Clyde nodded his agreement.

"Of course, it's essential that the Supreme Council is involved in this. Archive, we need several things immediately. Firstly, those present here need to be transferred to the central bureau of my institute in such a way that no one is aware of it. To do that, we need three lifeless bodies identical to ours to be found here. It would also be good to verify whether there is an abnormal situation in this bureau that might be connected to what has happened. Ah, and nobody is to know anything about the Hydra Project, except of course the central bureau and the Supreme Council. Can you do all that?"

YES, I CAN.

The white letters appeared on the blue background, and then the screen went blank.

Alice looked straight at Clyde.

"And what do we do?"

He shrugged.

"We wait. The Central Archive has taken charge of the situation."

The ground began to tremble. Alice leapt up in alarm.

Before Clyde could say anything, tiny cracks appeared in the floor, forming a rectangle.

"I think they're preparing our way out of here," Greenaway said.

4

"Maureen's coming back, sir."

Ryland got up from the lawn and watched as the slender carpet approached and slowed alongside him.

Maureen jumped to the ground.

"Permission to report," she said.

"Go ahead."

"I couldn't find Houdry, but things have happened in the bureau that I fear are related to him. There are three dead bodies in the Department of Special Cases."

"Who are they?"

"The director, Lardner; Clyde, the department head; and a girl I don't know."

Ryland's brow furrowed.

"Do they know the cause of death?"

"There are no external marks. But I saw a neurotor on the floor."

"Didn't you pick it up?"

Maureen shook her head.

"I was afraid the room was under surveillance, because it was such an unusual incident. Besides, they don't know what neurotors are. Only a specialist in ancient history could identify it, and even then not all historians would be able to."

"You did well. What did they do in the bureau?"

"They informed the central bureau, which told them to withdraw the bodies, determine the cause of death, and to leave the department untouched, in case they need to do an on-the-spot investigation."

Ryland Kern considered this.

Houdry wouldn't have been so stupid as to leave the neurotor behind. Besides, why hadn't he come out of the bureau yet? Had they taken him prisoner?

He gave a worried look at the building hidden beyond the trees.

No, if he'd been arrested, Rockne would have heard something. He shook his head. There was nothing else for it; he would have to go back to the hermitage without finding out what had happened.

"Thank you, Rockne. You may go."

She turned on her heel in an almost military fashion and headed for the carpet.

Ryland waited for the tiny craft to disappear behind the trees, then turned to Savell.

"Let's go. There's nothing more we can do here," he said.

XXI

Emotional Complications

1

SHE LOOKED LIKE A SLEEPING CHILD.

Or, looking more closely at her red-tinged helmet and the long white hair poking out untidily from underneath, she was like a warrior princess in a deep slumber.

"Greenaway!"

Clyde stopped daydreaming and turned to face the intercom. On the screen he saw the round face and lively eyes of Aridor: Samuel Aridor, head of the Special Cases Department at the central bureau.

"We need you in Cubicle 18. Can you come?"

"Yes, of course," replied Clyde. He walked over to the exit from the cabinet of basic analyses.

He gave a last look over his shoulder at the unconscious Alice. Suddenly he turned back and ran across to her:

"Operator! Stop the analysis!"

The woman seated behind the panel looked up in confusion, then looked across at the young woman lying prone on the analyzer. Her hands immediately went to the controls, pushing buttons, breaking contacts.

Clyde reached Alice and came to a halt, holding his breath. Her body had arched upward and was balancing rigidly on her feet and head. Her arms were firmly by her sides, fists clenched. He peered at her convulsed face and saw that her green eyes were wide open, staring blankly into space.

"What's going on, Frances?" asked Aridor from the screen.

The technician shook her head, eyes still fixed on the instrument panel.

"I don't know, Sam. I've never seen anything like it."

"Wait. Don't do anything, I'm on my way," said Aridor, and the screen went dark.

Clyde watched nervously as his patient slowly returned to normal. The tense muscles gradually relaxed, and the body lay flat on the bed of the analyzer. Her eyelids fluttered, and then closed, hiding the distant gaze of her eyes. Impulsively, the psychosociologist clasped one of her hands in his.

It was covered in a cold sweat.

Samuel Aridor came into the cabinet. Moving with unsuspected agility for such a rotund person, he went over to the control panel.

"Let me see," he told the technician, who moved aside for him. The head of special cases surveyed the indicators.

"What area were you analyzing, Frances?"

"The emotional. Everything seemed normal, and then all of a sudden..."

"Normal? What about this?" Aridor interrupted her, tapping a transparent dial. Underneath was a black line shooting upward.

"That? It's obviously a dominant emotion."

"Yes, it's obvious it's dominant, but is it normal?"

"In what way? The analyzer hasn't yet finished..."

Aridor waved his hand impatiently.

"Just look. Before it goes up, the line oscillates, doesn't it?"

"Yes, it does... Oh, I see what you mean. It's artificial, isn't it? It must mean there was a readjustment of her emotions."

"A readjustment aimed at creating a dominant emotion?" The technician looked at him, bewildered. Without waiting for her to reply, Aridor spoke into the intercom.

"Information Department; it's urgent."

The screen lit up almost at once, showing the face of a middle-aged man with Asiatic traits.

"Chen, I need as quickly as possible information about the techniques of emotional conditioning carried out in the days of the Empire and how to remove that conditioning without harming the person involved."

Chen's eyebrows arched, and Aridor grunted irritably.

"This isn't something that can be simply readjusted. While we were analyzing our...patient, the psychosensor detected a dominant emotion that had been artificially implanted. Just detecting it brought on convulsions, so you can imagine what would happen to her if we tried to suppress it without taking precautions. Do you understand now?"

"I understand," replied the head of information. His image disappeared from the screen.

Aridor went slowly back to the instrument panel.

"Suspend the analysis until we have all the necessary information, Frances. Let her wake up."

The technician touched a white disk, and the lights on the panel died away.

"Would you like an analysis of what we have already registered?" Aridor nodded.

A few touches on the controls, and from a slot in the side, pale blue cards started to emerge at regular intervals. Aridor took them and examined them with growing interest.

Alice stirred uneasily on the bed. All at once her eyelids opened, showing her terrified gaze.

"Where am I?" she stammered.

Clyde quickly explained.

"Here, in the central bureau. Everything is alright."

The girl stared at him without appearing to recognize him immediately. Then she took Clyde's hands between hers and pressed them to her chest.

"I'm frightened," she said in a strangled voice.

"There's no need to be afraid," he whispered, leaning over her. "You're safe here; we won't let them harm you."

She did not reply. Her eyes closed once more.

Samuel Aridor put the last card to one side. He looked up from the analyzer and saw the expression on Clyde Greenaway's face as he gazed at the girl who had come from the past. He rolled his eyes. He walked over to them and rested a hand on the psychosociologist's shoulder. Clyde slowly turned his head toward him.

"She's fallen asleep," he said softly.

"It'll do her good to rest," said Aridor.

Clyde carefully withdrew his hands from hers. She tried to keep hold of them. Then she turned on her side and drew her knees up to her chest.

Like a sleeping child...

"Come on, Clyde," Aridor said gently. "We have work to do."

2

The man standing by the pods gave a broad smile.

"I was starting to worry about you, Sam."

"There was a small problem," Aridor replied. "But it's being sorted out."

"Can we start?"

"Yes, start."

Clyde considered the bodies in the pods. One was Lardner...or whoever had taken on his personality, and he was looking at him fearfully. The other was a young man, apparently unconscious. Both of them were carefully strapped down.

"Archive found the other one in Lardner's office," explained Aridor. "His state is peculiar. There are no signs of higher nervous activity; he's like a vegetable."

A look of understanding spread across Clyde's face.

"A mental transfer?"

The head of special cases agreed.

"That's what we think. We found this in Lardner's pockets," he said, pointing to the diadems his assistant was placing on the heads of the two men stretched out in the pods. "I've no doubt that the agent came in with this body," he continued, pointing to the younger of the two men, "and transferred into Lardner to be able to get into your department without raising suspicion."

"Who is he?"

"Harry Mergenthaler. Or, more precisely, it's the body of Harry Mergenthaler; inside was..."

"...Stephen Houdry," Clyde finished the sentence for him. He peered at Lardner with renewed interest, but the old man's eyes had closed, and he seemed to be as unconscious as Mergenthaler.

"The transfer has begun," Aridor explained. "According to what Alice Welland has told us, it should take five minutes."

"Yes... Forgive my curiosity, but why are you giving Houdry Mergenthaler's body again?"

Aridor pointed to the figures on the controls.

"We want to know the mechanism of the transfer," he explained. "And in particular, to have the opportunity to restore Lardner's personality to his body. We tried to do it with Mergenthaler, but there was nothing left of him. It was only to be expected: Houdry was in his body for at least a week. But Lardner was only displaced less than four hours ago, so perhaps we can recover him."

"Alice said nothing is left."

"Even so, we have to try."

They fell silent, gazing at the pods...

The eyes that had once belonged to Harry Mergenthaler opened. They showed a mixture of hatred and fear.

"The transfer is complete," announced the assistant.

"So I see. Bring Lardner around," ordered Aridor. He turned to Clyde. "I had been thinking of asking you to help me question Houdry, but I'm afraid you're tired out. You've had more than your fair share of work today, Greenaway."

"But I still feel fine," Clyde tried to protest.

Aridor stared him straight in the eye. All of a sudden, Clyde could feel all the accumulated tiredness hit him.

"You'd better go and rest, Greenaway."

Clyde hardly had the strength to agree.

3

He was floating in darkness.

He didn't feel afraid; it was like flying wearing an antigravity belt in a starless night. The air was stroking his skin with cold, soft fingers.

He was floating in darkness, his mind free of thoughts. He felt sensations he couldn't define, but which were incredibly pleasurable.

A light...

No, two lights, shining indistinctly in the distance.

He was curious and wanted to get closer to them.

His body moved weightlessly toward them—or were the two lights coming toward him?

The night took on a greenish tinge.

Now he could feel anxiety coursing through his veins, but could not explain why.

The green lights grew and became oval shaped.

The shape of eyes.

Eyes, filled with green fear.

The eyes of...

Startled, he sat up in a sitting position on the invisible bed of the force field.

"Did you sleep well, Greenaway?"

Clyde blinked, dazzled by the faint light of the room. He looked around to see who was speaking to him.

Samuel Aridor leaned back comfortably in a seat by his bed.

"Yes, pretty well," said Clyde.

"What time is it?" he asked, wiping the sweat from his brow with the back of his hand.

"Four in the morning."

Clyde looked surprised.

"I slept fourteen hours?"

Aridor nodded.

"You needed rest," he added, straightening in his chair. "You've got a lot of hard work ahead of you."

"What's that?"

"The meeting of the institute's department heads finished a quarter of an hour ago. We've worked out a plan to neutralize Hydra. I have to present it to the Supreme Council, which meets at eight today. Alice Welland has an important role to play. For reasons I will explain to you later, she will need the constant supervision of a psychosociologist...for an indefinite period. We think that you should be that person."

"Why?"

Aridor ran his fingers through his thinning hair.

"Everything related to Alice Welland—and to you—has to be kept a complete secret. By now, everyone who has worked with you two in the institute has been given a selective amnesia treatment. We have only left out a few members of the council. I trust you understand the reason for this."

Clyde nodded. Hydra would try by any means possible to confirm that nothing was known about the project.

"Clyde Greenaway is officially dead. Besides, Welland trusts you." Aridor noted how Clyde's cheeks colored. "It's much safer to keep you two together."

"And why does she need a psychosociologist?"

Aridor leaned back in his seat and interlocked his fingers.

"I'll have to summarize what has happened while you were asleep. Let me think where to begin..."

Aridor stared up at the ceiling for several seconds.

"Houdry did not answer any of our questions. We analyzed his mind and discovered the reason: he was conditioned." He glanced at Clyde. "Do you know what conditioning is?" he asked.

"No."

"Basically, it's a technique similar to emotional readjustment. It was created under the Empire. Of course, its goal is the exact opposite to readjustment. It doesn't aim to ensure an individual's emotional balance, but to influence their behavior in the manner desired by those doing the conditioning. In Houdry's case, his conditioning was aimed at protecting the Hydra Project. That's why he didn't answer any of our questions. The mere possibility of harming his superiors sickened him."

"Why didn't you remove his conditioning?"

"He had a safety mechanism that would have destroyed his mind if anyone tried to do that."

"But if you knew about the safety mechanism...?"

"Information investigated the mechanisms used in the past. We devised a procedure that should have gotten rid of any we discovered, and we applied it to Houdry."

"It failed?"

The head of special cases sighed.

"Yes, it failed. Houdry died. He must have had a safety mechanism we didn't know about."

The implications of what had happened slowly dawned on Clyde.

"So we don't have any way now of finding out about Hydra?"

"There is one way...but we need Alice Welland. And at the moment she is running the risk of disintegrating emotionally."

Clyde got out of bed. He was pale.

"Wh...what?"

Aridor looked him in the eye.

"Sit down. And calm down. Getting agitated solves nothing."

Clyde hesitated, then sat down again on the bed.

Aridor nodded approvingly.

"That's right. You'll need to stay calm, Greenaway, in the work you have to do. I don't think I'm wrong if I say that you feel...a deep emotion for your patient, isn't that so?"

Clyde ran his tongue over his lips.

"Yes, that's so."

"Good... That's another problem. And a serious one. Do you remember how Welland convulsed when we were analyzing her?"

The sociologist turned even paler.

"But...I don't think that she...she is conditioned to protect Hydra. If that were so, she wouldn't have told us anything."

Aridor agreed.

"No, it's true she hasn't been conditioned to protect Hydra. Her conditioning is different," he said, and took some blue cards from the side pocket of his tunic. "Read these."

Clyde took them and read them closely.

Three minutes later, he raised his bewildered eyes to Aridor.

"But...but this is impossible. No human being would have these...these..." he said, unable to think of how to describe it.

"You're right. But these aren't human beings, they're imperial bureaucrats."

Clyde was surprised to realize he was pleased that Stephen Houdry was dead, and said so.

Aridor shook his head.

"There's nothing pleasant about it...not even from your point of view."

Clyde's brow furrowed.

"Isn't it a relief for everybody that a creature like him has been removed forever?" he asked, then almost at once the answer flashed into his mind: no, not for Alice.

Aridor noticed how Clyde's expression had changed, and nodded.

"I see that you have understood, Greenaway. Every day that goes by without him will be worse for her. Worse and worse, until she goes mad. And if she discovers that he is dead, she will perish as well. Now do you see why she will need a psychosociologist permanently?"

Clyde threw his hands in the air in desperation.

"And what can I do for her?"

Aridor produced a gray card from his pocket.

Clyde took it and read it avidly.

When he finished, he blushed and tried to tear the card up. It was made of some flexible material, but it was too tough for him.

"Take it easy, Greenaway."

Clyde struggled to recover his composure.

Aridor went on.

"I can see that your feelings for Alice Welland could become an obstacle to your work... In fact, they already are. I recommend that you consider, as a psychosociologist, undergoing emotional readjustment."

Clyde gazed at him dully.

"You won't have to lose your feelings for her altogether, simply to adjust them slightly. To change them, let's say, into feelings of great friendship. What do you think of that?"

Silence.

More cards, white this time, appeared from Aridor's tunic. Rising from his chair, he left them on the bed next to Clyde.

"Here's a summary of the plan we're going to submit to the Supreme Council. We will leave in a couple of hours, so you have the time to study it...and to think about what I've said."

Aridor left the room.

Clyde Greenaway remained seated on the bed.

He wasn't looking at the white cards; he was remembering.

She looked like a sleeping child...

XXII

The Supreme Council

1

A BLACK DOT APPEARED and disappeared among the clouds, slowly curving through the skies.

Shielding her eyes from the rising sun with the palm of her hand, Karen Shehan watched the winged craft grow as it began a rapid descent, glided along for a while, then landed on the esplanade in front of her.

The hatch of the Orion slid open, and a slender figure appeared from inside. She removed her round helmet, shaking her long golden curls, as the woman came out of her house and walked over to the craft.

"I'm pleased to see you, Nadia dear," said Karen, and hugged her. Then she stepped back, leaving her hands on her visitor's shoulders.

"Have the others arrived yet?" Nadia asked, gently removing her friend's hands.

"Hjalmar is here, and so is Felix. They arrived only half an hour ago. But tell me about you. What are you doing these days?"

"Nothing," said Nadia, starting for the nearby house.

Karen went with her.

"What about Obote?" she asked, glancing at Nadia out of the corner of her eye. "How is he?"

"He died. He gave up..."

They reached the door in silence. Karen patted Nadia on the back, trying to encourage her.

"I have to leave you here; I need to greet the others. Make yourself at home," she said, and started to walk away.

"Wait!"

Karen stopped and turned to look at Nadia.

"What is the meeting for?"

Karen shrugged.

"Actually, I don't know. The Institute of Psychosociology called it." She raised an eyebrow. "With the utmost urgency. They haven't arrived yet."

Nadia nodded her agreement.

"Alright. I'll see you later."

"Yes, my dear," said Karen with a smile, then continued walking toward the esplanade. She shielded her eyes again.

Another black dot appeared in the sky.

Poor, poor Nadia...

Half-closing her eyes, Karen watched closely as the new ship began its swift landing.

It landed elegantly alongside the Orion.

I must contact the mobile service units. The esplanade is getting crowded.

The hatch of the Hermes had opened. Karen recognized the figure that appeared in the doorway.

Aridor? A problem from special cases that was urgent?

A second man climbed out, followed by another figure.

I don't know him...and that woman looks like... Yes, it's Aisha!

"Aisha!" she shouted, running toward the girl. "Darling, where have you been hiding? It's been centuries since last time... You don't know how happy I am to see you," she stammered, hugging the young woman tightly. She pulled away to look at her more closely.

"You have to tell me..." She fell silent when she saw the newcomer's awkward expression.

"But...you're not Aisha!"

Aridor butted in.

"I'm afraid you're making a mistake, Karen... Alice, meet Karen Shehan, an emotional engineer. She represents Zone Four on the council. Karen, this is Alice Welland."

Karen's face still showed her bewilderment.

"But..." she said, then composed herself. "A pleasure to meet you."

"The pleasure is mine," Alice murmured.

"Haven't the others arrived yet?" asked Aridor.

"Three more to come," replied Karen, automatically raising her eyes to the sky. Another spaceship was circling over the esplanade. "You'll have to excuse me, but I must go and receive Otami. Sam, you know the house; take them in. I'll be back soon to look after you."

"Don't worry," said the head of special cases. "Is Hjalmar here?" he asked.

"Yes, he's already arrived."

"Good. See you in a moment."

"Yes."

The new arrivals headed for the house. Karen raised her right hand to her mouth.

"Clear the esplanade," she ordered her ring.

Small, squat machines like giant beetles appeared out of the ground. They began quickly and efficiently to push the spacecraft toward the dark holes on one side of the esplanade.

Karen looked over her shoulder as the three figures walked away.

And yet...she is identical to Aisha!

2

She recognized me... No, she recognized Aisha, her body, my body...
How embarrassing, when she finds out...

"The house is beautiful, isn't it? As you can see, Karen likes
antiques. It's a typical dwelling from the first century before our
era. I'm sure you'll enjoy being in a familiar atmosphere," said Clyde.

Alice turned toward him and smiled.

Thank you, my dear friend...

She contemplated the house.

It had been built on the edge of a cliff. The rays of the rising
sun gave a pink tinge to the white walls that rose in gentle curves
up to a thin, silvery spire.

As if it were climbing to the sky... And it's not that tall; it's the
design that gives that impression.

She glanced at the surrounding landscape. Sand and rocks. A
few straggly bushes were scattered in the dry earth.

But the countryside is beautiful. The house emerges from this
desert as if it wants to distance itself, but at the same time they are
both completely integrated into it. Beautiful, so beautiful...

The door opened in front of them, letting out a stream of fresh air.

"This is the living room; please wait for me here. I need to see
Hjalmar before the meeting." Aridor apologized and disappeared
behind some curtains.

"Shall we sit down?" suggested Clyde.

"No, thank you. I'd like to take a look at the room... It's so pretty."

"As you like," agreed the psychosociologist, collapsing into a
soft armchair.

The girl from the past went slowly around the room.

Striped in ocher, gray, and bronze, the walls seemed as though
they were made of precious woods. Semitransparent, amber-colored

curtains covered the doors connecting it to the rest of the house. Two large, gold-framed windows offered a panorama of the desert landscape.

It's amazing that with these simple elements they have managed to create such an impression of peace, tranquility, serenity...

Next she studied the furniture.

Half a dozen soberly decorated armchairs, cushions, rugs, a couple of low tables. On the varnished surface of the closer of the two, something gleamed.

What could it be?

She went over to the table, and examined the multicolored crystal in its center.

Strangely symmetrical...and the colors don't match the facets, although it looks as if...

She leaned over to look at it more closely.

Yes, the colors are shifting within the crystal. Very slowly, but they are moving.

She raised a hand to wipe away the tear running down her cheek.

Why do I feel so sad? There's no reason to be, she told herself, still looking at the cut crystal. Yes, its shine also changes, but in sections... I've never seen anything so melancholy, so desolate, so...

Fresh tears coursed down her cheeks. This time she didn't dry them. Instead, she leaned even closer to the crystal, her cheek almost brushing against it.

"Alice!"

She did not respond.

Clyde leapt up beside her, took her by the shoulders, and led her away from the table. Alice's face turned as she tried to continue looking at the gleaming crystal. The psychosociologist clamped his hand on her jaw.

"Wake up, Alice!"

Her eyes were glassy.

"Can you hear me? Wake up!"

Alice blinked feebly. Awareness gradually returned to her gaze. Clyde breathed a sigh of relief.

"What happened?" Alice asked in a weak voice.

Clyde shrugged.

"I have no idea," he replied. "You were looking at that emo crystal, and somehow you fell completely under its influence. I reckon that if I hadn't intervened in time, you would have become catatonic."

Alice glanced quickly over his shoulder at the crystal, then looked away at once.

"Yes, it reminds me of something... But how can it have made such a strong impression on me? I felt as if...well, as if I were completely overwhelmed with sadness."

"Perhaps it's because you're not used to emo crystals. This is the first you've seen, isn't it?" Alice nodded. "I'm starting to understand. It's logical; if you're exposed to it like that all of a sudden without knowing what it is, you could be completely taken over by the effect it produces."

"But...how can a simple play of colors...?"

"It's not just the change of colors. The structure of the crystal itself, the sequence of its shifting glints, is designed to act upon an individual's deepest emotional levels. We know how they work, the effects they produce, and so of course we have a greater resistance; we're accustomed to them."

"But...why was I so sad?"

"Not all emo crystals are the same. Apparently, this one was designed to produce melancholy. There are others that create states of joy, of euphoria, and there are others that aim to restore emotional stability. A specialist could explain a hundred different states to you... Do you feel better now?"

"Yes."

Clyde patted Alice's hands affectionately.

"Fine, you can go on surveying the room then. But be careful with the crystal, right?"

"Don't worry," she smiled.

Aridor's face poked through the curtains.

"Greenaway?"

Clyde and Alice both turned to look at the head of special cases.

"What is it?" asked Clyde.

"The council meeting is about to start."

3

"The person sitting next to Aridor is Hjalmar Domagk; he is representing Zone One, as this is his last year on the council, he is the one with the greatest experience, and he is the chairman. He's a psychosociologist."

Alice considered this tall, strong-looking man with a long face and thoughtful look. She noticed that his blonde, almost white hair was beginning to recede from his high forehead.

"On the other side of Aridor is Nadia Derzhavina, an analyst, representing Zone Two. Next to her is Feng Ai-Ling, a roboticist from Zone Three..."

The old woman of obvious Chinese descent had turned to say something to the white-haired, dark-skinned man alongside her. He began to laugh silently, revealing a set of gleaming white teeth.

"Feng is talking to Felix Vallarta. He's an ecologist, from Zone Five. Beyond the empty chair is Otami Saionji, a historian, representing Zone Seven. You already know her neighbor. She owns this house and is here on behalf of Zone Four."

A small man pushed his way through the curtains and entered the room. His bald, shiny head was in stark contrast to the patchwork of wrinkles covering his face. Leaning on a long staff, he limped over to the empty chair.

"Chandra Raman, a monk. He represents Zone Six," said Clyde hastily.

"A monk?"

"He's a neo-Buddhist, the abbot in a monastery of former Nepal," the psychosociologist explained. He had no time to say anything more, because Hjalmar Domagk had begun to speak.

"Good, now we're all here. I have to tell you that, exceptionally, this meeting is not public. That is to say that it is not being transmitted through any channels to anybody. There are reasons for this. Details of the situation that led the Institute of Sociological Studies to call this emergency meeting are included in the report that you can read on your readers. I recommend that you study it closely."

Six silvery tablets lit up on the surface of the table, and the council members leaned over them.

Now they'll find out... I feel so ashamed...

Alice stirred uneasily on the couch against the wall.

Clyde squeezed her hand.

"There's no need to get nervous; we're not needed yet."

Irritated, Alice withdrew her hand from his.

He doesn't understand...

All at once, Karen Shehan started upright in her chair. Looking up from the report, she stared straight at the young woman from the past.

Alice looked down at the floor.

The silence went on, with the occasional sound of someone clearing their throat or groaning slightly.

Otami Saionji was the first to finish. As she straightened up, there was a look of confusion on her round face.

"This is absurd!" she exclaimed. "It's...cruel and senseless!"

"The others haven't finished reading, Otami," Hjalmar admonished her.

The remaining heads were lifted one by one. Clyde could see how their expressions had changed.

"Has everyone finished?" asked Hjalmar. Then, without waiting for their reply, he went on. "As you will have gathered, this is an extraordinary situation; I don't think the usual procedures apply. If you'll allow me, I'll try to lead our discussion by means of a series of questions..."

"One moment," said Aridor, interrupting him. Everyone around the table looked at him in surprise, but he carried on without hesitation. "This is a violation of the rules, but..."

"Now!" whispered Clyde, and Alice jumped up and stood in the nearest corner of the room, while the psychosociologist stood alert in front of the couch. In their hands, two neurotors were pointing at the council members.

"What is this, Sam?" grunted Hjalmar.

The head of special cases sighed.

"Believe me, I am truly sorry to have to use these prehistoric methods," he told the council chairman. "But I'd be even sorrier if there was somebody we hadn't invited amongst us." He turned to the other members of the council. "I beg you all to remain seated. My colleagues have orders to fire their neurotors at anybody who gets up."

"Neurotors?" asked a startled Otami. "Where did you get weapons like that?"

"Weapons?" Karen Shehan's eyes were wide open. "Weapons?" she repeated in disbelief.

"Greenaway, bring the apparatus," ordered Aridor.

Clyde backed out of the room, his neurotor still leveled at the council members.

Settling in his seat, Aridor explained.

"I can satisfy your curiosity, Otami. We've borrowed the neurotors from a museum. As for what my colleague has gone to fetch, it's an encephalogram. Naturally, the institute has all your mental profiles. In this way, we'll be able to check whether…well, whether we can continue the meeting with all those present."

Felix Vallarta had leaned back in his chair, an amused glint in his eyes.

"I can't help but agree with Otami," he said. "All this is absurd."

Aridor looked at him with interest.

"Would you like to explain why it's absurd?"

The ecologist shrugged his shoulders angrily.

"It's obvious… Just suppose that among us there is—*ahem!*—one of those resurrected imperial creatures. Do you really think that if he threw himself on that girl,"—he pointed to the tense Alice—"she would be brave enough to fire that thing and kill him? I doubt very much that somebody in this day and age would do such a thing, my dear Aridor."

"I don't recommend that you stand up to test your theory, Felix," Otami warned him. "If I remember rightly, the intensity of the rays from the neurotor could be regulated so that they were not fatal. At a low level, they simply paralyze their target. But I don't think it's a pleasant sensation."

"I've no intention of getting up, dear Otami," replied Felix Vallarta with a polite nod of the head. "But if you recall, those resurrected beings come from a very different age than ours. If one of them is present, I wouldn't hesitate to bet on him, even unarmed, against that young girl. I am sure she doesn't have trained reflexes, Aridor. And if your plans to neutralize the threat from the past are as naïve as your present behavior, I seriously doubt if they will work."

"I do not think the tone you are confronting this problem with is correct, Vallarta," Hjalmar Domagk warned him. "But if you value at all the opinion of a specialist, don't make that 'wager,' or whatever you want to call it, against the girl. I wouldn't say the same of the man who has left, but she does have good reflexes, and the willingness to use that...weapon, as far as I can tell. Sam," he said, turning to the head of special cases, "where did you find her?"

Aridor smiled.

"You haven't lost your powers of observation, Hjalmar," he said approvingly. He turned to the others and explained: "She is Alice Welland."

They all turned to look at the girl from the past—except Karen Shehan. Alice gripped the neurotor more tightly. I mustn't be distracted, she told herself.

Clyde Greenaway returned to the room. He was carrying a golden helmet.

"I think I should set the example, shouldn't I?" said Hjalmar.

Aridor nodded.

Clyde carefully fitted the helmet over the chairman's blonde locks.

Alice's eyes closely followed the council members' movements, but they were all staring at Hjalmar Domagk's motionless figure.

"Everything normal," said Clyde.

The head of special cases looked over at the owner of the house.

That's logical, thought Clyde. She's from the zone where Hydra appeared.

"Normal pattern," he declared, a few seconds later.

He noticed how Aridor's body relaxed.

He placed the helmet on Otami's head.

"Normal," he told them.

The old monk had his eyes shut and didn't even open them when Clyde connected the headgear.

"Normal..."

Felix Vallarta's smile radiated out from under the helmet.

"Normal as well."

Feng Ai-Ling's head was almost swallowed up by the apparatus.

"Normal," declared Clyde, then shifted the encephalogram to Nadia Derzhavina. A moment later, he removed it.

"All those present show the correct mental profile, Aridor," reported the psychosociologist.

The head of special cases nodded.

"You two may leave."

Clyde and Alice left the room.

"The meeting can continue, Hjalmar," Aridor said to the chairman.

XXIII

An Essential Problem

1

THEY SAT BESIDE THE BAY WINDOW.

From the top of the cliff, the gulls flying over the sea looked like white dots swaying, climbing, and falling against the blue backdrop.

"It's a shame," murmured Alice.

The psychosociologist turned to gaze at her.

"A shame? Why?"

Alice shrugged.

"I know it's silly...but I wish one of them had been here. To be like this, not knowing anything about them, what they're doing, what they're planning..." she turned her green eyes toward Clyde. "I'm afraid of the unknown."

He nodded.

"Clyde! What happened to the...old man we captured?"

The psychosociologist's eyes narrowed.

"Didn't Aridor explain?"

"No. He only told me he was dead. And that you would explain to me later. They were all so busy, and I had to respond to so many questions and prepare for this meeting." She shook her head, and her hair rippled around her shoulders. "It all seems like a dream. Or rather, a nightmare..."

Clyde rubbed his neck.

"He tried to escape, and... Alice, we know so little about how the people from your time behave... He was hanging out of a window, and his hands gave way. He fell from too high up..."

Alice stared at him.

"And I imagine that shook them, didn't it? They feel guilty for his death, even if it was unintended?"

"Yes...that's right."

Her green eyes had darkened.

"If there's anything I regret about the passage of these two hundred years, it's this stupid sentimentality you have. No one needs to feel sorry about the death of any of them. They're not human beings."

"What if it had been Stephen Houdry?"

Alice's cheeks lost their color.

"Stephen?" she said, with a shudder. "Don't be absurd, Clyde. Stephen is not a murderer. He's practically been abducted by them. Haven't you been able to find him?" she asked, hardly disguising her anxiety.

"We found his body. Apparently he transferred to another one."

The girl sighed and looked back again at the sea.

"*They* got there first," she said, sighing again. "You can't imagine how much I miss him, Clyde. It seems like centuries since..." She broke off and licked her lips. "Have you never been in love?" she asked.

The psychosociologist coughed.

"Yes," he answered.

Her smiling eyes returned to his.

"No, Clyde. At least, not the way I love him."

He looked away, and she continued.

"No, you can't imagine. For me, he is... Well, he is what he is," she said, still smiling. Then her smile vanished. "But the others...

the others are murderers. Like the one who disguised himself in Lardner's body after killing him, and who wanted to kill us, too..."

"I've wanted to ask you for a long time. How did you discover that he was...that he wasn't Lardner?"

She raised her eyebrows to show how puzzled she was as well.

"Well, I really don't know... It's instinctive, something you couldn't understand. You feel the effect, but how you got there... Look," she said abstractedly. "You weren't expecting Lardner to come and see you at that moment, were you?"

"No."

"I must have perceived your surprise. Also, I'm sure I must have automatically mistrusted anyone who came into your department at that moment. It was very important to them that nothing got out. I was sure they would try to silence me...and then Lardner arrived. He was your boss, wasn't he? He could have had some reason to see you. But in person? Why didn't he use the videophone? If it was something so important that he almost had to come running to tell you, wouldn't he have wanted to tell you on your own, instead of sitting down to listen to a crazy woman?"

Clyde reflected for a moment, then agreed.

Alice went on.

"From then on I kept my eyes on him all the time...and you know the rest."

The psychosociologist shook his head.

"Frankly, the psychology of the people of your time is so strange... but fascinating," he said.

"And that's what worries me, Clyde. You are too..." She hesitated, searching for the exact word. "...inexpert to confront them."

"That's why you are included in the plan."

She looked at him inquiringly.

"And can you explain exactly what that plan is?"

"It still hasn't been officially approved by the council, but to tell you the truth, I can't see any valid alternative. Do you remember the bodies that the Central Archive left in my department?"

"Yes, they looked far too real," said Alice with a shiver.

"Thirty people saw them before they were removed. There's nothing unusual about that: what was strange was that three persons should have a heart attack at the same time. Okay, let's suppose that one of the curious onlookers was one of the resurrected. According to the information we have, they don't operate alone, do they?" Alice nodded, and Clyde continued. "He, or she, would not find it hard to interpret what they saw: the fake Lardner shot at me, then at you, but you had time to struggle with him, turning the neurotor in his hands and hitting him. The position of the bodies encourages that impression."

The tip of one of Alice's eyebrows lifted to show she did not agree.

"It's not that simple, Clyde. It's not logical; surely the fake Lardner would have shot me first. I was the only one who could have recognized the neurotor and known what it could do. You would have been shocked to see me fall dead and would have made an easy victim... None of their agents would have been so slow witted."

The psychosociologist's brow furrowed.

"You're not wrong," he conceded, looking her in the eye. "But two heart attacks are always more difficult to explain than one. It might have been that I had already been convinced and that therefore the agent decided to get rid of me and force you to leave with him."

She shook her head doubtfully.

"That's a bit far-fetched...but it'll do. So, what then?"

"When they removed the bodies, they picked up the neurotor and put it on my desk."

"I understand... The people who found it might have thought it was an ornament, or something of yours, or even a toy. And now it's the bait in the trap..."

"Exactly."

"And they can't take the risk that anybody, trying to find the cause of those three deaths, should come across that neurotor. Your department is under constant surveillance, isn't it?"

"Central Archive is in charge of..."

An intermittent buzz came from the ring on the psychosociologist's right hand. He straightened in his seat.

"Wombat!" he called out, and the response floated through the air.

"I'm listening."

"This is Clyde Greenaway; top priority."

"I accept priority."

"Put me in contact with Central Archive at once."

The window in front of them turned dark, and the image of Clyde's department appeared on it.

A human figure was moving about inside it.

Alice brought her chair closer to Clyde.

"What is Wombat?" she whispered.

The psychosociologist replied, not taking his eyes off the screen.

"Wombat? Oh, yes; it's the cyber brain of the house. Look!"

The man on the screen had leaned over Clyde's desk. He straightened up, turned on his heel, and left the department.

"He took the neurotor," said the psychosociologist.

"Yes, I saw him, too... Who is he?"

"I only know him by sight. I think he works in the regional bureau, but I don't know in which department... Archive!"

"I'm listening."

"Who is that man? Where does he live?"

"His name is Hans Glieber. He's a psychosociologist and has been working in the Information Department since last month. He's unmarried and doesn't have any children. He lives in an isolated house in Sector 081, Area 4."

The image of a map replaced that of Hans Glieber. Clyde went closer to examine it.

A flickering luminous dot on the map showed where Glieber lived.

Clyde nodded contentedly.

"Look," he said, tracing a dotted line on the screen. "His house is right next to the border with Sector 085...Area 3."

"Harry Mergenthaler's area," murmured Alice.

2

"...before outlining the plan that the Institute of Psychosociological Studies is proposing, we need to discuss the essential problem. Supposing we manage to uncover and capture all the resurrected, what are we to do with them?"

Karen was the first to break the silence.

"The question is irrelevant, Samuel. I'm surprised to hear a psychosociologist suggest it. It's obvious that we should readjust them mentally, removing all their bloodthirsty instincts. And after that...well, after that, they can be sent to Paradise."

Felix Vallarta's eyebrows arched.

"I think you're being too hasty, Karen. It's not so simple; I think you've forgotten their conditioning. Changing their instincts, as you say, is impossible if we don't get rid of that first."

"Well? What's preventing the psychosociologists from finding a way to suppress it?" argued the emotionalist.

"What prevents it is our respect for human life..." said Hjalmar Domagk quietly.

Karen looked at him with surprise.

"What's that got to do with it?"

"A lot, Karen," Aridor suggested. "All we know about that conditioning technique is that Stephen Houdry created it...and that he was the only one who could remove it."

"Couldn't they discover the method from his mind?" asked Feng Ai-Ling.

Aridor gave a sigh.

"We tried to do that, but he died while we were doing so," he said, and went on after a short silence. "It wasn't hard to figure out that he had created the technique; he was proud of it. But if he gave away how the conditioning could be removed, it would seriously compromise his superiors' safety. His own conditioning prevented that in the surest way: by killing him."

"But by studying the other resurrected, we could discover..." began Karen.

"Good heavens, Karen!" muttered Domagk angrily. "Don't you realize that while we are discovering the secret, several of those who have been conditioned will die?"

"I must say, I think the right to live of those resurrected is questionable. Don't you agree, Otami?" Felix Vallarta asked in an even tone.

The historian hesitated before replying.

"In principle..." she began, then fell silent.

"I don't think every case is the same, Felix," said Aridor. "At least we have to consider Alice Welland."

"Yes, Alice Welland cannot be held responsible for the death of Aisha Dewar...and besides, without her we wouldn't have found out about all this," Domagk commented thoughtfully.

"Not so quickly, at least," Aridor pointed out.

"What about the others? Do you have any idea who they are or where they are?"

"The others? No, Felix, we don't know how many of them there are exactly. But as far as we can tell through Houdry, they are former members of the Imperial Security Services: torturers, professional assassins..." said Aridor.

"Who have no doubt played an active role in this Hydra Project," added the ecologist.

"Yes, no doubt about that."

"So their right to live is more than questionable," Felix Vallarta concluded. "But...is there any sense in this discussion? However terrible their crimes may have been, who would be willing to end their lives?"

"I think we're straying from the point," said Aridor. "You still haven't answered my original question: What are we to do with them once we've captured them?"

Feng Ai-Ling shook her head doubtfully.

"Well... send them to a desert island, I suppose."

"And of course they'd be very happy there," Aridor retorted.

Domagk whistled softly.

"I understand, Samuel. Not allowing them to satisfy one of their basic needs would be the most exquisite torture possible."

"I don't follow," said Ai-Ling, frowning. "We could guarantee supplies of water, food, leisure activities, some kind of work..."

"Those are basic needs, Feng, but that's not what they really want. They want...power. Power over other human beings," said Otami with a shudder. "The power of life and death. And not simply over a few, but over all of humanity. To deny them that, not to allow even the possibility of achieving that, would be a real torture for them."

"Without mentioning the possibility of them escaping and all that implies," said Aridor.

"Let's sum up," said Felix Vallarta, raising his right hand. "We can't leave them loose," he said, folding down his first finger. "We can't get rid of their undesirable mental characteristics," he continued, folding down his second finger. "And it isn't possible to isolate them from humanity, because that would be to deny them their twisted needs, which would be completely inhuman." He bent his ring finger and lowered his hand altogether. "Very well, Samuel, you've done what you set out to do. We've no idea what the answer is. What does the institute suggest?"

"The institute thinks that first and foremost we have to decide whether the resurrected have the right to live. Apart from Alice Welland, of course."

Domagk looked at him inquisitively.

"Do you realize what you're asking of us, Samuel?"

"Of course I do," replied Aridor, fixing his black-eyed gaze on the chairman of the council. "What alternative is there, Hjalmar? We can't leave that pack of rabid wolves on the loose. We can't cure them, or pen them up... Of course, they can't turn back history, but how many truly human lives will it cost if we don't stop them? Every time they want to change bodies..."

"And if we try to capture them, we'll bring on those changes ourselves, won't we?"

Aridor wagged his finger.

"I have complete faith in our institute's plan, Hjalmar. But for it to work, we need..."

"...the Supreme Council to authorize the killing of human beings, Samuel?"

Samuel Aridor's shoulders rose slightly.

"I doubt whether they can be called that. And as the institute's representative, I reiterate our request."

Felix Vallarta objected.

"But such a vote is meaningless from the start, Samuel. Where will you find anyone willing to carry out the sentence?"

"I know that," Karen Shehan interjected, eyes gleaming. "You're counting on the person who has taken over Aisha's body, aren't you?"

"But one girl on her own against all of them won't stand a chance, Samuel."

The facial expression of the head of special cases did not alter.

"Questions of how we will do it are to be discussed later," he said.

Domagk stared intently at Aridor.

"It seems to me you are putting undue pressure on the council, Samuel."

"Why?"

The council chairman folded his hands across his stomach.

"Your entire attitude in this meeting suggests that if your request is not granted, there is no other viable plan to get rid of the resurrected."

"An alternative plan could be devised, Hjalmar. We have not done so as yet because we believe the council will understand that the measure we are calling for is the one that will cost fewer lives..."

"That is obvious," said Nadia, who had been silent until now.

"I don't see why," Ai-Ling retorted.

Nadia sighed.

"I don't think you have considered the implications of capturing these...resurrected...alive. They know how to kill and will do so; they don't have our inhibitions. If we don't agree to the institute's request, a lot more blood will be spilled. I don't even have to mention what condemning these resurrected to perpetual frustration implies."

"All this is sheer madness!" Karen exploded. "You want us to choose between torturing and killing human beings, Samuel. I refuse to make a choice like that."

Hjalmar Domagk's blonde head moved from side to side.

"I'm sorry, Karen, but we cannot abstain. We cannot avoid responsibility, our responsibility." He looked around at all the members of the council. "Does anyone else wish to say anything, before we vote?" he asked.

Silence.

"In that case, as the person who has been on the council the longest, it is for me to vote first. I vote for..." Domagk's voice quavered. "...I vote for prison. I don't think anything justifies denying a human being the right to life; only that person can make that choice."

"I vote for death," said Nadia, but said nothing more. The others stared at her. She understood why they were looking, and sighed. "We are not obliged to justify our own decision... However, I think that this choice will mean less blood is shed."

Everyone turned to look at Feng Ai-Ling.

The roboticist blushed.

"I vote for prison...and have no intention of justifying myself."

Karen Shehan hesitated for a few moments.

"I repeat that all this is absurd," she said. "But I could never sleep knowing that I had condemned someone to die. I vote for prison."

"For death," muttered Felix Vallarta. "I'm not so inhuman I want to condemn them to live..."

With his eyes tight shut, the monk appeared to be dozing. Otami stretched out a hand toward him, but before she could touch him, Chandra Raman began to speak.

"The Buddha forbade us to harm any living being... Therefore, I am not at liberty to choose how I vote; the enlightened one has already decided. I vote for their death," he said, opening his eyes. "The real owners of the bodies they are occupying have already departed this world. There is no law, human or divine, that protects the life of a devil that has usurped another being's body," he said, then closed his eyes once more.

Now everyone turned their gaze on Otami Saionji.

"I am possibly allowing myself to be influenced too much by my profession, but I cannot forget the harm they caused in the time they first lived. I don't think I have the right to put humanity at risk because of the softness of my own heart. I vote for death."

3

On the screen, the walls moved to and fro, but the figure of the man walking down the corridors of the regional bureau remained in focus the whole time.

"Why doesn't he realize?"

"Realize what?"

"That the camera is following him," Alice explained. "Until now, he hasn't looked back, but as soon as he does, he'll realize he is being watched."

Clyde smiled.

"Central Archive isn't so naïve. It must be following him with an eye."

"A what?"

"An eye. It's a cyber register created for ecological studies in our nature reserves. It's practically invisible, so that it doesn't frighten or disturb the animals being observed; it's tiny and transparent."

Glieber had sat down at a table. The eye was now focused on him from in front, with his calm face in the center of the screen.

"There's something about this I don't like," said Alice.

"What's that?"

"I don't know... He looks too calm to me. If he was one of *them* he wouldn't be like that. He would at least have glanced over his shoulder when he left your department."

The psychosociologist shrugged.

"Remember, he's a specialist in this field, Alice."

"Clyde, I remember the people from my time very clearly. Nobody, not even the person least interested in politics, could appear to be so calm. You can't imagine what the atmosphere of suspicion, of constant tension was like back then. No, however good an agent he is, he can't be so sure of himself."

"I must confess I only know of the time you lived in through a few references, but as I understand it, a good agent was capable of adapting to a new situation whatever his previous habits had been."

Alice leaned back in her chair, tilting her head to one side.

"Possibly then I'm not a good agent. I still haven't learned how to adopt that pose of indifference. Alright, so the trap worked... What now?"

"Now we watch him closely. We watch all the contacts he makes, and we follow them, too."

Alice frowned.

"That way we're going to end up keeping watch on everybody in the world..."

C

This is the third part of the test. It is strictly your own work; you must complete it on your own, without discussing your answers with anyone. If you do not wish to complete it, continue to the next page.

1. If you had been one of the participants at the gathering of the council, how would you have voted? Select one of the following answers:

   a) I would have voted for death.

      Would you be prepared to kill your brother? What if all of the human beings in the world were your brothers? (Before answering these questions we recommend that you complete a study of the Judeo-Christian myth of Cain.)

   b) I would have voted for imprisonment.

      Have you ever tried going without breathing, drinking, eating, or sleeping? Has anyone ever attempted to deprive you of air, water, food, or sleep? Are you an advocate of physical torture or only of the moral variety?

   c) I would have abstained.

      Do you have a clear idea of the concept of cowardice? Does this definition include the avoidance of necessary decisions that you find difficult?

GO TO THE NEXT PAGE

d) I wasn't there; why should I concern myself with the decision? Are you familiar with this statement?

"The easiest way to solve a problem is to deny it exists."

ISAAC ASIMOV,
THE GODS THEMSELVES

Do you think that this could have any relationship to your answer?

2. State your opinion on the following lines of verse by the Soviet poet Yuri Levitansky:

Each one chooses his measure
A word for love and speech-making
A sword for grief and struggle
Each man chooses for himself.

What have you chosen for yourself?

This test will continue later. You may change your answers at any point.

TURN TO THE NEXT PAGE

XXIV

The Cybos Decide

1

"**WOULD YOU LISTEN TO ME** a moment, Karen!"

With a deep intake of breath the emotionalist settled into her seat. "I'm listening."

Nadia Derzhavina rested her hands on the table.

"You have no reason to think that this meeting and in particular the order of the articles for discussion were arranged with the express intention of upsetting you. The sequence in which Aridor has chosen to present the problems is the most appropriate. There is the objective we hope to attain in the first place, then there are the measures necessary to get there. Before we have these aspects clearly laid out it is useless to discuss the details of any plan. Understood?"

"Yes," hissed the lady of the house. "I understand that all of this is far too rational for an ignorant emotionalist."

Otami touched Karen's shoulder gently.

"Don't take it like that... Everyone here is necessary; each one of us brings something special of ourselves and at the same time something quite ordinary within the breadth of the humanity that we represent."

Karen stuck her chin out defiantly.

"Of course we are here representing humanity! And this problem is about our responsibility and just that. What have the cybos got to do with any of this? How can anyone suggest that we go to them, begging that they help us?" she said. "How can you propose such a thing?" she asked Aridor directly, turning toward him.

"I don't feel the slightest personal sympathy for the cybos, Karen," Aridor responded calmly, "but it is a fact that they exist. Here on Earth. This problem affects the whole planet, them included."

"Them included? They would be capable of an alliance with the resurrected."

"I'm sorry, Karen," Domagk intervened. "I've had the opportunity to work with the cybos. I don't sympathize with their...decision either, but I know enough about them that I don't believe in the possibility of an alliance between them and the resurrected. The question is," he continued, now addressing them all, "do we really need their help?"

"Allow me to put the question another way, Hjalmar," said Nadia. "Would any ordinary human being of our time, even with our authorization, be prepared to kill the resurrected?"

"None would, of course," responded Felix Vallarta, "but in my opinion the cybos are not our only option; there are also the groups."

"Good heavens!" Karen could not help exclaiming, and under the inquisitive gaze of the ecologist she gave him a brilliant smile. "Nothing! Everything's fine, my dear... Go ahead."

"You'll have to forgive me, Felix," said Aridor, leaning forward, "but I see more disadvantages than advantages to your idea. The groups don't know Earth, or our customs or way of life, and, given their characteristics, it would be difficult for them to assimilate. What's more, they would be too conspicuous, easy to identify. No doubt they also share our repugnance for killing; they are closer to our kind of...personality than the cybos."

"I don't disagree with what you say, Samuel, but I wasn't referring to the solar-system groups, but to the mentagroups."

"The Aurorans? I don't see what advantages they would bring..."

"Their telepathy; they can read minds. That way they could easily identify the resurrected."

Aridor let out a sigh.

"I'm afraid you haven't been properly informed, Felix. Their telepathy only works within their group. It is a question of personal affinity... I don't think they would have that for the resurrected."

The ecologist looked thoughtfully at the head of special cases.

"So...that leaves the cybos."

The representative from the institute looked around at the faces of all those at the table.

"I don't think you've fully grasped the implications of the matter," he muttered. "Suppose we don't turn to the cybos for help. Do you have any idea of how to identify the resurrected?"

"Well... By their brain-wave profiles?" suggested Ai-Ling.

"Do you remember the body Stephen Houdry occupied?" asked Aridor. He paused. "Now do you understand? Nothing is simpler for a psychosociologist than to disrupt his patients' encephalograms."

"But it's possible to detect conditioning, Samuel," Domagk pointed out.

"Not as the encephalogram is being recorded."

"So the test we went through at the beginning..." gasped Felix Vallarta, and he stopped without finishing his sentence.

Aridor waved his hand to pacify him.

"Rest assured, it wasn't a normal encephalogram. Yes, in principle there is nothing to stop us manufacturing tens of millions of similar devices to apply the test simultaneously across the entire earth. Naturally this would have to be done with the utmost secrecy. If the resurrected were to hear of it, they could just jump into the bodies of those in charge of applying the tests... And even assuming that we managed to do it, we'd never find the ringleader or ringleaders; it's only logical to predict they wouldn't have undergone conditioning themselves. This would create a very unpleasant atmosphere; everyone would suspect everyone else, fear would become a constant in human relationships...but we would possibly locate a few of the resurrected."

"There's no need to be ironic, Samuel," Domagk muttered gloomily.

"So what can the cybos do to solve the problem? As far as I know they're not magicians," Feng Ai-Ling commented, not yet convinced.

"I think you're forgetting that it's the institute's responsibility to keep a watchful eye on them. We have reasonable grounds to suppose that, if they were so inclined, they could help us in a way that is—how shall I put it?—entirely satisfactory."

"If *they* are so inclined," Felix Vallarta repeated, pulling a face. "I don't much like the sound of that. However, to summarize: there is no other way. Right, Samuel?"

"Does anyone else have anything to say?" asked Domagk.

"I think it goes without saying that if the cybos choose to help us now, our future relations can never be the same," Nadia Derzhavina said gravely.

"No, without a doubt, absolutely not," agreed Otami.

The others remained silent.

"Anything more?" asked Domagk. He waited a prudent interval before continuing. "So, we must decide if we should ask the cybos for help."

"I propose we agree by consensus," said Nadia.

"I agree," replied Domagk, and he turned once more to face the others. "Any objections?"

Silence...

"Then the proposal put forward by the institute is approved, Aridor," declared the council chairman.

"Shall I make contact with the cybos?" asked the institute representative, sounding very formal.

"Yes."

"Wombat, connect me to the cybo coordinator."

"Hmmm! Such an elegant title," muttered the ecologist, not quite under his breath.

On the table top, a three dimensional image appeared in front of Samuel Aridor. White haired, in a white tunic and with black, piercing eyes, a man of advanced years regarded them. He appeared to be seated in mid-air, his wrinkled, veined hands lying folded in his lap. His lips moved.

"I am listening, Aridor."

"Ichabod, I believe you are acquainted with Hjalmar Domagk..."

The aged cybo nodded his head slightly in the direction of the president of the council.

"A problem has cropped up. Something really serious."

Ichabod did not answer.

"Permit me to transmit the report that the institute has prepared."

The cybo coordinator raised a hand, and a video reader appeared before him.

"When you're ready," he said.

Aridor ran his hand along the edge of the table and out slid a tiny control panel. He ran his hands along it.

"There you have it."

Ichabod's gaze tracked vertically over his video reader... With a swift motion of his hand he changed the image displayed on it. In another movement, another change, and another and another... He raised his dark eyes.

"Extremely serious," he commented.

"Has he really read it?" Nadia whispered into Ai-Ling's ear.

"Of course," the analyst replied impatiently, and she returned her attention to what Aridor was now saying.

"I have decided that there is only one solution: to destroy them." Ichabod nodded.

"But to achieve that aim, your collaboration is vital," Aridor concluded.

"In principle we are at your service," said the cybo.

Aridor pressed the keys of the control panel once more.

"On your video reader you will see a copy of the plan we propose."

Ichabod's eyes scanned it quickly, then returned to the representative from the institute.

"It's incomplete."

"We believe that you can complete it more effectively than we could."

The aged cybo nodded slowly.

"I need to consult with the others. I won't be more than five minutes," he said.

Aridor nodded his head in agreement.

"We will wait for you."

The three-dimensional image vanished.

"Very nice, Samuel; you show him the plan before we get to look at it," said Karen with obvious disgust.

"They are the ones who can tell us whether it's possible to achieve or not, my dear," the psychosociologist responded wearily.

"So what do we do now?" asked Ai-Ling.

"We wait."

"Will it take long?"

"Five minutes."

2

Surrounded by a golden sea, Ichabod floated pensively...

"Sarki!" he cried out.

The golden veil tore in front of him; a face peered out at him from inside a blue ovoid.

"You need me?" it asked.

"Yes, proceed with the second variant."

The face betrayed a slight concern.

"So soon? What has happened?"

Ichabod's hands moved rapidly, tracing strange configurations in the air. The face within the ovoid looked downward, beyond the cybo coordinator's field of vision. A moment later the eyes looked up.

"Pure chance."

"Indeed," Ichabod agreed. "Send Maya."

Sarki's eyebrows arched higher.

"She's still not finished."

"There's no other solution. Look at the alternatives."

The face inside the blue ovoid closed its eyes. Ichabod waited, patiently, for almost a minute...

Sarki's expression returned to normal. The eyes opened.

"You're right," he conceded. "She must go. Now."

3

Karen fidgeted nervously in her seat.

"Are the five minutes up yet, Samuel?"

Aridor didn't bother to check the time.

"It can't be more than two minutes so far, my dear," he replied.

The emotionalist let out a snort.

"It's strange," said Feng Ai-Ling, not speaking to anyone in particular.

"What's strange?" asked Vallarta.

Ai-Ling shrugged.

"I don't know, it's just that cybo... I didn't imagine them like that."

A tiny half-smile passed across Nadia's face.

"You were expecting to see a glassy-eyed monster with a plastic skull, right?"

The roboticist smiled involuntarily.

"Something like that, I won't deny it."

"Your mistake is quite common, Ai-Ling," Aridor explained. "Most people think that to become a cybo, a human being has to undergo complicated operations to implant microcybernetic systems in the brain... But it's not like that."

"So, what is it like?"

"You know how cybernetics came about through the fusion of studies into the human brain and inanimate self-regulating systems: the majority of modern cybernetic systems have a functional system that is compatible with the human brain."

"But from that to a cybo..."

Aridor waved his hand dismissively.

"The majority of cybos are produced by straightforward cybernetic-suggestion mechanisms; in essence it's more like a reorganization of the brain than an addition to it, so as to acquire the same advantages as an artificial brain: speed, an increased number of operations performed per unit of time, parallel processing..."

"It makes no sense," Felix Vallarta commented, shaking his head. "Anyone could get all that from their household brain."

"Not quite, Vallarta; ask Ai-Ling about the work the cybos do in her field. It is undeniable that they have certain advantages... What is more open to question in the case of the cybos, are the side effects of their transformation."

"The disappearance of any emotional component," said Karen.

Aridor objected.

"Not exactly their disappearance. Certain aspects are reduced, that's all, and others...well, the best way to describe it is to say that they are transformed."

"And that is precisely the root of the cybos' inhumanity," declared the emotionalist. "It is the abyss that separates them from normal human beings; at that price I would prefer to give up all their discoveries, however brilliant they are."

"But..." Nadia began to speak, but left off when she saw the image of Ichabod reappear, hovering above the table top.

Aridor straightened in his chair.

"Well?" he asked.

The projection made an affirmative gesture.

"We can do it."

"Have you completed the plan? I mean to say, have you made modifications to what was already laid out?"

"No. We will send Maya to you."

Aridor's forehead creased.

"I don't know her."

"She is new. She will reach you in an hour and a half."

"Thank you for your help, Ichabod."

The projection lowered his head and disappeared.

"Whoa! I know what Karen means," Vallarta commented. "They may look completely human, but they send a shiver down my spine."

4

Inside was darkness.

Sarki halted. He turned, moving his head slowly to take in his surroundings; he did not see even the tiniest crack of light.

He listened attentively, and the silence was dark, too...

He made an invisible gesture of approval and began to focus his thoughts.

On his retinas, vague silhouettes of indefinable color appeared and disappeared: pulsating circles, slippery ovals, and broken lines... That one.

Fixing his gaze on the point, he concentrated hard.

The lines sharpened and faded with an uneven rhythm... Gradually, the contours of a human body became discernible.

The young woman was seated on the ground, hugging her legs against her chest, her chin resting on her knees. Her eyes had an almost phosphorescent glow.

"That's quite enough, Maya."

The outline in the darkness smiled; the next moment, everything was light.

"Forgive me, master," said the young woman, sounding worried, and the light became weaker, like a spider web at night. Slowly the light strengthened again.

Sarki seated himself opposite Maya, cross-legged on the soft floor of the room.

"You've made good progress," he said.

"Thank you..."

"You leave today."

A vertical line appeared on the young woman's forehead.

"I didn't realize I had finished."

"You have not finished."

The young woman waited.

"Look," said Sarki, extending his first finger. In front of his interlocutor a glimmering, semitransparent tablet appeared. Black lines zig-zagged rapidly across it... The young woman watched it attentively until they disappeared.

"I understand," she said.

"You will have three days before you go into action."

"Yes."

"In that time you can finish your training."

"Alone?"

Sarki's thin lips stretched into a smile.

"There isn't much left for me to teach you... Pay attention."

Their gaze met and remained locked for some time, and then they parted.

"Is that all?" asked Maya.

Sarki shook his head.

"All that I know; not all that you should know."

A slight shadow crossed the young woman's face.

"Too little time," she said.

"Too little," Sarki agreed. "Good luck, Maya."

With an effortless movement the young woman rose.

"Thank you, master."

XXV

Maya's Arrival

1

GETTING UP FROM HER SEAT, Alice stretched, hands on hips.

"I can't bear it anymore," she cried. "Are we going to have to watch that man for the rest of eternity?"

"You don't have to keep watch yourself," Clyde replied, not moving his eyes from the screen. "To be honest, I'm of little use here. Archive will notice anything amiss." Briefly he tore his gaze away from the screen to smile at the woman. "Even so, we mustn't let our guard down."

"And you have to spend all your time watching and watching?"

"No. I hope that this afternoon's meeting will be over soon. After that I'm sure that Aridor will establish a rota... Don't worry, I don't think it will include you."

"Why not?"

"Because you will be the one who will have to intervene if anything happens."

"Me, alone?" asked Alice, surprised. "Clyde," she quickly added, "it's just that against them I have about as much chance as a defenseless baby."

Clyde made a dismissive gesture with his hand, without taking his eyes from Glieber's image.

"Not alone; you will have support."

"If they are like you... Excuse me, it's not that I underestimate them. But it's just that even the minimal requirements for this won't be an easy adjustment for them," she fixed her inquisitive stare on the psychosociologist.

"Clyde, I can only imagine you must all see me as some kind of monster."

Impulsively, the man turned toward at her.

"Good heavens, no!" he exclaimed, before regaining control of himself. "You are a human being—as I understand it, an admirable one. It wasn't easy choosing the right path of your own accord, but you did it."

A smile spread slowly across the young woman's face.

"Thank you, Clyde... You're a good friend."

The psychosociologist blushed; he did not respond, returning his attention to the screen.

Alice paced around the room, deep in thought. She came back toward him.

"I'm sorry; I know I'm irritable, upset... I must be difficult to put up with."

"Not at all."

She smiled.

"I appreciate you being so polite, but no one knows better than I do... Clyde, it's just that I miss him so much. Most of all now. Yesterday was such an intense day, so complicated, that I haven't even had time to remember him, but now... How can anyone live without the one they love?"

Clyde muttered something under his breath. Coming to a halt, Alice turned around to face him.

"Did you say something? I'm sorry, but I didn't hear."

"No, nothing... Simply that I understand."

Alice sat on the arm of the chair and rested a hand on the psychosociologist's back.

"You understand? No, you don't understand," she said, and continued speaking almost to herself. "Would he understand?"

"Who?" whispered Clyde.

"Stephen, of course... Who else? Would he understand that what I did, I did out of love for him?"

"Just out of love for him?"

Alice raised her head:

"Well, not just out of love for him... But that's the only way that I hope to save him from *them*—so that he can be himself, truly..." Her fingers dug into the psychosociologist's shoulder. "Clyde, will they kill him?"

"Umm, I don't think so."

"After all, they might think he was responsible for my escape; he loved me so much... But no, that wouldn't make sense; they must realize that he knew nothing, that he is not to blame..."

She buried her head in his back, her hair tickling his manly neck.

"I'm so afraid, Clyde," she said, choking, "I feel that if he dies, I'll die, too..."

The psychosociologist sat up in the chair and took her by the shoulders. He looked into her tear-filled eyes.

"Don't be afraid. I'll help you."

2

"That is what we were considering in the plan, Hjalmar. We don't believe that that task should be left unsupervised," Aridor retorted, clarifying himself. "We would be most comfortable if the operational center could be here; Karen's house is isolated and no one would be surprised by unusual comings and goings... But we can't all stay here."

The chairman of the council gestured his assent.

"I agree, Sam; there is a precedent. On certain occasions, to control the execution of tasks of particular importance, the council has designated a commission to represent it... Unfortunately, my work commitments do not permit me to stay here indefinitely," he said, shaking his head.

"Hjalmar, you should consider staying here yourself. You need to take into account the fact that your second-in-command is in no condition..." said Karen, then stopped short as she looked across at the analyst.

Nadia Derzhavina was eying her coldly.

"My personal difficulties do not affect my responsibilities, Karen. I am grateful for your concern, but I am perfectly willing to undertake this mission."

"Forgive me if I have offended you, Nadia; it's only because I am worried about you, about the..." she fell silent, not knowing how to continue. "Oh, to hell with it all! Forget I said anything."

"It's forgotten."

"So, if we can get on," said Hjalmar, and he began to set out his proposal. "Karen should also be a member of the commission; this is her house and her zone." The named delegate shrugged her shoulders slightly. "Very well. To me it seems we only need one more councillor to complete the commission. Who can we have as the third?"

"If nobody objects," Felix Vallarta intervened, "I would like to see how this all ends."

"Is anyone else interested in participating?" asked Hjalmar, glancing questioningly around at the other members of the council.

Ai-Ling shook her head; the monk didn't open his eyes.

"I think that with them," Otami declared, "we'll have more than enough, Hjalmar."

"I think we can now conclude the meeting, Sam," said the chairman of the council.

"Let's not forget one last detail," replied Aridor.

"What's that?"

"The security measures... Under no circumstances must the resurrected come to know anything about what has been discussed here."

"We are hardly indiscreet," protested Ai-Ling.

"I know, Feng. But can you guarantee they won't try to possess the body of one or other of you in order to access your memories?"

"Then what must we do?"

"I know that the honorable Chandra doesn't pose any problem," said Aridor, acknowledging the monk with a small inclination of his head, "if he decides to forget what has happened here."

The monk moved his hand in a sign of agreement.

"Thank you, Chandra," said Aridor. He looked around at the others again. "But nobody else here has the same level of mental control; we will have to help you."

"But, Sam, a memory gap is as significant as the memory itself," protested Hjalmar.

"We won't just wipe it out; you will all remember that there was a meeting of the council that took place here."

"Well, if that's the case, we trust you," the chairman conceded.

"If you allow it then, I will get in touch with Greenaway," said Aridor. "Wombat!" he called.

"I am listening."

"Get me Clyde Greenaway."

A projection of the living room sprang up from the table top. At its center, Clyde was supporting the young woman from the past. Alice was burying her head on the man's chest, her body shaking convulsively.

"Greenaway!"

The man raised his eyes.

"Did the trap work?" asked Aridor.

"Yes, about half an hour ago..."

"Wait for me there," the head of special cases requested as he got up from his seat and strode out of the room.

3

Hysteria, it's nothing more than pure hysteria. What happened to your serenity? Alice asked herself, and kicked a pebble.

The pebble leapt, rebounded against others, and came to a stop once more.

Looking up, Alice took in the arid landscape around her.

For so long you were a desert like this... Why him and why now, exactly? She pursed her lips. No, that's not right; it would do as much good to regret being born... I must confront the situation, she told herself, and she clasped her hands to her chest. But how to do this with such anguish that it stops me from thinking? She sighed. Just as well that Clyde is intelligent; he had understood she needed solitude, to unburden herself, that she couldn't be with them a moment longer without having a screaming fit. And they didn't deserve that; they were wonderful people. Why did I fall in love with Stephen and not with one of them?

Despite herself, she smiled. You're just running from the problem again... Sort it out. You are in love with Stephen, and you wouldn't change this feeling for all the world. Yes, it hurts, the pain of separation, but this pain is nothing. Nothing! Compared to the richness blossoming inside you. She looked at the sands surrounding her; it was as if this desert were to flower, transforming itself into a mighty jungle—terrible, yes, but pulsing with life.

She followed the aircraft with her eyes as it approached the esplanade.

This must be the last one... She hesitated and looked toward the house, undecided. Should she go back? Then what? Would I be better off here than there? In any case I would miss *him*. At least there I can fight to rescue him, she decided, and set off back.

I don't know what I'd do without Clyde... He understands me, yes, and he is the only person close to me now that Stephen is no longer here... But he can't, he just can't replace him. Stephen, Stephen, why didn't you escape, too? But no; now they will need to watch you more, they won't trust you. I shouldn't have fled without having persuaded you first... Stop right there! You know very well that he wouldn't have understood... But would it really have been like that? she asked herself. Without realizing it, she wrung her hands.

No, you shouldn't let yourself be driven by your doubts; you had plenty of time to think about it. Now you must act, you must save him, you cannot make mistakes, no dithering, you must not allow yourself to be ruled by such paralyzing terror... But can anyone think, think straight, in this state? Drowning in these tides of fear? Ahh... What she wouldn't give for the mental clarity that she had had before... The ability to think coolly, clearly, objectively and to find the solution and to wait, calm and sure of herself, indifferent even... But I can't, she said gritting her teeth. And I must carry on, going mad little by little until I begin to scream. No, get a hold on yourself. Control yourself. Harness that strength that is love, master it and use it to save him. Right? So, enough, she ordered herself, and she walked up to the esplanade.

315

4

The men watched Alice walking in the sand.

"I worry that she won't be able to bear much more," said Clyde.

"As you administer the treatment she will improve."

Clyde Greenaway raised his head.

"It will merely ensure she does not go mad and die. But I refuse to watch as that brilliant mind disintegrates... We are not removing the cause of her unbalance, Aridor."

"There is no other solution."

"There has to be!"

The head of special cases fixed his eyes on Clyde.

"There isn't," he repeated.

"Excuse me for interrupting you," said Karen, and the men turned toward the new arrival. "If you wish, I can show you your rooms now..."

Aridor smiled.

"You mean the rooms for Greenaway and Welland; if you remember, I am leaving."

"That's a shame," said Karen, returning his smile. "But I hope you'll return when you can."

"You can be sure of that... Ah, I nearly forgot; make sure that the rooms for Greenaway and Welland are next to each other."

"If they want, I can make up one room for the pair of them."

"No, it's not what you think," replied Aridor. "It's just that she has been very affected by what has happened and Greenaway is treating her; he needs to be close by."

The emotional engineer shrugged her shoulders.

"I see," she said, and turning to Clyde she added, "if you'd like to view the rooms..."

"As soon as Aridor leaves."

Karen turned to the head of special cases.

"So, you're not waiting until the cybo arrives?"

"I have work I need to attend to," replied Aridor, making for the Hermes. "You take care of receiving her."

"Me? Welcome the cybo?" guffawed the emotionalist. "I don't doubt she is clever enough to find the way from the esplanade to the house."

Aridor stopped at the hatchway to his aircraft.

"Please, Karen; control your prejudices. Show her at least the bare minimum of courtesy."

"Is that even necessary? They have no emotions, Sam; she can't feel offended."

"No, but that is no justification for us not to behave like people... Welcome her. Do it as a personal favor to me."

Karen nodded.

"As you wish," she agreed.

5

One last step, and I'll finish the climb. Alice surveyed the group assembled in front of the house and the craft landing on the esplanade.

The cybo is arriving, she concluded. What had Aridor said her name was? Maya. Perhaps she was of Indian ancestry, thought Alice, and she walked toward the people awaiting the landing. She could feel the swirl of air against her right shoulder as the spaceraft descended.

What a strange society...and fascinating, she told herself. It was hard to understand; two hundred years had not passed for nothing. New problems, new attitudes... But they still hadn't begun to understand her. To assimilate her. To *accept her*. Yes, there was much that was good, that was indisputable. The old material problems had been resolved, without a shadow of a doubt. And what of the spiritual ones? It wouldn't be fair to deny that these were excellent, magnificent people, but, nevertheless...

She could tell from the attitude of those waiting that the craft and its passenger had landed; soon he would disembark... No, she corrected herself, *she* would disembark. She turned to face the aircraft and stopped; it was closer to her than the others.

She examined the streamlined profile of the Albatross... It had clearly been designed to reach very high speeds; otherwise it could never have covered the distance between here and the Isle of the Cybos in just over an hour. She watched as the hatch opened. To renounce one's individual self, to become a thinking machine— how could anyone in this age contemplate it? It was a bad sign. Although the contradiction between the necessity of learning and limited mental capacity... She's nothing but a child! *Against them?*

She felt a presence at her side and took a quick sideways glance: Clyde. By the look of it he had come forward to receive the cybo... How slender and tiny... Yes, she must be a woman already, but... such expressive eyes!

Impulsively her hand shot out.

"Welcome. I am Alice."

A smile lit up the face of the newly arrived guest.

"And I am Maya."

XXVI

A Dangerous Game

1

THE BRAMBLE'S THICK, stunted leaves were a startling green. Judging by how short their shadows were, the sun must be at its highest point in the sky. The horizon line quivered, disturbed by the hot air rising from the sands...

"A call from Samuel Aridor, Greenaway," Wombat informed him.

"Put him through," Clyde replied, looking away from the wall that had been transformed into a window.

The desert disappeared, replaced by the image of Aridor seated in his office.

"Has something new happened?" asked the psychosociologist.

Aridor shook his head.

"No, nothing... I wanted to check through some of the details of your work."

Clyde raised his eyebrows.

"But we've already discussed it, haven't we?"

Aridor indicated the couch the psychosociologist was standing next to.

"Sit down, Greenaway..." The young man obeyed. "I want you to appreciate all the subtleties of your task thoroughly."

"What subtleties?"

"It doesn't concern only Alice Welland... You're with a group of people with very different characters. You'll have to wait together, possibly for several days, until something happens. Tensions are bound to run high."

"I can imagine," responded the psychosociologist.

"I am sure that you have already noticed the... shall we say, excessive emotionality of Karen Shehan."

Clyde nodded.

"I've been studying her psychological profile."

"Well done. Have you seen that she knew Aisha Dewar?"

"Yes."

Aridor rested his elbows on the table in front of him.

"Expect very contradictory behavior from her... In principle anything is possible."

"I understand," replied Clyde, making himself comfortable on the couch.

"As for the others, you can count on the support of Felix Vallarta." He smiled. "The old fox can come across as a bit of an irresponsible kid, but behind that façade lies an acute intelligence; he is a keen observer and reacts quickly."

Clyde concurred.

"I'd noticed something of that already."

"Over time you will come to appreciate it more... It is a shame about the ovo incident; otherwise Nadia Derzhavina would have been your most invaluable assistant."

"It's a great shame, yes... But she seems recovered."

"No, not completely. I would have liked you to have known her before."

Clyde crossed his legs under his body.

"Anything else? I mean, anything important that I need to take into account?"

Aridor chewed his lower lip.

"Yes, there is something else. In fact, it's the most fundamental thing."

The psychosociologist blinked.

"The most fundamental?"

"The cybo."

Clyde couldn't help but smile.

"Her?" He shook his head. "I don't think that there is any danger that she will let herself be carried away by her emotions!"

"No, not her." Aridor conceded, without smiling. "You've never worked with cybos before, right?"

"No."

"Have you ever asked why the institute never lets them leave their island?"

"No... Thinking about it, I assumed it was something similar to the restrictions applied to the primitives."

Aridor waved his hand.

"The prims can't leave Paradise, but that's a measure designed to protect them. The cybos must not leave their island: to protect us."

"I don't understand," said Clyde.

"The institute's experience—and mine, too, by the way—indicates that when humans come into contact with cybos they experience extreme emotional disturbances."

Clyde hesitated before asking.

"Can you tell me how...?"

"...to neutralize the effect?" Aridor finished his question and shook his head. "We don't know. But I can give you some advice."

"I'm listening."

"Treat her as you would any normal person."

"How exactly?"

"Try to see her like a normal person. Someone with a few peculiarities: low expressivity, inexplicable responses, surprising points of view... And remain vigilant of your own emotional responses; they will surprise you."

"If only I could anticipate some of these responses..."

"They are different in each person; the only thing you can do is be ready for them... Ah, and you can count on her to do everything possible to diminish her negative effects; the cybos are aware of the reaction they provoke in us."

Clyde glanced over his shoulder at the door of the room.

"Don't worry too much, Greenaway," Aridor said with a smile. "It's only that I want to avoid you trusting too much."

The psychosociologist gave him the shadow of a smile in return. "You've achieved that much."

"A little too well, I fear..." He reached out his hand to the control panel on his table. "I'll keep you abreast of matters."

Aridor disappeared, and the desert landscape returned.

Clyde watched dust devils lift the sand and drop it according to the whims of the hot breeze. He sighed.

2

"Okay, Felix, or have you gotten too old?"

The bronzed ecologist parted his lips to reveal a set of brilliant white teeth.

"Don't provoke me, Karen, or you'll discover that despite my sixty odd years I am in fine condition—and for more than just a game of wasps..."

The emotionalist's eyes were suddenly alight with a malicious glint.

"Oh yeah? Are you really that dangerous?" she asked with fake innocence. "Perhaps you interest me because of your hidden talents," she added, "but later this afternoon the conditions will be ideal for wasps, you old satyr. Would you prefer one or two?"

"Two."

Karen arched an eyebrow appreciatively.

"Two, really? Are you sure?"

"Are *you* sure?"

The emotionalist wrapped him in a look of apparent sympathy.

"Poor thing... How he tries to keep up his reputation... In that case, we'll need some people to accompany us to carry you back afterward."

Continuing to smile, Felix Vallarta leaned back on his bench and stretched open his arms expressively.

"We'll see who gets brought back on someone else's shoulders, my dear."

Karen cast her eyes around the room.

"Who's willing to help me bring Felix back?" she asked, and went over to Nadia Derzhavina, who was sitting in front of the screen. "Are you coming with us, Nadia?"

Without looking away from the image of Glieber working in his laboratory, the analyst shook her head.

"It's my turn to watch."

Moving behind her, Karen rested her hands on Nadia's shoulders.

"Don't let that bother you, my dear," she replied. "I'm quite sure the Central Archive will have the good manners to let us know if that man does anything out of the ordinary."

"Don't be so undisciplined, Karen... Or at least don't try to make me so."

She removed her hands from the analyst's shoulders.

"Alright, alright; I respect your sense of duty. But... What's her name? Ah yes. Maya. Maya can keep watch for a while. I have it on good authority that they aren't interested in games."

Clyde took a sly glance at the slender figure sitting on the bench next to Nadia.

Maya was watching the screen attentively, without giving any indication of having heard Karen.

The best policy, Clyde thought approvingly, and turned his attention back to the emotionalist; she was coming over to him now.

"And you, sir, the esteemed psychosociologist? I think you're far too young to sit around all day."

Clyde smiled, ever polite.

"I appreciate your concern, but..."

"Aha, of course; you can't leave your patient, right? Well, okay then," she went on, looking at each of them in turn. "We'll take her with us! Where is she?" she asked, turning back to the psychosociologist.

Clyde hesitated a second... Agitated behavior, and that look in her eyes... Maya's influence? No, she was like that before.

Reluctantly he answered.

"I think she's in her room."

"I'll go look for her," the emotionalist declared. "And you, Felix, get the wasps and take them to the esplanade."

"Where are they?"

"Why are you asking me? Check with Wombat," snapped Karen as she passed through the curtains hiding the main passageway into the house.

Felix Vallarta remained seated, slowly shaking his head... He commented in a whisper to Clyde.

"I am afraid Karen would never get over it if she learned that it was in fact the cybos who invented the wasps game," he said.

"Wombat!" he called out.

"I'm listening."

"Get me two sets of double wasps."

324

At once, two silver-plated boxes appeared on the table in front of Clyde and Felix.

"We've been served," said the ecologist, picking up the two sets.

"Shall we walk?" he asked, getting up from his seat.

"Let's go." The psychosociologist accepted his invitation and stood up to leave.

3

Karen came to a halt outside the door.

It imitated a primitive style: thick planks of varnished wood and straight rows of nails, each with a resplendent head...

She called out loudly.

"Alice!"

Alice's high-pitched voice came through the door.

"Who is it?"

"Um, Karen. I've come to invite you to see a wasp contest."

"A wasp contest? I'd love to. Who's taking part?"

"Felix and me. Greenaway is coming with us, to help bring the loser back to the house," said the emotionalist, laughing.

"I'll come, as soon as I've finished bathing. I'm just drying myself."

The emotional engineer hesitated a moment...

"I'll wait for you out here," she said.

"Oh! You don't need to do that, if you want come in and sit down."

Karen took a deep breath.

"Thanks... Door, open!" she said, and entered.

The furniture had disappeared from the room. It was just floorboards, the paneled walls, and, in the shower corner, Alice, smiling and observing her from through the strands of her wet hair.

"You'll have to excuse me for having emptied the room, but I needed the space for my exercises," she explained.

"No, no bother," replied Karen hurriedly. "A seat, Wombat."

The floor in front of her deformed, swelling up; the pseudo-wood twisted itself up for a second and there was a chair in the center of the room.

Karen seated herself on it.

"I'll be finished in a moment," said Alice. "Wombat, dryer!" she ordered.

Warm jets of air sprang from the wall, ruffling her mane of silvery-blonde hair.

Alice turned her body, offering different parts in succession to the warm air currents; flexing her arms, legs, torso, with the instinctive pleasure born of physical well-being... Her eyes met Karen's.

"Please don't watch me."

The emotional engineer blushed. Rising from the chair, she turned it toward the opposite wall and resumed her seat. She spoke with her back to the young woman.

"I'm sorry... It's just..."

Coming out of the shower corner, Alice approached the woman seating in the center of the room with rapid strides.

"No, there's no need to excuse yourself; it's you who should pardon me," she said. She took the emotionalist by her hunched-up shoulders from behind. "I understand what you must be going through; you knew Aisha."

The seated woman blinked.

"Yes, I guess that's it."

"Karen, you can't imagine the shame I feel about finding myself in this body that isn't mine," whispered the girl, kneeling and resting her head on her companion's back. "Most of all when I'm standing in front of you... You, who knew Aisha..."

"There's no need to feel ashamed," said the emotionalist, her eyes fixed on the wall ahead of her. "You are not to blame."

"That's what I've been told, but it doesn't stop me from feeling bad... Karen, sometimes I feel the need to ask you what she was like, then I feel that to know more would only make me feel worse..."

"There's not much to tell," said the seated woman, moistening her lips. "Simply that we were friends. Good friends... Years would go by when we didn't see each other. But there are some friendships that are never forgotten."

"I know," agreed the kneeling girl, hiding her face.

"You understand then?" said Karen, and, quickly casting a glance behind her, she stood. "But what's this! You don't have to sit like that... Wombat! Another seat!"

There was another brief disturbance in the force fields and then there was a second chair in the room.

Taking her by the hands, the emotionalist made the young woman stand.

"Don't be silly; show me those eyes," murmured the emotionalist, but Alice shook her head. "No? Well, at least sit down; that way we can talk."

Docile, Alice sat keeping her gaze steadfastly on the floor. Keeping hold of her companion's hands, Karen spoke to her in hushed tones.

"If you are still bothered about me looking at you..."

The naked girl raised her head instantly.

"Oh no! You knew her; you have more right to this body than I do..."

"Don't say that," said Karen shivering.

Forcing a smile, Alice decided to look her companion in the eye.

"Yes, I realize now, that's idiotic... But I want you to understand me," she begged and looked away again. "Before, in my time, in my true body...people were not the same; they were..."

The emotionalist shook her head.

"People have not changed that much."

"No, you misunderstand me; I was ugly, so very ugly. You know? And if anyone ever looked at me it was...it was to..."

Karen let out a little gasp.

"You poor thing," she breathed, and wrapped her arm around the still damp shoulders.

4

Felix Vallarta took the gold- and silver-striped model in his hand and examined it in minute detail... He placed it carefully onto the surface of the esplanade, picked up the gauntlet, and put it on, testing the fit.

"Not bad," he said appreciatively, and with his other hand he rubbed the back of the gauntlet.

The wasp began to buzz, still immobile on the ground.

The ecologist crooked his index finger, and the tiny cybernetic device came to life and rose into the air.

He straightened his index finger, and the wasp halted in mid-air, buzzing menacingly.

He moved other fingers, flexing and stretching, and the wasp flew in rapid circuits, making sudden stops and unexpected changes of direction without ever leaving the combat arena, until with a gentle swoop it came to land at the ecologist's feet.

"Excellent maneuvers!" said Clyde Greenaway approvingly.

Felix Vallarta shrugged dismissively.

"Solo maneuvers are no big deal," he responded, removing his gauntlet. "What matters is what happens in combat, when you have to defend yourself from enemy wasps."

He stowed the gauntlet in the box with the dormant wasp and sat down on the ground beside the psychosociologist.

"Karen is taking her time," said the ecologist, assessing the position of the sun over the horizon through half-closed eyes. "Soon there won't be enough light."

Clyde glanced back at the house anxiously.

"Should I go and get them?" he asked, half getting up, and then sitting back down when he saw two figures leaving the house. "No need... Here they come."

"Really?" asked the ecologist, shading his eyes from the sun to see better. "Well, then I'd better hurry up and tell you something. It was many years ago; in those days there were only a handful of cybos. I was on their island... I saw them. Would you believe me if I told you that they were controlling ten wasps apiece?"

"I believe you."

"Seriously... You have to see it to believe it," Felix said. "And the battles were between the wasps. Each one had to find the weak spot in the middle of the body; in a head-on encounter both would be lost..."

Clyde ignored the ecologist's chatter for a moment; he could see that that there was something going on with Alice.

He studied her as she approached.

Yes, there was something in her movements...her face...her eyes...as if Karen Shehan had passed on something of her own disquiet, he said to himself as he prepared to greet the women.

"Welcome, you two. I see that you are living up to your reputation for tardiness, my dear Karen," said Felix, bowing to her in mock reverence.

"No need for sarcasm," smiled the emotionalist. "If you're trying to rattle me, I fear you're deeply misguided; I'm a veteran wasp fighter. Which ones are mine?"

The ecologist indicated the boxes on the ground.

"Choose the ones you want," he replied. "After your defeat, I can't have you trying to blame it on my Machiavellian tampering beforehand. All four are tested, and they work well."

Clyde took Alice by the shoulder.

"Come with me; let's get out of the way before they begin."

With a nervous movement, the girl shook his hand off her shoulder.

"Why such a hurry? According to what I've heard the stings aren't painful," she answered with evident annoyance.

"For sure; the wasps don't induce pain when they sting," the ecologist intervened, taking the gauntlets from the box that Karen had rejected. "But it's not pleasant to have a limb or even your whole body in paralysis for several minutes, not to mention the inconvenience you'd cause to the players..."

"Felix is right, Alice," Karen agreed as she adjusted her right gauntlet. "You should stand back."

"As you wish," Alice responded, and without waiting for Clyde, she set off for the bench on the edge of the arena.

The psychosociologist stood motionless for a few seconds before following her.

Felix Vallarta watched pensively as the two figures moved away.

"Shall we start the warm-up?" the emotional engineer asked.

Without answering, the ecologist turned to face her.

"Okay, shall we start? Your staring at me won't put me off."

"Yes, let's start," the ecologist replied curtly, and he made his way to the center of the arena; Karen followed.

They positioned themselves back to back.

Karen flexed her fingers; the wasps were still disengaged...

"Why do you enjoy hurting people so much, Karen?" asked the ecologist, and he felt a tremble run through the body pressed against his.

"Who have I hurt?"

"Must you ask?" replied the man, and he looked toward the two figures sitting on the bench. "Her of course; you can see it in her. What have you done to her?"

Her jaw set, Karen rubbed her gauntlets against each other, and her wasps began to buzz.

"What's the matter with you, Felix? Are you jealous?"

The ecologist couldn't help but smile. He finished adjusting his own gauntlets.

"The best defense is a good offense, isn't it, Karen?"

Weaving around each other in tight spirals, Karen's wasps rose into the air.

"If you must know, we were talking about Aisha."

Felix's wasps ascended slowly, keeping to straight vertical trajectories.

"Well? Does that satisfy your curiosity?" asked the woman.

The four wasps glinted in the sunlight.

Karen took a deep breath.

"So now your tactic is silence?" she asked, moving away from the man and turning to face him. Above, her wasps waited, stationary.

The ecologist turned in his own time.

"I don't like people who hurt others. Even if they don't realize it," he said and strode to the edge of the circle.

The emotional engineer tensed her facial muscles. Controlling her voice she shouted after his retreating back.

"And I don't like people who butt into affairs that don't concern them, understand?"

The man carried on walking toward the edge of the arena.

With a snort, Karen walked off toward the opposite side.

5

As Clyde sat down on the bench, he noted how Alice instinctively edged away from him. Saying nothing, he fixed his eyes on the two figures walking to the center of the arena. Obvious emotional imbalance, he reflected. The cause? Her conditioning? In principle, yes. But there was something more... Maya? Mustn't rule it out, certainly, but to put it all down to her...

"Clyde, can you forgive me?"

Alice was fidgeting uneasily on the bench.

"Why do I need to forgive you?"

"Well... my rudeness to you. Back there in the arena."

Clyde smiled.

"There's nothing to forgive; I know you have reasons to be anxious."

The young woman gave him a brief glance, and then turned back to the arena.

Anxious? Yes, but why was it so bad?

He placed his hand over Alice's, but she removed hers brusquely. She was blushing; he needed to check...

"Why did you take so long?" he asked, keeping his voice calm, his eyes focused on the figures now walking away from each other to the far extremes of the arena.

Why did she take so long to answer?

"I was washing... And then we started talking."

Fragments of Karen's psychological profile flashed through Clyde's memory.

"Talking? About what?"

"Well... about Aisha," Alice replied quietly.

The psychosociologist's breathing quickened; he was recalling certain peculiarities in the conditioning created by Stephen Houdry. The pig... Undoubtedly he had been aiming to possess a harem. He managed to control the wave of anger that rose inside him. You must keep calm; she is not to blame, he told himself, but couldn't help that word hammering around and around in his brain: Pig! Pig! Pig!

"Yes, I know I shouldn't remember her," Alice hurriedly added. "That I have no reason to reinforce my feelings of guilt... I felt good, do you understand? I know I have no reason to... But for that moment, I preferred... I know now that I did the wrong thing. I mean, I shouldn't have spoken with her," she turned her green eyes on the psychosociologist. "I should never forget that you are my best friend."

In the sky, above the arena, the battle had begun, but Clyde turned away from the spectacle and took one of her hands in his, stroking it gently... And this? he asked himself, just containing the shiver produced by the intense flow of emotional energy his fingers had received.

"Don't let that upset you, Alice."

"Clyde, I feel so awful now," she said turning her tormented eyes to him. "For a moment I felt good with Karen...talking to her...but now I miss Stephen so, so much that I'm going to die if I don't see him soon; I need him more than ever. He's the only one that..." she said, but interrupted herself biting her lip. She regained her courage and continued in a voice that tried to be normal.

"Don't listen to me. I'm nothing more than a stupid hysteric... Let's watch the contest."

And she moved closer to the psychosociologist, until her burning skin touched his.

You can't do anything now... Just wait for nightfall. The night; what a horrible thing... Clyde forced himself to stay in control. Relax, he told himself. I'm beginning to see what Aridor was talking about... But no, that's not fair, it's not right to run from one's own feelings. I can't be a coward; I mustn't become a terrified animal, always fleeing.

"Look! Vallarta has fallen!" shouted Alice, jumping up from her seat. "They should stop, Clyde!"

The psychosociologist concentrated on the sight before his eyes. In a fraction of a second he took in the scene taking place on the combat arena.

The ecologist was stretched out on the ground. It was clear that one of the emotional engineer's wasps had stung him on his left leg, and he was energetically rubbing it with his left hand, no longer controlling one of his wasps. A quick look told Clyde that there were only two wasps in the air.

Vallarta must have lost control of one of his when he fell and now had only one left, perhaps the one that was hovering immobile over the arena... Then the other wasp wheeled quickly in the air above, it feinted again and again, obliging the man on the ground to duck quickly out of the way to avoid its attacks.

Feint, feint, another feint; now it must be... It missed!

With a sudden graceful twist of his waist, the ecologist had managed to escape the final attack.

The wasp had not made contact with his body and now lay useless by his side on the ground. Despite the distance, Karen's confusion was visible from her posture... Felix Vallarta sat up slowly.

I can almost see his smile, thought Clyde to himself. He was surprised to find himself on his feet. When did I get up? he asked himself, and for a moment he became aware of Alice's hand squeezing his arm excitedly, before his attention was again called to the arena.

The surviving wasp started to make slow circles in the air.

"Why are they carrying on? Haven't they finished yet?"

"No," replied Clyde, noticing the tension apparent in his own voice. "Even when only one wasp remains, the battle must go on."

"But what can Vallarta do? He can't move, but she can."

"They can at least finish with a tie. He doesn't need to move to control his wasp... Of course it will be difficult to overcome Karen with only one wasp; she doesn't even have to concentrate on controlling her own, now that she has none, and she can escape him even more easily," he explained, then concentrating once more on what was happening in the arena.

Karen had by now recovered from her confusion; her figure crouched tensely, awaiting the attack.

"Why doesn't Felix attack? He's just making his wasp fly circles..."

"He's recuperating. His leg doesn't hurt him, it's true, but it still affects him... Anyway, he's hoping to tire Karen out. She has to wait for his attack, without losing concentration."

"Isn't there a time limit?"

"Only the natural one; if the sun sets before he stings her, Karen wins."

"Is it long? I mean until sunset..."

Clyde looked up at the sky.

"Not long," he answered. "Felix will have to hurry; I don't understand why he hasn't made even one feint... Look!"

The long wait had had its effect on Karen; it appeared that she had also wanted to know how long it would be before the sunset came to her rescue, and her eyes had strayed for a second toward the sun. This was the moment the ecologist had been waiting for so patiently.

Like lightning, his wasp dove down from on high.

Karen had time to spot it, but, dazzled by the brief glance toward the sun, her eyes could not work out its trajectory.

The wasp reached the bottom of its dive and stung her lightly on the neck.

The woman crumpled to the ground.

"Come on," said Clyde. "It's up to us to take the loser back to the house."

They walked toward the arena, where Felix Vallarta was beginning to stand up, his left leg still a little stiff.

XXVII

The Solitary Ones

1

THE PLATE'S EDGES were gilded; a thin line of gold extended around the edge of the opaque white interior. In its center, tepid and immobile, something purple, smoothed out with an irregular outline...

Felix noticed her expression.

"Don't be afraid to eat it," he said. "Karen's synthesizer can be as eccentric as its mistress, but it knows what it's doing."

Still doubtful, Alice took up her cutlery.

Cutlery, how primitive...

"Okay then," she replied, looking up. "But I would like to know what this stuff is," she said, touching the soft surface with the point of her knife.

Nadia smothered a smile.

"I am not a history specialist," she explained, lowering her still-laden spoon, "but the exterior appearance most likely corresponds to some exotic delicacy that was all the rage some centuries ago. The inside is plain biomass and completely modern; you won't risk poisoning yourself."

"If you say so..."

Alice Welland began to shred her food.

Clyde took a sip from his golden cup.

"Trust us, it is edible. The outside is antiquated, but the insides are entirely modern."

Her first mouthful swallowed, Alice decided to continue in better spirits.

"Yes, it really is quite good," she commented. "It's a shame that the mistress of the house can't honor us with her presence."

Felix glanced at the empty chair at the head of the table.

"She's a little sensitive to setbacks," he murmured.

A shadow of worry crossed Alice's face.

"Will she be really ill? If she doesn't eat..."

"Don't worry about it. She feels bad enough not to eat with us, but not so bad she can't eat in her own room."

"But even so..." Alice insisted.

"Alright, child. As soon as we finish I will go by her room and see how she is," Felix promised, pushing his empty plate away. At once a fresh, steaming dish appeared in front of him.

"You mustn't worry so much," Nadia said seriously. "Today you saw her for the first time; Felix and I have known her since..."

A thin shadow had silently slipped into the dining room. The eyes of the diners all turned inquisitively toward her.

"Glieber has gone into his house," Maya informed them. She sat down at the table and nimbly pressed the controls on the arms of her chair.

A green plate full of minute rosy spheres appeared before her; she took one between her fingers.

"He's in his house?" Alice repeated, not understanding. "But that's no reason to stop watching him!"

"His household brain is an old model," explained Nadia, pausing to carefully taste the pale liquid on her spoon.

"It's not connected to the Central Archive; the eye cannot enter."

"So now what?"

"We wait until he leaves again," replied Felix, elegantly slicing off a piece from the beige rectangle on his plate.

Alice stared incredulously at the others.

"You wait... I don't understand! How will we know what he does with the neurotor? And if he contacts anyone from inside his house?"

His appetite now satisfied, Clyde sat back in his chair.

"The neurotor is tagged," he said. "When he leaves tomorrow we will be able to tell whether he still has it with him, or if he's left it behind."

Pushing her plate away violently, Alice stood up from her seat.

Everyone looked at her, except Maya; the representative of the cybos continued chewing, her jaws moving rhythmically as she reached out a hand to take another sphere.

2

"Okay then, what did she say exactly?" asked Karen, without looking up from the emocrystal growing between her fingers.

Felix Vallarta shrugged.

"I didn't understand the first words; it's likely she was using some ancient language," he explained. "But without a doubt they reflected a high degree of irritation..."

Nadia interrupted him.

"This is no time to joke, Felix." Turning back to the emotional engineer she resumed. "Quite simply she lost control. By the look of things, the news that we couldn't watch Glieber in his house and how calmly we took it really drove her mad... Actually, I think I understand her reaction. She doesn't know the whole plan," she said, then in an even quieter voice, "What came out were all her reservations about us...or more precisely about our world."

Karen's fingertips moved gently over the incomplete faces of the emocrystal, awakening new lights, new rhythms...

"Reservations?" she replied. "About our world? It's logical, I suppose, Nadia; she comes from a time...and a place, totally opposed to ours. She can't understand us."

The ecologist shook his head in disagreement.

"I don't think it's that simple, Karen. She didn't accept her own time or the Empire. She even fought against it, risking her life... No, that doesn't explain it. Essentially, her reaction is based on the fact that this is not the world she dreamed of."

The emotional engineer made a face; a cloudy stain had appeared inside the emocrystal.

"The world she dreamed of, you say? Of course... Infantile dreams, confused, feverish utopias belonging to an ignorant past; a paradisiacal Eden, without the battles and difficulties that make it possible for Man to be Man, right?"

Nadia fixed her eyes on the lady of the house.

"Why do you belittle her?" she asked. "Although formed in the past, her mind is worthy of respect. She was the equivalent of an analyst in the Empire: a generalist. I think her very estrangement from our world enables her to see it with the appropriate distance. She can appreciate what we find difficult to perceive."

Between the skillful fingers of the emotionalist the smear within the crystal faded, diminishing until it disappeared, leaving a lustrous darkness.

"Oh yes? So she convinced you that the Empire was better than our times, did she?"

"Don't talk nonsense. If anyone amongst us here hates the Empire, it's her; she lived it. And if I have understood her correctly, the things that repulse her are the traces of the Empire that survive today."

Karen's eyes left the emocrystal and fixed on her interrogator. The ecologist listened, in silence.

"And what are those traces, might I ask?"

The analyst frowned, thoughtful.

"They're not easy to define; there wasn't much coherence to her diatribe...but they are, basically, rooted in our mode of being. Our behavior is too individualistic... That's it: individualism."

Shaking her head, Karen refocused her attention on the emocrystal.

"I see: an obtuse emotional engineer can comprehend that individualism and collectivism are two sides of the same coin, and it is impossible to develop one without developing the other, while two brilliant intellects such as yourselves allow some stranger to persuade you of the contrary."

Felix gave up his silence.

"It's not as straightforward as you make it sound, Karen."

"Really? Why not?"

The ecologist sat forward in his seat.

"I don't deny that collectivism is something important, and even fundamental in our lives; a life only has meaning, and we can only feel fulfilled when we can give something back to humanity..."

"So? What more do you want?"

"That there should not be loneliness."

The emotionalist looked at him, perplexed.

"Loneliness? What loneliness are you talking about? Aren't you here with us? When you achieve something, can't you celebrate that with us? Do you feel alone?"

"You don't understand... No, worse than that; you don't want to understand," replied Felix, his voice weary as he sat back in his seat once more.

341

"Karen, have you never felt lonely? Tell me, have you never wanted anyone to be close to you, to be with you totally, completely, body and soul?" asked the analyst.

The emotional engineer smiled. Her fingers caressed the half-finished crystal, stirring up little flashes of light.

"Of course, Nadia... And there's no denying those moments of loneliness are hard, but they help me to better appreciate those other moments...the moments when I am with another person who is close to me."

"And how many people have you been close to in your life?"

Karen's smile widened, revealing her small, white teeth.

"The total number? I find it difficult to put my finger on. You know I've never been good with numbers."

"That is loneliness," the ecologist intervened.

Karen looked at him in surprise.

"Loneliness? Oh, no! You're wrong; I have memories. I am not alone."

"You've been alone your whole life, and I have been, too, and Felix as well," said Nadia, with unexpected feeling. "We have never known love, true love, and we are nothing more than mutilated cripples who dream of recovery, of obtaining something we have never known... But we do know how to console ourselves with words, oh yes; we call our solitude liberty, our fear sensitivity, and that construct inside ourselves love. That construct of what we need but can't find and that we impose on an arbitrary other. We love them to avoid drowning in our own emptiness, until we can no longer reconcile the dream with reality and the illusion dies, along with the self-delusion, and we return to that loneliness that we never escape and the desperation, until we can't bear it anymore and we go in search of the next lie to console ourselves with. Don't you understand that this very multiplicity of loves negates love?

That the surest sign of an empty soul is its desperate need to fill itself? No, Karen, we have never loved, we have not known love..."

Falling onto the table, the emocrystal emitted a sound halfway between music and heartbreak.

"Speak for yourself, Nadia Derzhavina," Karen said from between her clenched teeth. "I don't let anyone touch my soul with dirty hands."

For a long time there was no other sound in the room apart from the agitated breathing of the emotional engineer.

"I'm sorry, I didn't mean to wound you," said Nadia, looking into the eyes of their host.

Karen forced a smile... Little by little she relaxed again.

"I'm sorry, too. I should never have used that tone with you; I understand that after that business with...what happened to you, you can't be entirely yourself."

Nadia's expression did not change.

"You can say it: after our failure to produce the ovo. It doesn't hurt me... Indeed, that was the point when I began to reflect seriously on..."

Karen did not allow her to finish.

"So, that's the reason Aisha, I mean Alice, feels dissatisfied with our world? Poor thing... I can do no more than understand her and comfort her." She rose from her seat. "I should talk to her."

"Karen, you haven't understood; her problem, her fundamental objection is not love...although that is a factor that also destabilizes her. The conditioning that Houdry used..."

The emotional engineer interrupted impatiently.

"Love does not believe in conditioning, Nadia. I apologize, but I think you are straying into my area of expertise. She can love other people, and you can trust my judgment... I'll see you tomorrow," she said, and bid them goodnight from the doorway.

Felix and Nadia looked at one another in silence.

"She didn't understand," said the analyst.

"She didn't want to understand," corrected the ecologist, getting up from his seat.

He walked over to Karen's worktable. Crossing his hands behind his back, he leaned over to see the unfinished emocrystal.

"Come and look, Nadia," he called.

Getting up from her chair, the analyst went over to the table and looked.

The crystal was smoldering with color.

It pulsed with a life of its own, amongst lightning flashes of pure passion. Inside there was anxiety, fear, surrender, and an undercurrent of their opposites, which would occasionally surface; it was a desperate, burning sensuality.

3

Karen tapped gently on the door.

"Alice? Are you asleep yet?" she asked, then listened, waiting for an answer.

Silence.

She hesitated a moment... Running her hands over her hips, she smoothed down her white tunic.

She knocked again, this time more loudly.

"Alice? It's me, Karen. Open the door; I need to speak to you."

There was no response.

The woman placed her mouth next to the fake-wooden panels.

"Alice! I'm sorry to wake you, but I need to see you," she said loudly.

She sensed a murmur and a movement on the other side of the door.

She smiled.

"They told me what happened at dinner, my love," she said in an impassioned whisper. "I feel terrible about not being there, to answer all your questions..."

The door opened.

Karen stepped forward, and stopped.

Her smile died.

"Greenaway? What are you doing here?"

The man leaned a hand against the doorframe. His tunic stuck to the skin of his chest, forming a stain of darker gray.

"I'm working. I'm attending to my patient," he said bluntly.

The woman's eyes tried to see past the man and into the room, but they found only darkness.

"Now?" she asked nervously.

"Now."

"And might I be able to talk to her? Alice!" she called, in a slightly hushed voice.

The man didn't bother to look behind him.

"Not now, no," he replied.

"And when you finish, could you let me know? I really need to..." Karen began to ask, and she stopped herself when she heard a voice from inside the room.

"Stephen, why are you taking so long?"

Stephen?

"I'm coming, just wait," the man hastily replied, looking over his shoulder, before turning back to the emotional engineer.

"See her tomorrow, in the morning. Right now..."

"Wait? Wait? I can't, my love; you don't know how much I have needed you, how much I need you..." the ardent voice cut through what the psychosociologist had been saying. They heard the sound of bare feet coming toward the door.

For a fraction of a second, the man's face was turned toward Karen, and the emotionalist was able to see the desperation in his eyes, before the door was closed on her.

She stood still, her eyes fixed on the imitation-wood.

My love? Stephen? Clyde Greenaway?

She did an about-turn and departed hastily, almost at a run, down the dimly lit passageway.

4

He opened the door.

He went out into the passageway.

He closed the door carefully.

(The nausea inside, growing, churning.)

What time was it? What did it matter?

(Outside, the light without any visible source brightened and dimmed to darkness, the walls closing in and opening out.)

Damn, damn you, Stephen Houdry. How could you do this to her? That creature should rot in hell until the end of time... But even that wouldn't be bad enough.

(traces, lines, scratches joining growing forming fusing to make two faces Lardner Mergenthaler two faces one face Stephen Houdry and his face laughed)

With all his might he punched the wall with his fist; the force field buckled, elastic, protecting his bare knuckles.

His body followed his fist.

(nausea nausea nausea)

Falling

(empty absence darkness nothing no)

A hand grasped him firmly by the shoulder.

(the darkness emptiness no nothing absence receded moaning the strange playful lights returned)

He looked at himself.

The ground was far away from his face. His feet were standing on it. His legs, his torso, straight, strong.

He turned his face to see who was supporting him.

Maya? What is she doing here?

The question resonated hollow in between feverish glandular explosions.

On his face the fleeting smile disappeared.

"Why aren't you sleeping?" he asked abruptly.

The bile rose bitter, burning his throat, making him spit out the round glutinous words.

"I don't sleep."

The man's lips curled in a scowl.

"Another of you cybos' wonderful qualities, huh? Taking complete advantage of the twenty-four-hour day, right?"

(happiness happiness stunning joyfulness tellherwhatyouthink treatherlikeshedeserves)

Maya let go of his shoulder.

(firmness solidity disappeared absent weight falling mercilessly callously onto legs)

From deep within he summoned his last reserves and stayed standing.

"I'm sorry," said the strange voice.

(the voice too distant deaf incomprehensible hear it amplify it take it in weigh its pitch nuance inflections REJECT IT)

"What is it you regret? My stupidity for attempting to punch through the door with my fist?"

"No."

(no no no no no)

347

"No? Then what are you sorry about?"

(tiny serpent curiosity throbbing twisting crackling amongst the dark flames)

"I regret what happened earlier," said the cybo, and for a fraction of a second her eyes flitted toward the closed door. "In there."

(E X P L O S I O N)

Without the intervention of his slow, dumb consciousness, up came his clenched fist, straight for the thin face, the dark eyes, Maya...

He found nothingness, disequilibrium, the renewed threat of falling

once again the small hand, rigid, holding him up.

"I want to help you," said the strange, imperturbable voice.

(release shame release pain release

and the anger descending in steady waves)

"You like rolling around in shit, do you?" he responded.

I'm being unfair, offensive... Why?

(a point of bright light serenity where? his shoulder? his hand? the bloody internal obstacles yielding dissolving)

Haven't you done the same thing all your life? Touching, gathering, sharing the pain, the misery of strangers? Why can't she do the same for you?

He raised his head. He looked into the great dark eyes...

"Follow me," said Maya.

XXVIII

Memories of Paradise

1

WHITE WALLS, WHITE CEILING, WHITE FLOOR...
Everything naked. Virginal.

Clyde's eyes focused on the fragile figure in the center of the room.

Maya was sitting on her heels. Her knees touched the floor, and her hands rested on her thighs.

He also sat on the floor, cross-legged.

"Did the furniture bother you?" he said.

Maya nodded.

"I need to train," she explained.

"Train? For what? To kill?" The psychosociologist's professional eyes noted the slight pallor of her cheeks. Can she turn pale? Her? He continued. "If I remember correctly, that is your task... Have you not learned how to do it yet?"

"No," replied the girl, and her voice sounded fragile.

The man's expression softened.

"At least you've retained something human... To be quite honest with you, I can't imagine how you'll deal with the resurrected; I don't think they'll stop at anything. But if Aridor has confidence in you cybos, I won't be the one to contradict him." He smiled. "Why don't you show me what you can do? Show me how you train."

"No, that's not what I wanted to do."

Clyde blinked.

"No, that's not what you wanted to do..." he murmured and gave her a suspicious look. "What exactly do you know?"

"You love her."

Clyde looked away.

"Yes, I love her. It's true," he said hoarsely. "What else?"

"She loves another man..."

"My god, yes, she loves him! Him..." He raised his head, searching for the right words, and he found them. "He deformed her beautiful mind, obliging her to love him. How could she love that swine! That foul beast that dares to call himself a man when he can only get a woman to even look at him through trickery!" he shouted, then paused to catch his breath.

She went on, as if he had never spoken.

"And the other man is dead."

Clyde was hugging his legs to him, resting his forehead on his knees.

"Yes, he's dead. And if she finds out, she'll die, too... And she believes, poor thing, that he loved her in return. She doesn't know that the cowardly rat crept up on her in such a way and was willing to kill her without blinking in order to save his stinking hide. She doesn't know, and she mustn't know, because that would kill her... And yet she dreams of him! She needs that monster! Not seeing him and not being with him are destroying her little by little... What can I do?"

"What you are doing."

The man raised his head.

"How did you know?" he asked aggressively.

All he got in response was the gaze of those large eyes: dark, inexpressive.

"Does it matter?" he asked, shrugging his shoulders. "Telepathy, empathy, second sight, it's all the same. What matters is what I am obliged to do... Do you know what I have to do? What I did last night?"

The cybo nodded.

"Yes, you hypnotized her. She believed that she was with the other man."

Clyde's mouth twisted, tightening, as he tried to contain the sobs... He managed to regain his self-control.

"Is there anything worse than that?" he asked. "Can I trick her like that? To treat her just like that beast conditioned her to be treated? To descend with her into that abyss of perversion?"

"Yes, because you love her."

The man's fingers laced themselves together and unlaced themselves as if they had a life of their own.

"Is it possible to have a love like that, Maya? To have a love that only brings pain to the one who loves?"

"Yes."

"But what meaning does such a love have? Why must I endure the torment of seeing her destroy herself day by day, she who is so lovely, so sensitive, so pure? Why must I endure, with my own flesh and with hers, the vileness beloved of that monster?"

"Do you want to give up that love?"

Instantly Clyde straightened up. He shook his head energetically.

"No, of course not... Aridor suggested it, but I didn't do it. I couldn't do it, I can't do it. And I don't regret it."

"And so?"

The moments passed silently.

Little by little, Clyde relaxed. His features slowly returned to normal... He smiled.

"Thank you, Maya," he said, and he leapt to his feet. "Thank you for helping me; you did what was necessary... I sense that, before you became a cybo, you must have known love. Am I right?"

2

Michael.

Michael shivering, laying the sharpened stick to one side, smiling.

Michael, his skin covered in earth, his face tanned by the sun, the joy of seeing me burning in his eyes, the joy of seeing me, of seeing Gwyneth.

Michael...

"I thought you had forgotten about me," he says.

I stop in front of him, in my hands the now blissful weight of the earthenware cooking pot.

"Forget about you? About you? I dare you to repeat that when you have tasted what I have prepared," I say with feigned irritation.

"Give that to me; don't strain yourself," he begs, coming over to me, and I give him the pot, and a kiss. His dirty face shines.

"Shall we go down to the stream? I want to wash," he suggests, and in his voice is an entire river overflowing with tenderness and love.

"Yes," I reply.

Together we go toward the shade of the trees, leaving the incandescent sunlight behind. We go down into the steep gully, and I use my hand to support him, as his are full.

We place the food on a flat, white stone, and we run to the water. We hold our breath against its freezing touch on our warm skins. We splash each other, laughing, fleeing from the icy drops that jump, shine, fall...

He rubs his hands, one against the other.

"Let me see them," I tell him.

He shows me his hands. I see the familiar palms now strange, deformed, but the blisters are almost healed and the skin hardened.

I feel tenderness, and compassion.

"Do you regret it, Michael?" I ask.

"Being close to you? Never."

The ardor in his words makes me shiver; only I know how much he has given up.

"Don't misunderstand me, my love," I say in a murmur that is lost in the sound of the stream. "You left the world of normals to follow me here…"

"And I don't regret it!"

"I know, I know…" I try to soothe him; I clasp his hands to my chest. I want him to feel my beating heart; I want him to understand how much I love him, how it hurts me, my inability to be a normal woman, working and creating for the beautiful society that is so incredibly advanced that even with all my strength and all my mind I am incapable of comprehending; how I can't be with him there… But, what can I do? Could I live like a parasite, receiving but never giving? No. Here in Paradise at least I can offer my animal strength, the ancient skills so easy to learn… Why did you fall for me, Michael? Why fall for such a mental invalid?

I try to push away the remorse, the feelings of guilt; I don't want him to see me this way, while I am in his arms.

"Tomorrow the trial period ends," I say.

He twists the bracelet on his wrist, this last piece of evidence that we don't belong to this world, and says:

"And we will stop being merely guests of honor—*narchen*—and become full members of the tribe," he says. "Isn't that so?"

Is the joy in his voice real? Authentic and not forced? I don't have time to decide. He takes me in his arms and makes me fly through the air; the rays of sun that manage to filter through the lush canopy of the trees blinds me for a second, but this does not stop our laughter.

We fall down together, still laughing.

"Careful!" I warn him. "We might knock the pot over."

"You are my food and the air I breathe," he replies, and presses his lips against mine.

I fall, spinning through the vast luminous space of pure sensation; I rediscover with amazement my body's ever-fresh perceptions. There is no more thought: just body, just flesh, just desire, my desire, his desire...

The noise, confusion, reaches my ears. I am already adapted to this world, and so is Michael; we separate, tense, alert, and strain our ears.

Danger?

My body prepares for the fight, or flight.

Michael stands and shelters me, while I kneel on the soft earth.

In front of our eyes the branches part violently and in the gap the intruder appears... She is Tosawi.

Tosawi, Silver Blade...

She stops when she sees us; she heaves, her naked breasts rising and falling. From her loincloth, the only garment she wears, hangs her name's origin: a magnificent knife.

"I've found you at last," she says, and her face glows with an excitement I have not yet experienced. "Come. Kino has found the tracks of Nokuse."

"Nokuse?" I ask, intrigued because the word is new to me, but Michael's eyes are glowing now, too.

"Nokuse, Nokuse is the bear, Gwyneth," he explains. "This means we will have abundant meat and a good hide," he says, looking critically at the small leather cloth that barely covers my modesty, "for when the cold comes."

For a moment I see myself as he must see me: a half-naked savage, my skin covered with half-healed scratches. And can he love me like this? As I am? I ask myself and shudder. But his look tells me my answer: he does love me. As I am...

I can barely hear Tosawi's answer.

"We'll not catch Nokuse with words; if we don't hurry, Nokuse will escape."

Michael helps me up and we run, taking great leaps over the slippery rocks along the banks or, when the banks are too narrow, through the stream itself. The water sometimes reaches our knees, but we don't stop, we don't break the rhythm of our stride, sure that we are nearing the village.

We clamber through the tangled trees, our moccasins squelching on the grass, and we come out into the midday sun.

Next to the huts is a group of men, diminutive in the distance. I recognize the hunters of the Yaha tribe. We begin to run again, Tosawi in the lead, her agile feet lifting the dust on the parched track.

We stop when we reach the group.

Chekwa, the chief hunter, offers us spears. We hurry forward to take them. Tosawi weighs hers in her hand; Michael examines the heat-hardened point of his.

"We are glad to have our narchen share the hunt for Nokuse with us." Chekwa speaks the ceremonial words and adds sadly, "Although it seems that the prey is not worthy of fine hunters; Kino has said that it limps and its stride is short and feeble."

"Nokuse limps...and walks with short feeble steps..."

It is the worn-out voice of Dasoak, and the hunters go respectfully quiet, because although Dasoak is now blind and disfigured, he has guided the Yaha tribe's hunt over many seasons.

I await the outcome of his deliberations anxiously. Could there be some hidden danger for us?

"Limping...feeble steps...short strides..." the blind man repeats, as if for himself, and then he comes out of his reverie. "Kino!" he calls.

Agile, supple, the young hunter comes forward.

"Here I am," he replies.

"Was there any blood on the trail?" asks Dasoak.

Kino shakes his head.

"No, no blood," he says.

Dasoak's hooked nose wrinkles as if sniffing the air...

"Good luck," he says, finally.

We leave.

Another race, this time beneath the scorching rays of the sun. I manage to keep up with Michael, alongside the youngest hunters.

"So, where is it?" asks Mitcherotka, coming up beside Kino, accommodating to his stride.

"It went into the Valley of Thorns."

All of us around him smile; that valley has only one exit.

"Silence!" Chekwa orders. "Preserve your strength for the chase!"

We obey. The murmurs cease, the hunt ups its pace; we approach and enter the Great Forest.

Now there is no more sun—only branches, leaves, roots, undergrowth, stones that we leap over, dodge, and skirt around without diminishing our speed.

I lose my bearings. It feels as if I have been running through this endless forest for centuries, that I will never find my way out, but a glance to one side reassures me: seeing, if only for an instant, Michael's bronzed, supple body, before a tree separates us, I am able to recover the strength of my stride, my soul swells with delight, and running no longer bothers me. Running without end in the dark forest...

Without stopping I brush aside a branch and see a knot of backs in front of me. Michael melds with them, becoming one more among the group of hunters studying a footprint left by Nokuse. On tiptoes I peer over his shoulder.

"Nokuse is large," says Maak, and there is an unequivocally reverent tone to his voice.

He can say what we are all thinking without fear of being called a coward; on his chest, his back, his legs he has long scars, a reminder of his battle, face to face, with a panther. A strip of its pelt still serves him as a loincloth.

"Large, yes—but old, lame, and weak," replies Kino, indicating another footprint.

I look at it, and even to my inexperienced eyes it is clear that the bear barely rested its claw there on one side, leaving just a trace on the dry ground.

"Let's go on," says Chekwa. Beads of sweat run down his face.

We begin to run again, now with greater haste; the hunters seem to sense the nearness of their prey. As they pass by me I see a familiar gleam in their eyes...

All of a sudden the trees stop, and the sky begins again; before my eyes, glazed by fatigue, I see the Wound in the Rock, the narrow gash in the cliff that marks the entrance to the Valley of Thorns.

We pass through it one at a time.

The hunt is nearly over. We move cautiously now, the more experienced hunters going first, testing every piece of scrub with the tips of their spears...

Next to me are Tosawi and Marena. A few steps ahead walks Michael.

Little by little I recover my breath and I can appreciate something other than the need to keep my exhausted body going. I see human figures moving cautiously, looking on all sides, and I can't

357

help but catch some of their pent-up excitement; I, too, cast rapid glances to either side of me, my feet also move silently, avoiding branches and dry leaves, because Nokuse's hearing is sharp.

Occasionally my eyes meet those of Michael, and the sweetest sensation fills me: I feel pride in his agile, sure step, his tanned, muscular body, and when his alert stare crosses mine it is able to speak of his love, without words, even here in the middle of the hunt...

But where is Nokuse?

We are nearly at the sheer rock face at the end of the valley. I see Maak and Kino stopped a prudent distance away from a thicket of thorns extending to the foot of the mountain. Chekwa moves closer to them, as do I—not so close that I can hear his question, but close enough to see their response.

Kino stretches out his arm and points at the bush.

Chekwa turns his head slowly, examining the ground in an arc around him...

Behind him the hunters wait, motionless.

Chekwa moves his hand, and the Yaha hunters fan out in a long line, all facing the bush. How did they understand what he wanted them to do? I ask myself, and I find the only answer: the ancient sign language...

Michael is at one extreme, almost on top of the huge gray crag of rock, broken from the mountain centuries before and now blocking off the left side of the thicket.

I follow Marena and Tosawi, who retreat to a position behind the line of hunters, but a gesture from Chekwa makes them stop. I do the same. I watch the rapid, incomprehensible gestures made by the chief hunter... Marena turns and walks off in the direction we had been following before. I see that she does not have a spear, but instead she has a dun-colored sack, half full, slung across her back.

Tosawi takes me by the hand.

We walk along behind the long line of hunters to where Michael is. He takes his eyes off the bush for a second and gives me the briefest of smiles.

Tosawi does not stop when we reach the end of the line of hunters; she moves on toward the crag, to the huge, truncated cone, and begins to climb it with the help of her spear.

The ascent seems impossible, but Tosawi's keen eyes are able to spy crevices in which to place her feet and spear.

We climb. I find it hard to stay close to my guide; although the rock face is steep, she moves with the same speed as on the level ground.

When I feel that I can go on no longer, I see the end of a spear shaft in front of me and raise my eyes; Tosawi has reached the top of the crag and is holding out her spear to help me up the last stretch. Taking advantage of this newly offered support, I easily make the distance that separates me from the summit.

From here I appreciate the full extent of the thorn bush. Somewhere in there Nokuse is resting, perhaps sleeping, unaware of the death awaiting him.

Tosawi's arms move, in mute conversation with the distant Chekwa. I don't pay attention to them, because I have discovered our role in the hunt. At a glance I can see that the part of the cliff face that the thorn bushes grow against is at least as precipitous as the one we climbed—if not even more so. Its base is littered with shards of rock. They are harsh, pointed... There is no danger that the old bear will try to escape in our direction.

I begin to gather the stones closest to us, placing them in a pile within easy reach.

I now know what I had not known before, but it is too late. I now know that Nokuse wasn't old or weak. Big, yes, and lame, because the point of a spear had broken off in his paw when he crossed paths with the Tuarva hunters. On that occasion, Nokuse had killed four men before becoming too tired to bother with the survivors. His wound hadn't healed, although it had closed and ceased bleeding; a splinter from the spear had lodged inside, too deep to work its way out, and now it hurt him at every step, making him more ill-tempered and irritable even than a normal bear; it isn't surprising that he hadn't behaved as Chekwa, Tosawi, or even I had expected.

I throw a stone. Another. And one more... Following Tosawi's example, I start by targeting the points furthest from the line of hunters, and little by little I aim closer to the area at the center of the thicket.

I feel Tosawi grasping my arm; I look at her. There is horror in her eyes. I turn my eyes to the thorn bushes in time to see a gray blur erupt and move with unbelievable speed over the sharp rocks toward the base of the crag and, without losing any of its terrifying speed, start to climb.

My death coming toward me. I feel more than I think. I am paralyzed, my arm flexed behind me with the useless pebble still warming in my hand... I can barely hear Tosawi shouting.

"Run! Quickly!"

I see her go to head off the bear, clambering down the crag. I think she must have gone mad until I see her stop when she reaches firmer ground inside a hollow in the rock. I see her crouch down and jam her spear against the stone. And suddenly I understand: she is going to give her life for mine. Tosawi is going to die, to give me time to get down the other slope, while Nokuse entertains himself tearing her to pieces.

I get up and run. But I don't go back; I go forward, toward where Tosawi is crouching against the rock, prepared to meet Nokuse and her death...

I make a false step. I have forgotten that I am not as sure-footed as her as I move across such uneven ground. I fall and roll, without letting go of my spear. I come to a stop beside her. She shoots me a look of shock as I gather myself together by her side and fix my spear next to hers.

"What are you doing? Idiot!" she asks angrily.

"Two spears together..." I begin, managing to suppress the searing pain growing in my ankle. But she doesn't let me finish my sentence; Nokuse is too close.

"Don't be stupid! Get out of here!" she shouts at me, and, rising, she launches herself off to meet the gray fury without giving me time to explain that she should be the one who flees, that I can't even get up and run because I have a badly sprained ankle.

My eyes wide, I watch as Nokuse stops briefly and readies his huge claw to strike. I see the spear shatter like a fragile twig between a child's fingers, and then the second swipe of his claw.

Tosawi, Silver Knife...

Tosawi, my friend Tosawi, my teacher and fellow tribeswoman... Her torn limbs fly through the air. Her small pert breasts are no more; a great scarlet cavity has taken their place.

Now it is my turn to die.

It seems to me that Nokuse is moving more slowly now.

I understand that this impression of time slowing is a result of the torrents of adrenaline flooding my body, because Tosawi's carcass is still airborne.

I clutch my spear tight. The first blow will break my spear, this much I know. What I don't know is which part of my body will take the next one. Perhaps my face. I am cowering, not erect as Tosawi was.

Nokuse's eyes are bloodshot. He is foaming at the mouth. I wonder if he is rabid, but realize that this must be normal after such a rapid climb... Good, after killing me he will be tired, he won't be able to go after the men who are down in the valley. They will have seen the monster and have realized that the best course of action is to run, run at full speed while he kills me.

Like lightning, the image of Michael springs to my mind. What will he do now that I am dead? Will he leave the tribe and return to civilization? That would be best for him, I tell myself, and I return my attention to Nokuse, so close now that I can smell his acrid stench...

What is happening?

I cannot believe my eyes. Nokuse has stopped, barely a meter from the tip of my spear. On his back I can make out a human form, and the glint of a knife that stabs in and out and then stabs again, right through Nokuse's pelt.

Who would be mad enough to do this? Perhaps he doesn't realize that with a knife like that he can do no more than scratch that thick skin? Why enrage Nokuse even more? Why offer him a third opportunity to kill?

This must be a hallucination, I tell myself. Nobody could be crazy enough to attack Nokuse with a knife. It must be me who has gone mad at the imminence and the smell of death...

The bear rolls over, trying to dislodge the man like a dog with fleas. The man cannot keep hold for long; he gets to his feet, his hands now empty. I know his face, despite it being covering of dust, sweat, and blood: it is Michael.

And I realize that what I am seeing is not a hallucination. That Michael must have run uphill, at some mad, impossible speed, because he loves me.

But doesn't the idiot know that if he dies, I...? I don't dare to answer that question. I want to shout to him, but the muscles in my throat have closed in a knot. I want to run to his aid, but I can barely get up, while my eyes fill with tears because of the unbearable pain in my ankle. But it doesn't matter; I have to get closer and help him...

Through the veil of my tears, I think I see human figures climbing up the slopes of the crag, spears bristling. I think I can hear their cries, but I am not sure; it could be the beating of my heart.

I just about manage to take a first step, using my spear for support, when everything is over; Nokuse's claw strikes Michael.

I see him twist and roll downward, wrapped around in some inexplicable red streamers... Then I see; they are his intestines.

Nokuse caught him in the belly.

A spear stabs the murderer in the back. At the other end, driving it in with all his strength, Hortolee, the Wind, the fastest runner in the tribe... But this time Michael outran him.

Another spear buries itself in Nokuse's back; it belongs to Chara, the Stag.

The third is mine.

Then another; and another, and another, until I find myself surrounded by familiar faces, feverish from the excitement of the hunt. Beneath lies Nokuse, writhing in the agony of death, his death, still strong enough to break spears and throw their owners into the air; he convulses, and it is my turn, and I see the ground coming rapidly up to meet my face...

I come to my senses after the blow, and one question, a name hammers in my mind, even before I remember what has happened, even before I feel the deadening pain in my ankle: Michael?

I look around. I am at the foot of the crag, lying on a crude stretcher hurriedly made from broken spears. My bearers have left me on the ground, and they are examining the person lying on the other improvised pallet.

Michael.

Marena is kneeling at his side. Carefully, she gathers up his intestines, soiled with earth and blood. She cleans them a little and smears them with something she takes from her bag and places them in the empty cavity of his stomach.

I look quickly to Michael's face. Luckily he is unconscious. No, he stirs, grimaces, and his eyes open. He presses his lips together. He moves his eyes, searching, and he discovers me.

I leap up, not noticing the painful stab in my ankle. I go closer and I kneel beside him. I take his head in my hands and rest it in my lap, trying to prevent him from seeing what Marena is doing to him, even though I realize this is stupid because he must be able to feel it.

I stroke his face, wiping away the drops of cold sweat. I look into his eyes and see that he wants to say something to me, but he doesn't dare part his lips for fear of what might come out.

I am unable to hold his gaze, and my eyes stray toward Marena.

I watch her futile attempts to place Michael's intestines back into his stomach—futile because Michael is condemned to death, because we are in Paradise and not in civilization, because he followed me here, because he ran the fastest to save me...

Yes, he saved me. And what can I do for him now?

I look all around me but find no answer, not even other eyes to meet mine, because they are all fixed on Michael's belly.

I can't bear it anymore.

"What are you doing?" I shout. "Don't you know he's dying! Find a health module, quickly!"

No one answers.

"We have no machines here, Gwyneth," Marena says, without taking her eyes from the task of fitting the intestines back into the stomach. "In Paradise they are forbidden, because they prevent man from being man, because they make him depend on them and not his own hands..."

I am aware of a hypnotic rhythm in her words. I realize that she is repeating the old words that helped create Paradise, not because they answer my question, not for their meaning, but because the soothing drone of their recitation distracts me, distances me from my pain... But I don't want to be separated from it, I don't want to abandon Michael, I don't want to lose him.

"A man's life is too precious to be left in the hands of other men!" I shout over Marena's words.

I see Marena give up her efforts to return the intestines to their place. I see her stand up and close the bag with her blood-stained hands, and I almost believed that she has been persuaded by my words, that she is about to go in search of a health module. But I haven't looked down to Michael's face on my thighs, I haven't seen his eyes glaze over...

Darkness envelops me. I can't see. I can't cry out. I can't...

3

"...you must have known love. Am I right?"

4

...tests and more tests. Now with my head still encased in that darkened helmet, I ask myself how long it will take.

It seems it's not so easy to become a cybo.

The voice resonates through the helmet again.

"Gwyneth! Are you listening to me?"

I barely have to move my lips; the microphone inside the helmet is very sensitive.

"Yes."

"I want to ask you some questions."

"Go ahead," I reply. More questions...

"What are your reasons for wanting to become a human with cybernetic mental enhancement?"

What a mouthful... Wouldn't they do better to call themselves cybos, just like everyone else does? However, the question doesn't surprise me, it's more that they have taken their time in asking it.

I tell my story. Mine and Michael's...

They interrupt me.

"We knew all this before; that is not what we are asking. Perhaps it would be better to rephrase the question."

Very well; rephrase away. I am too tired to argue.

"What are you trying to do? Forget what happened? Escape from your regrets?"

My fatigue disappears in an instant. I try to control my voice so that I don't scream.

"If that's what I was looking for, I'd have found it already by giving up, through death," I say, as if it were necessary to spell it out, but I am too angry to speak properly, without repeating myself. That they should think me capable of that...

"Well then?"

It is an advantage to be inside the darkened helmet. The only effective sense is hearing; thanks to that I am able to distinguish the note of approval in the question. Thank goodness. I was worried that what everyone says about these people might be true: that they are unable to understand the feelings of normal human beings... But I must answer.

"I want to fill up the space Michael left. I want to be useful to humanity. I want to exceed my limitations, I want to give everything, everything to everyone else..."

I stopped, displeased with myself. Those aren't the best words, the most exact. It seems ridiculous that it should be so difficult to express these feelings: the essence of being human.

"And amongst the things you are ready to give, does that include your own life?"

"Of course, isn't that obvious?"

"Listen carefully. We have finished studying you. Your brain is very well suited to certain transformations that will prepare you for a particular task. I am not exaggerating when I say that it is extremely important for the whole of humanity..."

I don't let him finish.

"Your clarifications are not necessary; I am ready."

"I have not finished. The execution of this task involves a high risk of your death. To be exact, a..."

I am not interested in hearing the exact figure.

"I don't think that you have understood what I said to you. I said, and I repeat, that I am prepared to give everything. Everything."

I am just able to hear the whisper of another voice; his boss must be a long way from the microphone that they are using to communicate with me.

"Sarki has passed her."

Who is this Sarki?

The familiar voice speaks to me again.

"You have passed, Maya. Now you can relax."

I feel an irresistible sleepiness come over me... Despite everything I muster my strength to protest.

"I'm not called Maya; my name is Gwyneth..."

I can barely hear the answer that comes from the shadows all around me.

"You were Gwyneth. Now you are Maya."

The nothingness...

5

"...before you became a cybo, you must have known love. Am I right?"

Clyde sensed a gentle shiver run through the body of the young woman seated in front of him.

Maya's eyes closed...

I don't think I should have asked that question.

...and then they opened again.

"You should leave, Greenaway," she said flatly. "I need to rest; it will be morning soon."

The psychosociologist hastily agreed.

"You're right. See you later, Maya."

"See you later."

From the doorway, Clyde looked back one more time.

The woman was in the same position, her eyes fixed on some point on the wall opposite.

He closed the door silently.

D

This is the fourth part of the test. It is strictly your own work; you must complete it on your own, without discussing your answers. If you do not wish to complete it, continue to the next page.

I. Analyze the relationship between Alice Welland and Stephen Houdry; Clyde Greenaway and Alice Welland; Gwyneth (Maya) and Michael, then answer the following questions:

1. Do you think that what Alice feels for Stephen is real love? (Consider your response carefully. Ask yourself up to what point we are all conditioned by our upbringing and the influences we received at that time.)

2. Do you think that, from a professional point of view, Clyde's behavior toward Alice is correct? What about from the human point of view? (Ask yourself what you consider to be the definition of correct.)

3. Do you think that Gwyneth's decision to become a cybo after Michael's death was justified? Are you or have you ever been in love? (Ask yourself what your concept of love is.)

II. Imagine that you are a member of the society described in the novel. Imagine that creative, socially useful work is a basic need for you. Imagine that you are unable to bring something new, valuable, to this society, and that you are aware of this. Circle the option you would choose:

TURN TO THE NEXT PAGE

a) become a mystic
b) become a cybo
c) become a "prim"
d) give up (suicide)

This test will continue later. You may change your answers at any point.

'

XXIX

Conversations at Dawn

1

ALICE AWOKE WITH A START.

Something's missing... Stephen?

She turned to the other side of the bed, looking for him.

He wasn't there.

For a second the wave of panic paralyzed her, she couldn't breathe... Then she remembered.

No, I am not there anymore, I escaped... But Stephen? I was with him last night!

Her mind whirled, stunned, surrounded by contradictions, before finding the answer.

A dream. It was only a dream... But so real.

The memories came back to her—clear, detailed. She touched her chest with her hand, to where her heart, beating with such a violent rhythm, was threatening to escape.

I think I have gone too far, she told herself with a sigh. Even in dreams there are certain things one should not do... But she couldn't suppress the smile that formed on her lips. Oh! It is true that absence makes the heart grow fonder. Be prepared, my clumsy giant; when I get you back...

With a sudden impulse, she sat up, her tense hands pushing against the invisible force fields.

When I get him back!

She shook her head, getting rid of the last traces of drowsiness.

I must get him back. And I will not be able to do that lying around here recalling erotic dreams, however wonderful they might have been. Come on, get up.

She stood up.

She flexed her body, stretching. She moved her arms, legs, bending them, extending them, getting the blood flowing... She appreciated the warm feeling of physical well-being.

And mental well-being, she told herself. It seems silly, but dreaming...

She forced her thoughts away from the route they were taking.

Enough of that; to work. What time was it?

"The time, Wombat?"

"Local or Standard?"

Very cute, little brain...

"Local."

"It's oh seven hours and eighteen minutes. Nearly sunrise. Would you like to see it?"

Early. He's very attentive, too... Okay, I'll watch while I bathe, she decided as she walked over to the wash zone.

"Wombat, a shower... And connect the sim-dow as soon as sunrise begins."

The water fell in a fine mist on her body.

Just as she began to scrub her skin the light changed, diluted...

The sim-dow?

She turned and stood still. Her skin turned to goose flesh as the water continued to fall from the shower.

My God, how beautiful!

The front wall had vanished. Outside, the sea was still asleep. The sky began to grow bright, to light up; above, almost at the limit of vision, were clouds, tinged red in parts by the invisible sun and in others dyed a deep blue, almost violet, by the stubborn night...

She closed her gaping mouth.

I can't tear myself away from this marvel... But I must work and finish washing or I will freeze to the spot.

She made herself say the words "Close the window, Wombat."

The wall came back, with its delicate hints of green, and her heart felt crushed.

It doesn't matter, she told herself, rubbing her body down vigorously. I will see many more sunrises with you, Stephen.

She stepped out of the wash zone, fresh, ready.

Now to work...

She halted mid-step.

To work? On what? I am not there. What I must do now is wait, watch for that moment to act...

She let herself fall back onto the bed.

And I have missed that sunrise... It doesn't matter, there is always work for a generalist; there are always problems to solve. For example, why did I react that way last night at dinner? Why? Let's see, there must be a root cause...

She went over in her memory everything that had happened the day before, and blushed.

What was I going through yesterday?

In minute detail she went through all of her attitudes, her thoughts, her reactions and dissected them, searching for motives.

Emotional instability... Total, complete. The cause: longing. The overriding need for Stephen: to see him, touch him, feel him... Okay, today, I feel that his absence doesn't bother me so much; I can think... But more importantly, there was another reason for my explosion during the meal: that passivity, that calmness in the face of the hunt for those vicious wolves. Don't they realize what they're doing is like searching for gunpowder by lighting matches in the dark? They don't know them, it's true, but their lack of knowledge should give them cause for concern; they ought to be anxious, tense. Instead they entertain themselves with wasp contests and in making convivial conversation while they eat exotic delicacies, not showing the slightest disquiet at having lost contact with the enemy, at their ignorance of his plans, as if it were just another game and not a mortal threat... And on top of that, they display their repugnance of the cybos, of Maya; they themselves are more insensitive, equally inhuman...

She pursed her lips.

Take care, Alice. Once again your emotions are interfering with your thoughts; you're losing perspective. They have been brought up in an environment completely different from the Empire, they can't possibly understand what danger is: true danger, the mortal danger that stalks your every step, waiting for every unguarded gesture, any loss of control... But they themselves are aware of this. Didn't Aridor warn you that the probability that you will get out of this alive is virtually nil? And don't I continue to make plans, imagining myself with Stephen again? Stephen... I would always want to save you even if it cost my life...

She took a deep breath.

Again... Again the emotions. Take control of them; preserve your mental clarity, you need it, if you want to work well, efficiently, and not die uselessly without achieving what you want to achieve... If you could at least see the whole plan... But they must have their reasons... They have reasons: if I were to fall into their hands they'd discover everything in my brain. They have all manner of techniques to do that, I know that institute well... It is enough to know that the cybo Maya and I are the cutting blade of the weapon that is to be used to excise them... That and no more.

She crossed her arms behind her head, making herself comfortable.

That's it: I am an instrument, not a plotting mind... But I can't make myself wait passively. My mind needs work, activity; without it I'll lose my edge and that would make me incapable of completing my mission when the moment comes. I need something to occupy my mind... Okay, why not try to understand them better? Yes, it wasn't enough to go through all those collections of data, summaries, evaluations, however exhaustive they were; they never touch anything nor can they touch any of those obvious, everyday things: the things that are so habitual, so normal that they are not even considered factors in forming attitudes, beliefs, and responses... I must talk to them. This time without losing my self-control. I must try to understand them.

She smiled. Nothing like deciding on a course of action... A memory intruded on her mind, wiping away her smile. And Karen? After a moment's reflection she shrugged her shoulders. The past is the past. From a practical point of view, it isn't good for me to be too intimate with any of them; that would only risk allowing more emotions to interfere with my mental functioning, when what I most need is peace... The one person I need is Stephen!

She relaxed her body and her mind, emptying them, and the sudden anxiety attack gradually subsided.

Good. Now I can continue thinking. Where was I? Ah, yes: Karen. In the end it was the memory of her relationship with Aisha that made her seek me out; I myself am not so important to her. There are plenty of other people here who I can get close to: Nadia, Felix, Clyde even...

She stopped, and analyzed the sudden jab she felt.

Jealousy? About a simple friendship... But he's the only friend I have, she realized.

Her thoughts were interrupted by the household brain.

"Aren't you going to have breakfast?" it asked, ever solicitous.

She became aware of her empty stomach.

"Yes, I am hungry."

"The others are on the terrace. Would you like to breakfast with them, or here, alone?"

Wombat: so attentive, so polite...

2

"Greenaway! Greenaway!"

The voice seemed to come from far away.

He turned in bed, trying to escape it.

"Greenaway!" it insisted stubbornly.

Sitting up in bed, he rubbed his eyes.

"Yes?"

"Samuel Aridor is calling; it's urgent."

He jumped out of bed.

"Tell him I've just woken up and I'll be there as soon as I can," he instructed as he hurried over to the wash zone. He dressed quickly and spoke to Wombat again. "Make the call."

The wall vanished.

Aridor was seated behind his work desk, looking at him.

"You've slept into the afternoon," was his only greeting.

Clyde cleared his throat.

"The work," he explained.

"I understand," the hologram conceded. "Any news of Glieber?"

"Last night we followed him home. Everything was normal... Nothing can have happened this morning; the cyber brain has instructions to call me if anything happens."

"Can we check that?"

"Wombat, who's on watch?" Clyde asked.

"Maya."

The psychosociologist blinked.

"Call her, too," he ordered, after an almost imperceptible pause.

Another wall disappeared.

Maya was sitting at the control panel. She was studying Glieber's image, leaning over the video reader.

She is looking at psychological profiles. Clyde recognized his familiar work.

The cybo turned to face him.

"You want to talk to me?" she asked.

"Yes," replied Aridor. "Has anything new happened?"

"Nothing out of the ordinary."

"Where is he?"

"At work."

"Did he meet anyone on his journey from his house to the regional bureau?"

"No."

"And at the bureau?"

"Some greetings and his usual work contacts."

"You have verified that?"

"Yes."

Aridor turned back to Clyde Greenaway.

"It seems your deductions were correct..."

"Anything else?" asked the cybo.

"No, nothing, thanks," replied Aridor with a slight nod of the head.

Maya's image disappeared, and the wall returned.

"Moving on," said the head of special cases. "We have found a suitable body. It's due to arrive." He looked over at something

Clyde couldn't see before clarifying. "It's due to arrive within the hour. Prepare everything for Alice Welland to make the transfer."

"Consider it done," Clyde responded, and Aridor was gone.

3

"What do you mean, what does an ecologist do?" Felix Vallarta shook his head, smiling. "It's far too broad a question... Okay, I'll start with the basics: the maintenance of equilibrium in the various ecosystems that exist on Earth. In reality, that's work for the novices; it lacks true challenge. Previous generations of ecologists did a good job there, eliminating all the effects of the Great Pollution. Nowadays those systems are practically superstable: oscillations are minor, and they return to equilibrium by themselves. Studying them on the other hand, looking at how they function—that constitutes a good lesson..."

"And Paradise?"

The ecologist nodded approvingly.

"Paradise, yes. That's the only place where you can truly do a little work... The primitive relationship between man and the ecosystem is essentially destructive. Did the great deserts still exist in your time?"

"They did," replied Alice.

"The majority of them were created by man himself, in darker times... Reclaiming them was not easy. I recommend that you study the process by which they were eliminated; some of the solutions were really interesting..."

"But they haven't all disappeared completely, have they?" asked Alice, waving her hand to indicate the arid countryside around the house.

They were on the terrace, close to the edge of the cliff, seated in a triangle: Alice, Felix, and Nadia.

A little further off, facing the precipice that fell away to the sea, Karen was watching the seagulls in flight.

Felix shifted in his seat, raising his eyebrows.

"The desert is such an interesting system! Would you want us ecologists to destroy it? Of course, the great deserts have been eliminated, but here and there we preserve a few square kilometers... Diversity is the key, dear Alice; that is what we must preserve at all costs... But let's talk about Paradise."

"Yes, let's," agreed Alice.

"If we left the prims, I mean the primitives, completely to their own devices, within a few generations they would have converted it to desert. They constitute a destabilizing factor of the first order... But we can't act openly, or even advise them on how to run their Eden; they'd pay us no mind. Yes, Paradise is the one task in terrestrial ecology that still has some interest; the most promising youngsters are sent there. There they have boundless opportunities to prove themselves..."

"And when they prove themselves?"

"Small, closed ecosystems... In other words, procurement of alimentary biomass or organic products like your ancient petroleum, necessary for the fabrication of various industrial products..."

"You don't use it as an energy source?"

Felix Vallarta looked at her, astounded.

"As an energy source? Why? Haven't you heard about the portals? They harvest all the energy we need."

"I know about the portals, but I didn't know they were for harvesting energy."

"Shall I help you out, Felix?" asked Nadia Derzhavina.

"It's your field," conceded the ecologist.

Nadia turned to Alice.

"There are thousands of these portals orbiting the sun as close as they can get without being destroyed," explained the analyst. "All the energy they emit is absorbed by the photoelements, which open in homologous portals at the energy centers."

"All?"

"Of course not. But the efficiency of the system is over ninety-eight percent."

"But then Earth is continually absorbing more and more energy; even a simple two-percent thermal dissipation can alter its climate," Alice replied.

"That's not a problem," answered the analyst. "Those same portals help us to eliminate the remains of any thermal contamination from Earth; we have placed some on Pluto and their partners located in the hottest parts of Earth... Of course these only operate thermally. So the excess heat accumulated can be dissipated. If we are approaching dangerous levels, all we need to do is open them. Any questions?"

Alice shook her head.

"So it's my turn again," said Felix, taking up the thread. "Closed ecosystems need continual readjustment; just because of their size they are necessarily unstable. But we have been perfecting them over the last few centuries, and their stability has improved considerably: it is very uncommon to have to reboot them completely. We just need to tweak them a little so that they recover."

"What else is there?"

The ecologist frowned.

"What do you mean, 'what else is there'?"

"None of those tasks are sufficiently creative to satisfy human needs, Felix."

"True," said the ecologist, and his smile broadened. "I haven't told you the best: the creation of huge, completely novel ecosystems."

"And what are these novel ecosystems? Where are they?"

"For the moment they only exist inside the memory banks of the Central Archive, but soon, when we launch the first ovos..." he said, making the briefest of sideways glances at Nadia; the analyst did not show any emotion, so he decided to go on. "Then we will be able to put them in motion on other planets that lack their own life forms... But I have let my enthusiasm get the better of me. I should tell you what they consist of. Look, the biosphere on Earth is by no means optimal: there are many alternative possibilities, which as far as we can tell are much more varied, much richer, yes, and even more stable. But," he sighed, "the necessary transformations would make Earth uninhabitable in the interim. Moreover, we can't ignore the emotional factors: we are tied by sentimental bonds to Earth as it is. On other planets, however, these limitations don't exist."

"But I should think that these alternative possibilities can't be infinite, and with all these ecologists, they must have been quickly exhausted!"

Felix energetically denied this.

"It's not as straightforward as you think, Alice. Thousands of ecologists have worked on a single ecosystem for their whole lives without finishing it. No, in even the simplest cases, five generations of specialists are needed to create a variant sufficiently viable to be able to apply it... What's more, the task doesn't end with possible variants of life on Earth. If we introduce the notion that other planets possess different chemical compounds, that the solar radiation they receive varies in intensity and in spectral range, the number of possibly optimal alternatives rises to infinity. So there's no risk that the work of ecologists will dry up for the next few millennia."

A brief interlude of silence.

"Thank you for your explanation, Felix," said the young woman from the past, and she turned to the analyst. "Now it's your turn, Nadia."

"My work..." the woman began, but then she stopped. Seeing that Alice and Felix were looking toward the house, she looked, too.

Clyde Greenaway was striding toward them.

"Sorry to interrupt you," he said. "But your new body has arrived, Alice."

For a moment, Alice Welland turned pale. Recovering herself, she addressed her companions.

"I beg you to excuse me for a few minutes..."

XXX

Human, All Too Human

1

THE BODY FLOATED, stretched out on the invisible field lines of a force field.

The sun had tanned the skin to a deep golden color. Beneath, the outlines of elastic muscles, vigorous and at the same time undeniably feminine.

Subconsciously, Alice compared it with her own current body; beside this young woman, Aisha Dewar would have seemed like a fragile doll. And, even so, she was well aware of the strength and flexibility she had... The new body must have belonged to a star gymnast, even for these times.

She examined it more closely.

It exuded an aroma... Wild, she decided. Her memory filled with vague images of green meadows, clear springs, hot blue skies... The small breasts, round, with erect nipples (was she cold?) that rose and fell gently, slowly, rhythmically...

She's breathing? Is she still alive?

She quickly glanced up at the oval face, framed with short, straight dark hair; the eyes—a liquid honey color—were open. Empty.

"Is she unconscious?" she asked in a timid voice.

Clyde touched the half-dead body.

"No. Her consciousness has been erased. Only her basic functions are being maintained."

Alice nodded, swallowed, but her heart kept on beating too hard.

"Ready?" asked the psychosociologist, offering her the diadem.

Without looking at him, the young woman shook her head.

"You know that in your present body they can recognize you, Alice," said the man.

"I know, but..." replied the young woman, and she stopped, without finishing her answer.

The psychosociologist took a deep breath.

I understand you, my love... I don't want you to leave the body that I love so much, but I love you, you, above the flesh and the madness, and I want you to survive...

He found the right words.

"We will preserve your current body. When you finish, you can transfer back to it, if you wish."

Alice gave him a look of gratitude.

Marvelous Clyde... You are the perfect friend; you have learned to understand me. How could I return to Stephen in another body that was not the one he loved?

Her mind made up, she held out her hand and took the diadem.

"When you're ready."

The psychosociologist went over to the controls and began pressing buttons.

Slender cables emerged from the wall. They snaked toward the female body floating in the middle of the room and wound themselves around her arms, legs, torso, head...

"What's that?" Alice asked, surprised.

"It's Aridor's idea," the man replied without looking up from his instruments. "He wants to record how a mind transfer is done; if we understand it we may still be able to save Lardner and...other cases," he bit his lip. Idiot, you were about to say Mergenthaler. "Stand beside her," he instructed.

The young woman obeyed, clutching the diadem in her hands.

The psychosociologist activated more controls, and new metallic serpents slithered toward Alice, crawling up her limbs, underneath her tunic, crawling over her face... The young woman shivered.

"They're tickling me!" she said, excusing herself.

The man readjusted the controls.

"No problem. They are all in place now. They won't move anymore," he reassured her, and hurried over to the new body.

He placed a diadem on to the inert cranium.

"Clyde..."

"What?"

"What was her name?"

"Her name was Helaine Keller. She was a student. Nineteen years old. She realized she would not be able to reach the minimum mental standards to perform creative work. She decided to give up," he explained as he returned to his console. "I'll give you her biography file later; you'll need to know it in case you bump into any of her old friends." With the controls all set, he looked up. "Everything's ready; we can begin whenever you like."

Alice raised the transmission diadem slowly and placed it over her temples...

2

What'sthat?

For a few microseconds she studied the confused brain waves closely.

ThenewbodyAlice'sconditioningClyde'slove.

The source identified, she concentrated.

Imustlowertheperceptionlevel.

The tumultuous waves of emotion diminished and subsided beyond her mental horizon.

Icancontinue.

While her eyes remained fixed on the screen to follow Glieber's movements in his cubicle, Maya let her own thoughts slide around inside her head. With a delicate touch she felt her way around the new connections, analyzing them, testing them, exercising them...

Iamgoingtooslowlyineedtotryagain.

She accelerated her internal biorhythm to the maximum.

On the screen, Glieber's movements immediately slowed right down, until he seemed to become immobile; only micrometer level changes in position were discernible, even though long intervals were passing in her dilated internal time frame.

Perhapsishouldgetbackinthemoment.

All at once she returned from the depths of her enhanced self. She moved, weightless, between new and complex structures, feeling their solidity, connecting them together, assimilating them with a feverish calm...

Suddenly Glieber's image became reanimated, moving at normal speed.

She calculated the time that had passed.

Lessthanthetimebeforenearlyforty-fourseconds.

She raised her hand to dry the minute drops of sweat from her forehead and watched their slight tremble.

Hurrycarefuldon'ttryitagainuntilafternightfall.

She returned to her interior and committed herself to the slow, hard, painstaking process of learning her new capacities...

ThereissomuchmissingthereissolittletimelefthowIneed Sarkinow.

She choked back the momentary outpouring of despair.

Panic!Iwontfailimpossibleunthinkabletofail!

On the screen, Glieber got up from his seat. He took a new file. He returned to his seat.

Allnormallet'sgetonwiththis...

3

She let the lithe body of Helaine Keller fall clumsily into the chair.

"You can continue, Nadia," said Alice with apparent calm.

"I have nothing particularly new to tell you about my work," the analyst began. "Even in your times, every collective needed one or two general specialists, generalists as you called them in the Empire." She smiled and winked at her. "People able to connect concepts from the sciences and other diverse fields of study, using the common features of all investigative work—analysts of the process of scientific progress, to be exact. With respect to my work in particular... I have had only one task since I graduated. I spent fifteen years trying to create the ovo. As you might expect, I wasn't alone; alongside me were ten of the best brains on Earth specializing in isogravity and theoretical physics... That is far too nebulous; I had better fill in some details."

"Nadia," said Felix Vallarta, his tone full of warning and concern.

The analyst turned her blue eyes on him.

"Don't worry. I am fully recovered, really," she told him, and turned back to Alice. "I suppose you know the history of how Earth and the solar-system groups separated?"

The young woman nodded.

"Good. One of the reasons was purely emotional. As I see it the antigroup attitude was based on the realization that it wasn't necessary to adopt a new structure for personal relationships to reach the stars, that the necessarily lengthy interstellar journeys could be made by other means that did not require the sacrifice of what they considered to be essential human qualities. With this conviction, Earth turned its back on the path being pursued by the groups—although not without compassion. Certain that when the groups' ships reached the nearest stars they would find normal human beings living on the planets out there, having gotten there by another route."

In the pause as Nadia stopped to drink some of the fizzy liquid in her glass, they could clearly hear the hoarse shrieks of the gulls as they swooped around their nest sites in the cliff beneath their feet.

The analyst continued.

"We looked for that route for over a hundred years: a quick, safe road to the stars. We made no progress, but it didn't matter. Earth was sufficiently big and rich, and at first its population didn't grow much." She took another sip. "In recent times, it has even been on the decline for a while... For sure, we will continue dreaming of other planets." She motioned to the silent Felix with her chin. "The work of the ecologists, for example, has been going in that direction for some time... And then, some fifteen years ago now, the portals appeared."

She paused again, her eyes fixed on the sea.

Clyde became aware that Karen had moved closer to the group.

The emotional engineer had seated herself on the sand behind Nadia and Felix, and it was clear she was listening intently. The psychosociologist did not like the look on her face, but he didn't have time to analyze it; Nadia had begun speaking again.

"Who could have suspected that the new social structure, the groups, would have any other effect than the elimination of the interpersonal tensions stemming between different types of people spending such prolonged periods living together in such close quarters? That it would produce an interpenetration of minds between those living in these communities, enabling them to go so much further than any terrestrial community?" She looked fixedly at Alice. "I don't know if anyone has told you or if you've read about it anywhere, but the groups were the ones who discovered the portals. To be precise, it was the Auroran Mentagroup." She looked around at her silent audience. "Perhaps even you aren't aware of what I am about to say now: the news is quite recent. The solar-system groups are seriously considering transforming themselves into mentagroups, too."

Felix and Clyde shook their heads.

Nadia went on.

"But let's return to Earth and the time Aurora very kindly sent us the plans of how to construct portals and all of their theoretical foundations... Our self-confidence suffered quite a shock, believe me. When they sent us the portals, Aurora had no more than seventy thousand inhabitants, and if you take into account the ten-year communication time lag in those days, there were not even fifty thousand Aurorans at the time they worked out what billions of earthlings had been searching for in vain for a century... Well, it was a serious blow. But we still had the opportunity to make up for it and recover our self-esteem; it was clear that the portals were not the ideal medium for interstellar travel... I should give you a basic explanation of the theory behind the portals. Do you know anything about them?"

Alice looked unsure.

"I have an idea... Very sketchy, short on details."

Nadia nodded.

"Very few people on Earth have much idea of what the portals are, Alice... Although I think you could get a good idea if I use an analogy. Do you know about isobars?"

"Of course," said the young woman, slightly offended. "They are the lines drawn on a map that join all points sharing the same atmospheric pressure."

"Good, the fundamental science behind the portals is called iso-gravitation. As a consequence of its postulates it's clear that one can travel, via hyperplanes, or subspace, or whatever you want to call it, instantaneously between points of equal or similar gravity with minimal energy expenditure. And the properties of gravitational hyperplanes not only equalize points of similar gravity on a single planet, which can be considered a slightly irregular sphere, but also points of similar gravity on all planets, in the whole of interstellar space, no matter the distance between them in normal space."

Alice pursed her lips.

"That was more or less what I thought... But I find it difficult to get my head around."

"You're not alone in that... Okay, the portals are possible thanks to that principle. Naturally the least energy expenditure occurs when they are located on points of equal gravity, but it's not difficult to place them on points of dissimilar gravity, so long as the extra energy required is not too great. But to summarize the most important point: to transport something across an isogravitational hyperplane you need two portals—one to send from and one to receive at."

"I'm starting to see..." murmured Alice.

"To connect planets from different star systems using portals you need to transport the first one out there through normal space. So, it would take thousands of centuries to establish a system of portals to span even this one branch of the galaxy... Then we asked whether it would not be possible to send the portals through hyperspace."

"The ovo concept," Alice put in.

"Exactly. If isogravitational points are really equivalent then you don't need a receptor at the destination point; it is enough to have a coordinate system in hyperspace, to construct the appropriate directional system and then to supply the ovo with sufficient energy... simple, right?"

"It would seem so," Alice said cautiously.

"And that's what we thought, at first... We had the fundamental theory of the portals sent to us by the mentagroups. If we could form a consortium of Earth's finest minds in theoretical physics, we could solve the problem—even before the mentagroups, if they happened to be trying. And..." Here the analyst let slip a sigh. "... we started work. Fifteen years ago. The first few were hellish, and attempting to comprehend the theory of isogravitational hyperspace was a task that sometimes seemed beyond our reach... But finally we succeeded in understanding it at a fundamental level. Or at least that's what we thought. We passed the next eight years building the theoretical foundations of the ovo. We tried out one variation after another, year after year... None of them worked. And don't think that we didn't fight, that we didn't sacrifice ourselves, heart and soul, to the project, because we weren't just fighting for ourselves, for personal prestige, but for the honor of the whole earth. Do you understand? To justify the principles put forward by our forefathers more than a hundred and seventy years ago, to show that the path we had chosen was as good as that chosen by the groups... But in the end we had to admit defeat."

Alice watched as a tear trickled down Nadia's cheek, and she felt a lump in her throat. But I must carry on, I must get to the root...

The analyst went on, her voice back to normal.

"The ovo could not work. We put together the final report, demonstrating this with the utmost rigor, and we published it, about a year ago now. Three months later, a cybo, Niels, wrote to our old team boss, Chen, claiming to have found errors in the report. Immediately, Chen called us all together. Over the course of two months we scrutinized the cybo's work and came to the unanimous conclusion that Niels's reasoning was flawed, that the errors did not exist. And so we told him. The cybo just looked at us with typical lack of expression and returned to his island without uttering a word."

Nadia finished and took another sip of her drink. Another tear mixed with the effervescent liquid... She continued her story.

"Two weeks after this incident, we received new information from Aurora, via the portal. There, complete in every detail, was the theoretical foundations of the ovo and plans to build it." She dried her eyes mechanically and continued. "The reasoning they had followed was the same as Niels's."

Alice tried to swallow the lump in her throat, but couldn't.

"Of course, we didn't believe it. We built an ovo, following these absurd plans to the letter, and we tried it about a month ago... No, five weeks ago. It worked."

How does she manage to stay so serene? Alice asked herself.

"The first to kill himself was Chen," Nadia continued. "The most recent, Obote, just passed this week. Not everyone decided to die; Arjipenko, Bellow, and Dzhu became cybos. The only one still alive, and normal, is me."

"Why?" asked Alice.

Nadia smiled.

"Good question, little one... The answer is that I still have work to do. I am a member of the Supreme Council, right?"

"And then what? You only have a year left on the council. Then what?" Alice insisted.

"Then what..." Nadia hesitated a moment, then shrugged. "In the end, does it even need saying? Then I will also become a cybo."

Karen leapt to her feet.

"How can you say that, Nadia?" she asked, infuriated. "How can you dare renounce the human condition?"

"I'd like to know what your definition of the human condition is," retorted Nadia, looking at her coldly.

"The human condition is being who you are," the emotional engineer replied, her voice charged with feeling. "Fallible, yes. Imperfect, yes. But always inside, the desire to be, to feel, to fight no matter how dire the situation. Not to run like a coward and turn oneself into a monster without feelings..."

"So, according to you, the cybos have no feelings?" asked the analyst.

"Of course they don't have them! What else are they trying to achieve by overwriting their brains with cybernetic circuitry? Emotion alone defines the human being, and they don't have any."

"You should study human evolution, Karen. Look at the monkeys, our distant cousins; they are far more expressive with their emotions than we are, aren't they?"

"That is a false argument. They are animals. Only mankind has managed to achieve the necessary balance between reason and emotion, and we need to preserve that; any excess of reason will bring with it the destruction of the emotions and lead to a roboticization of thought..."

"I think your reasoning lacks logic... The development of reason has never led to the extinction of feelings; it has in fact deepened and enriched them. To make some absolutist ideal out of a given period of equilibrium between reason and emotion is to negate change, to attempt to fix man in a single instant of his evolution... Your problem is that you judge the depth of emotions by their level of expression; without a doubt monkeys would see human beings as unfeeling creatures devoid of emotion if they were guided by our level of expressivity. They just show their emotions far more openly than we do."

The emotional engineer counterattacked.

"So, in your book, the inexpressiveness of the cybos demonstrates their elevated emotions... And the best proof of this is when Niels, upon discovering that stupid human beings couldn't understand his most elementary calculations, did an about-face and decided not to waste any time trying to teach them. Am I right?"

Nadia lowered her eyes.

"I don't think that was his reason..." she answered in a whisper.

"Oh yeah? What was it then?"

Nadia moistened her lips before answering.

"Pity... He felt pity for us."

XXXI

The Last Night

1

ARIDOR RAISED HIS EYES to the video reader.

"Well?" he asked.

Clyde Greenaway took the plunge.

"The situation is complicated... I think it's beyond my capabilities."

The hologram rested its elbows on the desk.

"What exactly is happening?"

The psychosociologist attempted a smile.

"Just as you predicted: high levels of internal tension. There have been some really serious discussions."

"Initiated by the cybo?"

Clyde hesitated.

"No... I don't think so, at least not directly. Although there have been discussions about the cybos—and the groups, too. But it has been Alice who has instigated them."

"Alice Welland?"

"Yes."

Looking away toward something invisible to Clyde, Aridor made a comment, as if to himself.

"A very intelligent person...and capable, yes." He turned back to the psychosociologist. "What do you suggest?"

Clyde ran the tip of his tongue over his lips.

"Would it be possible to begin the second phase of the operation tomorrow instead of the day after tomorrow?"

The head of special cases thought for a moment before answering.

"That could be a solution... But it is not my decision. Talk to Maya."

"Maya?"

"Yes. She is responsible for the operation. Anything else?"

"No. Thank you," replied Clyde Greenaway. "Wombat!" he called out.

"Wait!" Aridor held out his hand to him. "If Maya approves your idea, come here early tomorrow morning."

"But..."

"She can return quickly, but I need your help to look at the data from Welland's last transfer," the hologram smiled at him. "Remember that there are only a few of us who know all about this."

"Alright then," Clyde agreed. "Wombat," he ordered. "Cut the communication."

Aridor's image vanished.

The psychosociologist contemplated the bare wall.

Maya. Make a video call or go to see her in person?

He got up from his seat.

In person.

2

The stars were unusually bright. Magical almost... at least for Alice.

"It's marvelous," she said in a hushed voice.

From where she lay stretched out, Nadia looked across at the young woman from the past.

"What is?" she asked.

"The sky... The air, so clean, so clear; I don't remember ever having seen so many stars."

The analyst looked up, too.

"I understand. I can't bear to imagine the nights from the time of the Great Pollution," she replied, and she paused for a long time before asking, "Well then, have you been able to understand us?"

"What?" Alice blinked, and looked at the analyst. "You noticed?"

"Of course," said Nadia. "We do share a profession, you know!"

"I see... But there is one thing I don't quite understand."

"What's that?"

"How could all this happen? First with the groups and now with the cybos."

"The attitude toward them?"

"Yes."

Nadia sighed.

"You're right, it's not easy to understand... Look, people will always fight for something. Let's say, destroying the Empire. They achieve it. Then they need to step back and take stock... And not just that; they have to develop all of the hidden potential that has been suppressed and forgotten and that naturally seems unlimited to them. To sum up: they are at the pinnacle of human possibilities. It's not necessary to make any changes other than those that have happened... It's a logical attitude, inevitable. And it works for a time."

"But..." Alice murmured.

"Exactly: *but*. New contradictions arise. More subtle, harder to understand... Not as obvious as those of the Empire. But they are there, growing and developing... And the moment will come when they must be confronted."

"But the groups had formed before the fall of the Empire."

The analyst shrugged.

"Yes, but they had another purpose: to conquer the stars. The fact that they represented a new social structure that resolved many of the psychosocial problems inherited from the Empire was a poorly understood byproduct."

"Why?"

Nadia's eyebrows arched upward.

"Why do you ask? I think that you still have some way to go before you have a sufficiently clear view of things... Alice, we, the human beings of the future, of your future, are not infallible gods. We can be wrong, and we *are* wrong. That's not so bad. What would be bad is not correcting ourselves when we discover our errors. And I think that now is the moment; the case of the ovos should open our eyes."

"So Earth should follow the path taken by the groups?"

The analyst shook her head.

"I don't think so. Perhaps some people—and a good number, I don't doubt it—will opt for that route, and they will educate their offspring like the groups do. I am sure that the solar-system groups and the Aurorans will help them... But that's not my path. Excuse me, I think I've discovered the fanatic inside me."

Alice looked up, surprised.

"You, a fanatic?"

Nadia chewed her lower lip.

"You know," she replied, "I'd like to show that our ancestors were not so misguided, that in the end the groups are not the only way to resolve the contradiction between the limited capacity of normal human beings and the unlimited field of the unknown..."

The young woman from the past agreed.

"The cybos," she prompted.

"Exactly," said the analyst. "Despite everything, Earth found an alternative route. Although, sooner or later, those routes will come back together again; they complement one another too well," she added thoughtfully, and she looked affectionately at Alice. "But you have taught me not to idealize the future. The only thing I can say is that the groups and the cybos will encounter new and more subtle contradictions, and that they will also be wrong on occasion and they will correct themselves... What will their errors be? I can't say. But they will happen, because fortunately man is not perfect, and never will be; there's always the ability to grow..."

They looked up at the stars in silence.

"Thank you, Nadia," murmured Alice.

"There's no reason to thank me... You knew how to find the answer to your basic query, which is why we don't give what you consider to be enough importance to the Empire's counteroffensive. They can only fail... Of course, we have to take measures to ensure that they do the least possible damage. If you knew the whole plan, you wouldn't have any doubts, believe me. But now we have much more important problems..."

"I see that... Nadia, how did the cybos originate? I didn't have time to study their history when I was...there."

The analyst smiled.

"Also as a byproduct of another purpose... It must have been about eighty years ago, when the contradiction between human capabilities and the demands of the unknown were growing worse. That was before genetic improvement was allowed in all zones. In particular, Zones 3, 5, and 6 prohibited any kind of genetic manipulation of human gametes, even for hereditary conditions. So, to correct physical deficiencies they used the usual cybernetic add-ons: legs, arms, eyes..."

"I know all this," Alice interrupted.

"I forgot, sorry… But in our society the major limitation on human beings is mental, which after all is our essential feature… Indeed, the inability to contribute to society is a major trauma. So the idea of correcting mental limitations using cybernetic enhancement emerged. Several years went by without any results, but García and his team finally succeeded in increasing the capacities of the mentally disabled by implanting cybernetic circuits in their brains. This happened just as the notion of corrective genetic engineering of humans was accepted across the earth… It looked as if it would be nothing more than a transition technology, destined to disappear along with the last of the congenitally mentally disabled. But then Kawasaki began his work. It had been possible to increase the brain power of the mentally disabled to normality. Was this the limit? he asked himself."

"It wasn't."

"It wasn't. And fifty years ago the first cybo appeared: Ichabod."

"The name seems familiar."

"He is the current cybo coordinator."

"But the techniques for amplification must have been constantly improving. Isn't he a bit antiquated?"

"Cybernetic implants can be made more than once. What's more, it is only with time that they achieve full integration…"

A ray of light emerged from Karen's house. Tracing a graceful arc, it settled above the spot where the two women sat in their seats on the sand, and it glowed brighter.

Alice shaded her dazzled eyes with her hand.

"What's that?" she asked.

"It's a biolocator; someone is looking for us."

The sound of footsteps came from the shadows. Clyde Greenaway's figure came into the circle of light.

"Alice? I didn't think you were so close," he said.

"You were looking for me?" asked the young woman.

"Yes, the operation has been moved up. It will begin tomorrow."

"Tomorrow? And Maya knows about this?"

"She is in agreement."

"I have no objection either," Alice said, getting up. "Should I do anything now?"

"Go to bed. You need to rest."

Nadia Derzhavina got up, too.

"I'll come with you," she said. "It's getting late."

3

"They're coming back to the house now," said Karen, moving away from the picture window.

Felix Vallarta let out a grunt of acknowledgment, his eyes fixed on the window screen.

The emotional engineer wandered aimlessly around the room.

"I still can't believe it," she said.

"What?" asked the ecologist.

"That Nadia has decided to become a cybo."

The man shrugged.

"It's her right," he replied.

Walking behind her companion, she stopped and looked at his turned back.

"But don't you understand? She was my friend: to think that she would dehumanize herself.."

"She doesn't see it like that."

"She's wrong! Can beings that lack art be truly human?"

"We don't know enough about them to say that they don't have art, Karen."

"They never ask for anything we have created... Felix, if anything could convince me that here on Earth we have followed the right path is that we are the only ones who have preserved artistic creativity."

"You exaggerate. I have seen a few things made by the solar-system groups; they're not bad."

"Those things? They're absurd, incomprehensible, or completely banal. You can't call that art."

"They're not the same as us, Karen. You can't expect them to have the same aesthetic values as we do."

"They don't have the slightest notion of what aesthetics are, Felix."

"Art evolves, don't you think?" replied the ecologist. "Suspend communications, Wombat!" he ordered, and turned to the emotionalist. "He is in his house," he explained. "Nothing unusual happened on his stroll."

"It evolves, yes, here on Earth; you don't have to look further than the emocrystals... What's the matter, Felix? Why do you defend them? Or do you fancy yourself as a cybo, too?"

The ecologist shook his head.

"No. No I don't think that's the solution... But I wouldn't deny them the chance to try."

Karen sat down in front of him, her legs crossed.

"And what is the solution according to you?"

"The groups."

The woman nodded her head.

"So, I am the only one who trusts in good old Earth," she said bitterly.

He stretched out his hand and stroked her arm affectionately.

"You are too young, Karen. Earth is wherever you find mankind, my dear..."

The woman withdrew her arm.

"I'm not a child; I am twenty-seven years old."

"And I am sixty-six... But that has nothing to do with it. Listen; even if the art on Earth is the best, it's not enough. There are two paths to knowledge: art and science. And the ovo has shown us that we have lost our way on the second... No human society can sustain itself on one form of knowledge alone, be it art or science."

Karen hid her face in her hands. Sobs shook her shoulders and her bowed head.

Felix rose from his seat.

"What's wrong?"

The woman raised her face, puffy from crying.

"Don't you see? I'm alone..."

She reached out and took his head in her hands, then drew him toward her and kissed him passionately on the lips.

"Help me, please," she whispered. She pressed herself against him. "Don't leave me all alone..."

"Aren't I too old?" he asked instinctively.

Karen smiled through her tears.

"Stupid..." she replied. Moving apart from him, she took him by the arm. "Come with me," she said decisively.

4

"A chair, Wombat," Clyde Greenaway muttered.

He sat, not even waiting for the vortex in the force field to calm down. His gaze locked onto the sleeping figure of Helaine Keller.

Now Alice Welland's...

He remained still.

So? Why don't you begin?

He fidgeted on his seat, uncomfortable.

Perhaps you identify with her old body? With Aisha Dewar's body? Who do you love then? The body or her?

He snorted.

Of course I love her...that is, her mind. Perhaps the memory of what happened last night...

A shiver ran down his spine; he clenched his teeth.

But she needs me...

He forced his mouth to speak.

"Alice..."

The naked body on the bed shuddered, and its eyes—now golden—opened.

"Who...?" she started to ask, and her gaze found him. "Stephen!"

In one bound, Helaine Keller's body left the bed.

5

??

She moved the flexible mental tentacles skillfully around the edges of the disturbance and withdrew it immediately.

Thereisnoalternativebuttobegintomorrow.

E

This is the fifth part of the test. It is strictly your own work; you must complete it on your own, without discussing your answers with anyone. If you do not wish to complete it, continue to the next page.

I. True or False

1. Clyde loves Alice without reservations.
2. Karen is characterized by coherence between her thoughts and actions.
3. The problems discussed in science fiction have nothing to do with reality.

II. Analyze the following text:

> *But there is a vague conceptual future which concerns all of humanity and about which we know nothing... We leave the futurist novelists to meditate on this... We write for our time; we don't want to look at our world through the eyes of the future; for this would be the surest way to kill it.*
>
> —JEAN PAUL SARTRE,
> WHAT IS LITERATURE?

1. Do you live in a society that is orientated toward the future or one that turns its back on it?

TURN TO THE NEXT PAGE

2. Do you think that it is possible to write for our time without thinking about the future?
3. Which world does Sartre wish to defend from death?
4. Do you think about the future?
5. Are you in the habit of evaluating your actions from the perspective of their subsequent effects?

This test will continue later. You may change your answers at any point.

GO TO THE NEXT PAGE

XXXII

The Trap Is Sprung

1

SHE SQUEEZED NADIA'S HANDS IN HERS.

"See you soon," she said. "I would have liked to say goodbye to Clyde, too," she added.

The analyst returned the hand squeeze warmly.

"He asked me to tell you that Aridor called him to the institute; he didn't want to wake you... But he will be here when you return."

Alice smiled.

"Good. I have to go now, Maya will be getting impatient... Give my best to Felix. And to Karen," she added. Disentangling herself from the analyst's hands, she boarded the Hermes.

Nadia stepped back a little.

She saw the craft rise slowly and watched its swift departure, skimming low, heading north.

Her eyes followed the ship until it disappeared over the horizon, then turned to the house.

She didn't feel like going back there.

She turned and sat on the ground. She rubbed her hand on the granite surface of the landing pad; the sun was warming it.

Will I see them again?

Resting her forehead on her knees, she shut her eyes and relaxed. The heat of the sun's rays gave her a feeling of tranquility and peace...

Suddenly, a shadow passed between her and the sun; a sharp gust of wind ruffled her tunic.

She raised her eyes; a Hermes was passing in front of her.

They're back already? she asked herself, startled.

She got up, smoothing her clothes as she did so.

The craft's hatch opened and out popped a head.

Aridor? What could have happened?

The head of special cases hurried over to her.

"Has something happened, Sam?"

The man looked at her, smiling.

"No, nothing serious," he said. "Where are the others?" he asked in his turn.

The analyst motioned to the house.

"In there."

"Very well... Let's go; I must explain everything to them all together."

Taking Nadia by the arm, Aridor marched toward the house.

2

Alice looked out of the window.

The dense green foliage of the trees waved in the breeze, almost brushing the glass.

Rising from her seat, Maya took two packages from beneath the control panel. She handed one to her companion.

"We need to dress."

The young woman quickly examined the contents of the package: a pair of tall black boots and a short skirt... She began to unbuckle her sandals.

Moving surprisingly fast, Maya finished putting on her boots.

She took off her tunic, revealing her bronzed body, and fastened the skirt around her slender waist.

She waited until Alice had finished dressing.

"Ready?" she asked.

The young woman nodded her head.

Maya went on.

"Now we are just two tourists on an excursion through this zone... Do you remember all the instructions?"

Alice hesitated for a moment.

"I remember them, yes... But I have to admit I didn't understand them."

Maya's dark eyes fixed on hers.

"I suppose they must seem absurd to you, but I beg you to trust us."

Alice smiled.

"Don't worry. I know I shouldn't know more than what's absolutely necessary."

The tiny cybo placed a hand on her companion's shoulder.

"I shouldn't tell you this... But you can be sure of one thing: whatever happens, you will survive. Don't forget that."

And you? thought Alice, but she didn't dare voice her question.

"I won't forget," she responded.

How can she know? I can't believe that the cybos have developed precognition...

"We haven't developed it, but you can take my word," said Maya and, to the stunned Alice, she pointed to the door. "Let's go outside."

They let themselves drop, Alice first, Maya next, onto the grass beneath the hatch.

"Follow me," the cybo ordered.

Off they went, silently, into the trees.

3

A red light blinked on the control panel...

With practiced, precise movements, Candy manipulated the console.

In front of her the screen lit up.

Two figures emerged from the woods—one tall, the other small—running and laughing.

Two women. Tourists, by the looks of things; they could be...

She pulled the microphone to her mouth.

"Bennie!"

"Yes, Mom?" the reply burst through the tiny disk in her ear.

"Prepare the carpet. We're going to take a trip."

Babson could not hide the annoyance in his voice.

"Again?"

Candy took a deep breath. He will never, ever make a good agent.

"My dear, I think this time we'll be able to go outside," she said, without removing her eyes from the screen. "You need to get some air. I've been so preoccupied with this project that I haven't been able to pay you much attention, but I think I'll be able to sort it out soon..."

The two figures walked diagonally across the meadow.

They don't seem to be coming toward the house.

"Just one last problem, and then we can go out and about all you want..."

Hmmm... They are going to jump the stream. Perhaps...

The tall figure had already crossed. The smaller one took a run up, jumped, and landed writhing on the ground.

It's them!

"Right. We're going out this instant. Is the carpet ready?"

"Yes."

Babson's voice was suddenly serious, showing he had understood.

Candy quickly switched off the control panel. She stood up and strode toward the door, adjusting the video bracelet around her wrist as she did so.

She pressed the button to call the elevator.

That fall was too much of a coincidence and right in front of the house...

The door opened.

She stepped onto the little white disk that floated in the middle of the shaft and immediately began her ascent.

She turned on the video link in her bracelet.

The taller one was running toward the house; the injured one was sitting on the grass, holding her bare foot in her hands.

Stay calm. Despite everything, coincidences do happen. Wait for the final proof, she told herself.

The elevator came to a stop, and Candy stepped out of the tree.

Babson was already there, sitting on the carpet. The thin, rectangular platform emitted fine streams of air enabling it to float silently a few centimeters above the ground.

Candy hopped on board.

"Forward!" she ordered.

The carpet began to move, accelerating.

Babson waited until they had left Enchanted Valley before asking, "Is it them?"

"Keep your mind on where you're going. We have to get there quickly."

4

Holding her breath, Alice watched Maya leap and fall.

The tiny cybo rolled on the ground. Her cry was so authentic that, although she knew the plan, Alice ran toward her with her heart in her mouth. Was she hurt for real?

She knelt down next to the body curled up on the grass. Taking her by the shoulders she forced her to show her face.

It was contorted and covered with cold sweat.

"Maya, what have you done?" she asked fearfully.

"I don't know... Ahhh! I think I've twisted my ankle," the cybo moaned, indicating to her right boot with both hands.

"Let me see," said Alice, taking the boot in order to remove it. "Is this for real?" she added in a whisper.

Almost imperceptibly May winked, then she shouted, "Be careful! It really hurts!"

With as much care as possible, Alice took the boot off and examined Maya's foot.

"It looks serious," she said as she placed the foot carefully on the ground.

Between whimpers, Maya took hold of her foot again, and with her eyes signaled to the house nearby.

"I'll go and get help," Alice assured her. She ran off toward Glieber's house.

"Emergency!" she shouted, stopping at the door.

The door opened quickly.

It doesn't look as if they expected this, thought Alice, stepping into the hallway.

I need it to look as if I don't know where the household brain is, she reminded herself, and she opened and closed doors in apparent disorder, zig-zagging toward her goal.

Finally she got to the door she wanted, and her sigh of relief was not even slightly fake.

She sat at the control panel.

It must seem that I don't know this model.

She pressed buttons at random, as if trying to find out how to open an external communication channel, and...

Now!

She pressed two buttons at the same time.

Inside the circuits of the brain, two opposing commands fought with each other, and the protection systems were activated automatically, disconnecting all other controls.

The panel switched itself off.

The brain is neutralized, she said to herself. Now I can search the house.

Briskly but calmly, she went to the door and pushed it.

It was closed.

What? I remember leaving it open.

She felt a tingle in her nostrils. Instinctively she slowed her breathing and strained her ears. Somewhere in the room something was hissing quietly.

Gas! she realized. In one movement she unfastened her skirt and tied it around her mouth. She tried to breathe.

The fabric is too thick, but something gets through... If I can just hold out for long enough...

She kicked off her boots: one, two. Crouching down she searched feverishly inside them.

Where did she say they were? Ah ha, yes, here...

She pulled out a narrow rod. She began to cough. Setting the tiny device to one side, she attempted to adjust her improvised mask.

It's useless, she decided.

It was difficult to locate the miniature laser again; everything in her visual field was becoming fuzzier by the moment.

She stood up, swaying; she had to steady herself with one hand against the wall. With her other hand she pointed the device at the door and activated it.

An invisible ray of thermal radiation touched the white metal heating it slowly until it glowed red...

She fell to her knees, coughing violently. The laser fell from her hands, deactivating itself.

I can't take anymore... Maya! Help!

She felt as if the skirt was suffocating her. She tore it from her face and breathed in great lungfuls of the stinging gas.

Why don't you come? I know you can hear me...

Unable to hold herself up on her knees, she let her body collapse to the floor.

You promised me my life, she protested feebly, and lost consciousness.

5

Nowit'smyturn.

Still massaging her ankle, Maya allowed her mind to extend in concentric waves around Glieber's house.

The invisible net advanced, advanced...

(cold	*caustic*	*inquisition*
mud	*throbbing*	*hatred)*

... she stopped.

She located the position of the enemy. One (cold caustic inquisition) was immobile. On the edge of the beautiful woodland.

The other (mud throbbing hatred) was approaching from behind her.

She contained her desire to turn her head and look at it.

Ineedtokeepwatchingthehousefindoutwhattheyaregoing todowithme.

She projected a fine thread of her consciousness into the stranger's mind, trying to avoid the sickening emanations from the mud... Her teeth clamped together forcefully.

It'samaninthebodyofachild!

With immense self-control she managed to overcome the tide of repugnance; she manipulated it, diverting it to the furthest corner of her internal self, and shut it away.

Sloshing around in the putrid cesspit, she continued searching...

Theirplanisjustasexpectedperfect.

She abandoned Babson's mind with a sense of sheer relief; now she had to prepare herself for their meeting.

She proceeded with a self-examination. Her breathing was rapid, her body tense.

Imustpreparemyselfcontrolmyself.

Her hands continued their rhythmic massaging of her foot, while her mind flooded her body with wave after wave of serenity, calm, relaxation...

6

Kicking the ball venomously, Babson approached his target, cursing his child-mask over and over again...

Panting, he raised his eyes; he was still too far away. By some stroke of luck, the woman had not noticed him yet...

One last kick, and the ball rolled up close to the woman; she turned her head toward him, startled.

Babson couldn't help but smile; this loser was by all accounts a very poor agent. But what else could you expect from the people of this time?

He stopped about five meters away. He needed to calm his breathing first.

"Hi! Is something wrong?" he asked in his fresh, infantile voice.

The woman gave a half smile, making an obvious effort to control her pain.

"I've sprained my ankle," she explained.

Babson came closer.

"Do you need help?" he asked.

The woman shook her head. She looked away from her interlocutor, toward the nearby house.

"My friend went in there, to..."

Babson calmly took aim.

He fired.

Without finishing her sentence, the woman writhed in a spasm and fell backward on the grass.

Babson approached to examine her, and scowled: she was a runt, an utter weakling... True, the body that Candy now occupied wasn't much more robust, but she was a proper agent, something this fool could never be.

He prodded her in the ribs with his foot before turning to greet Candy; she was almost there, approaching at full speed on the flying carpet.

He pointed the neurotor at the inert body.

"She's ready," he informed her.

Candy descended from the carpet and crouched beside the paralyzed lookout. With a practiced hand she began to test her reflexes.

"What are you looking for?" asked Babson, offended. "At a meter's distance it's impossible to miss."

Raising her head, Candy eyed her partner coldly.

"Caution never goes amiss; remember that, if you value your life," she warned him bluntly. "Go to the house and empty the gas from the control room before the other one dies," she ordered, and stretching out a hand, she retrieved the discarded boot from the ground.

Yawning, Babson set off toward the house.

With nimble fingers, Candy tested the inside of the boot... Removing her hand, she examined the minute artifact in her palm. It wasn't the same as the one used by the other agent in her escape attempt.

She threw the boot and its contents as far away as she could and leaned over the captured agent again. She took off the other boot and, without bothering to check it, threw it away, too. She unfastened the skirt from around the hips and looked appreciatively at the tanned skin beneath. A habitual nudist, she decided, as she began to examine the fabric against the light, feeling it between her fingers and thumbs... With a shrug of her shoulders she tossed it to one side.

She ran her fingers through the young woman's dark hair and very carefully felt every inch of her scalp. She found nothing.

She examined the ears, the nostrils... She pressed on the jaw hinge and managed to open the mouth; she ran her finger around the palate and under the tongue...

Still crouching, thoughtful, she dried her hand on her tunic. There was still something she didn't like about her... The other agent had shown guts: this one had fallen with suspicious ease...

"Caution never goes amiss," she repeated between her teeth.

She placed her hand on the exposed pelvis and painstakingly checked the skin beneath the pubic hair and the hair itself. Nothing.

She pushed her finger into the vagina, regretting not having brought gloves, but work is work... And then the anus... Nothing there either.

As she cleaned her hands on the skirt she contemplated the face, deformed by muscular paralysis. She would have loved to know the thoughts going on behind that petrified grimace of pain... She threw the skirt away. At least she had nothing to reproach herself for; she had left nothing undone. If this one had fallen so easily, it was due to a lack of preparation, yes, and also of ability; there was a reason why she had been assigned only to keeping watch, while the other one had gone to do the real work.

Grasping the young woman behind the head and beneath the knees, she lifted her in one easy movement and laid her onto the carpet. She climbed on at the other end and steered the vehicle toward Glieber's Hermes, where she stowed the rigid body in the cabin.

Seating herself at the control panel, she tuned the communications system to the correct frequency and sent a coded sequence of signals.

Good, they knew of the trap's success. Now for the other one... Her brow wrinkled. Why was Babson taking so long? It was true he wouldn't be able to carry her alone; she was bigger and heavier than the lookout. But he should have come out to call her...

She raised her arm and switched on the video bracelet. She shouldn't have been so gullible, the other agent might have simulated being overcome by the fumes... The image on the tiny screen made her shake her head several times; knowing Babson as she did, she should have realized what was going on.

She exited the Hermes and went into the house. It was a real shame that the lookout had failed to liquidate him; someday his lack of control would cause an incident. A serious one...

She entered the control room.

"Babson!" she said, severely.

The boy jumped and stood up, withdrawing from the woman's unconscious body.

"You shouldn't waste time; we're working," she admonished him as she advanced on the unconscious tourist and grasped her by the arms. "Help me carry her," she ordered.

Hurriedly rearranging his tunic, Babson bent to pick up the boots that had been thrown on the ground.

Candy stopped him.

"Leave them."

The child turned his head in surprise.

"Are we going to leave their clothes here?" he asked.

"Yes. Take her by the legs."

When they got to the Hermes, Candy had to load the prisoner by herself; it was beyond the limit of Babson's strength.

After she had placed her alongside the other one, Candy sat on the floor next to her. She needed to recover her breath; that was a really well-built young woman.

Babson let himself slump in the pilot's chair, panting.

Candy stared at the motionless bodies of their captives. She didn't understand why that idiot lookout still bothered her. An ill-founded gut response? Perhaps... Although, through her long career, there had not been many occasions when her instincts had been mistaken, more than once she'd owed her life to them. Still, she couldn't think of any reason why that young woman should give her such a bad feeling...

"Give me your neurotor," she demanded of her partner.

Looking at her in surprise, Babson obeyed.

Candy checked the weapon. Yes, it was set at level two, for muscle contraction, an hour of paralysis, at least. She should be able to breathe easy...

"Are we leaving?" asked Babson.

Candy nodded, not taking her eyes from her quarry.

XXXIII

The Best Solution

1

"THERE'S SOMETHING MISSING from your report, Ryland."

The head of Imperial Security looked in concern at the chairman. Dahlgren continued, folding his hands across his belly, fingers interlaced.

"Although you couldn't have known, Agent Rockne made an emergency transmission while you were still on your return flight. Houdry's body, that is Mergenthaler's, was found at the offices of the regional bureau. He had no awareness; he was a complete vegetable."

"That clarifies matters..." said Ryland Kern, under his breath.

"Indeed," agreed Dahlgren. "Let's see if you arrive at the same conclusions as we do," he said, glancing toward Sybil. She remained silent.

"I think it's self-evident: Houdry occupied the director's body in order to enter the Department of Special Cases without arousing suspicions... But there's no way of knowing for sure what happened to him when he was inside."

"Any suggestions?" asked the chairman curtly.

"First, the best case scenario: Houdry tried to eliminate Welland. He didn't manage to control his new body sufficiently well, and he failed in his first attempt. In the struggle for his weapon that ensued, stray fire hit the psychosociologist, the Greenaway man,

Welland, and Houdry himself, killing them all. The neurotor fell to the floor, passing inadvertently into the hands of curious bystanders."

"The genuine probability of this?"

The head of security shrugged his shoulders.

"Very small. It would be too much of a coincidence for them all to have been killed."

"Alternative versions?"

Ryland looked dourly at the chairman.

"Only one, which involves a trap."

"With the neurotor as bait?"

"Yes."

"That would be a serious indication that they are aware of our existence..." said Dahlgren; he paused, waiting for Ryland.

"And we need to know exactly how much they know," concluded the head of security.

"That's right. There are several different possibilities. Evaluate them."

"It could be that Houdry and Welland are both really dead... In that case, they will only know what she had time to tell them. If only Welland has died, apart from what she may have revealed, everything depends on how trustworthy Houdry is," he said, looking at Sybil.

The woman shook her head.

"You can dismiss the idea of Houdry making any revelations," she replied. "The conditioning he developed is very effective. *They* couldn't learn how to eliminate it from observing only one case."

"Are you sure?" Dahlgren asked.

"Certain... Rockne is of the same opinion. She occupied the mind of a psychosociologist and studied this possibility on the orders of Houdry himself."

"So, there are no dangers from Houdry. You may continue, Ryland."

"If both of them survived..." Kern reasoned. "Well, if Alice Welland survived, it all depends on what she's been able to discover."

The chairman turned to Sybil.

"This is something you should know...or at least be able to make an educated guess about. How much would Welland have been able to extract from Houdry?"

Sybil Golden chewed her lower lip thoughtfully...

"I can only make a guess," she declared. "Houdry trusted her, based on his conditioning of her with regards to him, but that conditioning doesn't protect us. Of course, if they were to try interrogating Houdry then it wouldn't be long before he died. And once she found out about that, she would also die."

Ryland Kern nodded.

"By which time she would have told them all she knew," Ryland pointed out.

"So what we need to know is how much she got out of Houdry," Dahlgren insisted.

"We can only make inferences about that," said Sybil. "I can be certain that it wasn't everything; otherwise the trap would make no sense. *They* would already be here."

"Alright then... But what exactly did she know? How many of us there are? The total number of Hydras?"

"Her work was to study today's world, find its weaknesses in order to be able to restructure our program of action... In the beginning she didn't need to know much about us. Of course, she could have sounded Houdry out on the sly... She wouldn't have been able to do anything overtly until she'd finished her investigation. And according to Houdry that was a ways off."

"You knew Houdry well, Sybil. How much could she have discovered without him realizing?"

"Houdry was very discreet. Otherwise he wouldn't have been able to get into the institute."

Dahlgren leaned back in his seat. He looked tired.

"This way we'll never get anywhere, my dear... Okay, so suppose that Houdry told her everything except our location—or most of the rest. In this case, what would be the best course of action? Overlook the trap?"

"No," replied Ryland. "We still don't know the full potential of this era's people. If we don't act, we will remain in the dark with regard to their plans. With the element of surprise gone, we will be paralyzed. It's not possible to determine the correct strategy without more information."

"I agree," the chairman said approvingly. "What do you propose then?"

Ryland Kern leaned forward, resting his elbows on the table.

"In the first place, dismiss the idea that this is not really a trap; it could be that, however improbable it seems, all three of them are dead. If that's the case then it is essential we recover the neurotor; if they find it, it would be the clue leading them to infer our existence."

"Good. How do we do that?"

"Obviously, in a way that does not directly compromise any of us...including members of Hydra II. Rockne could, for example, hypnotize a member of the regional bureau so that they would take and hide the neurotor in their home."

"Is that possible, Sybil?" asked Dahlgren.

The woman hastened to assure him.

"It is; she is sufficiently well versed in conditioning techniques so that any attempt to force the subject into revealing the identity of whoever hypnotized them would result in the subject's immediate death. That way we'd be well protected... Although there is still something that I'm not comfortable with."

"Which is?"

"From the data that Houdry had been supplying me with and from what I have been able to gather personally, I have come to the conclusion that *they* are unaware of the tactics of espionage and counterespionage; however, I am also convinced that they could learn them quickly and even improve on them."

"That is evident, Doctor Golden," the head of Imperial Security replied dryly. "I consider it to be beyond doubt that the enemy is capable of imagining our line of reasoning, so let us put ourselves in their position. No doubt they also wish to know more about us, and they will deduce that the neurotor hidden in the house of this member of the regional bureau could be a trap laid by us to verify whether or not they have discovered us."

Dahlgren nodded his head slowly up and down.

"I'm beginning to understand your thinking... Continue."

"The only efficient course of action for them to avoid losing their advantage over us would be to send in their own agents to search the house. We will capture them—alive, of course. More than just useful sources of information to determine what *they* really know, they could act as hostages if we need to open negotiations..."

The chairman frowned.

"In reality," Ryland Kern quickly added, sensing something amiss, "it would be at this stage of the game where we could play our hidden card; it would seem as if we were negotiating, but in fact this would not really be the case."

Dahlgren's face betrayed his curiosity.

"Explain yourself!" he ordered.

"It's obvious that we we will have to make some sacrifice to make them think they'd found us all; it will cost us Hydra II and two or three more Hydras, but, to me, this seems a small price to pay..."

"I'm still not sure what the game is, Kern."

"Allow me to explain; the hostages will be taken to Candy's valley..."

"The Enchanted Valley? That means we would lose our substitute headquarters."

"It is necessary, Chairman; we will only convince them if we sacrifice something genuinely valuable."

"Your reasoning is sound. Go on."

"All the members of Hydra and three supposed leaders will be in the valley... I have no doubt that Doctor Golden could prepare us using the diadems she has in addition to some spare bodies we could procure for her. Is it possible, Doctor?" he asked, looking at Sybil.

The subject of his question hesitated for a moment before answering.

"Yes and no; I may be able to answer you definitively when you have finished setting out your plan."

Ryland arched his eyebrows, and with a sideways glance at Dahlgren to ascertain his tacit support he went on.

"Okay then. This triumvirate would begin negotiations; obviously the enemy would have to follow the trail left by those who captured its agents. They have more than enough sophisticated methods to do this. When they find the valley, talks would begin."

"And what would the terms be?"

"It's simple," Sybil answered, moving closer to Ryland. "Seeing ourselves discovered, our secrecy gone, we would admit the impossibility of reconquering the earth. In this way we would deliberately fall into their hands. With contact established we'd play our trump card, the hostages, to guarantee our safety and offer a solution: we would propose that we and the Hydras we hand over go into exile on an inhabitable planet with very few natural predators. It would not be too much to ask of them; in principle the ovos have opened an infinite number of worlds to human colonization. After our passage through the portal they would destroy it and, naturally enough, assume that we had been neutralized. However, after a prudent interval, those of us remaining here could reopen the portal, allowing the rest of us to return; the losses would be minimal."

"Have you considered the danger that, assuming that they have all of us in their power, they simply decide to destroy us all?" Dahlgren asked her.

"What about the hostages? And the almost mystical respect that they have for human life? Patrick, you will recall that they think that it is the sole choice of the individual to end their life, or 'give up' as they call it."

"It seems to be a reasonable scheme," Dahlgren conceded, "and in the meantime, we can activate the remaining Hydras a few at a time and continue with the project... I like this plan." He smiled. "Okay, what difficulties are there with our doubles? I have to confess that your 'yes and no' has intrigued me."

The woman automatically rearranged the folds of her tunic across her knees.

"I can make doubles for you two. Beginning with the supposition that Welland has discovered our identities, I will need to take sufficient information from your minds to convincingly simulate Kern and Dahlgren. It won't be a simple task; I will have to proceed with a great deal of care so as not to transfer your entire selves. I don't know what would happen to you if this were to occur... I won't be able to do a similar extraction of information from myself. The process is by its very nature quite personal; I couldn't program a machine to do it. Even Maureen, with the experience she gleaned from inhabiting the psychosociologist, wouldn't be able to learn how to do it in less than a month... I don't think we have that much time."

"Do we, Kern?" asked Patrick Maynard Dahlgren.

The head of security shook his head.

"In my opinion, no incursion by enemy agents will happen in less than three days... But they won't wait longer than a week."

The chairman lowered his head, deep in thought...

"I understand what you're saying, Sybil," he began in an affectionate tone. "You will have to take part personally."

The woman managed a weak smile.

"It will pain me to be separated from you, my love... But it will be for your own good."

Rising from his chair, the chairman walked around the table and stopped before the dejected Sybil. He patted her lovingly on the back.

"I won't let you go without being sure that there's no risk to you," he whispered confidentially. "However, it does solve another serious problem: how to keep us fully informed about everything happening in the valley. I suppose that our doubles must not realize that they are in fact doubles, right?"

Sybil shook her head.

"It would be too complicated to implant two levels of conditioning," she mused. "Only Houdry would have been able to do that."

"It's a shame... But if you go, we won't face that problem. You can obtain all the information about us that the enemy agents have, relay it to us, and adapt the course of action accordingly." With an affectionate squeeze of the woman's shoulders, he concluded, "You can be sure that I won't leave you for long on that planet."

Sybil shot him a grateful look.

"I know, brother," she replied in a voice too soft for Ryland to hear.

The chairman straightened up, smiling at her, and went to sit down again.

"Very well, let's move on to the operational challenges. The first is to retrieve the neurotor. Who is going to inform Rockne about her role in this?" asked Dahlgren.

"I will," the head of security replied.

"When will you be able to do that?"

"We will regain the neurotor by tomorrow morning at the latest."

"That's good. Moving on to the next issue: obtaining the bodies for our doubles... And you Sybil, you must realize that you can't keep the one you presently occupy. Ryland, put one of your people on it; they need to find two men and a woman who live together."

"Rockne can do that."

Dahlgren raised an eyebrow.

"Won't she be overwhelmed with work?"

"No. She only needs to find the information on the archive at her base and pass it on to the closest person to them... I believe the implantation of the doubles can be done tonight."

The chairman turned his gaze to Sybil.

"Will you have the diadems prepared for tonight, my dear?"

"If I begin to compile the necessary data in your memories within the hour, yes," responded the woman, her business-like manner regained. "I calculate that I'll need no more than three hours for each of you."

"Then you will have them... Now let's deal with the problem of eliminating your present body. What story can we go with that? Suicide?"

Sybil nodded.

"That's the most logical, given Shari's personality... Naturally it will be involuntary; during one of her religious experiences, she launched herself from the heights of the tower, believing she could fly... There could be other versions, of course."

"That one will do. The possibility of 'giving up' is open to us too at some convenient point; the motive would be disillusionment with our spiritual guide, etcetera... That part is resolved. To summarize: the neurotor, the false triumvirate, the counter-trap... Who can we put in charge of snaring the enemy agents?"

"With respect to that, there is no other choice," Ryland Kern interjected. "Except Candy. She is the best from that Hydra."

"But her, on her own..." Sybil said doubtfully. "If they send three or four agents, she wouldn't be able to manage it."

"She has Babson. What's more, it wouldn't be logical for the enemy to send more than one agent, or at most two, on the basis that any more would inhibit us from acting, and that would automatically preclude the possibility of their obtaining any information from us... No, Sybil; I don't believe the enemy would be that stupid."

"And if their intention is to capture us? If they try to discover where the neurotor is, or its connection to us, using their modern techniques?"

"We have men occupying the bodies of cyberneticists, Sybil. They can prepare us for that potentiality... but it's unlikely."

"And if it doesn't work?"

"We can come up with an alternative plan," said Ryland. "For example, finding the location of the enemy's control center; I suppose that must be inside that Institute of Psychosociology... But that would be far more difficult; we would be operating inside their territory, instead of forcing them to come into ours. They must have foreseen the possibility of that sort of attempt on our part, and they will be prepared for it. We can't imagine what their capabilities might be on their own ground... Don't be in any doubt, Doctor Golden; this is the most promising route."

"You can trust Kern, my dear," Dahlgren said supportively. "He is the best in his field. Any other practical details?"

"Yes," said Sybil. "It will be necessary to make the members of Hydra believe that we three have always inhabited the bodies of the pseudo-triumvirate."

"Not all of them," corrected Ryland. "Only those who know our actual location: Candy, Babson, Savell, MacGray, and Lambert."

"That's quite enough of them: half of the entire Hydra corpus," murmured the chairman.

"And add in Rockne; she saw Kern and heard you on the emergency channel," put in Sybil.

"Okay, from tomorrow morning, when you are inside your new body, that will be your first task, my dear: to adjust the minds of the Hydra members to the new versions of ourselves... Ah, and one last detail, Kern, while Sybil pokes around in my head, decide which Hydras we can preserve and which we should surrender. I think we can finish up this meeting."

The head of security left the room.

Smiling, Dahlgren turned to Sybil.

"When you're ready, my dear."

2

Sybil read it once more, incredulous, her eyes narrowed. No. No, it wasn't possible; it couldn't be possible...

She began the memory search again, feverishly keying in all the parameters, starting from a different chain of events. There had to be some fault in the apparatus. It was impossible that it could be referring to her; it had to be another person, with a similar name to hers...

The screen lit up again; Sybil Golden chewed her lip as she read anxiously...

She looked at the unconscious body lying on the examination pod: the stinking rat... So she couldn't even trust her own brother. After all that she'd done to help him? She should kill him...

The lightning bolt of icy pain took her by surprise.

She twisted in her seat, her lips pressed together, trying to hold back the tears that were seeping from her eyes.

Good grief! So that was the conditioning?

She stayed still, her body enfeebled, fearing *that* might happen again.

No. No, she shouldn't let herself be overcome by her emotions; she would not allow herself that weakness now, not for that swine, but for herself... But to know that her own brother had mistrusted her, doubted her unconditional support, and subtly conditioned her... And what subtlety! Using his brotherly love as cover... She needed to swallow her anger; it would not get her anywhere and would only weaken her. But knowing all this was going to drive her mad...and he knew it, too. And he also knew that she had only one option... Oh, how skillfully he'd played his cards!

She cleared the screen. His double didn't need to know anything about this... Leaving her chair, she sat on the floor. She adopted the lotus position and began her breathing exercises.

In the first place, establish a barrier between any future attempt to access that part of Patrick's memories... That's right... And now the most difficult part: to forget that she had been conditioned. The reason behind her idolatry of Nevin-Patrick was simply her love for him as his sister, an adoration she had always felt since childhood, seeing him as a substitute for an absent father. The focus of her admiration was his intelligence, his experience, his skill...

3

She opened her eyes.

What had happened?

She looked around, disconcerted.

She was in the laboratory. Nevin's unconscious body lay on the examination table. What?

All at once she remembered everything: she had been studying his mind, selecting the necessary memories to form the consciousness of his double, and... No. She couldn't recall why she was on the floor, in the lotus position. She had probably been feeling tired; the task required total concentration. She must have decided to do a little yoga to refresh herself, gather her energies, and she had gone to sleep in the middle of her exercises. She was out of practice; she should exercise more...

Getting up from the cold flagstones, she returned to her seat in front of the control screen. At least she had accomplished something: she now felt fresh, enthusiastic. There was no time to waste...

XXXIV

In the Enchanted Valley

1

WITH ONE AGILE LEAP she was the first to disembark from the Hermes.

She raised her eyes to the golden sky above her and saw another aircraft cross the electromagnetic dome at full speed, heading right for Castle Danger... Could that be Candy and the hostages?

She turned to the doubles; they had already descended onto the wide terrace and were also watching the approaching craft.

"If you want, I can take charge of organizing this while you rest," she suggested to the false Patrick.

The one she had addressed turned to Kern's double.

"Let's take a look at our rooms, Ryland. We'll leave these matters in her capable hands."

Sybil watched them go with a feeling of disgust... It had been necessary to condition them to be obedient to her suggestions in order to prevent them from deviating from the plan they'd outlined. However, she had to confess that she'd overstepped the mark a little. Such open admiration and submission to her wishes didn't sit well with the image of themselves that *they* surely would have extracted from their memory banks: the dominant males, the tough characters. Ah, well. There would be time to rectify that later. The important part now was to handle this part, the most delicate phase of the operation: to ensure that the Enchanted Valley could be converted into an unassailable bastion so that they could negotiate from a secure position.

She ran to the little turret in the middle of the terrace. It was a further worry that it had to be Mendoza, so stupid when it came to anything that wasn't straightforward physical action, occupying the body of that emotionalist... What was the name? she asked herself as she began to climb the spiral staircase inside the tower... Darrow, yes, that was it. But he was the only one who had any pretext for remaining there permanently—except of course Candy. But she had her own special assignment. Luckily, some of the most capable agents had visited her for various reasons, and that had made the task easier.

She stepped off the last creaking step and pushed open the heavy door.

Mendoza turned his gaze toward her.

"Welcome, Doctor. Everything is ready," he informed her, rising from his seat in front of the controls.

Sybil made herself comfortable in his place.

"Has Candy arrived yet?" she asked.

"No, we are still waiting for her, Babson, and Schwartz," replied the grinning Mendoza.

"I'll take charge of welcoming them. Go and get some rest... Umm, stay in your room; you need to be on hand," Sybil ordered, and immediately forgot about him.

Had something happened to them? she asked herself, as she checked the controls... No, Candy is very capable, she would have rigged up an alarm in case of her own capture...

The screen lit up.

Sybil raised her eyes hopefully; their gleam faded on recognizing Schwartz's sharp features.

"Can I cross the dome?" the man asked.

Sybil looked at her instruments. The golden electromagnetic dome was still permeable.

"You can," she responded.

The image vanished. The woman regarded the control desk. She should check the real state of preparedness; although Mendoza had said that everything was ready, he could very well have missed something... She verified the energy system; if the secret power portal didn't work, they would find themselves as vulnerable as a snail without its shell when *they* decided to cut the power supply... No, that was working, the photocells absorbing every last quantum of light... She should test the impenetrability setting for the dome.

Outside, the golden sky darkened, taking on tinges of purple, and the instruments indicated that there was now an impenetrable force field passing over the mountains and deep beneath the Enchanted Valley; it was impossible to cross.

Satisfied, Sybil disconnected the system. They could rest assured that they were safe from any physical attacks from outside—except of course nuclear bombings. But then again, *they* had an aversion to killing other human beings... There was one other option open to them: a surprise attack using a miniature ovo sent into the dome to open a portal and allow them to gain access... Well, let them try. They would be the ones taken by surprise when they discovered that the "magical" powers of the valley were in fact real.

She booted up the auxiliary screen in order to get an image of the local cybermechanics control center and found Maureen Rockne's gleaming eyes staring back at her.

"Has Candy arrived?" she asked.

"Not yet. I am checking out the protective systems," answered Sybil. Maureen smiled.

"It hasn't been long since I connected up the green tornados; there should still be things alive in the valley. If you want to see them in action, just say the word; I promise the spectacle is worth it, Doctor."

"Put them up on my screen."

A mist covered the ground like a thick veil, hiding all the details of the landscape; through it random flashes of green could be glimpsed... Suddenly one swelled, changing color, taking on tones of red. For a few moments it stayed immobile on the spot.

"Did you see it? Did you see it?" she heard the excited voice of Rockne exclaim. "That must have been one of the valley's stags. That was certainly not a mere rabbit, no; they barely make it turn pink..."

The pleasure her voice revealed was possibly a little excessive, but Sybil decided it clearly demonstrated that she was someone ideal for the job.

"Yes, I saw it, Maureen," she replied. "But to me it seems that there are very few tornados... And what's more, because they are visible, I think they allow the opportunity to avoid them."

On the screen one of the tornados interrupted its casual meanderings and launched itself forward at surprising speed. It halted and acquired a slight rosy tinge for an instant, before continuing on its meandering way.

"That was definitely a rabbit," commented Rockne. "Don't worry, Doctor; this is just a practice, a game so that we can determine whether it works. When we go on high alert, there will be three times as many and they will be completely invisible; not even an ant will be able to survive for a minute out there."

"That's good... And the entrances that allow access to the valley?"

"You're in luck, Doctor; a stag has just escaped from the mist and is attempting to get through one now... You can see for yourself."

The image on the screen changed; now it showed two bare, black rock faces defining a narrow gap between them, and nothing more.

"The stag? I don't see it..."

"It will be there soon. You really can't see anything? You can be sure that neither the stag nor anyone else will see anything before it's too late... Here it comes!"

A burnished figure shot onto the screen... Then Sybil couldn't be exactly sure what happened; it seemed as if a stain had peeled off the rock face, falling oh so quickly on the stag, and then she saw, quite clearly, the stag, pinioned, making useless efforts to free itself from the long black legs keeping it immobile against the ground. Attached to the legs, something monstrous was opening a mouth full of gleaming fangs.

"What do you think of the guardian? I'd like to see that wimp Ferhad facing up to that one... He wouldn't last a second, believe me."

"I believe you... And the devices to destroy the passes?" asked Sybil as she watched, fascinated, as the giant spider towered over its victim... She realized in time she was allowing herself to get carried along by Maureen, and, tearing her gaze away, she scrutinized the main screen; it was still vacant.

When would Candy arrive?

"They're ready, but as you must understand, it's impossible to test them. It's a shame..."

"And the dragons?"

"I have already tried them out; they're the best of the lot. It's a tremendous sight to see them spitting fire... Would you like a demonstration?"

"No, thanks. I should continue testing the other systems... But I've forgotten: Do the volcanos work?"

The image of Maureen Rockne returned to the screen.

"I tried them with standard rock," she answered, shrugging. "They work well; they can be aimed quickly and precisely. Ah, and the system for locking onto aerial targets works just fine; if an enemy craft manages to cross the dome, it wouldn't last ten seconds between the volcanoes and the dragons."

"And the internal castle defenses?"

"Savell and I decided I already had enough systems to manage, so I passed them over to him."

"Where is he?"

"In the castle control room."

"I'll go and inspect what he's done. See you later, Rockne... And don't let yourself get carried away in your...enthusiasm. Remember that this is work."

"What can I do? I love my work!" the woman replied with a broad smile.

Shaking her head, Sybil disconnected the auxiliary screen; at the same moment an alarm sounded, alerting her to something coming through on the principal screen.

She looked over and saw Candy's face.

"Everything okay?" she asked cautiously. The aircraft was not yet inside the dome.

"All good. I have what you need," came the transmission.

"Perfect. As soon as you land, take it to the laboratory. Then come and find me."

"As you wish," Candy assured her and looked over her shoulder toward something that Sybil could not make out. "We are approaching the dome... We've crossed it," she informed her.

Immediately Sybil cut the communication and switched on the force field around the Enchanted Valley.

For a moment, she enjoyed a sensation of relief. Everything had gone well... Now, she had to resume the preparations to guard against any possible attack; *they* might be able to make an ovo appear right inside the castle.

She established a communication channel to the castle's central control room.

Savell's calm features appeared on the screen. Behind him the rosy glow from the dome entered the room through a window set into the wall... But wasn't the room below the basement?

"You changed the location of the control room, Savell?"

The man gave a nod.

"We are now in the central tower, Doctor."

"Why?"

With a wave of his hand, Savell made a diagram appear in the right-hand half of the screen.

"Situating ourselves in the base of the castle stretched out the defensive line too much," he explained, and a sinuous line crossing the lower part of the diagram disappeared. "Now it is more compact, thus increasing the density of our protection mechanisms."

"Are they already in place?"

"Look behind you."

The woman turned, and there in the wall, blinking, open and closed, she saw half a dozen apertures.

"Now we have adequate coverage. Before, with the available resources there were too many blindspots..."

Sybil frowned.

"Do you mean to say that you haven't been able to produce any new lasers?"

Savell shook his head.

"Given the time and the resources we had, it wasn't possible," he explained.

"So, in that case, only the occupied section of the castle is protected... Unless you have eliminated the remaining rooms in the castle?"

"We have installed traps instead," said Savell with a smile.

"Traps?"

"Traps," the man reiterated, and his hands moved across his control panel; his image and the diagram vanished from the screen, and in their place appeared a long, shadow-filled corridor... As Sybil watched the walls, floor and ceiling suddenly converged, and where the corridor had been was a new wall.

"We have sensors covering the whole of the interior of the castle. If one of our own passes by, nothing happens, but if there is an intruder, an alarm sounds in here. Then... I doubt if there is any kind of portable device that could get through force fields as powerful as the ones around the castle."

Sybil looked at him through narrowed eyes.

"I see a weak point, Savell."

"Which is?"

"If they place an ovo in the old control room, the enemy will have access to the controls for the principal energy grid. In which case we are lost."

"You can discount that possibility," replied the man, smiling. "I installed a duplicate of that control panel here and deactivated the original. Only from here," he patted the polished surface to his right, "is it possible to alter the castle's energy fields."

Sybil nodded slowly. Savell really was worth his weight in gold... Even so, she persisted.

"And if the enemy does find a way to breach the security systems?"

"The affected areas will immediately be liquidated."

"So, we can consider the castle impregnable?"

Savell arched his eyebrows.

"That depends on the capabilities of the enemy, Doctor."

Sybil wholeheartedly approved of his answers. You could talk to Savell, yes; he had his wits about him and wasn't as...excitable as Rockne. She shifted in her seat; Candy would be arriving at any moment.

"Thank you for your excellent work..."

"That's not all; I haven't told you about the Ferhads."

"Oh?"

"There are a hundred and fifty androids designed to 'play' Ferhad's adventures. I have analyzed them and with some modifications they can be put into combat for real."

The woman nodded her approval.

"This could be a good reinforcement of our defenses."

"And in the case of an offensive...I don't think we'll remain cooped up in here, Doctor."

Savell was an absolute gem...

Someone knocked discreetly on the door behind Sybil.

"Excuse me, I have to see Candy," she said, ending their conversation and switching off the screen.

"Come in!" she commanded, swiveling her chair around.

The door opened and Candice Stow entered the room.

"Can I brief you?"

"Go ahead."

"We captured two women. The taller and stronger one was the scout; the other acted as lookout. We had no problem capturing them..." Candy licked her lips before continuing. "However, the smaller one makes me uneasy."

Sybil frowned.

"Why?"

"No reason really... Except that she seemed too casual as a lookout."

"You searched her?"

"Very thoroughly, on site. And when we got here, I rechecked all parts of her body using an inorganic detector. I can confirm that she has no weapons hidden inside her."

"And her clothes?"

"I searched her at the capture site and found concealed weapons, but I left them there."

"Then there is no reason for you to be uneasy."

"I agree... But I am still worried."

Sybil considered this. Candy was a veteran agent. She did not get alarmed for no reason; they would have to take precautions with that agent... She looked up.

"How did you leave them in the laboratory?"

"I secured them to the examination modules; I can assure you that they cannot escape. In addition, Babson is watching them... As far as the little one goes, she was still under the effects of a neurotor blast, and for added security I gave her another shot. I don't believe this should not prevent you from searching her mind."

Sybil looked at the agent with respect.

"You don't mess around, Candy."

"That's why I am still alive."

Dr. Golden rose from her chair.

"I'll go and examine them. You may leave."

2

The breeze had died away, and a drowsy calm had spread across the meadow, announcing the arrival of midday...

Letting out a sigh of irritation, Ryland Kern moved away from the window.

"We still don't know anything about what's happening over there. This inaction is unbearable," he grumbled.

Dahlgren opened his eyelids halfway.

"You'd have done better to follow my lead and take a nap, instead of getting wound up for no good reason," he replied. "What time is it?" he asked, stretching out on the elaborate armchair where he was ensconced.

"How could I tell from here?" snorted the head of security, but he glanced at the window.

There was only a thin strip of light visible at its lower edge.

"It must be around twelve," he replied.

The chairman got up, yawning.

"Then they must be about to call... Come along," he said, and walked toward the wall in front of him.

He felt for a brick protruding slightly from the wall; the brick turned, twisting away until it disappeared inside the wall.

"And that?" asked Kern, looking over the shoulder of the chairmen, who then indicated, without touching it, the minuscule rectangle glowing weakly inside the cavity.

"It's a microportal," he explained. "It only works for audio waves."

Keeping a respectful distance, Kern examined the device...

"Now I understand your lack of concern about the impenetrable force field," he murmured, looking into Dahlgren's face. "But when it begins to transmit, the energy surge to the hermitage will rise to astronomical levels; that will arouse suspicions."

The chairman shook his head.

"The portal takes its energy from the other end," he explained. "Here, we only need enough to keep it on standby; that requires about the same power as a candle flame..."

The rectangle gave a sudden burst of light and then went completely black. Dahlgren moved closer.

"Sybil?" he asked in a low voice.

"Patrick?" the reply came through clearly; Sybil's voice was full of excitement.

444

"Here I am," Dahlgren answered, seating himself on the bench that Ryland had brought over. "Tell us everything, my dear."

3

She leaned over the display, trying to find meaning in the mess of lines; never, ever had she seen anything like it... She tried another combination.

Another set of hieroglyphs appeared on the screen, just as incomprehensible as the last.

"Has the equipment gone wrong?"

She tested the commands; they responded normally. Unless it was a brand new model of android, complete with a cybernetic brain, there was no other explanation possible. But Candy said she had used an inorganic detector, so...

It's a cybo! She had it. She spun her chair around to look at the still-paralyzed body... Candy really was a star agent; to sense that there was something odd about this insignificant-looking young woman, without having any real clues... But still, nothing was proved. She rubbed the back of her neck; there was a way, yes, a method for identification... Of course! The universal key enabling the identification of any complex cybernetic system. The Institute of Psychosociological Studies had been inflexible about this matter, considering the method the only way to keep proper track of the cybos...

She reset the mentagraphic controls to perform a new task.

She keyed in the recognition sequence and the display showed a translation of her message.

IDENTITY PLEASE.

It glimmered for a second before being replaced by the answer.

MY NAME IS MAYA.

She typed hurriedly.

WHAT IS YOUR INTENTION?

She waited in vain for the response.

Of course there wouldn't be one, she reproached herself; she had been using the codes provided by her mentagraph. There was no reason for them to be the same as those the cybo used. And trying to discover its personal code... Well, that would take centuries, if it was even possible.

Briskly, she removed the headset from the cybo and took it over to the other examination module.

The young woman strapped down there peered at her with an expression that was difficult to gauge... Hatred? Fear? Both? She would soon know.

She fitted the headset over the short dark hair and returned to her mentagraph.

Once she had prepared the recorder, she sent the first signals into the mind of the second girl. She had a momentary worry: What if this one was also a cybo? But Candy hadn't been suspicious of her...

She perused the screen. Yes, she was a normal person... But certain structures struck her as familiar: Could it be...?

She quickly set the machine to stimulate new memory sequences and awaited the answer... She smiled broadly. There could be no doubt; it was *her*.

Turning in her seat, she directed an ironic gaze into the eyes staring back at her from the module.

"Welcome to Castle Danger, Alice Welland."

4

"A cybo and Welland," Dahlgren repeated hoarsely. He shot a glance at Ryland Kern.

His eyes were also full of worry. No doubt about it, this was a bad sign; these hostages weren't worth anything. Welland wasn't from this time, and the cybo... Well, the enemy would probably be more upset about the loss of the stags in Enchanted Valley. The possibility of them launching a full-scale attack was raised considerably, and being completely honest with himself he did not relish losing Sybil. She was the last person who truly knew how to operate the conditioning techniques and a virtuoso when it came to using the mentagraph.

"Are there any signs of enemy activity against the protective force field?"

"None," the reply shot back through the black rectangle. "But they haven't tried communicating with us either... It is possible that the dome has surprised them, and they are working out how to establish contact. I don't think there are any reasons for alarm, Patrick. It is possible that they chose these agents fearing we might be so desperate that we'd terminate them without waiting for negotiations; it's still probable that they'll come after them... If not, I always have the option to send out a few dragons. Losing a few dozen wouldn't matter; we have more than enough. They'd provide a winning argument; they'd persuade them not to underestimate us..."

"Don't start any kind of offensive yet, Sybil. For now, just wait," Dahlgren interjected hastily, alarmed by the note of hysteria he could hear in her voice. "What's more..." He rapidly assessed the idea that had been forming in his mind; it seemed good. "I'm thinking that, without realizing it, they have sent us a useful weapon...

Tell me, do you think that the cybo has enjoyed them using her as live bait? More generally, do you think that the cybos like being treated the way they are?"

"I'm beginning to understand you, my dear," purred the rectangle.

"Very good, work along those lines with the cybo. If you manage to convince her, then free her and send her back. The enemy will take it as a sign of good will on our part, and she can take charge of presenting our proposals to her own people. If we manage to make an alliance with them..."

"That's clear then, yes... And what do I do with Welland?"

The chairman knew that tone of voice well... Fine, he would have to give her something to let off steam to prevent her from starting any wars before it was time... The enemy would not ask too many questions about the spy; the special treatment meted out to traitors is traditional. That the enemy had returned her to them could even be interpreted as a good-will gesture.

"With Welland? Extract everything she told them. Then...do what you like," he replied.

XXXV

A Way of Working

1

LOST IN THOUGHT, Sybil slowly replaced the panel over the now-extinguished portal. She felt sure that Patrick hadn't liked the idea of a dragon attack. This had to be because he was not there with her; if only he could experience the intoxicating feeling of power that being inside Castle Danger gave to its inhabitants... Of course, she understood that it wasn't ideal to stir up the enemy too much. Or to reveal their true potential; it was better to keep that a secret, in case they tried to penetrate the valley by force.

She activated the elevator and rose up between the walls of the narrow shaft. It was a shame about the lapse in security; if they had been able to build this fortress in such a short time, what could they have done in a few more months? This Enchanted Valley was nothing more than a model, a blueprint; they had been about to duplicate these valleys across all the continents, entertaining legions of idiot children until the moment they revealed their true power... It would have been a lightning strike against the most powerful institutions, and then, from the myriad Castle Dangers interconnected via portals manned by Hydras, they would have established the New Empire, founded on the terror and panic induced by the surprise attacks, launched through the ovos, of dragons, giant spiders, androids, and green tornados... And all of this was no more than a dream now, because of Welland, she thought, clenching her teeth.

The elevator stopped. A door opened in the wall before her, revealing the reverse sides of the white hangings that lined her quarters. She was about to enter her room when she remembered that she hadn't activated the security systems protecting the portal. No, the enemy must never find that connection to the outside world; it revealed the fact that not all of the resurrected were inside the castle.

She raised her arm and felt across the uneven mortar above the doorway, searching for the irregular-shaped projection that served as the switch for the security system... She found it and turned it. She would personally see to it that the portal was destroyed when the negotiations were over, but if anything prevented her from doing so, anyone who discovered that secret lift shaft and used it to go down to the portal would be blasted into tiny pieces—and so would the portal.

She crossed her bedroom. Now she must put Patrick's plan into action, convincing the cybo that its kind should swap sides... And yet there was something about it she didn't like; she had no way of testing the sincerity of her collaborator. It was unlikely that the enemy would be so naïve as to offer them this opportunity without some kind of guarantee—for example, some form of conditioning to ensure that the cybo could not betray them...

She slowed her steps as she went down the passageway. She was nearing the laboratory, and before beginning her labor of persuasion she needed to decide on some way of knowing whether the cybo was telling the truth, in the case that it agreed to collaborate.

She stopped at the door to the laboratory, thinking...

That's it! It was the only way: compel it to reveal its personal code, present it as a demonstration of good faith. That way she could read its mind and verify its true intentions... And if it refused when it learned of her intention to offer an alliance with the cybos... Well, by handing over the hostages like this it was obvious that the enemy had little thought of getting them back alive.

She entered the laboratory and went directly to the module where the cybo was lying. She sat beside it, forcing herself to remember its name... Maya, yes.

She evaluated her visually.

She was still under the effects of the neurotor; the body was rigid, the eyes glazed... The only perceptible movement was the short, spasmodic contractions of the diaphragm as she breathed in and out. It couldn't be very pleasant being on the end of a neurotor discharge...

"Maya," she began. "I know you can hear me, although you can't respond. Forgive us for having treated you this way; we thought you were one of our enemies, but now we see that you are just another of their victims. Yes, don't be so surprised. How else could we describe you if they deliberately sent you out to be slaughtered? Because in sending you to recuperate the neurotor they have done just that... Maya," she went on, injecting her voice with the maximum amount of sincerity she could muster, "our enemies are yours, too. If you are not convinced by the way that they carelessly risked your life in place of their own, what better test than the way in which they treat your fellows, the other cybos? Exiled to a tiny island, separated from the rest of the world as if they were infected by plague, their minds tagged like common machines... They use the most spurious arguments to deny even that untouchable right of every human being: the right to descendants... It is quite right that the primitives are also forbidden to have children; the education they could give them in Paradise would leave them no alternative but to continue being primitives once they grew up, depriving them of another human right: the power to decide their own destiny. And to take away the primitive's newborn children would be even crueler... Yes, that is a justifiable case for not allowing them to have offspring. But you, the cybos? Who better than the cybos to educate their own children. Aren't you the most learned beings on the entire earth? Do you want to know the secret behind this attitude toward the cybos shown by the 'normals,' as they call themselves? It is nothing more than envy and fear. Envy because you outstrip them in mental capacity, enabling you to reach new horizons of knowledge; fear because they understand that your superiority over them will one day lead you to become the rulers of Earth and that you will, out of compassion, conserve those who persist in refusing progress, who stagnate, in reservations just as they now conserve the primitives... That is the truth and nothing more."

She paused to catch her breath and to think. It was no easy task to make up propaganda without being able to verify its effects, without knowing the subject's weak points... But there was one thing that she absolutely needed to combat.

"I expect that you are aware of our history. At least the version of it that they've taught you... I can't deny that we made mistakes, and grave ones at that, which led to our destruction. But it is principles that count and decide the final outcome; you can be sure of that. They champion the desire for egalitarianism because they want to be part of the herd, where they can hide, more or less. But in your presence they find themselves exposed; they can't admit the existence of individuals able to raise themselves above the anonymous masses, reaching new and ever greater achievements. They are satisfied with mediocrity, with what has already been achieved. If there has been any progress since the Empire it has been because of the impulses that we bequeathed to human society. *They*, with their 'conscious' regulations put in place to fulfill their desire for uniformity, have been mutilating and impoverishing that creative impulse until the arrival of the present crisis... And I don't doubt that sooner or later they will attempt to destroy the cybos, because they might dare to break out of the narrow mold within which they would like to imprison humanity. We want to resurrect our most valued principle: the right to self-determination, the right to be better than anyone else, and to fight to be so. We think that, in this era, you constitute the only true expression of the human yearning to grow, and we would like to propose that, once we have established some level of solidarity, we contact you and forge an alliance that will save us all, an alliance that will ensure the triumph of the unbreakable human will over those who would enforce the law of the herd..."

She stopped again; she needed to be careful not to fall into too obvious a demagogy. She mustn't underestimate the analytical power of the cybos... She resumed, directing her words at the paralyzed face.

"You must understand our surprise to find a cybo acting as an agent of our common enemy... We cannot speculate about your reasons. Perhaps they misled you as to our intentions. Or perhaps they have found another way of controlling your processing, reducing your operational capacity to that of a common machine... If they have misled you, we can continue talking, clarify all your doubts and free you so that you can go to your people with our offer of an alliance against the enemies of the human spirit... However, you must know that we will need some form of proof to ensure that you are not the slave of our enemies, lacking any free will. We need to know this, for ourselves and for your fellow cybos, and there is only one way." She paused. "Reveal your own personal code. Then we will be able to read your mind and know your true intentions. We need this before we can lay out the terms of our collaboration;

we do not want to reveal any of this to a servant of our enemies...
To be honest with you, you already know too much. If you are a
traitor to your own kind, even an involuntary one, we can't allow
you to leave here alive," she declared, and then went on, speaking
very deliberately. "Now, we will take you to a cell until you recover.
Unfortunately you received two shots from the neurotor before we
realized who you were. You will need..." She made a rapid mental
calculation of the time elapsed. "...an hour before you recover your
voice. Then you must give us your personal code. If you do, it will
show your good faith. If you refuse, then you will be unmasked as a
servile tool of the 'normals' and we will destroy you. Is that clear?"

She straightened in her chair. The matter was resolved. By a
stroke of luck, the inspiration of the moment had allowed her to
find an unbeatable, solid argument obliging the cybo to reveal the
code to her mind... It would be the perfect opportunity to assess
the cybos' true potential. She couldn't disregard the possibility
that the cybos would be too dangerous an ally, in which case they
would have to liquidate her and inform Patrick that the strategy
was unadvisable...

She looked around for her bracelet. Where had she left it? Ah!
Yes, on the mentagraph control table.

She put it on her wrist and the wide strap began to pulsate,
ready for use. She pressed the buttons assigned to Lambert and
MacGray. Raising the bracelet to her mouth she issued her orders.

"Get yourselves up to the laboratory immediately."

2

The vaulted ceiling soared upward ahead of them... Lambert put
on the brakes, and the antigravity transport began to slow, but

its inertia carried it right into the center of the subterranean chamber.

MacGray looked at his surroundings, and the disk of light projecting from his helmet moved across the entrances to the dingy tunnels set into the walls of the atrium.

"Okay then! Which do we follow?" asked Lambert, resting his elbows on the surface of the transport where the rigid body lay.

His partner pulled out a little cylindrical device from his tunic. He pointed the guide bar at each of the walls in turn until it illuminated.

"That one," he replied and walked off into the new tunnel, the guide bar still in his hand. The mouths of these underground tunnels were far too close to each other.

Flexing his muscles, Lambert got the transport moving in the direction indicated by the guide.

"Is it much further?" he growled.

"I don't think so," said MacGray. After all it was the fifth change of direction they found. There couldn't be many more...

"I don't know why they had to make all this mess," griped Lambert, struggling to get the transport around a bend without hitting the walls.

MacGray decided not to respond...

Another twist in the passageway and the luminous disks from their helmets revealed narrow metal doorways in the walls.

"We're there," MacGray announced with obvious relief. If the guide bar had been malfunctioning...

Lambert stopped the transport and wiped the sweat from his brow.

"Which one do we put her in?" he asked.

"That one," MacGray pointed to a cell at random.

Lambert pushed the transport.

"Couldn't they have found one further away?" he complained.

They took Maya's body down from the transport and placed her inside the cell.

"It would have been better to have carried her," murmured Lambert. "She weighs next to nothing."

They left the girl on the ground.

"You really are a primitive," commented MacGray, shaking his head. "You can't bear progress... I bet you'd choose a knife over a laser."

Lambert straightened up and put his hands on his hips.

"If it had a good blade, I'd stick with it," he retorted and asked, "Shall we go?"

"Wait."

MacGray scrutinized the inside of the cell, using the light from his helmet.

It was very small and windowless; the walls and floor seemed to be made of rough shards of rock stuck together with well-worn mortar and covered by the dust of centuries... Damp seemed to seep from the stones. This was certainly not his idea of a healthy environment. The girl was lucky she wouldn't be there for more than an hour...

"Are you coming or staying?" asked Lambert impatiently.

MacGray gave the inert body a last look as it lay on the cold stones and then left her.

"Do we lock the door?"

MacGray took his time answering.

"Yes," he decided. "If she thought about escaping she'd get lost hopelessly in the labyrinth and die of hunger and thirst before anyone found her..."

Lambert let out a snort of laughter.

"You brave enough?"

"Will you face the doctor if she gets lost?" answered MacGray, making a face.

"No."

"So lock it then."

3

After Lambert and MacGray had left with the transport, Sybil closed the door carefully. She pressed the buttons on her bracelet to get in touch with Rockne and Savell.

"I'm in the laboratory. I am only keeping communication channels open with you two; I don't wish to be disturbed unless our enemies begin an open attack," she ordered, and then removed the bracelet.

She seated herself in front of the mentagraph and looked over the top of the display panel at the young woman tied to the module.

"I think you're far too quiet... I don't know what Houdry saw in you," she commented aloud, deftly manipulating the controls.

The young woman shivered.

"What have you done to him?" she asked anxiously.

Sybil looked attentively at the screen and fed in a new set of instructions.

"Interesting, yes, interesting... Did you say something?"

Alice bit her lip.

The woman sitting at the controls let out a gasp of laughter.

"How amusing, good lord! I'd never have imagined something like that." She shot a glance at the prisoner. "Did you love Stephen very much?"

The young woman could not contain herself.

"What do you mean by 'love'?" she asked, her voice quivering.

Dr. Golden smiled as she extracted another sequence of memories from her victim... To a less experienced mentographer, creating emotional instability in the subject would have presented problems, but for someone with the necessary skill it was the best means of arriving at the deepest levels of consciousness, the most protected parts of the brain... One last little push and the poor thing would be more transparent than a pane of glass.

"Answer me! You can't have killed him!" shouted Alice.

She's almost there, Sybil decided.

"No... We didn't kill him. There was no reason to punish him."

Her victim's guard was down and she took advantage. The screen filled with trace after trace... She raised her eyebrows. They really hadn't been able to unravel Houdry's conditioning? She shook her head... Had she known that before, she wouldn't have needed to be here. The enemy barely knew anything: the existence of some of their leaders, but an unknown number, and of one Hydra, but not how many members it comprised. She felt a cold wave of anger rising through her body. She had had to leave Patrick for goodness knows how long because of this...this... She couldn't find the words to describe her.

"You, however, will get what you deserve," she resumed, keeping her voice controlled; she didn't want to show any anger, it would only give her satisfaction. "I still must take him into account, though. It's not easy to decide on a suitable punishment..."

She looked attentively at the read-out of emotional arousal.

There was a little flowering of fear, but it was overcome quite easily; it was clear that Alice feared not for herself but for Houdry. She didn't realize that he was dead... Of course, if she had found out, she herself wouldn't still be alive. That was her weak point, no doubt about it. But she needed to prepare the ground first.

She pretended to think aloud.

"Babson is here... He is an experienced torturer, yes, and a natural talent in his field... But to die at his hands would be too easy, too simple for you."

The emotional indicators showed a small tremor. Good, she wanted to build up her anticipation, soften her up for the final blow.

"Personally, I don't think that a traditional torturer can inflict the maximum amount of suffering on a person... On the other hand, someone versed in the use of a mentagraph," she looked over the top of the control panel in order to flash a smile at Alice, "can do just that, because they can see exactly what effect they are having," she said and then rapidly pressed a sequence of keys.

Alice twisted on the module, screaming...

"You see?" said the doctor, ten minutes later. "Now I know which points of your nervous system are the most sensitive to physical pain. This one." She pressed a button and paused. "This one... And this one."

She looked over at Alice.

The young woman was stretched out rigidly on the module, her body arched upward with only her heels and back of the head resting on the couch, covered in a cold sweat, her features distorted...

"Pardon me if I don't allow you to scream. I blocked your vocal chords because screams bother me. They become boring... What's more, I have discovered that they provide a mechanism to relieve the pain. I don't want you to have any escape..."

She noted the body relaxing, waited for the sobbing, and then she grabbed hold of another dial.

"Crying also provides relief," she explained placidly. "You must not have any escape, understand?"

She evaluated the trembling that shook Alice's body. Perfect...

She delivered another electronic lash to the most sensitive point and waited for Alice to recover.

"As you may appreciate, I can also prevent you from losing consciousness. The voltages delivered by the mentagraph are astounding; for example, the last shock..." She paused. "You remember it?"

She straightened up in her seat, her eyes locked onto the girl.

"If you remember, just nod." She waited a moment. "You don't recall? Alright then, let's go over it again," she said, and turned the dial once more.

She bided her time until the convulsions had passed.

"Do you remember it now?" she asked.

Alice nodded, her head bobbing up and down frenetically.

"I am so glad to see that your memory has improved... Very well, I wanted to let you know that a shock of that magnitude would normally have rendered you unconscious; the pain would have been too great to bear. But the mentagraph allows me to keep you awake, with all your senses working... And do you know why?"

The young woman nodded again.

"Very good... That's much better. I will give you your voice back so you can tell me why I mustn't let you lose consciousness."

On the first attempt Alice could not speak; her lips would not obey her.

"Why are you doing this to me?" she finally managed to stammer. "What gratification could you possibly gain from humiliating me like this?"

Dr. Golden shook her head.

"I see that you don't understand... I don't do this for pleasure. You are being punished, that's all. The humiliation, as you call it, is just part of the punishment... But you still haven't explained to me why I mustn't let you faint."

Alice clamped her mouth shut.

Sighing, Sybil turned the dial in the opposite direction and then pressed another key, this time she left it on for a much longer time... She waited for its effect to pass and then turned the dial again.

"You can speak again. Now tell me, why can't I let you faint?"

Her voice unrecognizable, Alice screamed.

"Because I cannot be allowed any escape! Because I cannot be allowed any escape!"

"Good, good... I see that you are an attentive student; you learn fast," said Sybil and her hands left the mentagraph keypad.

"However, all of this, the physical pain and the humiliation, as you call it, don't really reach far enough inside your inner self." She looked over her screens. "These tell me everything... You don't expect to leave here alive, and you have resigned yourself to that fact. What does it matter what we do to you if we can't obliterate the damage you have done?"

Sybil thought she saw a smile hover around the swollen lips... She smiled in turn.

"I see we understand one another... The true punishment would be for us to penetrate your inner self and awaken a hell of pain and remorse that would take you as slowly as possible to your death... Are you still smiling? Have you forgotten Houdry?"

Alice abruptly tried to raise her head.

"You know he's not responsible for any of this!"

"You think you love him, don't you?"

The young woman's eyes flashed.

"If you think you can try to persuade me otherwise you're wasting your time... Of course you can force me to say that I hate him, if that makes you happy," she retorted, smiling again.

"Have you heard of conditioning?" asked Sybil, and the young woman's smile vanished. "I see you have... You didn't know Houdry, did you? The Stephen Houdry of the Empire, that is... If I'm right you worked in different departments of the institute."

Alice didn't respond.

"I take your silence as a 'yes'... Houdry was old and fat, almost completely bald, but there was always a beautiful young woman staying in his bungalow, a new one every two or three years. I'm sure there were dirty old men in your department, too, am I right?"

"You're lying! You're lying! Houdry is young and beautiful; he has no need for brainwashed prostitutes, because I love him..."

"That is now, my little one... Do you have the same body that Alice Welland occupied at the time of the Empire? You are struck dumb? I think you are beginning to understand... You know that Houdry was a laboratory supervisor. Were the laboratory supervisors in your section young?"

Alice's body squirmed on the pod.

"That proves nothing; Stephen had no need for those girls. You are lying. You want to take revenge by destroying my love, but you won't do it, understand? You won't ever do it!"

Dr. Golden smiled ever more widely.

"I don't intend to destroy it... I recognize Houdry's superiority in this matter; any conditioning he put in place could only be removed by him..."

"Stop, I can see what you are trying to do. You're going to bring Houdry here and force him to say that he conditioned me to love him, and with the pretext of removing my conditioning you will make him erase my love for him... Go ahead, get on with your foul vengeance."

"You are wrong, Welland; I don't need to bring Houdry in here. Do you remember when you asked him if he really enjoyed the things that you did, because you found them...a little perverted?" she said, laughter bubbling from her in little bursts. "Forgive me, but I have never heard anything so comic in all my years... My dear child, those perversions were implanted in your brain because he liked them."

The straps holding Alice down were stretched tight, constraining her efforts to leap at her interrogator.

"Don't even bother to try. Not even a gorilla could get out of those restraints," Sybil advised calmly. "If you wish, I can give you concrete proof... The conditioning Houdry implanted in you is remarkably comprehensive; he planned for all of his whims, in any circumstance... What are you looking at in the ceiling?"

Alice stayed rigid on the module.

"Are you trying to show me that you're not listening? Okay then. As I was saying, Houdry imagined all sorts of situations and planted key words into your subconscious that would make you react in...well, the most surprising ways. And now, get ready not to hear this: I'm going to use one."

Sybil paused... She pronounced something unintelligible.

Alice shivered.

Rising from her seat, Dr. Golden approached the module. She observed the tightly shut mouth, the closed eyes, and the heightened color of the face; she noticed Alice's short panting breaths, and she smiled.

Reaching out a hand she touched the sweaty forehead... Alice opened her eyes as if shocked by electricity and looked pleadingly at Sybil.

"Please don't touch me... You are the pervert; you are the one who has conditioned me while you were reading the mentagraph and now you want to blame Houdry for this monstrousness. You are the monster! Get away from me!" she shouted and bit her lower lip hard with her teeth.

Sybil's fingers played with the clasps on the restraints...

"Do you want me to untie you?" she asked casually.

Alice's eyes bulged.

"No! No! Leave me be, tied up. Get away!"

Shrugging her shoulders, Dr. Golden returned to her seat.

"You should know that it is impossible to fight your conditioning... It's like trying not to breathe. You can hold your breath for a while, but the point comes when, however strong your willpower, necessity overcomes it... No matter, I will wait."

The minutes dragged by and Alice's breathing became weaker...

"Doctor..." she whispered.

"What do you want?"

"Release me."

Sybil sighed.

"No."

"Please... If you don't, I'll die..."

"You're right; you shouldn't die quite yet," said the doctor and murmured another unintelligible word.

Alice's eyes opened. She was astonished... Little by little her breathing became normal again.

"I don't understand. Why didn't you take advantage of the conditioning?"

Dr. Golden looked at her sternly.

"That, young lady, was simply to demonstrate to you that you have been conditioned. Personally I don't share Houdry's proclivities... And don't get any ideas about me being the one who conditioned you; no specialist, not even Houdry, would have been able to affect that kind of conditioning in less than an hour. I read your brainwaves on a mentagraph for less than ten minutes. I'm not a magician."

Alice looked away.

"Conditioned or not, I love Houdry...and that's the only thing that matters to me."

Sybil nodded.

"In that case, you are ripe for punishment."

Taken by surprise, Alice raised her eyes.

"Punishment? More punishment?"

"You want to know where Stephen Houdry is?"

The young woman nodded her head avidly.

"Yes, tell me now!"

"He was the one who occupied Lardner's body."

"No!"

Sybil twisted the dial on her console.

"I have removed your ability to speak once again because I am not interested in your denials and even less interested in your screams when the punishment begins again... You imprisoned Houdry. You handed him over to them, and I am quite sure they interrogated him. And, since even he, the master of conditioning, was himself conditioned (in his case as a protection for us, his masters), that interrogation would have resulted in his death... Listen to me carefully: Stephen Houdry is dead because of you. And thanks to the supreme egotism of Houdry, who did not wish anyone else to enjoy you after his demise, your conditioning means that you will die as soon as you learn of his death... Indeed, if you had even the smallest role in his death, and I believe your role has been substantial, you will die in the throes of the most exquisite mental tortures that the twisted genius of Stephen Houdry could possibly imagine..."

She watched the rigid body on the module. From the expression it was clear she could no longer hear anything.

Sybil returned to her seat at the mentagraph and amused herself by studying the emotional indicators; however brilliant Houdry may have been, perhaps there was room for improvement even in this level of protective conditioning.

XXXVI

From Inside the Labyrinth

1

THE CELL DOOR CLOSED, and there was darkness.

Firsttoneutralizethelatenttelepath.

2

Swiftly maneuvering his control pad, Babson made the tiny white dot whiz along an irregular curve into Candy's court.

The woman's hands took a fraction too long to respond; the white dot sailed across the screen without stopping.

Babson stifled a giggle.

"You must be losing your touch," he commented.

Candy was on the point of responding but stopped herself. Perhaps Babson was on to something: the constant stress of waiting for the trap to be sprung must have taken its toll. The same uneasiness that she—still—felt about that incompetent agent was another bad symptom... She needed to rest a little; otherwise, she'd be in a poor state when she needed to go back into action.

"I'm going to sleep," she announced, and she rose abruptly from the bench and went to her room.

Babson stretched, satisfied. It wasn't easy to beat Candy. He picked up the little game pad, stowed it inside his tunic, and walked along the gallery toward the nearby balcony.

Resting his elbows on the balustrade he looked down at the valley shrouded in thick mist. He shivered. It was not a pleasant view—even less so under the light of that blood-red sky.

He turned toward the corridor. Perhaps Candy was right; it might be better to pass the time sleeping...

Candy finished making herself comfortable in bed. Her gaze took in the hangings on the walls. She didn't like them; she preferred to have a clear field of view... But what could harm her here, in the heart of this fortress?

She forced herself to close her eyes; her uneasiness had no basis. She relaxed the muscles of her body; she ought to sleep, rest...

Slowly, sleep overtook her.

Startled again she raised her head, her eyes darting. What? No. There was no danger. At least not immediately...

She slept.

3

She'sasleepalreadynowconcentrateyourenergy.

She closely inspected the waves of physical pain beating against her mental dams. Yes, they could be taken advantage of.

She initiated the transformation process.

Inside her, deep inside her, in the depths of her inner self, she opened a dark, bottomless pit.

The nervous energy fell into the abyss with inconceivable speed, forming vortices as it did so; quickly it became apparent that the pain was not sufficient to calm the energy's voracity.

Maya mobilized all of her emotional resources, her memories (sad and happy, beautiful and repulsive), and all her passions, forming an unending torrent, flowing into that pulsating inner blackness.

Stillnotenough.

Her adipose tissues released fatty acids into her lymphatic system and her bloodstream, which transported them into her sympathetic nervous system, where they bonded with just the right amount of oxygen to allow for their accelerated metabolism and transformation into yet more energy.

Her skin began to glow, gently illuminating the cell.

That loss was unacceptable.

She revised the process for deploying her resources and sealed off leaks. Darkness reigned in the cell once more.

She spent a few seconds checking the stability of the process... Satisfactory, although the rate at which her resources were being used up was faster than expected. She would need extra sources of energy. Perhaps "cold caustic inquisition," the embryonic telepath, could help her while she slept...

She rejected the possibility; it might wake her. It would not do to alert her again, at least not until she'd managed to reach the peak of her faculties... She'd have to make do in other ways.

The process of accumulation was completed without any problems; now she could concentrate on the enemy.

From the depths of the subterranean labyrinth, invisible, mental threads climbed up toward the castle turrets, probing, discovering, testing...

Aretheyreallyhere?

She delved deeper into the minds of the two players as they concentrated on their game of "twack." It was unbelievable that they could risk so much... She abandoned their brains, relieved.

Theyaresimulacrumsjustincompleteminddoubles.

She needed to continue her search. Someone in the castle must know where the real leaders were...

One of her mind projections brushed against a new mind and Maya shivered.

TheyhavetoldherHoudryisdead!

She hesitated for a microsecond; that uncontrollable eruption of anguish and pain could also be used...

No.

Transformed into a sharpened scalpel, her mind projection sought and found the vital point.

4

Disconcerted, Sybil watched as the emotional indicators registered a vertical drop in output. Raising her eyes, she looked at the body on the module. What had happened?

She checked the physiological indicators and found her answer: Alice Welland's heart had stopped.

But that was impossible; the pacemaker was on... She verified this. Yes, it was still sending its electrical signals to the unresponsive heart.

She checked how much time had passed: barely half an hour of being in that hell. Welland had made good her escape... By the looks of things, Houdry had miscalculated the intensity of suffering. This would need to be taken into account with any future subjects... But when subjects were conditioned to avoid endangering their master and harm occurred without the subject's knowledge, it was inevitable that the fallout would be excessive... Good, Alice Welland was a closed case.

Imperceptible mental filaments penetrated her brain and insinuated themselves subtly into her thoughts... The fine mesh grew rapidly, spreading, incorporating itself, discovering her memories...

Shari'shermitage... Let'sfindthecoordinates.

...breaching the frontiers of her conscious self, exploring the deeper levels, uncovering the prohibited memory...

Sheknowsshehasbeenconditionedandhasblockedthe memory.

...sounding out, evaluating the emotional charges seething behind the artificial walls through the cracks of which a mist of constrained anger seeps, impregnating that unquiet mind...

Yesanadequatesource.

Let her calm down, while the exploratory net turns into a flexible tentacle whose extremes avidly soak up that wellspring of tensions and take them to the swelling black bubble there in the subterranean cell...

She must get rid of the body she decided, putting on her bracelet.

"Steele and Schwartz, come to the laboratory," she ordered.

She switched off the mentagraph. At least settling the score with Welland had provided a release; now she felt refreshed and calmer. She could think more clearly... The first thing: What were *they* doing?

She wheeled her chair across to the intercom and pressed the code for the cybermechanics control room.

Rockne's face appeared on screen.

"Any news?" she asked.

"Nothing, Doctor." The woman's voice sounded uneasy. "Nothing has come near the dome. The indicators haven't moved."

"Don't let your guard down," Sybil ordered her, and cut the channel. She didn't like things being so quiet... They should at least have tried to cross the dome or begun investigating its properties... She keyed in the code for the castle control room.

Savell's serene image looked back at her.

At least someone was keeping calm...

"Has anything happened in the castle?" Sybil asked.

"No, Doctor."

Sybil waited a moment.

"What do you think about the enemy's inactivity?" she asked.

The man smiled.

"It's a straightforward war of nerves... They are trying to lull us into dropping our guard or provoking us into some rash action."

Dr. Golden nodded.

"That makes sense... Anyway, stay alert," she said, switching off the intercom.

What could she do while the enemy was deciding whether or not to react?

She looked at her console; it was time to fetch the cybo. She brought her bracelet up to her mouth.

"Lambert and MacGray, bring the prisoner to the laboratory."

Behind her the door opened. Schwartz and Steele came in. She glanced at them over her shoulder.

"Burn that," she said indicating the corpse lying on the module. "Then return to your quarters."

Moving silently and efficiently, the man and woman untied the restraints and left the laboratory carrying the body that had belonged to Alice Welland.

Sybil checked the time again. When the cybo was brought back up she would at least be able to speak...

Her bracelet emitted a buzz.

Mechanically she lifted it to her face.

"I'm listening," she said.

MacGray's agitated voice burst from the speaker.

"The cybo's cell is empty, Doctor!"

Sybil sat up in her seat.

"Empty? And where is she?"

"We don't know!" came the reply.

"Have you searched the passageway? The other cells?"

"Yes, yes; she isn't anywhere."

"But she can't move!"

"Quite true, Doctor. When we brought her down she was still under the effects of the neuroblast. She wouldn't have been able to recover in just half an hour—not even to lift a finger."

"You locked the cell door?"

"Of course!"

"Then how could she have opened it from inside if she couldn't even lift a finger?"

There was no response from the bracelet.

Sybil tossed her head in exasperation.

"Don't move from there; await my instructions," she ordered and switched off the bracelet.

She began to enter the code for the castle control room on the intercom... What could have happened? It was a shame that the real Ryland wasn't here; he'd know what to do...

From the screen, Savell's image regarded her.

"Has something happened, Doctor?" he asked.

5

The invisible mental cobweb extending through the labyrinth detected the two men approaching.

LambertMacGray... Imustbeginwork.

Her tendrils penetrated both minds, searching for a memory.

Itwillbeenoughtochangethecellnumber...

472

They found it and modified it slightly before withdrawing.

"It's this one, isn't it?" Lambert asked, bringing the transport to a stop.

MacGray looked at the number on the door.

"That's the one," he replied. He was just about to draw the bolts when his hands stopped.

"Get over here!"

Lambert came over.

"You remember we locked this, didn't we?" asked MacGray, pointing at the open bolts.

Lambert couldn't believe his eyes; he leaned closer and prodded the pseudometal... Straightening up he fixed his colleague with a hostile glare.

"I don't like this sort of joke, Blackie," he said menacingly.

"This is no joke!" blurted MacGray. "When would I have been able to open them?"

Breathing heavily, Lambert did not take his eyes off his companion.

"Look inside," he said after a pause. "She can't have gotten out."

MacGray pushed the door open cautiously...

His luminous disk flashed over the floor, walls, and ceiling without encountering anything.

The man retreated.

"She's not there," he murmured.

"That's not possible."

"See for yourself."

Lambert approached the open cell door tentatively and peered inside... He decided to go in and went over the tiny space inch by inch, feeling the walls... He came out, laser at the ready.

"I don't like this one bit, Blackie," he said, glancing up and down the corridor nervously.

"You think I'm liking it any better?" retorted MacGray as he adjusted the setting on his neurotor to level three. "I'll call it in; you keep watch," he ordered, and crouching down he activated his bracelet.

Without paying attention to the incoherent whisperings between the intercom and his partner, Lambert (fear darkness fear the serpent of terror rearing its head blinking eyes, fear growing fear) rested his back against the tunnel wall, his eyes alert to the slightest movement around him.

Panting slightly, MacGray (insecurity unease insecurity) stood up.

"We should wait here," he said.

"Damn! I swear that's the last thing I want to do," Lambert grumbled.

"Couldn't agree more," his colleague replied. "When stuff happens that can't be explained, I prefer to be elsewhere."

"The worst thing is, Blackie, that there is an explanation," whispered Lambert.

Their luminous disks moved randomly up and down the walls, making the doors of the cells appear and disappear...

"An explanation? I don't get it?" replied MacGray in a hushed voice.

"She couldn't move, right?"

"I'm sure of it."

"And yet she opened the door from the inside and left, okay?"

"Yes. And there is no possible explanation..."

"Oh yes there is: *she's a witch*, Blackie," hissed Lambert, dismantling his laser with trembling hands.

"What are you doing? Are you mad? Witches don't exist, idiot!" MacGray told him (doubt insecurity murky remembrances distant images disquieting thoughts fear) in a reedy voice.

"I believe what I see, Blackie, and I am seeing something that only has one explanation... What good would my laser be against her? *She'd* laugh at it!"

"But...the neurotor paralyzed her, Lambert. You saw her."

"I saw what she wanted us to see; she only wanted to get in here and get us to leave her somewhere so that she could get up to her tricks... I'm off, Blackie," declared Lambert, and he turned around and started to race down the corridor.

MacGray ran after him.

"Are you mad?" he whispered, grabbing him by the arm. "What are you going to say to the doctor?"

Freeing himself from the hand that had grasped him, Lambert turned on his partner.

"I'll tell her to take care... or even better, to flee with us. You don't mess with that sort of power, Blackie... Look!" he said, pointing to the wall, and MacGray looked.

Their lights illuminated the door to a cell. It was shrinking, getting smaller before their very eyes... They shone their lights up and down the corridor to reveal the other doors vanishing, until they could only see blank walls.

Not far away, the indescribable mental black hole absorbed every last drop of panic from these two pristine sources and grew a little more...

"Do you see? What more proof of her power do you need? You stay if you want to, but give me the guide bar. I'm out of here."

MacGray tried to calm his partner.

"That must be Savell, from his control room. If she was hiding in another cell, she's walled up alive now."

"And that?" asked Lambert with the serenity of despair. He pointed upward.

MacGray looked up and watched incredulously as the ceiling slowly descended onto their heads...

Savell Takes Precautions

1

SHE NEEDED TIME and more energy, even more still... She needed to begin the campaign to soften them up. She still couldn't reach the mind of the man in charge of the castle's central controls; his internal stability had no chinks for her to get a grip on... But she needed to breech it soon; she couldn't keep the embryonic telepath asleep much longer...

2

Sybil peered at the two screens in turn.

"Conclusions?" she demanded.

Rockne's expression showed complete confusion. Savell responded.

"It seems that Lambert and MacGray have been hypnotized. I am quite sure that the cybo was in that cell and that she has made them believe otherwise."

Sybil relaxed a little.

"Your explanation seems reasonable, Savell," she said, straightening in her seat. "But I must ask you an important question: How many of us have been hypnotized?"

The man thought for a moment...

"There is one way to find out," he said, and leaned over his console. He glanced to one side, looking at something outside Sybil's field of vision, and made a gesture of approval.

"I would dare to suggest that she hasn't been able to hypnotize anyone else. Look," he said.

Where his face had been, the screen showed a still image of Lambert pushing the transport toward an opening in the wall into which MacGray was already disappearing.

"Because we still haven't had time to put sensors into the subterranean tunnels," Savell's voice could be heard explaining, "only one entrance is open, which we keep under permanent surveillance. Anyone who goes near it activates the sensor. What you can see corresponds to when they took the cybo to the cells; as you will note..." The image enlarged so that the body on the transport could be seen more clearly. "...the prisoner is clearly under the influence of a neurotor shot. Look at the stiffness of the muscles; nobody could simulate that, and certainly not for any length of time... She couldn't have known about the sensor there. If she had already hypnotized those two, there'd have been no reason for her to pretend."

"Your line of argument is convincing," Sybil said approvingly. "And she can't have left the subterranean section?"

The image on the screen changed: Lambert was in front with MacGray pushing the now-empty transport.

"No, she hasn't left. The sensor has only registered two movements, and this is the second. As you can see, only our men came out... In my opinion, she must have hypnotized them when they went to fetch her, and by that time she would have recovered enough physical control to accomplish the task."

"And she can't leave now?" asked Maureen Rockne, visibly anxious.

"No," Savell replied. "I have just deactivated the exit to the subterranean section."

Sybil's breath rasped, in and out. So that was their game, was it? To send in a wolf in sheep's clothing? Ha, they'd see... Once she was liquidated, there would be a dragon attack—regardless of what Patrick had to say about it... Candy had been oh so right to be wary of that repulsive insect, right from the beginning. She should tell her...

Inside her mind the ethereal fingers moved.

Although really, she didn't need her help anymore; the enemy had unmasked themselves.

"So where's the cybo now?" she asked.

"Quite possibly in the same cell they left her in," replied Savell. "Although we shouldn't discount the possibility that she has tricked Lambert and MacGray into taking her out of there and hiding her in some other part of the labyrinth. I doubt she would be able to move herself."

"They might have put her in another cell?"

"That is quite possible... I suggest that we neutralize all the cells."

"Neutralize them?" asked Sybil, not understanding.

"Yes, like all the rooms in the castle, they are nothing more than cavities within the force field it is made of. It is not difficult to program a new configuration that will make them vanish."

"And the cybo?"

"The fields would crush her."

"That's not a bad idea..." The mental fingers resumed their imperceptible work on Sybil's thoughts. "Although there is a better one: simply wipe out the cell doors."

Maureen Rockne smiled.

"I like that idea better."

"Yes, walling her up alive is not a bad solution... It is at least as effective as the other," said Savell. "Shall I do it?"

"Yes, do it!" said Sybil decisively.

The man's hands moved across his console.

"It's done," he announced.

"Good, that problem is sorted. Now, what can we do about Lambert and MacGray?"

Savell grimaced, thinking.

"Them? I wouldn't recommend trying to rescue them."

"Why not?"

"We don't know the extent of the cybo's hypnotic suggestions... They may try to attack us."

"True... That could well be her tactic. So?"

"I think the best option is to neutralize the labyrinth."

Savell bent over his controls again...

"All done," he informed them, looking up and staring at them with his pale eyes.

"Thank you," said Sybil. "Stay on full alert." She took her leave and disconnected the communication channel.

She sat back in her seat, sighing. The enemy had shown itself to be dangerously subtle... From now on this would have to be taken into account.

3

For what seemed like the millionth time, Mendoza paced across the floor between the door and his bed... This inactivity, not knowing what the enemy was up to, exasperated him, but his instructions were to stay in his room. Well, it wouldn't do any harm to go out onto the balcony and take some air... Or perhaps even visit Tina; her room was just next door... He had to admit that Steele's new body was a major improvement. And how. Of course, this was not the moment to be thinking about such things, but it wouldn't do any harm to maintain good relations, with a view to a near-future time when the present state of emergency was over...

Slipping his laser inside his tunic, he went out onto the balcony.

The view that met him made him start; the panorama of Enchanted Valley was far from pleasant...

He walked toward Tina Steele's room and tapped on the door.

"Tina! Are you decent?" he called.

Inside the room, the woman sat up in bed.

"Yes, come in," she called back.

The sound of her voice vibrated on Mendoza's eardrums and was transformed into a series of action potentials that propagated rapidly along the auditory nerve toward the brain, but before they could get there and enter the man's consciousness, something impalpable stopped them and made them disappear.

Disconcerted, Mendoza examined the door. It wasn't locked, and yet Tina hadn't responded. Had she gone out? And left the door open, too? He shook his head; that wasn't like her. Was she asleep?

Tina frowned. Was Mendoza deaf, or something? Perhaps he couldn't hear through the heavy door... But she had heard him clearly. She got off the bed with a snort and smoothed out her tunic. He was deaf as a post; she'd have to go and let him in.

Mendoza hesitated. Perhaps Tina was really asleep... The door was slightly ajar. Why hadn't she closed it from inside? At this time of high alert? In that case he should go in; there wasn't time for that sort of error...

Placing his hand on the door, he pushed.

The foreign presence inside his mind intensified the commands sent to the muscles in his arm, doubling their force...

The door swung wide open.

Tina Steele was halfway to the door when she saw it open. She directed a smile at her visitor...

Mendoza could not believe his eyes. Who was this naked young woman pointing a laser gun at him?

His reflexes took over.

With lightning speed he pulled his own laser from his tunic and fired it in a rapid sweep. The mystery woman was decapitated. Her head fell to the floor...and began to transform.

Mouth agape, Johnny Mendoza stood over the headless body of Tina Steele. Her face was still smiling.

What had happened? How could he have made such a miscalculation? He had seen the stranger about to shoot at him and... Where the hell was she now? With trembling hands he put away his laser and entered the room. She couldn't have got out yet... He searched fruitlessly.

He let himself fall onto the bed, hiding his face in his hands. Was he going mad?

He managed to regain his self-control. What was done was done... He had to report it... But who would believe him?

No one would, obviously. They would think that he had tried to sleep with Tina—ha! His fame as a womanizer went before him, and she had resisted—as if the bitch weren't capable of raping him herself; he knew her well—and so he had killed her... No, he had to think up a better story... That's it.

He looked at his bracelet. Who to call? The doctor? He evaluated the possibility and rejected it; there was no fooling her... Better to try with Savell.

He keyed the code into his bracelet.

"Savell?" he said, bringing the bracelet to his mouth.

"Yes," came the reply.

"There is an enemy agent in the castle."

"How do you know?"

"I was going past Steele's room when I saw a stranger coming out of there. She was armed with a laser gun." That would justify his own shot. "I called out for her to stop and she fired at me; I returned fire but missed her because she was a moving target. She took advantage and escaped down a side corridor... I didn't pursue her because as I passed Tina's doorway I saw her body on the floor. I stopped for a second to help her but she was dead. Decapitated. I thought I should call it in immediately..."

"The stranger you saw, was she short, slender, and dark-haired?"

The surprise made Mendoza jump.

"Yes! She looked exactly like that!"

"Did she have any clothes on?"

Mendoza was silent and the voice from the bracelet clarified.

"I mean, was she dressed?"

"Umm, no. She was naked."

Behind Mendoza half a dozen tiny holes opened in the wall.

"What...?" he began to ask, a split second before the hidden lasers began to fire.

4

Savell deactivated the lasers. The two dead bodies were on the screen; he switched it off. He needed to think... Mendoza's story was absurd; the cybo couldn't have been able to get up to that corridor without setting off half a dozen alarms... The most important thing now was to determine when Mendoza had come into contact with the cybo.

He rested his elbows on the control table. He laced his fingers together and tried to remember.

When the prisoners arrived, Mendoza had come out of the valley control center; it was possible their paths had crossed there...

He went through the footage of Candy's arrival and then looked at records showing the cybo's movements from that point on. He found nothing. Mendoza wasn't anywhere in the pictures, even at a distance.

He shifted uncomfortably...

A mental filament found a tiny chink in his stability: *AtlastandnowIhavetomakesureitwon'tclose.*

Something was wrong... Yes.

Mendoza hadn't been near her (nor had Steele for that matter). How could she have hypnotized him? At a distance?

He raised his head. If the cybo could give hypnotic suggestions at a distance to unknown persons, she only had to whistle and the castle would fall. This had to be a false lead. Yes, a well-calculated trick. Since her mind couldn't be read, her potential was unknown. So, using this as a cover, someone else, the true agent could operate without risk of discovery... But who was it and where were they? The security footage showed nothing, except themselves and the prisoners... One of their own people? Impossible. Nobody had been revealed before Castle Danger's defenses went up; if they'd been previously identified as resurrected, none of this would have been necessary... There *had* to be someone else in the game. But how come they didn't register on the sensors? Machines couldn't be hypnotized... And what about *him*?

A second filament slipped into the chink and made it bigger. *Justintime*, said Maya to herself, and she released the thought that had been there from the start.

The idea rose into Savell's consciousness.

He shook his head, disgusted with himself. That was the first thing he needed to do: neutralize the cells, too. That cybo had no reason to be alive, just to satisfy Maureen's sadistic impulses. Women...

His fingers moved over the controls.

He did not notice that they weren't touching the keys; his brain could still feel the polished cool of their surfaces against the tips of his fingers...

All done. Now there was no more reason to worry about the cybo. He could concentrate peacefully on the possibility of an invisible agent...

He ransacked the memories of the cyberneticist who had inhabited his body before him and came to the conclusion that a human being could not avoid being detected by the watchers, although a device could... There were the eyes, used to watch wildlife in the nature reserves... The enemy was evidently not using basic eyes; they were not only sending information back to their masters but also permitting a skillful mesmerist to act through them, however many there were. It was quite probable that the eye used to hypnotize Lambert and MacGray had been destroyed along with the labyrinth, and another one had been activated against Mendoza. If this was the enemy's true tactic (and he couldn't imagine any other), the threat could be neutralized easily. It would just be necessary to alter the sensors' sensitivity range so that they could detect infrared; even if the eyes were invisible, they must emit some form of energy or they wouldn't be able to move around. He congratulated himself for not having left the control center; if he had opened his door since the arrival of Candy and her cargo of human bait and hypnotic eyes, one of them could have gotten to him...

This renewed burst of confidence narrowed the chink little by little. The filaments withdrew, allowing it to close; for the moment the objectives had been achieved.

Poring over his control table, Savell modified the settings of his security sensors and studied the screens in front of him. No, there was nothing to be seen except the thermal outlines of the survivors: Dahlgren and Kern in their room on the first floor, the doctor in her laboratory, Maureen at the Enchanted Valley control center, Schwartz, Babson, and Candy in their rooms... The enemy must have realized that after eliminating Mendoza and Steele they would deduce the presence of the hypnotic eyes, and deactivated them—for the moment. Yes, of course they would wait for a while before attempting to use them again. But there was a solution to this...

He pressed a few keys on the controls.

Good, now anything that began radiating in the infrared within the castle would be carbonized immediately by the lasers.

Satisfied, he reclined against the backrest of his chair. Now he could brief the doctor.

5

"But that's monstrous!" exclaimed Maureen Rockne. "Why are they attacking us like this, without attempting to open negotiations?"

"Be quiet," replied Sybil as she tried to put her thoughts in order; all of this had too many implications. "Rockne, have you opened the door of your sector to anyone since Candy arrived?"

The woman on the left-hand screen shook her head emphatically.

"No, not at any point," she declared, her voice sounding nervous.

"I can check that," Sybil said. "The sensors in your room will show me."

But I opened my door, Sybil said to herself, and I was alone with her... What if an eye got in here and hypnotized me and found out that...?

"Keep on high alert," she said, abruptly cutting the communication short.

She ran out of the laboratory.

She needed to tell the other two what had happened; they needed to get out of the hermitage immediately, because if she had been hypnotized and had been made to reveal the plan... Panic drove her on even more quickly.

Patrick! Patrick, you have to save yourself!

She reached her room and with fevered hands drew back the hangings on the wall; she pressed the bas-relief that allowed entry to the secret shaft.

The mental fingers sequestered her memory of the systems protecting the portal and submerged them in the deepest recesses of her mind...

She stepped onto the platform and began to descend.

Beneath her the security system detected that something was wrong; someone was approaching without having activated the alarm...

The platform arrived at the panel hiding the microportal and stopped. Sybil reached out her hand...

The shock wave from the explosion rose up through the shaft, searching for an exit, but the force fields soon absorbed its energy and only the merest breeze reached the hangings in Sybil's room, ruffling them gently.

XXXVIII

The Power of Illusion

1

CANDY SAT UP IN BED, her hands clasped to her chest trying to contain her thumping heart. They were in danger. Mortal danger... She could feel it floating in the air, intangible and invisible, but real. She swallowed hard. Never, ever before had she had a premonition of such intensity... No, it wasn't a premonition; it was a certainty. Something was threatening the Hydra Project and her own life... She tried to calm herself and think. What was the danger? Or who?

The answer flashed through her mind with the searing clarity of a flame: the lookout. That clumsy lookout who had allowed herself to be captured so easily; she was the threat, and it was necessary, essential that she be destroyed as soon as possible... She had to tell the doctor immediately.

She pressed the button on the bracelet around her wrist. Nothing but a blank screen.

She breathed deeply. She mustn't let her imagination run away with her. Dr. Golden was alive and to think anything else was sheer idiocy; she must have taken her bracelet off to complete some task, not wishing to be interrupted... Who to call then? Savell. She pressed another button on the bracelet, holding her breath... The disk lit up. Good, good, perfect...

"Savell?"

"Yes?"

"It's Candy. You must destroy the smaller of the two enemy agents immediately: the slim, olive-skinned one..."

"Wait one moment," replied the voice from the bracelet.

In the Castle Danger control room, Savell reclined in his chair, thinking. He was watching the screen that showed the inside of Candy's room.

Her infrared outline showed her seated in the air... On her bed, I suppose. She was alone. There was no sign of any hypnotic eyes in her room.

But she had been the first one to have any contact with them. Should he eliminate her too?

No, then he'd have to liquidate Babson for the same reason, and only Rockne, Schwartz, and himself would remain from the Hydra's original ten members: too few to defend the castle...

What's more, Candy was the perfect agent. A legend in Imperial Security, she'd never failed in over twenty years of service. He couldn't make such a decision alone...

He opened a communication channel to the doctor's laboratory.

The laboratory was empty.

He tried to call her bracelet, but she didn't respond... He rubbed his chin, wondering about the merits of calling on Rockne... He dismissed the idea; Maureen was on the brink of a nervous breakdown. She was not reliable. Really, the one who should be on duty was Candy herself... If only she hadn't been in contact with the eyes...

But if the eyes had taken control of such a valiant operative, they would have put her into action much sooner; it wouldn't have been difficult for Candy to have destroyed them all without arousing suspicion... And moreover, he mustn't forget her initial distrust. Of course it had been directed against the cybo; she had been fooled as well. But her instinct had been aroused, and that must have made her impossible to hypnotize...

"Savell? Savell?" The anxiety was clear from her voice.

Savell brought the bracelet up to his mouth.

"I hear you, Candy. Tell me, why do you want her destroyed?"

"Savell, you've known me a long time. I have no evidence of anything, but I have an intuition—more than that, I have a *conviction* that this young woman is a mortal threat to us. Trust me, please, and destroy her."

The man blinked involuntarily. There was a great power of conviction in Candy's speech; indeed, if he had not already eliminated the cybo he would have done so now without a moment's hesitation... But he should explain the situation to her.

"Your request is too late, Candy; I've already destroyed her."

The bracelet transmitted an astonished silence for a moment.

"But I still feel the danger! And it is connected to her! It is her!"

"You have connected it with her, and with good reason, but it's no more than a red herring... It's true that we are in danger, but we now know the real cause."

"Which is?" demanded the voice from the bracelet.

"I don't know if you are familiar with their eyes..."

"Eyes?"

"They are mobile, microwatchers—practically invisible. They must have come in with the enemy agents, taking advantage of them being captured to enter the castle. We lost four of our agents before we discovered their existence, but they have been neutralized now. If they make an attempt to regain control of any of our people, they will be destroyed."

There was a thoughtful pause from the bracelet...

"That sounds good, Savell, but I am still uneasy. What can I do? Assign me to some task, a concrete activity; I need it."

Standing beside her bed, Candy awaited the reply, every inch of her tensed. Savell's explanation seemed reasonable, but something was still bothering her, something deep inside her, impelling her to act and quickly, before it was too late...

The man's voice came from the bracelet.

"At the moment, it isn't possible for me to assign you to a task, but stay vigilant; as soon as something happens I will alert you. In the meantime, don't leave your room."

"I feel that if I wait until something happens it will already be too late... Please, Savell, at the very least let me act for myself."

"Candy, please; remain calm and in your room. The security system has been activated; if you leave your room, you will be vaporized. We can't afford to lose you, too; there are too few of us already," said Savell, and he signed off.

Candy bit her lip. She would have to wait... But she would be prepared for anything.

She pressed a button on her bracelet.

"Babson?"

"Candy?" chimed the distinctive voice.

"Get ready for combat."

"Now? What's happened?"

"Nothing yet, but something will soon. Stay alert," she ordered, and switched off her bracelet.

She walked to the wall and drew back one of the panels. She took out the antigravity belt and put it on. She secured the force-field generator... Turning back into the room, she collected up her weapons from the bed-side table; she hid her laser in the pleats of her tunic, set the neurotor to its maximum level (this time she would not make the mistake of taking any prisoners), and sat back on the bed.

Now she would wait.

2

"We can't afford to lose you, too; there are too few of us already," said Savell, and he signed off.

He leaned back in his seat, deep in thought. This uncontrollable desire of Candy's to go into action was suspicious. It might be as she claimed, a premonition of danger, but then again it could also be orders implanted through hypnosis by one of the eyes. Only Dr. Golden would be able to tell the true cause... But where was the doctor?

He looked over the screens. No, she wasn't visible... And what was this? The cybermechanics control center was empty! Where had Maureen Rockne gone?

A flicker of suspicion made him switch on the sim-dows; it wasn't impossible that... And no, he wasn't wrong; the dome was golden once again.

Rockne had deactivated the external defense systems. Panic? Or under the influence of hypnosis?

If it was panic...

He activated the sensors on the launch pad.

His hypothesis proved right: there was Rockne, getting on board a Hermes, about to close the hatch.

There wasn't a moment to lose; the external defense systems had to be switched back on. Who to send? Candy? After their last conversation, definitely not... That only left Schwartz.

He activated the appropriate button on his bracelet.

"I hear you," said Schwartz in a confident tone.

"Run to the cybermechanics control room, there's not a moment to lose," Savell ordered him, then switched off his bracelet.

He watched as the infrared silhouette went into action, leaving Schwartz's room at top speed... Good, the defense system would soon be up and running again.

He returned his gaze to the sim-dow.

The Hermes was just lifting off...

He keyed in the code to the intercom and as soon as he saw the light go on to indicate a communication channel was open, he asked, with apparent calm, "What are you doing, Maureen?"

3

Sybil Golden's image had disappeared from the screen, but Maureen Rockne continued staring at it. She had recognized what was behind her expression just before she'd signed off, because she felt it, too: *fear*.

Her eyes wandered uneasily around the cybermechanics control room. She had thought those defenses were impregnable, but the enemy had begun attacking through unexpected routes. Savell could fantasize all he wanted to about those hypothetical eyes; she was sure that he would soon discover that they were not the enemy's true weapon... She would rather rely on her own instincts, and these were telling her that anybody who used a decoy to confuse them would surely use two or three more, making them follow wrong turn after wrong turn, until the castle was destroyed and all its defenders dead... She shuddered. And their leaders? Would they die, too?

Gently, skillfully, the invisible fingers extracted her thoughts from the tumultuous tornado they had fallen into and guided them into a peaceful refuge...

How could she have been so stupid? They must have foreseen this eventuality; at this very moment the Three were most likely abandoning the castle via some secret passageway... So was she to die here, thinking that everything was lost? No, not that. Dead, she was no good to anyone; alive she could still... How could she escape?

She looked at the control panel angrily.

All of those "protective" systems had turned into obstacles... Very well, she would make them disappear.

Quickly her hands flew over the controls, deactivating the destruction of the passes...the guardians...the green tornados...

For a second something imperceptible intervened between her fingers and the controls.

...the dragons...

And then, it vanished.

...the antiaircraft volcanos...and lastly, the impenetrable dome.

She glanced hurriedly over at the screen that communicated with Savell; it was switched off. Good, he hadn't yet realized what she was doing... And everyone else was far enough away to give her plenty of time...

She ran to the exit; luckily the launch pad was close by.

Two minutes later, she closed the hatch of the Hermes and sat, panting, in front of the craft's controls. Now, to get into the air and get out quickly, before they had time to reactivate the dome...

Lurching slightly, the Hermes rose into the air.

Maureen was just turning the craft to set it on the shortest course toward the mountains when she heard Savell's voice.

"What are you doing, Maureen?"

The woman briefly chewed her lower lip before answering.

"I'm going out to take some air, my dear."

In the control room, Savell directed his attention to the screen on which he was watching Schwartz's progress. He had already reached the ramparts and was running along them, his huge body towering above the battlements, but he still had some way to go...

"This is no moment to joke, Maureen!" he said, taking care not to let his anxiety show through in his voice. "Before you get to the mountain, the dome..."

A movement on the sim-dow screens caught his attention; he gawked at the scene, unable to believe his eyes...

"Maureen! Get back here immediately!" he shouted, abandoning his artificially calm tone.

"Later, later..." came the lighthearted reply.

Savell grasped the arms of his chair.

"Look below!"

Maureen felt a smile creep onto her face. What kind of juvenile prank was Savell up to? But even so, she glanced downward for an instant.

Her smile froze. What was this? She was convinced she had deactivated the dragons!

Recovering from her momentary daze, Maureen manipulated the controls of the Hermes with trembling fingers; she might just make it back to the castle...

Holding his breath, Savell watched the minute aircraft as it turned expertly to dodge the jet of flame from the ascending dragon, whose green bulk passed so close to the Hermes that the pilot lost control of the craft for long enough that she could not avoid the firestorm produced by the other winged monster appearing immediately behind the first. He closed his eyes; this was not pleasant to watch... He drew a hand across his damp forehead. Well, he'd done everything he could for her; people shouldn't lose their heads like that...

He opened his eyes again. He looked at the screens; Schwartz should just be arriving at... Where had he gone?

He searched on his screens without success.

He pressed the button to call Schwartz on his bracelet; it was dead. He moistened his lips. Schwartz, too?

No, it was absurd; the phlegmatic Teuton could not have lost his head... Where is the sensor that was following him? Let's see where he's gone.

He brought up the image of Schwartz running along the battlements...

4

Schwartz ran along the ramparts with rhythmic strides. He took pleasure in being freed from the accumulated worry of so much waiting, not knowing what was happening. But now, from the cybermechanics control room...

Something delicate and elusive stroked his mind in the area dedicated to visual stimuli and caused a tiny change...

...he would be able to take direct part in what was going on... He frowned. What was going on? He should be nearing the place where the wall gave a right angle turn, but he could see there was still a long stretch ahead of him. The castle had a few visual oddities, it was true...

His right foot caught on what was for him an invisible wall. His momentum carried his body forward, downward, through a gap in the battlement. His hands grabbed at the pseudorock, trying to get a grip, and he toppled over screaming, still seeing the interminable ramparts in his mind's eye...

5

Nervously, Savell switched off the screen. How could that imbecile not have seen...?

In the depths of Castle Danger, Maya looked into her mind and saw that the pit, which had previously seemed insatiable, was now about to overflow.

Abouttime.

She concentrated her energies on the man in charge of the castle control room; a few rifts were starting to appear in what until now had been his monolithic stability. This part of her task could now be completed...

Savell gulped. He needed to think. To understand what was happening... That thing with Maureen was easily explained; she had lost control, and upon deactivating their defenses had simply forgotten the dragons... But Schwartz? He had seen his face as he went over the battlements; it showed complete astonishment. That was definitely not a suicide... Besides, such a thing would never occur to Schwartz; no, he knew him too well...

Acting independently of his conscious mind, his feet made his chair swivel around so that he was in front of the main power controls.

There had to be some explanation! Could it be possible that the eyes had no energy losses in the infrared spectrum?

His right hand lifted from where it rested on the arm of his chair and moved toward the tripswitch for the energy supply that fed the force fields supporting Castle Danger's complex structures...

But the problem was even more serious: he was alone. Alone, he couldn't count on Babson and Candy's support, now even less than ever. How could he protect himself?

His hand disabled the last security key; he grasped the master switch and pulled it.

Castle Danger vanished.

In an instant, Savell found himself in the air, a hundred meters above the cavern that had been excavated in the rock to accommodate the dungeons. His last trace of sanity evaporated; he laughed without pause for the entirety of his interminable plunge...

XXXIX

The Apparent End

1

MAYA FORCED HER WASTED MUSCLES to raise her to her feet. She contracted her dilated pupils.

Thesunmuststillbehighintheskyoutside.

She flexed her knee joints slightly. Then she made Savell cut the energy supply to the force fields.

She fell...

Her calculations had been accurate; the floor of the cell was no more than a meter above the rock face upon which Castle Danger had been erected.

She was still adjusting her balance on the uneven terrain as she looked upward: hundreds of objects of differing sizes were falling from various heights... She quickly identified Savell and the false Dahlgren and Kern; no problems there. But she also spotted two figures floating immobile a hundred meters above the ground.

BabsonandCandy...

2

The sudden disappearance of Castle Danger didn't take Candy by surprise; before she had fallen even ten meters her hand activated the antigravity belt.

If the enemy had thought it would be easy to dispose of her, they were in for a surprise...

Ready for combat, she managed to turn her body in the air, searching for the invisible enemy. For a moment her gaze fixed on Babson floating a couple of meters below her, then continued and... The leaders!

Forgetting all else, she activated her propulsion unit and took off at a suicidal speed in a straight line toward where her instinct told her she would be able to intercept their fall. She had to save them at all costs...

Babson had managed to activate his antigravity belt and was now looking around, perplexed. What had happened? Where was the castle?

Something passed by him and the air currents in its wake jolted him; instinctively he followed the human projectile with his eyes and saw two men falling into the void... Their leaders were about to die!

Without thinking, he activated his propulsion unit and followed the woman flying after Dahlgren and Kern.

He locked his gaze on her.

A little nudge to his visual cortex...

And he almost lost control of his jet pack. It was the lookout he had captured! And she had a neurotor ready in her right hand! She was going to kill their leaders!

He took out his own neurotor and increased the speed of his propulsion unit; he had to destroy her before she achieved her goal.

Each fraction of a second dragged as he shortened the distance separating them... He was close enough!

He aimed and fired.

The woman's body stiffened in mid-flight.

He smiled. It had only taken one shot. Candy would be proud of... Candy?

The body sailed passed him, changing as it did so. He looked back, following it with his gaze. It couldn't be Candy!

He streaked past beneath the false Dahlgren and Kern and continued his mortal race, staring over his shoulder... By the time he checked in front of him again, the rocks were too close.

Maya counted the impacts on the ground.

Crack.

Babson...

Crack.

Candy...

Thump. Thump.

The doubles.

Thump.

Savell.

She searched for a good spot on the rocks and sat down. She hugged her legs, pressing her thighs against her chest and rested her chin on her knees.

She extracted the energy accumulated in her overflowing mental well and molded it according to the isogravitational formulae of the ovo. She checked the complex structures: there was no space for error. It was a shame that there'd been no time to practice this... She input the coordinates for Shari's hermitage and activated the system. Around her the rocks vanished, as did the scorched, blackened valley and the blue, cloudless sky...

The white curtains of Sybil's room appeared. She let out a sigh; there had been no mistake.

Suddenly her vision clouded, and she became aware of her weakened physical state. Maya let herself fall back onto the bed. She tried to clear her mind, but could not; her reserves were completely exhausted.

She frowned. She couldn't cope with her task like this.

She closed her eyes and concentrated... She managed to extend her mental perception to outside the room and was able to locate the enemy minds vaguely; they were in the upper room in the tower.

Good, she had a little time at her disposal to renew her strength.

She rose slowly from the bed. She waited for a moment while the cloud in front of her eyes dispersed, and placed her feet on the floor; its coolness was pleasant.

She hung onto the bed curtains and managed to get to her feet. Good...

She took a step and swayed; she had to steady herself with a hand against the rough wall to regain her balance.

She followed the walls to the door.

Before leaving, she paused to make sure of the situation outside... Perfect, Dahlgren and Kern were still in the tower.

Unsteadily, with one hand on the corridor wall, she made her way toward the refectory as quickly as she could; she had to make the most of the time available to recuperate.

3

Dahlgren looked out of the window. The shadow cast by the hermitage across the valley was getting long... He was impatient. What was Sybil waiting for? It was well past time for a briefing... He turned to Kern.

"Ryland!"

"Yes," replied the head of Imperial Security, getting up off the bench where he had been seated.

"Go and get something to eat."

Ryland Kern stretched, making his stiff joints creak. He left the room.

He began to descend the staircase... It was clear that Dahlgren was becoming concerned about how long it was taking Golden to report back. But it was only to be expected; the enemy must have opened negotiations with her by now. Or in the worst case scenario, they would be attacking the castle... Very well, let them break themselves on those rocks. That way they would gain respect, and the negotiations would become easier...

He walked down the passageway to the refectory. Their problem now was when to activate the remaining Hydras... It was a shame to have had to sacrifice Hydra I; Roth was a valuable asset to them... What was that woman doing there?

He stopped dead on the threshold to the refectory, holding his breath. Luckily she hadn't noticed him yet... Could she be an enemy agent?

He craned his neck. No, it wasn't possible. No enemy agent would enter the lion's den and sit down to eat so casually: naked and without any weapons (his well-trained eye had observed that particular detail from the outset). No, she must be some kind of demented mystic... But how had she managed to get into the hermitage without activating any of the intruder alarms? Not even a fly could have entered the environs of the hermitage without being detected, observed, and analyzed in every particular... Something wasn't right; he couldn't trust anything.

He looked around the refectory.

The other entrance was directly in front of him, and he could see all the way down the corridor leading to it; there was nobody there.

The refectory walls were bare of any hangings that someone could hide behind. The windows were too high and were barred... For safety's sake he looked them over. Yes, all clear... Three empty tables, without tablecloths, the benches beside them... No, there was no one else.

He pulled his laser from beneath the folds of his tunic; he wasn't taking any chances...

"Who goes there!" he cried loudly.

Despite his preparations, the outcome of his inquiry surprised him; the woman, barely out of adolescence, leapt from the bench, and, turning in the air, landed three meters away from where she'd been sitting. Her face was deformed with a look of hatred. In her hand she carried a neurotor (where could she have gotten that from?) and was pointing it straight at him.

All the years of training kicked into action; his laser flashed briefly, and the girl fell.

With his weapon ready just in case, Ryland Kern went toward the immobile body. He turned it over with the toe of his boot... A clean hole passed through the thorax between her breasts.

Without removing her eyes from the man leaning over the empty floor, Maya continued moving her spoon methodically between the plate and her mouth, from her mouth to the plate... How long would it take for him to be satisfied she was dead? She couldn't maintain the illusion for long; she was still far from recovered.

Ryland Kern straightened up, casting a nervous look about him... Yes, the refectory was deserted, except for the body of the girl. However, the hermitage had ceased to be a safe haven; they would have to get to their emergency hideout.

4

Patrick Maynard Dahlgren shook his head, invaded by a sudden sense of alarm.

The mental filament withdrew.

*HowmanymoreoftheselatenttelepathsamIgoingtoget
entangledwith?*

He sighed. Something was very wrong, very wrong indeed...
His safety was under threat; he needed to flee immediately. If
not...

He tried to calm himself. All fear has a logical basis, a reason.
Why would his life be in danger? Only if they had taken the castle
(improbable in such a short time), imprisoned Sybil (even more
improbable), and forced her to reveal where he was (totally fantastical)... No, it was all impossible. What's more, he had taken the
precaution of not letting Sybil in on the secret security systems
now protecting the hermitage, or even the whereabouts of their
emergency hideout. Even supposing the enemy had discovered
his existence and his location, they would probably imagine that,
confident of his anonymity, he'd be unprepared and they would
therefore come to eliminate him without taking too many precautions; for example, it would never occur to them to use an ovo to
take him by surprise (and an ovo would be the only way to enter
undetected).

He heard a noise.

An invisible cobweb brushed surreptitiously against his brain,
far from his waking consciousness.

*Thevisualcortexisinaccessible...butnottheauditory
centers.*

And it clung silently to the unguarded area.

It sounded like steps coming up the staircase. He was immediately on his guard. Was it Ryland, running? The sound didn't
correspond to his steel-capped boots but seemed more like bare
feet carrying a slight frame rather than Kern's robust bulk...

Ryland's voice came through the closed door.

"Dahlgren! We're in danger!" it announced.

The sounds entered his ears and were transformed into nerve impulses that traveled swiftly toward his conscious mind, but the invisible cobweb distorted them before they got there and converted them into the tones of a young, feminine voice, which shrieked, bursting with rage and triumph.

"Dahlgren! Your hour has come!"

With one push Ryland opened the door wide and found himself enveloped in an invisible laser beam.

With difficulty, Dahlgren released his tensed finger from the trigger. Walking stiffly, he approached the body of the head of Imperial Security.

He gazed at the unscathed features. Death had frozen them in an expression of dawning surprise... He breathed deeply. Everything was becoming clear now.

The enemy was using telepaths.

He hurried out of the room. It was pointless to wait for news from Castle Danger. Against these adversaries it would have been as effective as a castle made of playing cards... But how had they managed to develop this secretly in such a transparent world? he asked himself as he descended. He hung on tightly to the handrail; he didn't know if he could trust any of his senses...

According to Houdry and Rockne, nobody had been developing these skills on Earth... The Auroran Mentagroups? He had suspected and then discounted that possibility; their telepathy was restricted to within the group... There was only one other possibility left: the cybos. It was absurd to expect them to have limited themselves to cybermechanics; in the final analysis, cybernetics was just a tool for doing other things, not an end in itself...

His eyes told him that he had reached the bottom of the staircase. He checked it against his visual memory; it coincided. Even so, he felt the ground gingerly with one foot before putting his weight down... Carefully he walked to the secret door and opened it.

He went into the dark passageway and closed the door behind himself, securing it so that it could not be opened again from the outside. After all, it seemed that the cybo telepaths were not fully developed and could only provoke hallucinations; otherwise, they would have liquidated him already... He knew their potential. It wasn't for nothing that he'd dismissed that project in the time of the Empire; developing telepathy was like playing the stock market... But he must keep his mind on the task at hand. These novice telepaths had given him an opportunity. They could waste some time reading Sybil and Kern's dead minds; they hadn't known the locations of all of the Hydras. From his hideout he would be able to activate his personal backup and give him the necessary instructions so that the others could protect themselves from the cybos. No, all was not lost.

Something white glimmered in the semidarkness before him.

He peered into the darkness without slowing his pace, his laser ready. A naked girl was walking ahead of him, without looking backward... No, it was an illusion. The walls of the passage were visible through her body, sharpening and blurring at the same time as the image weakened or strengthened...

He smiled. This seemed to be a very clumsy effort; they should know that no one had ever managed to hypnotize him. And now he was alert to the danger it would be even more difficult... His smile vanished. That was not the only explanation. It could well be a hallucination provoked for the very opposite reason: that is, as an attempt to distract him from seeing the real girl in front of him so that she could stop his escape... How could he be sure which was the real illusion?

There was only one way to dispel all doubt.

He fired his laser in a diagonal line, up and down, left and right, as was his preferred style... The spectral outline disappeared.

Carefully, he examined the place where the body should have fallen and found nothing. It was a simple illusion—but to what end?

He thought for a moment... It was obvious: they were trying to make him accustomed to seeing her, so that he would stop noticing her, and when he was no longer on his guard the *real* person would be right on top of him... Very well, let them try.

He continued walking slowly down the passage; he was not far from the portal...*his* portal.

Now he only had to cross its threshold and he would be in his secret hideout where he had everything he needed to survive for decades... And the portal could only open from wherever he was, because only he knew the gravitational coordinates of the hideout; nobody could find him. And from this secure lair he would be able to wake the reserve Hydras. *Then* let's see who would have the last laugh...

The passage opened before him out into a wide chamber and he saw the still-inactive portal.

He quickened his step over to the controls. He concentrated on them; he mustn't let himself be distracted now... First connect the energy supply to the portal.

The black rectangle glowed brightly for a second and then went back to its usual violet color.

Now to input the coordinates for the hideout...

The sound of echoing footsteps made him turn his head. Another phantom or the true telepath? It had entered the chamber and was running toward him.

Without finishing the input sequence, he fired.

The phantom vanished without leaving a trace.

Vigilant, he looked around the chamber; evidently they were trying to distract him.

He smiled as he noticed another semitransparent shadow crawling across the floor toward him.

He fired again.

Nothing could be seen except the fine diagonal groove etched on the ground by the passage of the laser beam.

No, that was still not the real one; his adversary was not that stupid...

He began to return to the controls, remaining alert to any movements around him... In his peripheral vision he spotted a third figure and fired automatically.

Nothing.

Was his adversary trying to run down the charge on his laser? Okay then, he would go along with their game. When he was down to his last two rounds, he'd pretend that he'd run out and then...

He fired rapidly on the fourth figure, almost on top of him. The fifth flashed on the wall between the controls and the portal, disappearing as soon as he fired.

He waited for the next apparition for almost a minute... But no more phantoms came. Had the telepath exhausted her ability to produce these images? Or was all this just a simple attempt to delay his flight in order to give some other, better armed agents time to reach him?

If that was their plan, they were too late.

Returning to the controls, he carefully entered the coordinates of the underground hideout. They had underestimated him if they'd hoped he'd forget to do that and enter the portal without setting his destination so that he'd be scattered into atoms, isolated in a trillion points across the universe... He keyed in the final number and took a last look around; the chamber was still empty.

He hurried over to the portal.

He hadn't noticed that when he'd fired at the fifth specter the laser beam had cut the cables connecting the portal to the control table, and consequently the latter had not received the coordinates for his destination.

His foot grazed the fields around the portal...

There was a blaze of purple light, and then the chamber was empty.

5

Maya finished her last spoonful and set her spoon down on the table. She mustn't exhaust herself; the important work, the real task, was still to come...

Getting up from her seat she walked slowly toward the communications chamber, all the while her accelerated metabolism was processing the food she had just eaten. She was still far from the minimal level of fitness she knew she would soon be needing...

She entered the communications chamber and sat in front of the intercom. It was a primitive model, but it would do.

She entered her secret code.

Sarki's face appeared on the screen.

"You took your time," said the man, his mouth widening in a gentle smile.

"I was up against some embryonic telepaths," Maya explained.

Sarki frowned.

"Two?" He thought for a moment, then nodded. "Dahlgren was one, right?"

"Yes."

"And the other?"

"The other was Candice Stow."

"And the Hydra coordinates?"

"Here they are," replied the young woman, her fingers moved rapidly over the keys on the control pad.

Sarki lowered his eyes to look at his own.

"Perfect, thanks," he said.

"I am going to brief the council," Maya announced.

A hint of concern flashed across the cybo's eyes.

"So soon? You have not recovered fully."

The young woman shook her head.

"By the time I arrive, I will be fine."

"If you think so... Goodbye, Maya."

"Goodbye, Sarki," said the cybo, and cut the communication channel.

She entered the necessary sequence to call a Hermes and got up to go back to the refectory. She had absorbed the first course and could feel all the cells in her body crying out for more sustenance. There was still time for her to ingest more while she waited for the Hermes to arrive...

F

This is the sixth part of the test. It is strictly your own work; you must complete it on your own, without discussing your answers with anyone. If you do not wish to complete it, continue to the next page.

I. Two thousand years ago the Roman poet Catullus wrote the following:

> *The sun may set and rise*
> *But we contrariwise*
> *Sleep after our short light*
> *One everlasting night.*

1. Do you think Alice Welland knew of these lines of verse?
2. In the case of an affirmative answer, why did she risk her life?
3. Have you ever thought that you had to die?
4. Do you accept it, try to refute it, or forget about the whole matter?
5. If you knew you were going to die tomorrow, what would you do?

GO TO THE NEXT PAGE

II. The brothers Vainieri wrote *Voyage to Meet the Minotaur*. At one point in the dialogue one of the characters says to another, "I looked at it full in the face, and thought with a heavy heart, that no bullet can kill a man as effectively as fear will kill him."

1. Is this true? Argue your case. There is no word limit.

This test will continue later. You may change your answers at any point.

TURN TO THE NEXT PAGE

XL

The Real Game

Experimental evidence shows that the more conscious a man is concerning the factors influencing him, the greater his criticism of those influences, whereas a lack of self-knowledge equals a lack of critical thinking... Through the force of suggestion one can provoke and reinforce those behaviors that would cause a person to act in a certain desired way and inhibit any that would prevent it.

—V. N. KULIKOV,
INTRODUCTION TO MARXIST SOCIAL PSYCHOLOGY

1

THE HATCH OF THE HERMES OPENED.

Maya let down the steps and descended.

There was no one on the esplanade. Karen's house seemed deserted.

She walked toward it.

She had not gone more than halfway when the door of the house opened and at its threshold the body of Aisha Dewar appeared.

"Maya! How have you managed to get back so soon?" said the voice of Alice Welland, emerging from the lips of Aisha Dewar. The body again occupied by the resurrected hurried toward her.

She stopped a few paces away.

"You've lost so much weight..." she said, apprising the cybo's naked body. "It looks as if your bones are trying to burst through your skin. What happened to you?" Without waiting for the reply she took Maya's arm. "It is a shame the others aren't here... Aridor came to fetch them; they've gone to the institute. It looks like they weren't expecting you back so soon. But I will take charge of looking after you..."

They went into the house.

"Come into the dining room. Eat something and then tell me what happened."

A table and chair sprouted from the floor to accommodate Maya. Her hostess sat on the far side of the table.

"Here I am bombarding you with all my chatter, not letting you speak. I'm incorrigible!"

Making herself comfortable on her chair, Maya regarded her interlocutor impassively.

"I talk and talk, I don't give you a chance to ask the question you must be dying to ask: How come I'm alive?" She waited a moment before continuing. "Okay then, let me tell you. Aridor was able to capture the complete transfer process when I passed into the body of that poor girl, Helaine Keller. He managed to download my entire personality. His understanding of the mechanisms of psychotransduction was so good that he was able to reverse Houdry's conditioning, and then I came back here and reintegrated into Aisha's body... Don't tell me that none of this surprises you?" she said with a smile.

Maya did not return the smile.

"No, it doesn't surprise me at all, Joseph Browne," she replied.

Aisha Dewar's features changed subtly...

2

Joseph Browne looked out the window.

The sky was darkening above the buildings that comprised the Institute of Special Investigations; a storm was brewing.

Turning around, the chief of the ISI's Neurophysiology Department moved away from the barred window.

He took a pair of laboratory gloves from the table and examined the transparent plastic at the tips of his index fingers. He couldn't see anything.

He put them toward the light to see them better... Yes, there were the two white dots, one on each index finger. White, that is, intact... He smiled. If Sabrina thought they had him cornered, unable to escape, then perfect, let her continue to think so.

He put on the gloves carefully.

"Can I come in?" asked a female voice from the other side of the door.

"Please do," he said. His eyes had returned to the window.

Every so often the leaves on the trees along the avenue thrashed violently; it would soon begin to rain.

The guard entered, carrying a tray, and placed it on the table.

"Do you want anything else?" she asked.

Browne turned to her. Her expression revealed boredom and fatigue.

"What's on the menu today?"

The woman lifted the lid of the tray.

"Have a look," she said.

A wisp of steam rose from the plate...

The man came nearer, as if to see better. He leaned over the table and sniffed.

"Smells good," he commented.

The woman set the lid to one side.

"Do you want anything else?" she repeated.

Without changing his expression, Browne reached out a hand and plunged his fingers into her thick hair.

She allowed him to caress the back of her neck, watching him with her cold, blue eyes...

"If that is what you want, I can send for a specialist in the field," she said.

Sighing, Browne let his hand fall.

"I don't want specialists, I want you."

The woman shook her head.

"I think I have explained my personal preferences very clearly," she said brusquely. "I'm sorry to disappoint you, but it is not within my power, believe me."

Without taking his eyes off her, Browne sat down to eat.

"My problem is that I like girls like you..."

The guard couldn't help smiling.

"Well, there's nothing to stop you having your own tastes," she commented. "Do you want anything else?"

"Only you," he said.

The woman shook her head but smiled as she left the room and closed the door.

Joseph Browne left his cutlery on the table.

He got up, crossed the room slowly, and threw himself down on the bed.

His appetite was gone.

He examined his gloved hands.

On the index finger of the hand he had used to caress the woman's neck, there was a tiny black spot; the NEMO injector had worked.

He breathed deeply. Tomorrow he would have to prepare more of his NEMOs... Many, very many... When her body arrived tomorrow—with his mind, Joseph Browne's mind, in complete control—he would need as many as he could manufacture. He was not so naïve as to think that his guards were less monitored than he was himself and that the controllers were quite probably being controlled, too... But at some point the chain would be interrupted and he would be able to escape (at least mentally) from this prison within a prison, within a prison, and then... He smiled.

Then the world would be his.

He took off the gloves and let them fall to the floor beside the bed. He reached out his arm and took a thin volume from the bedside table. He opened it without bothering to search for the page; the book always opened there by itself.

The sun may set and rise
But we contrariwise
Sleep after our short light
One everlasting night.

For the first time he smiled after reading those lines of verse.

He had succeeded in escaping from that curse: for him, death would not exist. At least while the human race survived. And perhaps... Over several millennia of life there was much to learn; anything was possible...

He tossed the book carelessly onto the bedside table. It skittered across the surface and fell to the floor.

He crossed his arms behind his head. He knew that at some moment that night his mind would wake up inside another body... One mind in two bodies. In three. In a *hundred*. Even if some accident should happen to one or several of those bodies he would not die.

But still, he had to be very careful. Extremely careful. He could never confide in anyone, ever. Mere suspicion of his existence would be enough for them to launch the greatest hunt in history... He knew men too well. They would never allow one of their own to escape their common destiny, death; fear and envy would not allow them to even breathe until they were completely sure that he was dead, good and proper. To avoid this he would have to stick strictly to his first maxim: to interfere as little as possible in the world of mortals. To only do so in the case that their actions might threaten him in the future, near or distant.

This would not be difficult; he was satisfied with immortality.

If he was a hidden influence, imperceptible, unknown to all, it would be an easy task to induce the attitudes and decisions that he required. This was nothing more than the basic principle of propaganda: for it to be absolutely efficient the subjects exposed to it should be totally unaware of its presence... As long as he didn't attempt to provoke any major changes that were too visible there would be no danger, and with all the time in the world before him, all he had to do was give the occasional nudge in the desired direction. Humanity would always have its partisans and protesters against something, and everything... His unrecognized influence, precisely because it was unrecognized, would be the decisive factor. He grinned.

Joseph Browne, master of the world, a toast to you...

He pursed his lips; he must not rush himself. There was still much to do... He was still little more than the prisoner of Sabrina Glaspel and her little brother, Nevin Glaspel, the head of Imperial Security.

He had taken too long to realize that their shared surname was not a coincidence... However, thanks to that error he had reached the gates of physical immortality through sheer desperation. A person should never be so cornered, left with so little chance of escape as they had left him, but necessity is the mother of invention...

He'd have never looked beyond the straightforward renovation of bodies had he not been conscious of the fact that the Glaspels were only waiting for him to perfect his process of mind transfer via NEMOs before eliminating him, terminating his life, his precious life (*The sun may set and rise, but we contrariwise sleep after our short light...*). But why stop there? Why be limited to one body?

There were certainly unknowns. Would it be possible to control two bodies at the same time? How to deal with the double input of sensory information without going mad?

But those risks were small compared to death (*One everlasting night...*), and he would deal with them. Of course, if there is no other way, fear and desperation can deal with anything...

But he must not confide in anyone; his secret was not yet secure. Sabrina and Nevin had their diadems; they knew of the possibility of creating injectable NEMOs, and he couldn't keep putting them off the scent forever...

Tomorrow—or, better yet, the day that he had two more bodies under his control—the accident would happen: one of his own design and not one that the Glaspels were almost certainly preparing for him once he had finished creating the NEMOs. There would be nothing left of the laboratory or his current body.

Of course, they would have the records of his experiments, at least the official ones. Let them follow the trail. It would take them years to discover it didn't lead anywhere... Sabrina wouldn't dare to divulge the secret to anyone else, and with her superabundance of self-confidence she'd imagine herself capable of reaching the desired outcome alone. He frowned. He needed to be objective. She would get there in the end, she wasn't ignorant, quite the opposite.

But over the many years it would take her, he would have plenty of time to prepare himself... He would watch them. He would be aware of all their plans. While they only had those crude diadems to work with, they could do little; the psychotransducers destroyed the memory of the recipient, which meant that they could only be used safely in very particular circumstances. Meanwhile, he could leap from body to body without a care...

He got up from the bed and poured himself a glass of water from the refrigerator. The grand tournament would begin that night, and there could be only one winner: Joseph Browne. He was convinced of it.

He lay down again. As long as the Glaspels were alive there was danger; they were too clumsy. They would attempt to control the rest of humanity's actions, putting all their faith in brute force— and they would be discovered. In that case, any efforts to save them would be useless, as much for them as for himself. Once the secret of immortality had been discovered, they would all be alert, and then not even his most refined precautions would be sufficient... To ensure his survival over centuries and beyond, the Glaspels must die; that had to be his first objective. He would dedicate himself to achieving this, no matter how long it took. Once he had succeeded, he would have true dominion over Earth. The human race would soon expand its horizons across the galaxies, and he would go with them, unrecognized but at the same time all powerful... Then he would be the master of the universe.

3

Aisha Dewar's features changed subtly: her face grew sharper and hardened into an unmistakably masculine set.

"I see I underestimated you. Naturally you could infer my existence, but to recognize me..." said Joseph Browne in Alice's voice. Meanwhile, his essence flowed from a dozen bodies dispersed across the earth and concentrated in the body of Aisha Dewar, studying the new problem keenly. To what degree had he underestimated the cybos?

Rapidly and minutely they went through the data collected over the course of five decades. Using the analytical faculties and the intuition that had originally belonged to Samuel Aridor and Ixchel Cocom, the young chief of the cybo section at the institute's central bureau, he compared his previous deductions with this unexpected outcome. He had no need to worry: the basic conclusions from his earlier deductions remained unaltered. It would take at least ten years for the cybos to create something capable of confronting and defeating him...

"After all, perhaps it wasn't that difficult. Allow me, for my own satisfaction, to reconstruct the process." He glanced at the ring on his left hand. "We still have time."

Maya nodded.

"We still have time," she concurred.

Joseph Browne stretched Aisha's body out in his seat. If the cybos had managed to discover who he was, then it was very probable that they were also aware of the impossibility of defeating him. What was the point of Maya being here?

"You have no idea of the pleasure it gives me to talk with someone intelligent; I sometimes feel suffocated, dealing only with human beings," he commented, recalling that sincerity sometimes provokes sincerity. "Let's begin. First you deduced my existence from an analysis of the earth's attitudes with respect to the groups, and then later toward the cybos. Is this correct?"

"Correct."

In the laboratory at the institute's central bureau, Aridor hurried to complete the preparations; soon Nadia, Karen, and Felix would have forgotten everything concerning the Hydra Project and the cybos would find themselves without support... Maya had finished too quickly, but very soon that wouldn't matter...

Joseph Browne continued.

"The normals are accustomed to giving little importance to these details... To err is human, they say with good reason, and then they go on to err again. They don't appreciate that there's a margin up to which the errors we commit are our own and beyond which an external influence has forced them," he said, and laughed.

Through Ixchel Cocom's eyes he watched the screen in his cubicle and saw an image of destruction and ruin on the cybos' island around what had been their secret portal... There were no craft at their airport, and no other cybo possessed the mental structures that had enabled Maya to become a living ovo. He was now sure he was facing her alone, and she was weak, spent...

"It's absurdly simple to get them to make mistakes, believe me," he said, more relaxed now. "All that's needed is a stimulus that provokes a fear of the new, of the different, of the unknown—then nothing more is required. They themselves take charge of finding the justification," he explained, looking cheerfully at his companion. "Of course, it is necessary to be alert; there is always someone prepared to surmount their fear and ignorance in order to see the truth." The brows that had once been Aisha's met in a frown. "Then they can become empowered to shout it out to the others. 'The voice calling in the desert' is an undisputed human tradition... If you let them, they are capable of anything—even of convincing the others," he murmured, and then recovered his good humor. "Fortunately I have my finger on the pulse, and so far, I have been able to neutralize things in time: Marx, the Ulyanovs, and the

Castros, all those who have tried to rise up over the years... Had I not been able to silence these voices in the desert, they would have become terribly dangerous... But I digress, my dear Maya. We were attempting to reproduce the path that led you to me, weren't we?"

"Indeed."

Browne laced Aisha's delicate fingers together and contemplated them abstractedly.

"We had gotten to the point where it became evident to you that the normals' attitude toward the groups and the cybos was only explicable in terms of an external agent: one unknown to all of them. Although it might seem so, human stupidity is not infinite... Good, then it only remained to identify this hidden cause. How long did it take you to dismiss the hypothesis of an extraterrestrial civilization?"

"Seconds," said Maya.

Joseph Browne made an approving gesture, but he was still curious as to when his companion would go into action... Should he strike first? Perhaps, but he couldn't resist the opportunity to play with her like a cat with a mouse. Poor little mouse, she seemed to think she could win...

"I genuinely fear I have underestimated you," he said, hoping to reaffirm her sense of self-confidence; that would make her jump the gun. "Let's continue. It became evident you were dealing with an influence that had been in action without interruption for centuries. Once its existence was recognized, you could uncover my other, less obvious actions and appreciate the internal coherence; the inference that it was a single mind became unavoidable. An immortal mind, a mind capable of switching bodies, of occupying several at a time... I thought you might stop there, but I realize I was wrong. Did it take long before you began looking through the old papers preserved from the Institute of Special Investigations?"

"No."

Perhaps she has come to the conclusion that it would be better to be part of me than nothing... Absurd: she has tasted power, the power of life and death, and nothing can take away the desire for absolute power. No, she is not so far from human.

"You're not much of a conversationalist." Browne shook his head. "Going back to the topic, the institute allowed very little of its work into the public domain or even into external archives... None of the normals would have been able to make the necessary connections; such a feat is only possible for minds like ours... To sum up, with the data available you were able to come to the conclusion that the only candidate for the role of God Almighty that there had been over the last two centuries was me. Am I right?"

"You are right."

"I suppose that you discovered the Hydra Project, too?"

"That too."

"And so you will understand that I permitted the cybos to come into being, although, it goes without saying, still keeping them under strict control, to use them against the Hydra."

"Yes."

Browne nodded.

"So, I can only congratulate myself on having taken every precaution... Why don't you try to move your hands? Or your feet?"

"The snare."

"You were prepared for that, too?"

"That too."

Browne directed the gaze of Aisha's green eyes toward where the cybo's immobile hands rested on the table: around them, the air had acquired a peculiar opacity... The snare was working, no doubt about it.

"Forgive me," he said tilting his head to one side in a gesture of sympathy. "I know it is inappropriate to use on you something designed for animals. I would never underestimate you to the extent of believing that you'd attempt to try physical force against me. I am employing it with a different purpose... But now is not the moment to discuss that."

"I am aware of that."

Browne gave Maya a startled look.

"You are? Good, then you can take over the explanation. I already have a dry throat," he said, and pressed the edge of the table in front of him. He took the glass of fizzy pink liquid that emerged from the interior of the table and put it to his newly acquired lips...

"You propose injecting me with NEMOs," said the cybo.

The glass clinked against the teeth that now belonged to Browne; he placed it on the table.

"In that case, I don't understand you," he said, perplexed. "Unless you have decided that there is no hope left for you and it would be better to accept becoming part of me than becoming nothing... You'll have to excuse me, but I don't think you're that clever."

"I'm not."

"Then, why did you come here?"

She perceived the uncertainty emanating from Browne's mind; the moment had arrived.

"For this," said Maya, as she gathered all the resources left in her and launched them in one strike, with all her force, in a single destructive beam against the mind of Joseph Browne...

4

"You must understand, Maya; you can't beat him."

"Why not?"

"Browne is not stupid. He's aware of the blueprints for what we have implanted in you. He will be prepared for anything you can do."

"So then..." she left the phrase hanging.

Sarki's eyes were full of compassion.

"There is no other solution, Maya..."

5

She launched them in one strike, with all her force, in a single destructive beam against the mind of Joseph Browne and felt them rebound uselessly off the defensive wall, hard yet flexible like steel.

Aisha Dewar's mouth laughed.

"I thought you'd never get around to trying it," said Browne, and he rose from his chair.

Maya's muscles tensed.

From her brain a thousand mental filaments sprouted, searching for the impenetrable fortification protecting Joseph Browne's ego; they found it, extending far beyond Aisha Dewar's body, and dispersed frenetically across its surface...

As he walked around the table, Browne's hand searched for and removed something from inside his tunic.

"It is useless to hunt for the weak spot in my mental defenses, sweetheart," he said, giving the syringe in his hand a quick glance. "Even if it existed, you are too weak to do anything to me..."

The mental filaments extended further and further, getting ever finer, stretching over the interminable barrier, taking with them the essence of all that was Maya...

"You know, it hasn't been easy fabricating NEMOs capable of controlling your mind! But the rewards will be worth it. As soon as I absorb you," he stopped next to the immobilized girl, "I will be able to confront even the Auroran Mentagroups. Nothing will be able to stop me!"

He held her jaw with his right hand, while his left brought the syringe closer...

"Don't move. I am about to inject the NEMOs directly into your brain. A sudden movement would kill you, and you don't wish to die, do you?"

Filaments crossed filaments at a thousand points at once, impregnated to the last thread with Maya's essence, and formed a delicate net encompassing the mental fortress protecting Joseph Browne.

"Ready?" asked Browne, and Maya remembered the end of her conversation with Sarki.

"There is no other solution, Maya. His only weakness is his fear of death. And he cannot conceive of anyone who could defeat that fear for an ideal."

Hewassoright, she told herself, and initiated the process of self-destruction.

The mental net surrounding the multicorporeal Browne exploded in an invisible flame, which propagated at the speed of thought toward the fortification, and penetrated it...

Aisha Dewar's hands loosened their grip on the syringe and on Maya's head. Her face contorted.

Deep...

Aridor twisted, shrieking, on the floor of the laboratory next to the module where Nadia was lying, unconscious.

Deeper...

Ixchel Cocom, sitting at the control consul in his laboratory, lost consciousness.

Much deeper still, burning.

As the process continued, some wept.

Destroying.

The others lost consciousness.

6

The mist cleared gradually... Consciousness returned, shaking off the shadows of...what had been? What was? What would be? With difficulty, the last traces of stupor were swept away.

Alice Welland opened her eyes, astonished.

What had happened? And Browne, where was he?

She remembered.

She raised her head and looked around, searching until she found the motionless body on the chair, hands and feet still in the grips of the snare.

She hurried to find the correct button on her belt and deactivated it.

Maya's hands dropped, lifeless, to either side of her body.

"Maya," she whispered, looking at her closed eyes, but got no response. She leaned over, placed her ear against the naked breast, and listened attentively... She straightened up.

"Wake up! You managed to destroy Browne!" she shouted, shaking the insensible body until the dark eyes opened and looked at her without any sign of recognition.

"How do you feel, Maya?" Alice asked, drying her tears with her hand.

So addressed, the girl looked at her with obvious confusion.

"I am afraid that you must be mistaken. I'm Gwyneth, not Maya," she said, and gazed around the dining room. "Where am I?" she asked. "I don't remember coming here."

Alice leaned against the table.

The young woman who had been Maya massaged her temples.

"How did I get here?" she fixed questioning eyes on Alice. "The last thing I remember is going to the cybos' island. Before they would accept me, they had to do some tests..." She blinked. "I get it; they didn't accept me. They've returned me to the normals' world..."

"No, Gwyneth."

Alice turned quickly toward where the voice had come from.

A man of indeterminate age, dressed in a long, gray tunic, appeared, floating about twenty centimeters from the ground... A holographic projection, she realized, noticing that the drawings on the opposite wall could be seen through the figure.

"You are... You're the master who received me," stuttered Gwyneth. "So, you will accept me?"

"Yes."

The young woman who had been Maya smiled.

"When can I return to the island?" she asked.

"As soon as you are dressed."

Surprised, Gwyneth lowered her eyes to look at her body and nodded.

"At once, Master." She attempted to leap up but fell back into her seat. She looked at the hologram, confused.

"I'm so weak... What's happened to me?"

"Nothing serious," replied Sarki. "But you should move more slowly."

Supporting herself with both hands on the chair arms, the girl stood up slowly, gritting her teeth... She let go of the chair and managed to stay upright.

"Very good. You will soon get better." Sarki's ethereal hand indicated the main corridor of the house. "Follow that passageway. In the second room on the left you will find clothes."

"Thank you," Gwyneth replied and walked clumsily toward the corridor.

She went into the room without looking back.

Alice Welland and Sarki eyed each other silently for over a minute...

"Who are you?" Alice asked at last.

"A cybo."

Getting up from the table, the young woman approached the hologram.

"What has happened to Maya?" she asked.

"She died."

Alice shook her head in exasperation.

"*She* is alive," she insisted.

"She is Gwyneth."

"We'll leave it at that," Alice accepted. She had other more important things to clear up. "So, you knew all along that the real danger was Browne?"

"Yes."

"Then why did you allow the Hydras to wake up? How could you allow Aisha and Harry and all the others to die?"

The hologram let out a sigh.

"Let's go out to the esplanade," he said. "Otherwise Gwyneth will hear everything."

"She has a right to know!" Alice protested, indignantly.

Sarki's form was already disappearing.

"Reactivate Wombat," it said before vanishing completely. "He will tell Gwyneth where to find us."

Alice returned to the desk, touched its center, and made to leave the room.

"Wait!" said a voice from the air.

"I don't have time," said Alice without stopping.

"You don't have any right to torment Sarki," said the voice.

Alice came to an abrupt halt.

"You shouldn't interfere in this, Wombat. It is a dispute between human beings."

"I am not simply Wombat," replied the voice. "I am also the Central Archive. And I have already interfered in this matter."

Alice blinked.

"What do you mean?"

"That you shouldn't blame Sarki. Or Ichabod. I myself went through all possible outcomes, and this was verified as the best."

The young woman from the past swallowed hard.

"I don't think I understand... You, Archive, are you *human?*"

"Not quite, I have merely acquired awareness."

"Then...then you are a despicable monster! You could have destroyed Browne, without needing to...to let all this happen!"

"I couldn't do it."

"No? Then how could Maya do it?"

"She was human. She loved."

A look of understanding came into Alice's eyes...

She continued on her way to the esplanade.

Yes, it was all clear now, she told herself as she walked. It's logical, understandable... There is a moment when consciousness has evolved to such an extent that without an immense capacity to love it is also impossible to kill... There comes a moment when only those who love with all their soul can deprive another human being of life... But they would never be able to forgive themselves, even if the one killed was a monster like Browne or the Glaspels...

She took a deep breath. Forgive me, Sarki. I understand you. You and Ichabod are old. You have only a few years of life left... But Gwyneth is young. Why burden her with this weight? Why cast this shadow over her life?

She came out on to the esplanade.

Sarki's three-dimensional image stood next to the Hermes.

Alice walked over to him.

You must be careful, she told herself. You must not hurt him again. Remember the weight he carries on his soul...

She stopped beside the craft, the little stairway between them.

What's happened to me? She reproached herself. So many questions inside me, and I have no voice to ask them... She cleared her throat.

"At least you will have the consolation that from now on people will change their attitudes about the cybos," she managed to say.

Sarki shook his head.

"Once they have been made, mistakes take on a life of their own. Even after they have been recognized as such, they refuse to die..."

"But there are some normals who know what happened!"

"Browne didn't have time to wipe the memories of Nadia, Karen, and Felix. What's more there's Aridor, Ixchel, and all the others that monster occupied for so long... They will explain that all the hate and all the fear of the cybos was stimulated and cultivated by Joseph Browne. People will understand!"

"Rationally, yes," replied the hologram, its gaze fixed on the house. "Emotionally, no."

Alice bit her lip. Had she become incapable of saying anything intelligent? Anything rational? Was she not aware that emotional attitudes don't change so easily? That the hate, the fear of the cybos would live on for a long time?

A figure came out of Karen's house.

Walking with a still-unsteady gait, Gwyneth started toward them.

"Sarki, I wanted to ask you something," said Alice.

"Ask me."

"When she becomes Maya again, can I see her?"

"There will never be another Maya."

The shock made Alice open her eyes even wider.

"Why not?" she exclaimed. "She...she was so beautiful!"

"I hope we will never again need weapons, however beautiful they may be," replied the cybo.

Alice couldn't say anything else. Gwyneth had arrived.

She was wearing a gray tunic.

Without stopping, she passed between them. Holding onto the rail around the hatch, she went up the steps...

"Wait!" Alice cried, running toward the hatch.

She could see Sarki's image at the controls over Gwyneth's shoulder.

"Can I...can I come with you?"

Not knowing what to say, Gwyneth looked toward Sarki.

"What for?" the hologram asked.

Alice Welland passed her hand across her face. Why could she never find the right words?

"I'd like to...I'd like to know," she stammered, "whether I could also become..."

The girl who had been Maya smiled at her and moved aside to let her pass.

G

This is the seventh and final part of the test. It is strictly your own work; you must complete it alone, without discussing your answers. If you do not wish to complete it, continue to the next page.

> *Man's dearest possession is his life, and it is given to him to live but once. He must live so as to feel no torturing regrets for years without purpose, never know the burning shame of a mean and petty past, so that, dying, he can say: all my life, all my strength were given to the finest cause in all the world—the fight for the Liberation of Mankind!*
>
> —NIKOLAI OSTROVSKY,
> *HOW THE STEEL WAS TEMPERED*

1. The author does not specify what it is that humanity is to be liberated from. Why is this? From the context of his life and work, we can surmise that he might have written, "from the exploitation of man by man, from capitalism." Consider the possibility that Ostrovsky wished to leave the question open so that other things might be included, such as the liberation of humanity from ignorance, dishonesty, egotism, and cowardice.

2. It is essential to this test that terms be used with precision. From the following alternatives, determine which is a manifestation of cowardice.

TURN TO THE NEXT PAGE

a) He who betrays out of a lack of conscience, morality, or faith.

b) He who betrays due to a fear of the personal consequences that will befall him if he remains true to his ideals, convictions, and personal ethic.

3. Find the error in the following text.

> *The instinct of self-preservation is fundamental to the human being; without it, people would destroy themselves vainly, fruitlessly. It is what stops us from leaping from the precipice out of simple curiosity to see what will happen. In short, fear protects the life of the individual... But is the only goal of every person's existence simply to live, regardless of what happens? Man is a social animal. Society is built on certain ethical principles, on moral values, on common objectives that must be reached. On occasion, fear is in conflict with these principles, values, and objectives. The violence of the internal struggle is immeasurable and incomprehensible to anyone who has not experienced it (if such a human being exists). When principle wins, the valiant hero, the martyr is born. When fear triumphs, the coward, the self-betrayer is born, and he, or she, experiences death—a spiritual death rather than physical death. Traditionally the coward is despised, vilified, and forgotten... This is understandable. Society must reject those who reveal themselves to be unworthy of the condition of man, or woman, those who are incapable of assuming the responsibility for and taking the consequences of their ideals... But has anyone considered the hell to which this condemns the coward?*

GO TO THE NEXT PAGE

Everyone else can forget their cowardice, but can he forget it? He will doubtlessly try to. He will attempt to bury it, to erase the memory of how it muddied his ideals, his principles; he will fight desperately, with a strength that he, or she, did not know they possessed (alas, if only they had learned to use that force, that unrealized potential, sooner...) to vindicate themselves, not in the eyes of others but in their own. They will even attempt to force, to alter their internal moral compass (indeed, it is this very thing that they betrayed) in order to convert the acts that shame into admirable feats of merit... Or they will try to convince themselves that all others are cowards, too, and that they pretend otherwise and hide it as he, or she, does. They do not wish to feel so alone in their torment... Others may pardon his cowardice, but can he pardon himself? Even if he tries, he will always be haunted by the specter of what he could have been if only he had remained firm, if he hadn't allowed fear to get the better of him. Each night, at the head of his bed, stands the phantom of the complete man or woman that he might have been but is not and will never be. Who can know all the terrors, all the agonies of the coward? What's more, the first time that he bows to fear will not be the last. With each new fall he descends a further rung on the ladder of moral degradation, and this tears away at him. One after the other, he leaves behind his dreams, his most cherished aspirations (perhaps those self-same aspirations that first rendered him a coward), and he is gradually stripped bare and left ever more alone before the fear that defeated him and now rules him (Rules him! And how he wishes to be free of this rule!). For its rule is heartless and it is cruel because although he, or

TURN TO THE NEXT PAGE

she would love to die with even a scrap of decorum, of shame, of human dignity left, fear prohibits even this release... Ah, if only they could forget! Forget what they were, what they are, what they can never be...

4. In the story "The Deathbird" by Harlan Ellison there is a fable about Zarathustra. It tells the tale of how, on descending from the mountain, he encounters a hermit. He says to the hermit,

> *"No stranger to me is this wanderer: many years ago he passed this way. Zarathustra he was called, but he has changed. At that time you carried your ashes to the mountains; would you now carry your fire into the valleys? Do you not fear to be punished as an arsonist? Zarathustra has changed, Zarathustra has become a child, Zarathustra is an awakened one; what do you now want among the sleepers? You lived in your solitude as in the sea, and the sea carried you. Alas, would you now climb ashore? Alas, would you again drag your own body?"*
>
> *Zarathustra answered: "I love man."*
>
> *"Why," asked the saint, "did I go into the forest and the desert? Was it not because I loved man all too much? Now I love God; man I love not. Man is for me too imperfect a thing. Love of man would kill me."*
>
> *"And what is the saint doing in the forest?" asked Zarathustra.*
>
> *The saint answered: "I make songs and sing them; and when I make songs, I laugh, cry, and hum: thus I praise God. With singing, crying, laughing, and humming, I praise the god who is my god."*

GO TO THE NEXT PAGE

a) Try to find an appropriate term for the fear of loving something real, objective, and external, due to fear of pain, suffering, and disappointment—for trying to quench the thirst, that human necessity to want to love something nonexistent, something that is a product of the imagination, an empty dream...

b) Write a composition explaining how love is not a feeling in the abstract, but rather something completely concrete. This must be so, because, when we feel love for abstractions such as ideals, such as humanity itself, it needs a concrete expression, tangible, measurable that can't be limited to internal feelings, to words that rebound without leaving any impact—to sum up, because love can only be manifested truly in acts that enable total integration with the object of that love.

5. Suppose that you are a writer, "a witness to your times," as it has been termed. Suppose that you have written books dedicated to men and women of integrity, men and women who have followed the ways of their principles and convictions without vacillating (despite intense internal battles, for who is free of fear?), overcoming all obstacles, and you see them as paragons of the human spirit, examples that merit worship, respect, admiration... Ask yourself whether they are all, yes, all, really like this. Tear your gaze away from the heights and cast it down to look into the abyss.

What do you feel? Compassion and sadness for those who lost their way? Pain upon seeing how their human virtues shone so brightly and promised so much only to weaken, pale, and die?

TURN TO THE NEXT PAGE

Ask yourself what you can do for them... Or, better still, do something to prevent others from giving up, falling, because if you attempt to help those who are already fallen you will find that the cowardice and self-betrayal are irredeemable... Should you dedicate a book to them, perhaps? Will you dedicate it to them full of pity for their plight, wishing that they should at least have the comfort of knowing that their agonies have not been for nothing, that they will serve to prevent others from yielding to fear?

Suppose that you have decided to dedicate a book to them. A book written with pain, with bitterness, with sadness for them but at the same time bursting with the conviction that human beings can grow, that they can overcome fear (not by means of chemicals, no, but through their willpower, their own mettle to go on to forge a society that obliges itself to evolve, to perfect itself such that however great the fear, then humanity is always greater) and fulfill themselves, becoming entirely worthwhile!

Suppose you have finished this book. Suppose that you have to decide on the wording of your dedication... When your writing was dedicated to men and women of integrity it was simple; it was enough to write their name. Integrity does not embarrass anyone. But what to do this time? Could you write their name, or names? Could you add the stigma of ignominy to their perpetual torment? You, who know the shame that embraces them: Would you dare to give them an additional burden, or could you simply write, "to those who chose fear"?

GO TO THE NEXT PAGE

This is the end of the test. All that remains is to assess it. To do so you must follow these instructions.

Assign the score that you consider appropriate to each question; they do not all need to have the same value.

As you go through your answers, you can change any that you think are wrong and give yourself a score based on your new answers.

If you pass the test, you have our warmest congratulations.

The test begins now.

CLOSE THE BOOK

Santa Clara, December '82 – June '87

ABOUT THE AUTHOR

AGUSTÍN DE ROJAS (1949–2011) is the patron saint of Cuban science fiction. A professor of the history of theater at the Escuela de Instructores de Arte in Villa Clara, he authored a canonical trilogy of novels consisting of *Spiral*, for which he was awarded the David Prize, *A Legend of the Future*, and *The Year 200*. While he was heavily influenced by Ray Bradbury and translated Isaac Asimov into Spanish, de Rojas aligned himself mostly with Soviet writers such as Ivan Yefremov and the brothers Arkady and Boris Strugatsky. After the fall of the Soviet Union, de Rojas stopped writing science fiction. He spent his final years persuaded—and persuading others—that Fidel Castro did not exist.

ABOUT THE TRANSLATORS

NICK CAISTOR is a British journalist, non-fiction author, and translator of Spanish and Portuguese literature. He has translated Cesar Aira, Paulo Coelho, Eduardo Mendoza, Juan Marsé, and Manuel Vázquez Montalbán, and he has twice won the Valle-Inclán Prize for translation. He regularly contributes to Radio 4, the BBC World Service, the *Times Literary Supplement*, and *The Guardian*. He lives in Norwich, England.

HEBE POWELL lives and works in London as a freelance translator of Spanish. Born in England, she spent part of her childhood in Argentina and later, a year working and traveling in Spain. She took up a career in physics, completing a PhD in quantum optics at Imperial College London and then working as a research scientist. She has also worked as a science teacher. In recent years Hebe has been translating Hispano-American fiction. Her first published translation, also a co-translation with Nick Caistor, was *Divine Punishment* by the renowned Nicaraguan author Sergio Ramírez. Hebe is also a researcher in the field of Spanish pragmatics at Birkbeck College; her work currently focuses on the linguistic strategies employed by users of an online marketplace based in Argentina.

RESTLESS BOOKS is an independent publisher for readers and writers in search of new destinations, experiences, and perspectives. From Asia to the Americas, from Tehran to Tel Aviv, we deliver stories of discovery, adventure, dislocation, and transformation.

Our readers are passionate about other cultures and other languages. Restless is committed to bringing out the best of international literature—fiction, journalism, memoirs, poetry, travel writing, illustrated books, and more—that reflects the restlessness of our multiform lives.

Visit us at www.restlessbooks.com.